I0843016

Overstuffed

A Living Pillow Collection

Sylvia Morrow

Copyright © 2025 by Sylvia Morrow

All rights reserved.

Cover by Impyeu

Interior art by TeeGenevaReads

No portion of this book may be reproduced in any form without written permission from the publisher or author, except as permitted by U.S. copyright law.

Stuffed

by Sylvia Morrow

Content Notes

Tentacles, rapid aging, food, extreme devotion, insect death, mention of bird death, sexual harassment, landlord bothering for money, body horror, build a perfect man scenario, fictophilia, fear of germs, tics, extreme dislike of touching, dislike of people, loss of virginity, discussion of genital size, multiple sexual acts.

The author will happily answer any further questions via her social media inboxes. Just be warned, she's a chatterbox!

Chapter One

Anne

"Holy shit, dude, ever hear of personal space?"

I dodge some creep on the sidewalk who walks way too close, nearly brushing up against me. He looks sweaty and grimy. I shudder as I walk away from him. That was way too close of a call.

After some fancy footwork, I make it up the busy sidewalk without touching anyone. My apartment building is a relief to see. I know once inside, I'll nearly be to my little place where I can be all alone, just how I like. I open the front door to the building, only to bump chest first into Jimmy, my landlord.

"Hey there, little Annie. You got your rent? Or you gonna make me come get it from you?" Jimmy winks a glassy blue eye at me.

I back away, my hands itching to toss off the jacket I'm wearing. I can't stand the idea of wearing something he touched. Being stuck with him is killing me.

"Rent isn't due for five days, Jimmy. I'll have it in by then. You know I always do."

"Never hurts to have a reminder though, right, girly?" He licks a worm-like bottom lip which sets my teeth on edge.

My fingers feel so itchy I start rubbing them against one another furiously. It's a tic I can't help doing when I get too upset or anxious. I used to have a lot more obvious tics, but I've worked on them over time through therapy. This particular one just stuck.

"Okay, see you later, Jimmy," I say with a fake smile I really freaking struggle to put on. Thankfully he moves to the side so I can squeeze past and up to my apartment.

I slam and lock the door, throw off my clothes, and get into a hot shower where I scrub myself with antibacterial soap. Once I feel good and clean I get out and decide to have a nice night watching a show or two and just chilling. I'm admittedly a bit obsessed with anime but I'm not worried about it. Everyone has a hobby, plus it calms me down and I could really use some relaxation.

The butler character in the anime I'm watching tonight is fighting with a reaper in a scene I've seen a million times before. This is my favorite show. I watch this one like every other night. Some people might think it's weird that this character in particular gets me so physically excited but, well my body reacts, and it reacts *strongly*.

Now, I don't like *real* people. I really, really don't. Aside from my small family and online friends, that is. Those particular folks are awesome because I don't have to *touch* them. I get to enjoy their presence platonically and from at least several inches away. But dating? Gross. My hooha dries up at the thought.

The industry I work in, game design, is overwhelmingly male. Even surrounded by men there aren't any I want. There are never any I want *anywhere*, and I'm glad about that because dating seems like the worst. It just doesn't appeal to me.

The thought of sweaty hands groping me, people's germs all over me...eew. I hate germs and touching, and sex is packed with nothing but bodily fluids and I can't think of anything worse.

But fictional characters are a whole other story.

I watch the colors move across the screen, clutching a pillow between my legs—my favorite pillow.

It's the perfect firmness, soft enough to lay my head on at night but firm enough to do this naughty thing I like to do. More like an embarrassing thing, actually. If anyone saw me, I think I would die, but it just feels so, so good. With my perfect pillow between my legs and my fictional boyfriend on the T.V., everything is just right in the world.

My satin pajama pants feel so smooth against my thighs, my ass...along my sensitive folds. They're already slick with the juices the animations have drawn from me tonight. I grip my pillow tighter, imagining it's the mysterious butler from the television, and sliding myself slowly up and down against it.

Fictophilia. That's what it's called when you're only attracted to fictional characters. I can't help it. Thinking of actual skin touching me is just repulsive. But this pillow between my thighs, riding it, is perfect for me. No skin, no germs, no potential for disease. Only stroking and grinding just right while thinking of my animated man.

I push harder against the pillow, letting the satin of these pink pajama pants slide against my slippery pussy. I'm really wet now, and I dip my hips against the pillow, opening my legs wide for a moment to slip along my core where I'm leaking for my butler.

My legs close tight as I grind as hard as I can against the pillow, soaking through my pants—and into the pillow itself at this point, I'm sure. My clit is forced against the layers of fabric, relentlessly ground against the firm block of feathers and cotton, over and over until my legs squeeze and shake. A silent scream forms in my mouth as my eyes close tight. My cunt spasms against the pillow; I come hard.

After my moment of release, I fall down onto the bed, relaxed, and pull the pillow up against my head. It's slightly moist but I don't care, I just flip it around. I'll change the case tomorrow. Right now, I'm exhausted.

I'm not sure if I'm actually a *fictophiliac,* or if it's just that I know I won't ever find anyone real I can be with. I guess it doesn't really matter either way. I like an orgasm as much as anyone, so yeah, it would be cool if there were some way for one of my beloved characters to help me out, but I'm sane enough to know that's not going to happen. My television, my imagination, and my favorite pillow will just have to do. After all, there's no way I'll ever have a real man to be with.

I set my glasses on the side table. The remote is within reach and I grab it, turning off the television.

"Goodnight, my darling," I whisper into the dark.

As I'm falling asleep, I swear I imagine I hear the same returned.

Chapter Two

Pillow

O h Anne. Anne, my *darling*. My *wondrous* Anne.

She made use of me again tonight, and it was glorious. It had been ages since she'd gripped me tight and run me between her warm thighs. I was beginning to worry she had forgotten about me. I don't know what I would have done if that would have happened.

Anne is my reason for living. Well, if you could call what I'm doing now living, which I wouldn't. At this moment, I'm simply existing.

Though I was part of something alive once, I barely recall it. A phoenix, it was. Once upon a time, this phoenix—a powerful and ancient creature known for its ability to regenerate—fell in love with...a goose.

How disappointing. How uninspired.

You'd think a creature of legend would choose something more *interesting*, but I guess a phoenix is just a fancy bird when it all comes down to it.

And, well, to make a sad story short, the goose got cooked, so the phoenix died of sadness. Too heartbroken to be revived, it perished in a funeral pyre of its own making.

However, before it died, a single one of its feathers fell amidst the goose's own down. When the humans gathered them and stuffed them into their "organic, free range, all natural goose feather pillows" the phoenix feather got scooped up along with it.

And that's how my existence began.

In just one feather there is a tiny spark of regenerative power. A Phoenix can't come back from one feather alone—there's no *bird* left. There's no *anything* left in me, aside from the tiniest potential for life. I would have been only a feather in a pillow if it weren't for *her*. The passion she projected onto me added a bit of spark to the little flicker of life in the plume, just enough to give me awareness.

And to give me an aching desire for *Anne.*

On its own, it's not enough to give me a physical form. It's not enough to give me *Anne.* But ever so slowly, I'm building up more life, more mass, more energy, *more* for *her.*

Just now, a fly buzzes into Anne's room; this will be perfect if things go just right. I wait patiently to see where the insect will go. Not that I can wait any other way. After all, I'm an inanimate object.

The fly drops down onto Anne's head, all its disgusting legs touching her glorious mane of golden-brown hair. *How dare it touch her.* I wait as it flits about around the bed until, finally, it lands on *me.* It takes less than half a second for the fly to drop down, dead, and for me to feel a little more alive.

Alive. Someday I'll have enough life stored inside to turn myself into a creature Anne could love. She'll hold me, caress me, and I'll *feel* all of it and I'll give her every bit of pleasure she deserves.

As long as she doesn't give up on me, doesn't throw me away before then, of course.

I concentrate on using the energy I absorbed from the fly to keep my fabric cool, and my feathers fluffed just the way she likes them. To make sure she never throws me away, I need to remain perfect until I can become the man she needs. Because I know she *does* need me, and I need her. Things will be so wonderful when I'm *alive.*

Chapter Three

Anne

Finally, it's five o'clock and I can go home. Today has been the worst day at work. There were so many meetings, all of them in packed rooms where I was jammed next to tons of coughing, sweating, *leering*, people. I just want to take a shower, order some food, and relax. No people, no deadlines, just me and whatever I feel like watching tonight.

I start to smile as I pack my bag, thinking of the relaxing night ahead of me. Maybe even an upbeat night to wash away this negativity. I can put on some Sailor Scouts—fight the evil feelings by the moonlight.

Heck, I could even turn on the PC and play a game with my online friends. We could get the guild together and just nerd out. It's been way too long since I checked in on them, I should make sure they're okay. As I finish packing up, my budding smile turns to a frown as I think about how antisocial I've been with all the stress from work.

"Hey there, little miss grumpy."

The interruption shocks me from my thoughts, causing me to jump and spill the contents of my bag all over the floor. *Argh*, all my favorite Copic markers roll under the desk. Those things are expensive, and I'll be damned if I lose any of them. I close my eyes and take a deep breath, trying to calm myself before replying to the jerk who broke me away from my pleasant thoughts.

"What do you want, Todd?" I ask in a tone that admittedly does nothing to disprove his claim of my grumpiness.

"Just wanted to see if you'd be interested in going out with me tonight? We could go get some drinks, go back to my place, play some games...who knows what else? Could be fun, right?" Todd asks in his perpetually phlegmy voice.

He leans one bony shoulder against the wall of my cubicle and I can see the sweat stains under the arm of his vintage band t-shirt. One of his fingers trails along my forearm. I pull away. *No touching. No, no, no.* I begin to hurriedly pick up my scattered items, avoiding his gaze as much as possible.

"I'm not interested. I've told you already, I'm here to work, not find a date. Please respect that," I tell him, trying to retain my composure.

I tend to cry when I get upset and I don't want to do that. This is a professional environment, even though it doesn't seem like it half the time, and I'm the only woman working on this team. I can't be seen crying.

"You can do both, you know, Annie Banannie. In fact, I think it might even help your work to experience a little romance. Relax and let your mind free to new ideas or whatever." Todd brushes against my arm again and this time tears build in the corners of my eyes.

Please stop touching me.

I pack up the rest of my items and sling my bag over my shoulder. "No. End of it."

My jaw clenches as I walk out the door, fingertips frantically rubbing against one another. Todd scoffs behind me. I think tonight I'm not feeling fun or social after all. Watching something will be better. Something to represent my mood. Tonight, I need to go home and scrub all the parts where he touched me with antibacterial soap, and then I'm going to turn on my television to watch my old friend Ryuk.

On my way home my murderous impulses only increase. Okay, that's an exaggeration. I don't want to kill anyone, but I do want some of these people to fall in dog shit and scrape their knees or something.

I'm just trying to walk home from the bus stop, already stressed out from *Todd*, but I grit my teeth as I see these teenage morons standing on the corner of my block. They hang out there most days, always harass me, though I don't get why. I'm too old for them! I'm a grown ass woman and I'm not exactly a hot babe. I work hard to appear as bland as possible so I don't stand out, in fact. My clothes are plain and loose, my hair is in a simple bob, and I don't wear any makeup on my bespectacled face. But every time they're on the corner, which is most days, they catcall me and say gross stuff. It's so frustrating.

Today is the same as any other in that regard.

"Hey little mama, miss librarian with those glasses on, looking all smart and shit. Come here and give me a kiss," one of them hollers at me.

I grit my teeth and keep walking past. They never hurt me, just say stupid stuff. I'll just go past, get home, and relax with my television.

But today, things are different. Today they *touch me.*

"Hey, slow down sweetie, you don't got to look all mad. We just want to talk, you know?" A second one of them laughs and *grabs my arm.*

He steps up close to me and he smells like sour milk. I can see dried flecks of saliva on the corners of his pale lips, mysterious brown flecks in the stubble of his sparse, blonde mustache. *No, no, no.*

"DO NOT TOUCH ME!" I scream, pulling my arm away.

"Damn, crazy bitch," I hear behind me but I'm already running away to the middle of the block where my building is.

I unlock my apartment door and run up the stairs. As soon as I'm inside, I strip off my clothes and get in the shower, scrubbing my skin so hard it burns.

I fucking hate humans.

Chapter Four

Pillow

My Anne is not holding me in her delightfully passionate way tonight. As soon as she lay down on the bed to place her head on me, I could tell things were off. She smells like the strong soap, the one she uses when she's sad. She lays flat on her back, barely moving, only quietly observing those shows she likes. After hours of this she turns to her side, sniffles, and I feel a tear drop onto me.

If I had a heart it would break, seeing her like this. I want to hold her, to ask what's wrong, to help her, but I can't; I'm not strong enough yet. She's so sweet, so beautiful. She doesn't deserve any sort of suffering. She *needs* me, I know it. Insect energy barely keeps me firm and cool, it's not nearly enough to make myself *more*.

Oh, my Anne, my Anne, how can I help you?

A knock sounds from far outside the room. Anne sits up, holding me to her full chest, staying still, until another knock sounds. She sets me down and walks away.

Come back, please.

I immediately miss the warmth of her touch and I do not trust the knock at the door this late at night.

I hear voices coming from the other room, one of them hers, one of them male. If I could growl I would. Anne has never taken a mate since she's owned me, and I think I wouldn't be able to stand it if she did. She is *mine*.

"Yeah, you must have dropped it when you spilled your stuff like a silly goose. Thankfully your address is on your I.D. so I could bring it right over to you tonight. Would be a shame to not have your wallet if you needed it. Might even say you owe me a favor, right, Annie Banannie?" the male voice says.

"You could have given it to me tomorrow at work too, Todd. Thanks though. I'll see you later," Anne bites out.

She sounds much different than I've ever heard her. Granted, I usually only hear her when she's on the phone with her mother, playing online games with her internet friends, or making her sexy little noises when she uses me. But the way she sounds now is like none of those by far.

She sounds...upset.

"You know, I think I need to use the restroom. I'll just be a sec," the male voice says.

"That's not a good idea," Anne insists, but I hear heavy footsteps start down the hall nonetheless, footsteps that do not belong to her.

"I'll just be a second. Oh, hey, is that your bedroom? Where the magic happens, am I right?" he, *Todd*, says.

His footsteps come even closer.

"Dude, get out. You said you had to pee, not wander my apartment. What the fuck?" My Anne raises her voice, and I can sense fear there.

This man is raising her alarms. Mine as well.

Then I see him. He enters her room and looks around, a lascivious grin on his pasty face as his eyes meet the bed. His disgusting cologne fills the room. I want to strangle him for covering the scent of my Anne for even a moment.

My Anne steps next to him, and he turns to face her, his grin only growing wider.

"Nice bed. I like your setup here with the T.V. and all. Why don't we sit here and watch a movie? Netflix and chill," he says with a creepy little laugh.

Todd sits down on the bed. My excitement builds.

Come a little closer. Just a *little* closer.

"Get out. This isn't funny," Anne cries.

She *cries.* This bastard is bringing tears to the eyes of my precious love. Now I'll feel no guilt at all when I do what I need to. *Not that I would anyway.*

"Oh, you're so silly, Annie. Come on, have a seat," he says.

He pats me to invite her over. *Yes.*

HE TOUCHES ME.

When his hand lands on me I suck the life out of him. It's much more difficult than with the bugs, I find. He struggles much harder. He tries to lift his hand but can't—I won't allow it.

"What the hell?" he forces out through choked breath.

If he's speaking, that means I'm not pulling hard enough. I yank on his life force, dragging it into me. I can see his skin dry out, become thinner, lose the glow of youth.

The power inside me grows. I'm strong. It feels *so good.*

"Todd? TODD!" Anne screams, wrenching him off of me.

He stands for barely a moment before collapsing to the ground. In the flash that I'm able to see him, I can tell he looks older, much older, though I didn't age him enough to kill him. *Oh well.* He *does* look old enough for death to come soon.

Thin, gray hair, hollow cheeks, frail body, nearly skeletal...he won't be hurting my Anne any longer.

Anne looks around frantically, wiping her hands on her pants as she searches for her phone. Seeing it finally, she grabs it, then drops it before picking it up with a growl of frustration. She sobs as she dials a three-digit number. I feel bad—for a moment; I don't want her to be upset but I know I did what had to be done. *It will be worth it, my love.*

"Please send an ambulance to 1775 Barkersville Lane. This guy collapsed I don't know what the fuck happened. Please hurry."

She talks some more for a few minutes on the phone, pacing up and down the hallway, occasionally peering down at Todd to make sure he's still breathing. Eventually some strangers arrive to take him away, and other strangers question Anne for a bit. It's late before they leave. She's so worn and tired that she doesn't even change into her pajamas before collapsing into bed with me.

She holds me as she sleeps, unaware that I'm doing something incredible inside of me. Something that will change both of us forever.

Tomorrow we'll be together. Anne, my Anne.

Chapter Five

Anne

Everyone stares at me all day at work. I can't freaking handle it, so I fake a migraine and leave early. They all know about what happened to Todd, somehow. I don't know how; I didn't tell them. Hell, I don't even really know what happened. One second he was on my bed being a creep and the next he was halfway to being a corpse. I didn't do anything to him, but I could tell by the way people looked at me that they certainly thought I did.

Why wouldn't they? I was the only one with him. *Whatever*, I'm going home and taking some me time away from their judgmental stares.

I stop by the market on the way home to grab my favorite brand of triangle-shaped corn chips and a bottle of peach Ramune soda. They're my comfort foods, and I could really use some comfort right now. I just want to go home, eat my snacks, sit in bed, and watch something I've seen a hundred times before. Nothing dark—I already feel gloomy as it is. I think I'll just find some magical girl show to keep me company.

As soon as I open the door to my apartment, I can sense something is off. There is a feeling in the air, this vibration, just something *wrong*. I know it's coming from my room. I have seen enough horror to know not to head toward what the weird thing is, but I can't help it. This is my apartment, and I can't just run away because there are some bad vibes, right?

It's probably just me being paranoid because of last night. I shake my head and walk toward my room instead of the kitchen like I'd planned, needing to prove to myself right away that I'm just being a scaredy cat.

When I get to my room, my hand clenches in surprise, causing my bag of chips to burst, making a loud *pop* sound. The smell of nacho cheese wafts upward. I drop the soda bottle from my right hand, shattering the glass. Sweet, carbonated beverage sprays all over my feet, all over the walls, and in the direction of my bed.

My bed, where some horrible thing is pulsing and stretching.
What the fuck is it?

Chapter Six

Pillow

My Anne stands in the doorway in shock. I understand why she's upset; I'm not fully formed. She isn't supposed to be home for hours and I haven't finished building myself yet. *Damn.*

As of right now my lower half is mostly formed. I have feet, legs, hips, even pants. None of it is fully detailed, but it's started at least. My upper half, however, is a mess.

My chest, arms, and head are simply four pillows. They aren't even particularly firm or attractive pillows at the moment, they're only blank placeholders for upcoming pieces. It's quite embarrassing to be seen this way after spending so many years making myself into the perfect pillow, I must say.

Not all of my upper half is blank though. Part of a face is formed on the topmost pillow—a dent of a mouth and eyes only, but that's it. The eyes are well formed, sitting in the center of the topmost pillow, turning toward Anne to watch her as her face drains of color.

Oh, dear. I can imagine having fully formed eyes rolling around in all that white space probably looks quite gruesome. *Damn, again.*

All the rest of me is soft, feather-filled cotton that is bubbling, growing, and stretching—the process which will make me into a fully formed man. But for now, that form is more of a...pillow sludge.

All of that is to say, I look like a goddamn monster.

I open what I have of a mouth to try to speak. Out comes something that doesn't help me seem any less monstrous. My "voice" sounds as if a creaking door and an old air conditioner had a child and shat it into my mouth. Anne begins to hyperventilate. I begin to panic. What do I do now?

Alright, I'll focus on building my communication skills.

I put all of my effort into all the parts of me most responsible for speech, until I can at least make a sound that won't send her into cardiac arrest—I think. She looks like she's going to faint by the time I'm done, even though it doesn't take me long, so I try to choose my words carefully.

"Anne," I rasp out. My voice isn't perfect yet but it's not horrible. It's whispery and rough but it's getting better. "Don't be afraid, please. I won't harm you. Please forgive me for my appearance, I shall fix it shortly."

Anne blinks once, twice then to my relief, speaks to me. "Oh. Okay then."

I smile as much as I can with a mouth that's hardly more than two folds in fabric. She accepts me.

My Anne, of course, would accept me. She's meant for me. My Anne is...

...on the floor. She fainted. *Damn.*

Alright, time to make a functioning body so I can help her. I'll worry about appearance later I suppose, though I hope I don't scare her again.

Why did she have to come home early? Of all the days.

I focus on working arms and legs, everything I need to walk and lift my Anne. I'm panicking by the time I get to her, knowing I still look hideous, but I do get to her, nonetheless. I lift her carefully and take her to the bed where I lay her down on one of her inferior pillows. I don't really know what else to do other than wait; I'm only a pillow after all. I don't exactly have emergency medical education. So, I just sit next to her and continue building myself.

Anne is out for a long time. I am able to finish my shape, however my details are not completed when she wakes. My hair is just a vague blob and I have little color to speak of. I have, however, been able to add some shading to my facial features with the ink that was on my tag, so I do look more human and less monster. Yes, I look like a sketch, a drawing, but a drawing of a human at least.

Anne opens her eyes and looks at my newly built face. I smile again, this time with a mouth that's more than just a few dents in woven cotton.

"Hello again," I say in a much clearer voice than before. "Welcome back."

Chapter Seven

Anne

I open my eyes and see before me a living animation. Or something. What the hell is it? Is that the thing from before? I slide away from whatever it is, until I am at the opposite edge of the bed.

"What are you?" I stammer out.

My body shakes. I feel like I should run but there's nowhere to go. If I wanted to leave the room, I would have to go past the...thing, so it's pointless. *Fuck.*

"Well, that's complicated," it says, smiling with a mouth that looks as if it were drawn with ink. "The simplest answer, I suppose, would be that I am your pillow. Your favorite pillow. I've just changed a bit, as you can see."

"No shit." One quick, hysterical bubble of laughter escapes me before going silent again. "What are you doing here?"

"I...upgraded myself today. I'm not complete. Building a person takes a lot of detailed work, but I'm getting closer. I am saving the fine details until I get your input. You see, I built myself for *you*, Anne. *You* should decide on my final form."

I'm silent for a while before replying slowly and carefully, "What do you mean 'built myself for you'?"

"Anne, I have been in love with you for years. I have kept myself firm and cool for you and tried every day to find a way to become *more*. Today I have done it. We can finally be together. You are my love; make me yours."

"Okay well that's pretty intense. And look dude, I'm not even sure I'm not hallucinating," I say as I rub my temples.

Either I'm going insane, or I have some kind of pillow monster who is moving way too fast in the relationship department in my bedroom. Neither of those situations seem appealing.

"I assure you I'm real. I'm too aware that I'm inhuman and appear to be as such, quite so, but I am working on changing that. Just give me a short while, please. It will be much easier to accept the reality of the situation when I don't appear so...strange."

He looks embarrassed and I actually feel kind of bad for him. I can't imagine being in his situation.

"So, uh, what can I do to help?" I ask. I cross my arms over my ample chest nervously, not really sure what else to do.

He perks up, sitting straight, his face seeming to light up as much as cotton and ink can. "Please, just tell me what your ideal man would be. I want to be everything you desire. My only reason for being is to please you, Anne. Help me."

"So, that's a lot," I begin, standing up and moving away from the bed. "I hope you understand that I don't exactly like people."

"I know, Anne, I know you. That's why you must understand that I'm not like them. I'm not flesh and blood. When you touch me there will be no sweat, no germs, nothing to fear. I'll only appear how you want me to. I'll only touch you how you want me to. I'll never make you sick. never betray you or insult you. I'll never hurt you. I'm yours, Anne. Please, complete me."

My mind races as I think of all the possibilities. I could have everything I've ever wanted. But this...this is *wrong*. Isn't it? It can't be right to mess with the universe like this. And yet, I want the ability to *touch*. But I've wanted only animated guys—yet here is someone with *a drawing for a face* telling me he'll be anything I want him to be.

I nibble on my thumbnail, trying to prevent myself from messing with my fingertips. They've gotten dry as hell from all the stress rubbing lately and it's distracting. I need to think right now. If I could finally have the ability to touch someone, maybe even a boyfriend type someone, shouldn't I take it? And if I could create him to look however I want, what would I do? *This is tough.* I lower my hand and nod as I make my decision.

"Well, there's this anime butler," I say. "I think that's a good place to start if we're working on appearance."

Chapter Eight

Pillow

My Anne and I work for hours to get my form correct. She requests that I be tall and lean, my brows arched, handsome in a nearly androgynous way. I'm provided with the markers she uses for sketching design ideas to absorb colors for my pale flesh. Of course, I'm easily able to create the perfect designs for my elegant clothing; I'm made of fabrics after all.

When I'm done, I'm precisely as she requested. My dark hair falls over one eye. I bite a pouty lip seductively as I watch her inspect me one final time for anything she may have missed. She's so, so beautiful and now that I'm complete I hope...I hope she'll accept me.

"Wow, you look great," she exclaims.

I exhale powerfully, relieved beyond measure to hear those words.

"Obviously if anyone got too close, they'd see you're made of fabric. I mean, I think the being made of fabric thing is awesome, but you'll just have to not get super close to other people I guess."

"That's not a problem. I don't care about anyone else, only you."

"Man, you're really killing me. You seriously only exist because of me?" She crosses her arms over her chest again in that way that means she's nervous.

I don't want her to feel anxious around me, but I can't help coming across a bit…intense. Being aware but unable to move, communicate, or even let anyone know I was sentient for years may have had a small effect on my sanity. Or at the very least my ability to properly tone down my feelings for the comfort of others.

"Oh, Anne. You have no idea how much you mean to me. You are the reason I exist and the reason I want to keep existing."

"Well, I feel kind of weird. I mean, how long have you been sentient? Because I've, uh, done stuff…" Her face turns bright red, and she holds herself even tighter than before.

I can only assume *stuff* means her wonderful *grinding* sessions.

"I've been sentient for quite a while now. If you're wondering whether I've been aware when you've ground your gorgeous cunt against me the answer is *yes*."

Anne takes a sharp breath and covers her face with her hands.

"Oh my god," she whispers from behind those small hands. "I'm so embarrassed."

"Don't be. It was beautiful. You brought me to life, Anne. I hope one day to experience that again, to have you grind against my face, as I thrust my tongue into your wet center, and rub your throbbing clit. You wouldn't have to do it all yourself anymore, my darling. I'm here to serve you."

I take a risk and slowly, tentatively, step toward her. Watch her reaction so, so carefully to make sure she doesn't panic. I raise my brand-new hand to caress her rosy cheek. She doesn't pull away. My heart races.

She doesn't pull away.

"Anne, let me serve you." I run my fingers through her brown hair and her eyes close. "Come with me."

I step back and hold out my hand. The decision is now hers. My feather heart pounds as I wait for her to decide.

Please, please, take my hand.

"I should be afraid but you're...irresistible. What is it about you?" she asks as she takes my hand.

Yes, my heart rejoices as she takes my hand. How do I answer her?

Because we're meant to be together. Because I am literally made for you. Because I will do anything it takes to claim you, serve you, and keep you.

No, I know what she would like to hear. I grin as I reply in a partial quote I know she'll love.

"I'm simply one hell of a pillow."

Chapter Nine

Anne

I take his hand and a sharp breath; the feeling is so strange, though not uncomfortable by any means. Normally I would be flinching away in disgust at any touch, but this is different. He's not flesh, he's not greasy and sweaty. When I touch him it's just cool, firm, fabric. I sigh in relief and let him lead me to the bed where we sit on the edge next to one another. He sets our hands on my knee, his on top of mine and smiles at me silently.

"What now?" I ask with a soft, nervous laugh.

"Whatever you'd like. You have a man who would do any-thing for you, a man you've built to your specifications, who can't make you sick, who'll never hurt you. What would you like to do with me?" He speaks in a raspy voice right against my neck, sounding as if his every muscle is tense with anticipation.

"Whatever I'd like? What if I just want to do stuff that isn't super...sexual?" My face heats when I say it, but I don't know how else to phrase it. "I mean, I just met you."

"Well, you haven't just met me; I've been here for years. I understand what you mean though," he says with a soft laugh. "I said we can do whatever you want, and I mean it.

"Just because I came off strong doesn't mean you have to do what I spoke of. I only know what I've been taught by you, I should let you know that. Everything I know about the world came from what you've said to visitors, on your phone, what you've watched on your screens, et cetera. I admit I have a fondness for the hentai you watch and perhaps that influenced my initial enthusiasm."

He smirks as my cheeks heat.

"But I know how much you love so many other things, and I love them too because of that. I will be your partner in all things. Just tell me."

"You've watched the hentai? Oh no. Oh no, no, no. Even the stuff with the tentacles?" I cover my face with my hands and lean forward.

"Oh yes. I have a special fondness for that, actually. I've seen everything you've watched here, Anne, and I've been here every time you've touched yourself to it. Think of how many times you've ground yourself against me until you came. Don't be embarrassed; you've made me so, so happy."

I flop backwards onto the bed and stare at the ceiling. I have one of those ugly lights that looks like a boob, the kind you find in like every apartment. The landlord keeps saying they're going to replace it with new more energy efficient lights, but they also said they were going to replace the air conditioner, and it's eighty degrees in here, so yeah, right. Why am I focusing on the light?

I turn back toward the pillow and my breath catches as I really, fully take in how gorgeous he is. As I was working to design him it was like a puzzle and though I paid attention to the pieces, now that I am looking at the completed man, he's...wow. Every dreamboat in my favorite anime–or anything else real or fiction–has nothing on him. I might literally swoon.

"Maybe we can, um, hold hands for a little while?" I manage to squeak out.

He grins with a perfectly white smile. "Of course. Come here, we'll lay on these inferior pillows."

We climb up onto the bed next to one another, sitting propped up on my pillows, and I hold his hand. I feel silly but considering I haven't willingly touched another person in years, this is a pretty big deal. I clear my throat and decide to make conversation.

"Do you have a name? I mean, I can't call you 'Pillow' forever."

"I do not. Perhaps you'll give me one? I would like that a lot." He smiles at me, and I notice he has a dimple.

I didn't suggest the dimple but it's perfect.

"That's a pretty big responsibility, but I guess someone has to give you a name and I'm the only person you know. Let's see."

I look him over and take in all of his features: dark hair, bright eyes, pale skin, long and lean body, soft and full lips, elegant hands, broad shoulders, big feet. I realize as I'm looking that I didn't build his...uh, *disco stick*. He created his pants before I paid attention to that part. I wonder if I'll be in charge of that or if he'll do it.

"Anne?" He interrupts my thoughts and I realize I have been thinking for a long time.

Oops, caught thinking about dick.

"Sorry, just thinking hard. What about Ori? It's an actual name, a really pretty name, and it kind of sounds a little bit like 'pillow' in French, if you mangle the word a lot. I think. I haven't taken French since high school. That's fun, right? Or is it dumb? It's pretty either way though, I think."

"I love it. *Ori.* I am now a man with a name. Who would have thought only hours ago I was simply a place to rest your head? You can still do that, of course, but now we can do lots of other fun things." He smiles again, showing that adorable dimple and squeezes my hand.

"Yep, you can order Starbucks now that you have a name for them to put on your cup. Very cool." I nod my head with a faux serious expression on my face.

"Oh, yes, of course. That is exactly the sort of thing I had in mind." When he laughs at my little joke it's deep and throaty.

It's the kind of laugh the hero in a story has, the one that swoops the love interest away at the last minute when she gets nearly overwhelmed in battle; the one she nearly kisses episode after episode but never quite does until the very last season and when she does it's absolute fireworks. I squirm in my spot at the sound of it. *Is anything about him not perfect?*

Ori sits up, faces me, and reaches out to stroke my cheek. "Anne, I—"

His head flops forward, his neck bent over in an entirely flat seam. A wheezing, burbling sound releases briefly before there is only silence. His head wobbles flat against his chest.

"Ori!" I panic, pushing him down to the bed.

He looks normal, except there is a crease in the fabric of the center of his neck, cutting off his breathing.

His eyes swivel to my face. He grimaces. His hands push against his chest under where I am bent over him. I move away to watch what's happening. Slowly he pushes whatever fills the volume inside of him—feathers if he's still mostly pillow—into his neck, filling it back up again. He lets out a gasp and sits up, wrapping his arms around me, holding tight.

"Ori, what the hell happened?" I squeak out.

"I think I need a little more power. Being both pillow and man is fine, good for *us* even, but I think I might be weighted a little too heavily on the pillow side currently. I'm afraid if I don't get a bit more power I might fall apart." He takes a shuddering breath. "I'm a little frightened, Anne."

"Ori," I say as I unwrap his arms from around me. I put my hands on either side of his face and look him square in the eyes. "Tell me what we have to do to keep you safe."

Chapter Ten

Ori

Oh dear. I don't want her to reject me, but I do need her help. I knew this could be a problem, though I hoped it wouldn't be. I really don't want her to think I'm a monster but if I want to be more solid, I have no choice.

Here goes nothing, as they say.

"Anne, to get my life I need to take bits from others. I was—I know this may be disturbing but forgive me—I was surviving on the life energy of *insects* until recently."

"Oh, that explains all the dead flies and stuff I find in my bed sometimes."

"Yes, my apologies." I grimace before continuing. "It wasn't enough to build myself into more than the rectangle I was, however, so I needed something larger. When that man came over, that disgusting *Todd*, I may have sipped from him a bit."

I rub the back of my neck and shrug my shoulders.

Anne sits silently for a moment before barking out a laugh. "That's what happened to that creep? He got drained by a vampire pillow? I mean, I should feel like scared of you, or bad for Todd, or something but he's a massive asshole. I have no doubt he was going to try something *really bad* with me that night so like...good job."

She holds up her hand for a high five and I give her one, breathing out a sigh of relief. There is more to tell her but at least that part is covered. Now, onto the next.

"I'm glad you're not upset. I am continuing to have a problem with my body, however. I am not quite man enough, yet—too much pillow. I'm going to continue to have these..." I point to where my neck was flopping earlier, "...episodes if I don't get a bit stronger."

"Okay, so how do we do it then? I don't think we can get Todd back over here," she says with a snort.

"No, I don't believe so. I don't suppose you know any other 'massive assholes' you wouldn't mind being drained of their life forces?"

I laugh until I notice she isn't laughing. *Oh dear.*

"I wasn't serious, please don't be upset."

"No, it's okay. I think I do know other creeps. A lot of them. You can just take a little at a time though, right? It doesn't have to be a whole bunch like with Todd?"

"Yes. I can take *very* small amounts. I believe I can, at least, I haven't tried it on a person but the amounts I take from insects are so small I am assuming I can take the same from people."

My Anne grins in a way that reminds me of a certain classic, animated, green Christmas creature looking to steal presents. She rubs her hands together and *cackles.*

"Let's go for a walk."

Chapter Eleven

Anne

I'm not a cruel person, I swear, I just really don't like people who grab onto me without permission. The idea of having a tiny bit of revenge is too delicious to resist. Grabbing my purse and Ori's hand on the way, I grin like a fiend as I march toward the front door.

"Where are we going, my love?" he asks so sweetly.

"You won't *really* hurt anyone, right? And you can take the life force, or whatever it's called, fast?" I ask as I shut the door behind us and start down the street. "So, let's say you just brush up against someone. You could take a little bit, right? You only need a little more mojo, meaning you'd only need a few people, so if we just took from a handful of jerks, it wouldn't be too bad of a thing."

"Yes to all of that but what are you planning, Anne?"

"Follow me."

Ori follows my commands blindly and for a moment I feel a little guilty, like I'm bossing him around, until he stumbles next to me. I nearly tumble down with him when he dips downward. When I look in the direction I'm falling, I see that his thigh has bent flat in half.

"One moment please," he pleads, falling to one knee as he adjusts his stuffing to refill his thigh. Once he's finished, he stands up and retakes my hand. "My apologies. Let us continue."

I don't feel so bad pulling him along now. He needs this, he needs me to take him to these guys. Ori is a sweetheart, and I can't let him fall apart just because I'm too chicken to be a little bit ruthless. The thought of him getting hurt—or worse—because of my hesitation frightens me more than I thought it would.

So, I take him to the corner where the teenage jerks hang out and sure enough, they're there. A little before we get to the corner, I drag Ori over to the shadow of a building where I can talk to him a little more privately. My fingertips itch to be soothed but I grab Ori's hands instead.

"See those guys? They called me names and grabbed my arm and stuff. They're really young, like nineteen years old I think, so if you take just a tiny bit, they won't miss it. They're huge jerks and they deserve it anyway. Okay?"

My stomach kind of hurts when I say it. I mean, it's definitely not like I'm Light Yagami or something, I'm not killing them, but it's not a nice thing to do.

A flapping sound distracts me. I see Ori's ear blowing wildly in the breeze, nothing more now than flat fabric against his head as he smiles his adorably dimpled smile and tells me, "Of course. I would do anything for you, my Anne."

No, it's not a nice thing to do but for Ori it's the *right* thing to do.

Chapter Twelve

Ori

Anne and I walk to the corner of her street where some hooligans are crowded near a bus stop. The ruffians begin shouting as soon as they see her.

"Hey look, that crazy girl has a man."

"Girl, when'd you get a man? How about a real man, huh?"

My anger flares hot inside me. Oh, I'm going to enjoy taking life from them, even though it won't be much.

Anne is silent as we walk through their group, silent even as they *touch her face.* Yes, one taps on her cheek as we walk past, and if she would have allowed it, I would have done whatever I could to have torn that man's arm right off. *No one touches my Anne but me.* But no, she wouldn't want that. Instead of indulging my more violent fantasies, I subtly drag my fingers across their exposed hands and arms, incredibly lightly, as we walk past, enjoying the shivers and brief flare of dullness in each of their eyes as I touch them.

By the time we pass they're all silent, confused looks on their faces. We turn the corner and head around the block, back to her apartment, unspeaking the entire way.

When we get inside she stomps to the bathroom, slamming the door shut. I hear the water running and I know she must be washing the touch from her face.

The memory of his dry, cracked fingers on her soft, freckled skin makes my stomach feel like it's filled with lead and my fists clench. If I could return I would take more life from them. *Bastards.* But no, I will always do what Anne desires and she told me only to take a little, so now the only thing I take are deep breaths until I'm calm. I work on making myself more solid.

When Anne returns I am built up much more strongly than I was before. There should be no falling apart now. There's only one bit of me left to create and I've saved some energy for that. It's important I have her input on that part more than any other, however, so I'll wait until she's ready to help me.

"How are you feeling, Ori?" she asks as she walks into the bedroom, drying her face, now red from scrubbing, and sets her glasses on the small table next to her bed.

"Wonderful. Our mission was a success." I raise my arms and do a slow spin with a wide grin on my face, showing her that I am whole and solid.

"That's fantastic, because I want to take you up on your earlier offer." Anne tosses the towel into her laundry basket and shakes her damp hair out.

"What do you mean?" My heart rate increases; she can't mean what I think she means.

My darling Anne wraps her arms around my neck, gazing up into my wide eyes. "It's time I finally experienced real touch, Ori, and I can't think of anyone better to try it with than you. I know I've just found you but you're perfect. When I thought you were hurt...I was scared, Ori. Even though I didn't know you, I wanted to help you so much. I would have been devastated to lose you. It's weird to feel like that so soon but I don't care, this whole thing is fucking weird as hell, right? So, let's go for it. Touch me, Ori."

My hands slightly shake as I tuck her hair behind her ears, run my fingertips along her jaw, my thumb across her barely parted lips.

"Do you want more touch than this?" I pause with my palm against her cheek.

Anne is breathing hard, her eyes closed. Her little pink tongue darts across her lips before she opens those bright eyes and looks into mine.

"Please. Touch me everywhere, Ori."

"Gladly."

Using my new strength, I grab my love under her thick rump and lift her until she is face to face with me. Her arms wrap around my neck and her legs wrap around my waist, pushing her body flush against me. I barely hold back a moan at the feeling. I take a breath of time to memorize this moment before I walk her to the bed, laying her down flat on her back. Her hair spreads around her face, chest heaving, and her legs remain spread wide around my hips as I loom over her. I've never had this view of her. *She's perfect.*

"Is this too weird? To move this fast?" Anne's adorable, freckled nose scrunches up in concern. "It's just, I mean, you're so hot and nice and I'm really excited to experience all the things I never have before, you know? But if you think this is bad then we can slow it down, okay?"

The hem of Anne's t-shirt slides smoothly over her stomach as I drag it slowly up her body.

"Why wait? We know what we want." I slip the shirt the rest of the way over her head and *tsk* when she crosses her arms over her chest.

"None of that now, I want to see all of you," I admonish her as I move her arms to her sides and reach behind her to unclasp her bra.

It's a bit harder with my inexperienced fingers than I expected but after a few giggles on both our ends I manage to get it undone. Anne lets out a shaky breath as I pull the bra from her body, revealing her full chest to me.

I can feel my new pupils expand as I gaze down at her lovely breasts. The large mounds of them fall heavily to the side as she's lying flat on her back. Her nipples are hard already, and the area around them is a soft pinkish brown. I can't resist dragging the pad of my thumb over one of those peaked nipples, making her arch up into my hand with a soft hiss.

"Your skin...it doesn't feel exactly like skin. I mean, it feels like how a thumb should be sort of rough, but it also feels like...well, fabric." Anne takes my hand and inspects it. "It looks much more like flesh than it did before we left the house earlier, and it does feel like it at first, but on my lips and, um, nipple I could tell it wasn't. On my sensitive spots, basically, it felt more like denim than skin."

"Did that upset you?" I roll off of her and lie next to her. *Have I disgusted her?*

"Oh no, not at all." She rolls over to face me, grabbing my face in her hands. "It's perfect. I freaking love it. Seriously. If this trend continues and I don't have to worry about you feeling like skin in my other sensitive spots then I am going to be ecstatic, Ori, for real. In fact, we should check right now to see if it's just your thumbs that feel like fabric."

Anne blinks her eyes slowly, moves her face closer to mine, pulling me toward her. *Yes.* Our lips part slightly, and we meet in a soft kiss. After several quick, gentle kisses, she slips her tongue into my mouth, seeking mine. I'm only too happy to greet her. She moans as our tongues tangle together, and she presses her unclothed chest against my shirt.

Pulling away finally she takes a ragged breath, brushing away the hair that has fallen into my eyes.

"Satin. Your mouth feels like the slipperiest, smoothest satin." She rests her head on my chest and lets out a breathless laugh. "It's too perfect. This has to be a dream."

I pet her hair and pull her tight against me. "Not a dream, my darling Anne, though I admit I question the reality of it myself every time you allow me the blessing of your touch."

Anne groans and pushes away from me. "You're too freaking sweet, I can't stand it."

She fusses with a button on my shirt, pouting. "Why am I topless and you're still fully dressed? Take off your clothes, right now."

"Gladly, dear."

As I begin to unbutton my shirt, Anne leans over and begins to kiss me, her hands running through my hair. I fumble through the work of unbuttoning, distracted by her perfect tongue, somehow managing after an awkwardly long moment. I work my arms out of the sleeves, pulling away from the kiss as I turn to toss the shirt onto the floor.

"I'll pick it up later, I promise." I laugh.

When I turn back to Anne, she isn't laughing one bit. She's staring at my exposed torso, her mouth slightly ajar, eyes wide. Anne reaches out her small hand and runs her fingers from my neck to the waistband of my pants.

"Damn, we really did a good job designing you didn't we? I mean, you looked good before but after you got that extra juice from those corner guys you really...wow."

I look down at my body to see what she's talking about and notice that I have become more defined. I look quite fantastic indeed. Smirking, I lie back on my elbows.

"I wonder if the rest of me looks as good, hmm?" When she goes to hastily grab the button on my pants, I stop her hand. "You first."

"Rude!" she scoffs, feigning outrage, but I can see the glint of playfulness in her eyes. "Fine."

She tugs her jeans off with no gracefulness, sticking her tongue out at me, making me laugh. When she's left in nothing but her blue, cotton underwear she grabs the button on my pants once again.

"Now it's you, dang it."

Still laughing, I let her undo my button, unzip my zipper, and slowly tug my pants from my hips. My laughter dies out when she straddles my thighs and runs her fingers along the waistband of my black undergarments. I'm forced to stop her hands once again, this time with a sigh.

"We have to talk."

Chapter Thirteen

Anne

"What's wrong?" I cock my head to the side, confused. I thought he'd want me to get into his pants. I mean, I noticed it's pretty, uh, flat in his underwear but I'm thinking maybe he's just nervous. Or maybe his parts are super small? Either way, I don't care, I want him to feel comfortable as much as I want to touch him.

Jeez that feels weird, wanting to touch someone. For the first time, though, I feel that desire.

"Nothing is wrong, my love, we simply need to finish something. You see, we still need to complete my cock." Ori blushes as he says that final word, then clears his throat. "And the rest of the bits too, I suppose."

"Ooh! Okay! So, I get to like decide what it's going to look like and stuff?" I raise an eyebrow.

"Exactly. You'll be the only one who gets to benefit from it so why shouldn't you get to decide its features? Just like the rest of me, it belongs to you, Anne."

I wiggle my fingers in front of me in a steeple formation. "Mwa, ha, ha. This is going to be fun."

I pause for a moment to think of what I should do until a thought occurs to me.

"Wait, I have no idea what I want, realistically." Flopping down next to Ori on the bed, I pout at my realization. "I thought I was going to be a sexy Doctor Frankenstein there for a second, but I don't know anything about sex that isn't from hentai or like movies."

We sit in thoughtful silence until Ori breaks it.

"We could start with what you do know, perhaps? We've seen them on the internet when you've browsed your laptop lying in bed. You only need to give me a vague idea of which one you'd like to start with. Then we can adjust from there."

"That's a good idea. I grew up on the internet, I've seen dicks before. I always quickly looked away because...ugh, people, but still. Okay. Maybe, uh, well there was that one picture that was kind of nice that I even paused on recently before deleting it that those trolls posted under my comment on the Visual Novels Creators Forum. It was like, I don't know, six inches and a little thick and it didn't curve much or anything, I guess. Can you try that?"

I put my hands on my cheeks, feeling how hot they are. *Ugh this is awkward.*

"Right away, my dear," Ori replies with a dashing grin.

Soon enough a bulge begins to inflate in his underpants. I stifle a giggle at the sight. It's less like a cock growing hard and more like a balloon inflating. It's just so silly, but when it's finally done the outline of it is definitely *not* a balloon. My mouth goes dry at the sight of it. My fingers itch to pull down that waistband—*finally.*

"Ori, is it time for me to look?" I manage to choke out.

"I believe so, yes. Remember I can change anything."

I slide my fingers under the waistband of his black under-garments and slip them slowly down. His freshly created cock springs free, and I gasp. It's exactly as I asked for, beautiful if ever one could be described as such, and balls to match.

"Is it alright then?" he asks, his voice barely above a whisper.

I look up to see his cheeks have turned shockingly pink.

"Are you feeling shy?"

My eyebrows practically raise to the ceiling. So far I've been the super awkward one but right now he looks nervous as heck. I can't resist poking at him a little bit; he's just too cute.

"No...I mean, a bit, yes." He crosses his arms over his chest, uncrosses them, then crosses them again, seeming as if he no longer has any idea what to do with his body.

"Well, you don't have to be nervous. You look super-hot."

Ori exhales sharply, tense muscles relaxing.

"However," I continue, and he inhales deeply again, eyes wide, "I think I should sample the goods before deciding if they're satisfactory, shouldn't I?"

I toss a leg over his so that his lovely cock juts up before me. I can see his chest rise and fall quickly as the speed of his breathing increases.

"That sounds like the correct choice, I believe. Only rational, yes," he chokes out.

I lick my finger and run the tip of it down the length of him, watching his face as he makes a strangled noise. I can't help but giggle at his reaction. If just that small touch made him react that way then what will even more bring?

This time I bend over, take him into my hand, and run my tongue up his shaft and around the top of him. Ori sits up so fast he nearly smashes his face into mine. He puts his hands on either side of my face and kisses the top of my head, my cheek, my shoulder.

"Sorry," he says as he lays back down. "Brand new equipment and all. It needs a bit of calibration I think. By which I mean I need a moment or two before I receive the focus of your attention or I'll just make a mess everywhere."

Ori runs a long-fingered hand through his increasingly messy mop of dark hair.

"Besides, I want to focus on your pleasure, Anne. I want to please you, to make love to you."

I lay my head on his chest and consider the next steps between us. This is all very fast but very exciting. His cock is pressed against my stomach. Feeling how hard and thick it is gets me a bit nervous about the whole sex thing.

"So, we can adjust as we go, right? I just want to make sure we're on the same page," I ask as I sit up, looking him in the eye.

If we're going to have fun I want to make sure I don't offend him by doing the build-a-dick thing during it.

"You absolutely will not offend me if that's what you're concerned about. I want you to make me perfect, tell me what you desire, my darling."

"This might be weird but what if we adjust it while it's, uh, inside me? I mean, we could find the perfect size if it's literally inside, right? Is that dumb?" I rub my fingers together nervously, waiting for his reactions.

"That's not in any way a foolish suggestion. In fact, I think it's brilliant. Who else in the world would have that opportunity?" He sits up and strokes the side of my cheek, eyelids heavy with desire. "Shall we give it a go then?"

Chapter Fourteen

Ori

"Um, I'll be right back." Anne jumps off the bed and sprints to the bathroom, shutting the door behind her.

Hmm. Well, she's either too nervous or needs a moment to clean up, I'm assuming. Then again, I know very little about women so who knows really? I lie back with an arm behind my head and wait for her to return.

It only takes a bit for her to come back to me. I watch only too gladly as she walks back down the hall toward me in her little cotton panties, her full breasts bouncing, her cheeks red with a shy blush.

"Come to me, my love, and lay next to me." I slide over and pat the bed beside me, and she follows my instruction. "Take off your panties and spread your legs for me, let me see your pretty cunt."

I decide to be forward with her, with it being her first time and all. She's likely to be a bit nervous and in need of direction.

I admit I'm a nervous virgin as well but, being a pillow, I don't have the virginity hang ups people do and so I feel it's my responsibility to take the lead.

Her breath comes out as shaky as her hands as she slowly removes her panties. She looks away shyly as she opens her legs for me, not saying a word. I climb between them, on my knees before her.

"You're magnificent, Anne. Spread your lips for me, I want to see all of you."

She makes a squeaking sound. "Ori!" she yelps before attempting to close her legs, but she can't when I'm between them.

"*Tsk.* Don't deny me now, please. Be a naughty girl for once, my sweet Anne." My lip curls on one side when she takes a sharp breath and opens wide again.

She places one hand on her breast and the other cups the dark curls on her enticing mound. She uses two fingers to spread the outer lips of her folds, showing me the inside of her offerings. I groan as I crawl forward, needing to witness that pink perfection as close as possible.

"Anne," I beg in a voice so strained I can barely scratch it out, "may I taste you?"

"Oh. Yes, please. That would be great actually." She giggles. I grin at the sound.

Inhaling her scent as I kiss my way up her inner thigh, the clean, light, fragrance goes straight to my newly formed cock. My eyes meet hers, seeking assurance one last time, and she gives a tiny nod. It's all I need before I playfully swat her hand away from her glistening cunt and plant my face there instead.

My satin tongue glides through her slippery folds, pushing deep into her core, teasing her, then out again to circle the firm bud of her clitoris. She pulls my head against her sweet heat and grinds against my face, using me roughly as if I were simply the pillow of before, only now I've got lips and tongue and teeth to further the pleasure.

She pulls me harder against her, so hard that a normal man wouldn't be able to breathe. Thankfully, being mostly a pillow I can last much longer without air and can survive her overpowering embrace until I feel her shake and tense around me. Wetness floods against me as she cries out in pleasure. *Yes.* This is what I've dreamed of for so long.

"Ori, oh fuck, that was amazing. I can't believe it." Anne pants when her climax is complete. She pulls me up by the ears to meet her eye-to-eye and when her barely focused eyes take in my face finally she yelps and pushes me away. "Your face!"

"What is it?" I look into the mirror on the closet door only to see I've been flattened a bit, mostly my nose. *Oh my.* "Oh, well, it appears I only need to fluff myself back up. Apologies."

I give myself a few pats and like a good pillow I am back in tip top shape.

"Okay. I keep forgetting you're a pillow. Huh. I suppose I was grinding kind of hard." Anne snorts out a laugh.

"Not that I minded one bit." I slide a finger along the seam of her pussy, feeling how incredibly wet she is, and making her hiss in surprise. "And you certainly enjoyed it. That's all that matters to me."

"I really did enjoy it. Very much, thank you." Anne bites her lip. "I think I'm ready to, you know."

"To what, Anne?" I fit myself between her thighs when she doesn't answer me, one of my hands goes to her hair as the other lazily strokes a nipple. "Tell me, you have to say it. You're ready to what?"

"You know what I want, Ori." Anne runs her fingers through my sleek, dark hair.

I put my mouth against her ear, run my tongue along that lovely shell until she moans.

"Say it," I demand. "I need to hear it. Do you want me to fuck you, my sweet? Do you want my cock inside you, the one you've created to be perfect just for you? I've spent years thinking of being inside your hot, wet, cunt and I need to hear you tell me I'm allowed to be there. My entire existence is for you, I want nothing more than your pleasure in all things, and I promise them to you, if only you'll allow it. So, say it, my darling. Say the words."

"Yes, please. Fuck me, Ori, now, I need it." Anne grips my hips and pushes me against her wet center.

I grin against the crook of her neck in relief.

"As you wish."

Chapter Fifteen

Anne

I'm begging for a pillow to fuck me. What kind of day is this? I mean, he's in man form but still. This has to be the first time in history it's ever happened. I'm seriously about to lose my virginity to a *living pillow*. Holy shit.

You know, this is kind of...awesome, actually. I'm not going to complain.

Ori runs a finger between my folds, making me sigh in delight, but when he inserts two fingers slowly into my pussy I find myself making a desperate, keening noise I've never made before.

"Is this alright?" Ori asks, sounding almost breathless as he carefully plunges his fingers in and out of me.

"Yes," I mewl. "It feels good."

"Are you ready for me then, my love?"

"Yes, I am." I look into his eyes and nod, reassuring him.

He smiles softly, showing that dimple I like so much.

Ori adjusts my hips slightly before aligning the tip of his cock against my center. I can see his throat bob right before he begins to enter me, and I have a brief moment to realize he might be even more anxious than I am, considering how long he's waited for this. It's only a moment of thought, because next thing I know, I feel him pushing inside.

He moves agonizingly slowly. I'm super wet and turned on, so it goes pretty easy at first, but after a bit it starts to hurt just a little.

"Wait, stop." I put my hands on his shoulders. "Be, uh, smaller for a second. You're kind of big I guess, and it hurts a little. Maybe we can get it in smaller and then see about going bigger?"

Ori chuckles softly. "Brilliant idea."

He shrinks inside me; it's a strange sort of relief.

"Is this alright?"

"Much better. Now kiss me," I plead.

Ori obliges by giving me the hottest, deepest kiss imaginable. I groan into his mouth at the fantastic feeling and when he starts moving into me again it's the perfect slippery compliment to his tongue.

"That feels so fucking good." My voice is so much higher than normal when he breaks the kiss to lick and suck my neck as he slips in and out of me in a slow, smooth rhythm.

"*You* feel so good," I add. "Your cock is like some impossible combination of velvet, silk, and latex. So soft and smooth, feels like nothing I could have imagined."

I moan as he breathes hard against my neck and begins to move faster. "Go bigger now, Ori, to what you were before."

"Yes, Anne," he replies with a choked voice.

He lifts his head to kiss me again. I can feel him swelling inside me, the sudden increase in friction making us both groan low in our throats.

He breaks the kiss and pulls my hair back, giving me a desperate look. "I can feel your pulse around me. It's as if your heart beats only for the swell of my cock."

"Faster, Ori," I beg, my voice a high whine.

"Happy to oblige, my sweet." Ori hooks my legs over his arms and pumps faster, making me shout.

"Bigger now. And deeper. And *fuck*—go harder," I cry out.

I don't know if I can handle it but *I want it.*

Ori doesn't answer in words, he just growls before tossing my legs over his shoulders, making me yelp in surprise. In this position he's deeper, thrusts hard and fast. His cock swells much bigger than before. Almost too big.

But I don't want him to stop. It hurts, but the manic look in his eyes, the way he grits his teeth, his hair falling over his brow, is too beautiful to interrupt.

"Touch yourself, Anne," he barks out in a command. It's so unlike what I've seen from him so far, so...*alpha* I can't help but comply.

I circle my clit between the two of us as he relentlessly thrusts into me. I arch into him and cry out.

"Oh fuck, it's too much," I yell.

"No, it's not. Come for me, Anne. Now."

Once again, his command is one that must be met. I clench around him with a silent scream. I've never had an orgasm this hard. I squeeze so tight around Ori he grunts, his rhythm briefly faltering. I'm coming so hard I can't even make a sound; my mouth hangs open while my body is one tense statue. When, finally, the orgasm ends, I gasp loudly, throwing my hands over my head as I watch the point where our centers meet.

"You're not done, Anne," Ori growls. "I remember the things you like to watch. I remember the tentacles."

"What?" I am wholly unable to grasp what Ori is saying.

He's still sliding in and out of me, albeit more slowly than before, and it's all I can focus on.

"What does the hentai have to do with this?"

"Everything, Anne." Ori presses a hard kiss against my throat, licking and sucking hard enough to surely leave a mark.

I moan, running my fingers through the back of his hair as he kisses me, rocking my hips against his as he moves. It feels good, wonderful, and then it feels like...tentacles.

There are tentacles touching my vagina.

"Ori? What are you doing?" I squeal as one tentacle rubs against my already overly sensitized, slippery clit.

"Anything you want, Anne. Remember always that I can be anything you want me to be."

Ori pulls back far enough to gaze at the point of our lovemaking, a crazed look crossing his perfectly created features. A second thin tentacle slips alongside Ori's cock, stretching me, and I cry out in perfect agony.

"I will always give you everything you want even when you don't know you want it."

A third tentacle nudges against my rear entrance unexpectedly and I flinch. After a few breaths, I relax and decide that if I am going to be a tentacle fucker, then I might as go all the way.

Come on in, the backdoor's open!

The feeling of the first tentacle rubbing my clit combined with the second pressed against his cock inside my hot channel is already so intense. When that third one works its way into my tight asshole, I just explode.

I am rubbed, rutted, worked on, and writhed against and it's beyond overwhelming. Ori groans as I squeeze, pulse, and shudder through my climax. His eyes can't stop flitting back and forth between my face and the place where he's fucking me. I finally manage to lift myself enough to look at what's going on down there and catch a glimpse of the tentacle rubbing my clit.

It's white, and smooth, and fuck *it's so weird, right?* But *damn* it feels good.

Suddenly the tentacles snap out of existence, or absorb back into his body, I'm not really sure. All I know is they're gone fast. I yelp with surprise. I'm left with my beautiful Ori, and his made-to-order cock. He kisses me deeply, running his fingers through my hair over and over before pulling back and rutting hard into me.

"*Oh*, Anne," Ori chokes out. "I'm going to come."

"Then come, please, fill me up."

I'm assuming he can't get me pregnant, so the whole breeding kink thing will be alright, right?

"You don't understand." His face screws up and he pulls out of me with a hiss, holding his cock above me.

Okay, coming on my chest is fine too. I close my eyes and wait for the onslaught of jizz...but it doesn't come.

When I hear him gasp and moan my name, I cautiously open my eyes. Something tickles my stomach and I give an incredulous snort as I see the white, fluffy things in the air.

I lift my head to see a final spurt of downy feathers float out from the end of his cock. They're everywhere in the air between us, landing on my nude body, my face, my hair.

I begin to laugh; I can't control it.

The blissed-out look on Ori's face falls at the sound of my laughter. *Oh no.* He slides backward on the bed, away from me.

"No, no, I'm not laughing at you. Come here, please." I hold out my arms and wait, hoping he isn't too upset.

After a moment his look softens and he settles into my arms, head on my shoulder. "You promise you don't think I'm disgusting? I didn't think about what would happen until I was nearly there and then it hit me. All that's inside me that would come out are feathers."

"Disgusting? How could I think you're disgusting? The feathers are so sweet! I laughed because of how much joy it brought me, not because I was making fun of you or something." I rub my face into his hair. "It's just another way you're perfect for me. It means you can never get me pregnant and since I absolutely do not want to ever get knocked-up that's like a huge plus."

I nip his ear and he laughs before settling his head on my chest.

"You're in charge of sweeping up all the mess though."

"Gladly. If a bit of housework is the only sacrifice I need to make to make love to the most beautiful woman on the planet, then so be it."

"You know, you haven't really met any other women."

"I don't need to. I've seen them on the internet when you're browsing it."

"Oh boy. You have a lot to learn. What am I going to do with you?" I ruffle his hair and giggle, thinking of all the things I'm going to have to teach him.

"Well, hopefully more sex. And you'll need to take me to buy at least one more pillow, as a replacement you know, since you're one short. For me to use, not you. You have me."

I roll my eyes. "Okay, Ori. Let's get a little rest and after that we'll learn about the world beyond the internet."

Chapter Sixteen

Ori

"And this is a kitten. Personally, my pet of choice. They're just so fuzzy-wuzzy."

My Anne and I are at the animal rescue shelter picking out a pet. She's wanted one for a while, and I need company while she's at work, so we think a pet might be good for us.

I'm not quite at the social level to venture into the world on my own for long periods of time yet so I'm stuck at home without Anne during the day. I really don't mind; it's not as if that wasn't my reality for my entire existence prior to becoming a man. It will be nice to have another living being around though, I will admit. I have a great urge to serve and care for Anne, as she's the whole reason I'm alive. When she's not around, it will be good to use some of that energy to take care of a being that was abandoned and needs it desperately.

"Here, you hold the kitty." Anne passes the wriggling kitten to me, and I wrap it in my arms.

It really is a wonderful creature, so soft and full of life. I scratch the top of its tiny gray head, and it vibrates with a purr. My face cracks wide in a smile. The kitten kneads my arm until its claw catches on my fabric and tears a small hole. I don't bleed but a small puff of feathers floats through the air. The kitten sits up to bat at them.

I quickly hand the feline back to Anne, who looks around the room to make sure no one has seen what just happened. Thankfully no one has.

"Well, perhaps we should get a hamster instead. Or a fish."

I feel bad, crushing her kitten dreams. But Anne simply laughs.

"It's alright Ori, I think fish are pretty cool, too."

The next day we finished setting up our goldfish. Anne goes to work. The sweet little swimmer was a great choice. It's a lovely fish, and we picked a great big tank, so it has a lot of room to swim around. Apparently, the person who had the fish before us kept it in a tiny bowl, which is quite sad, so I'm glad to give it a new life.

A knock on the door startles me, interrupting my enjoyment of Carl, which is what we named the fish.

I open the door and find none other than the landlord, an absolute asshole. He's been bothering Anne about me staying at the apartment and finally forced her to pay extra for me to stay here. I have no idea what he wants now.

"Yes, James?" I drawl.

"I've said twenty times now, it's Jimmy. Just checking on the place, seeing you ain't got no more people staying here." He looks past me into the apartment.

"I assure you we have no one else here. Have a fine day now." I move to close the door, but *Jimmy* puts his Croc-wearing foot in the way.

"Not so fast. I see you got a pet now. That means a pet fee. That's a pet deposit plus pet rent each month." He grins as he scratches a sweaty armpit. "Gonna need that right away, fancy boy."

"It's a fish, *Jimmy*. I'm sure you don't need all of that." I say through clenched teeth.

Jimmy pushes past me into the apartment and I can feel a hot rage burning in my chest.

"Well, if you got a fish, you might have something else. Let's see. You got a dog? A cat? Cat fee is extra seeing as they stink up the place and all."

He starts to head toward the bedroom. *Absolutely not.*

I take a step to follow him, but my leg gives out.

Damn it!

I haven't told Anne yet, but it appears I need to feed to keep up my life force. Those first times weren't enough; I need regular maintenance. I can't eat *food*, we've discovered, unfortunately, so that's no help. I need to drain life. I've been carefully skimming tiny bits from rude people when we've gone out without telling Anne, but everyone has been so pleasant lately. *Fuck.*

I rub my leg until I can limp along enough behind the landlord. By this time, he's made it to Anne's room and is bent over, searching under her bed.

"I don't see no cat but that don't mean you won't get one, so I'll be back soon," he says as he stands up.

I grab him by his thick, sweaty throat.

"I don't believe you will, James. I don't believe you'll bother me or my precious Anne ever again."

I begin to drain his life force slowly, relishing the feel of taking revenge on this parasite. I watch as he turns gray, feel my leg become stronger as he does. Before I am able to take all his life I stop, letting go of his throat. He falls, but I catch his limp form.

"No, you won't be coming back, will you?" I smile, pinching his sagging cheek.

As I leave the apartment, I check to make sure the stairwell is empty, then carry James to the bottom of the stairs, where I leave him seated, drooling, propped carefully so he won't fall. Someone will find him eventually and take him somewhere safe, I'm sure.

I return to the apartment and watch Carl again, happily swimming in his big tank. I feel a strange sensation on my wrist and lift my sleeve to see what's going on. *Oh no.*

Flesh. Real flesh.

It appears I took too much life force and started to become more *man* than pillow. This simply won't do. Anne won't like this one bit. I run to the bedroom and remove my clothes, checking in the mirror to see if any other parts of me have turned to flesh. Thankfully there aren't any. I sigh in relief.

When Anne returns, I carefully avoid letting her touch that particular area on my wrist. It will take a while for my life energy to fade down enough for that to go away but I'm sure it will. For now, I'll just be careful she doesn't touch it.

As for James, he was gone when she arrived, and no one came knocking at our door to ask any questions. Perfect.

"Darling, are you hungry? Do you want me to order you some tacos? Curry?" I ask my sweet Anne as I rub her feet.

She had a tough day at work, and I want to make sure she's as comfortable at home as she can be.

"Oh no, I'm good. I had some pizza at work for some dumb pizza party they threw as a bonus instead of actually giving us a raise. So, I'm stuffed."

My lip quirks up at the side. I lean back on our new pillow, one stuffed with artificial material—I don't trust feathers—and grin broadly at my Anne.

"Actually, I believe I'm the one that's stuffed."

Double Stuffed

by Sylvia Morrow

Content Notes

Tentacles, murder, attempted sexual assault, implied sex work, fear of germs, extreme devotion, chasing, tics, near accidental death of pet, loss of virginity, confusion about sex, eating food you don't like to please other people.

Chapter One

Ori

"Carl," I say to our goldfish. "Prepare yourself for a night of having to listen to loud and boisterous intercourse. Louder than usual, I should say."

My Anne. My darling Anne. She'll be home soon, and I can tell her of the wonderful thing I've discovered. Oh, how excited she'll be. I'm certain of it.

I brush my shoulders off and smirk. Anne and I have had a wonderful relationship these past few months and we've kept things quite lively in the bedroom. I'll do whatever it takes to please my Anne.

The lock on the door clicks as a key turns inside it. She's home! My love! I stand near the door, next to Carl, waiting as I do each day for her when she comes home from work. The door opens and I see her there. Her short brown hair is mussed, her eyes sleepy, even her glasses are a little crooked as if too tired to stay on straight. It's clear she's exhausted and I probably should let her rest before pouncing on her, but I can't keep this exciting news inside.

"Welcome home darling." I kiss her soft cheek, barely containing the excitement inside my feather-filled body. "I have wonderful news."

"Hi Ori," she says with a yawn, then turns to Carl and waves at his tank. "Hello Carl, sweetie. Alright Ori, can the news wait until after I have a shower?"

"I'll be quick," I reply, bouncing on my toes. "I found the most exciting thing on the internet today."

"Oh boy." Anne rubs her temples and sits on the sofa.

"I swear it's good. I promise I'm not being scammed or fooled by a creepypasta yet again." I cringe a little as I recall the times my naivety got me in trouble. Oh well, that's the past. This is the wonderful future. "No this, my love, is fantastic."

I drop to my knees before her and take hold of her hands. Anne flinches a bit and I know she must be thinking about how many germs are on her hands right now, and that I'm touching them. We've been working on that, however, her particular problems with germs, and she knows rationally all will be fine in a moment. She takes a calming breath and when she relaxes after only a second, I continue.

"Anne. I've discovered something we can explore together. I think you'll love it. It's called," I pause dramatically as I rise, take hold of her face, and look her directly in the eyes, "the Omegaverse."

Anne stays silent for a long moment, only blinking, before suddenly breaking out into wild laughter. Confusion crosses my face as I set my hands in my lap and settle to the floor. *Why is she laughing? This is a serious matter.*

"Oh, Ori. You're so sweet. I'll get in the shower, clean up, and we can talk after. I have some stuff we need to talk about anyway, okay? We can talk about your..." she breaks out into giggles for a moment again before continuing, "*discovery* in a bit."

Disappointed but relieved that we'll still address it, I stand to assist Anne in rising from the sofa. She's so beautiful and perfect I can't help but agree to anything she asks. She's the reason I'm alive, after all.

"Alright, darling. Shall I join you?"

Her gaze heats as she inspects my form. I watch as her breathing increases in speed and her pupils dilate. *Yes. There she is, my spicy girl.*

"You'll get all soggy. You're made of fabric. Won't that be an issue?" she asks in a near whisper.

"You know I clean and dry myself carefully in private. I can handle it. I'll stay mostly out of the spray. Let me wash you." As long as I'm careful not to get *too* wet I can handle it anyway. I hope.

Taking her hips, I press them against me so that she can feel how hard I am for her. She moans and grinds her pelvis harder against me. Our desire for one another has not lessened one bit over time.

"I take my washing very seriously."

"No one takes anything as seriously as I take pleasuring you, Anne," I tell her, and *I mean it with everything I am.*

Anne whimpers as I lift her and carry her to the bathroom. I set her on the edge of the far side of the bath while I run the water, testing it with one finger to make sure the temperature is right. When it's ready, I undress, as does my Anne, and I open the curtain, ready to properly welcome her home.

Chapter Two

Anne

"Oh, Ori, that feels amazing," I moan as he runs the loofah up and down my back. The scent of the antibacterial soap relaxes me after a hard day at work and the scratch of the loofah makes me feel like all my troubles are being scrubbed away.

Only lightly damp, Ori has managed to stay out of the spray, so when I turn around, he still looks just as gorgeous as always. His black hair sticks to his forehead from the steam and I reach up to smooth it back. Ori takes hold of my waist and presses me tightly against him.

"Nothing could feel as good as the way your skin feels pressed against me, Anne." Ori manages to bathe me in compliments just as well as water. "Nothing except the way it feels to be inside you, of course."

Ori's gaze lowers to my lips and my stomach flutters with delight at the knowledge of the impending kiss. I will never, ever tire of this man. The water sprays over my back, hot and stinging the way I like it, as he leans in for a kiss...then his hands slip off my waist. Ori steps back and raises his arms with a frown on his face.

"Damn," he says as he inspects the soggy clumps at the ends of his wrists that were his hands. "I held them too long in the water. Help me wring them out, will you?"

Ori grimaces with embarrassment and my heart aches for him. The poor guy has a lot of troubles due to him being made of fabric and feathers.

"Of course I'll help you, honey." I wring one hand out, then the other.

Ori steps out of the shower, carefully avoiding the spray, and shakes off his hands until they're more or less back into shape. Then, with a focused look on his face, he puffs them properly back up.

"There we are. Should be fine in a moment. No harm done. I'll stand here and dry off while you finish your shower, darling. Then we can dress and have our discussion."

"And dinner. I'm starving." As if on cue my stomach rumbles. I hurry to rinse shampoo from my hair. "Do you know if we have any more leftover pizza? I'm too tired to cook, ugh."

"Well, neither Carl nor I ate it so if you didn't then it should still be there."

"Oh, good point," I say with a laugh. "Then leftover pizza and a chat it is."

A few minutes later, we're snuggled together on the sofa in pajamas while I eat my reheated pizza, a popular boy band playing in the background. Ori is reading something on the phone I got him with a confused look.

"I still don't understand. Is it 'Boys' or 'Boy Scouts'? And what does 'Bulletproof' have to do with anything?"

I swallow my pepperoni and sigh. "Once again, I don't know. I'm not their army or whatever it's called or anything, I'm just a casual enjoyer. Okay, one more bite, then I'm done."

With the last bite, I stand and begin the walk to the kitchen to put the plate in the sink and give it a wash before putting it into the dishwasher. I like to clean my dishes thoroughly before washing and drying them as hot as possible in the dishwasher. You can never be too careful with food safety. When I make it back to Ori his phone is put away and he's sitting peacefully, watching Carl swim around. No one can sit as quietly and peacefully for as long as Ori; he had a ton of practice when he was a pillow.

I curl up next to him and snuggle under his arm, which he wraps around me. "Alright, I think we need to discuss something pretty important, Ori."

"Yes. The Omegaverse is quite exciting. We don't have a beta, but I think we'll be fine. Of course, I'll be the alpha, and-"

"Ori!" I interrupt. "That's not what I meant. We can talk about that later if you still want to. Though honestly you really should get off those fan fiction websites for a bit. I never spent that much time on them even in my high school days. And anyway, what I need to say is about our main life, not just the bedroom stuff."

"Oh, alright then. Go on, little omega." He pats me on the head, and I give him a dry look before I continue.

"I think it's time you get out of the house. Every day I go to work, and you stay home and it's not really any kind of life for you. I know I have my own problems, but I can't let them get in the way of you exploring the world. So, I need to be strong for both of us and work through my shit." I sit up straight and give Ori a determined look. "Ori. We're going to the mall."

"But you hate the mall. You've said so several times when your mother tried to get you to go with her," Ori replies, eyebrows raised in shock. He hasn't met my mom yet, but he's overheard plenty of the conversations between her and I.

"I know I do."

"Even when I told you that millennials statistically have a fondness for malls and want to see them return to their glory days you still-"

"Ori, I know. I remember. This is an example of you being home too much. You sat on the computer and looked up statistics about millennials and their shopping habits when you don't even shop. You should be out experiencing these things, not just reading about them. Don't you want to?" I plead with him.

Ori gives me a soft look and runs his hand along my jaw. "Of course, I want to, my love. I simply don't want to make you do anything you don't want to. If it pleased you, I would remain inside forever. It's not as if I know any difference anyway. The only other places I've been, besides our Sunday walks to the park, are the animal rescue down the street and the lingerie store two blocks away. I quite liked that place, by the way. We should go again soon."

My cheeks turn red as I roll my eyes. He liked the lingerie place *a lot* indeed. We spent all of my birthday money there, in fact. And *wow* was it worth every penny.

"Honey, I don't want you to be stuck anywhere. It's time you stopped living only for me and found something else that you love. And before you say something incredibly sweet, like I know you were about to, I know you'll never love anything as much as me. But you don't have to. You just have to find something you really care about."

He crosses his arms and gives me a grumpy look. "I care about things."

"Like what?"

"Like...Carl. I care a lot about Carl. His whole life depends on me, in fact, and I take very good care of him." He smooths the front of his shirt and straightens his posture.

"Yes, you do. I love Carl too. But I mean something outside of the house."

Ori slumps again. "Fine. I suppose I'm a little nervous. I don't want anything to happen that could get me taken from you. People would see me as a monster, you know. They'd study me in a lab. Take me apart. I'd never see you again if they found me out, Anne."

"We won't let them discover your secrets then, Ori. You forget that I love you just as much as you love me."

"Impossible." He scoffs.

"Hey! I took *seven* of your tentacles at once last night. If that's not love, I don't know what is."

Ori offers me a lascivious grin. "It was eight, Anne. If you lost count so easily then it wasn't enough."

I clear my throat as my cheeks heat. "Anyway, the mall. I think it's a good place to start because it has a lot of sensory experiences and different types of people. Plus, it will be good practice for me since I need to get used to loud sounds again. Any time I have to deal with them at work I just get overwhelmed and exhausted. And the mall is close so if things get tough it's only one short bus ride home."

"We should get a car." Ori frowns. "We could make a better escape if things went south."

"If you want a car, you better get a job," I grumble.

Ori grins. "Well, as your alpha I am meant to be the provider of the family so I suppose I should seek employment soon."

"Oh, boy."

Chapter Three

Ori

*H**alloween.* Anne insists we practice dealing with the public before our mall trip and that doing so while still at home is a perfect idea. This means standing on the outside stairs, handing out candy to *children* while in *costume.*

The costume part is mildly entertaining, I suppose. I've been Anne's "butler" all along and it's nice to switch things up for a night. It's quite simple for me to get into costume, as I can change appearance at will. It does take a bit of power, however. Thankfully, on our walk last Sunday someone was harassing an elderly woman ahead of us and I took a few sips from the hooligan as we passed them by without Anne noticing. We did have to purchase some bits of the costume though since I couldn't produce the accessories myself. I'm not enjoying wearing them.

"Must I wear this mask?" I ask as I adjust it once again. The white mask only covers my eyes, yes, but it's quite annoying.

I prefer to have my vision unobstructed in every direction so that I may be on guard to protect Anne all the better.

"If you don't wear both the tuxedo and the mask the costume won't make sense. If I can deal with this ultra long, itchy, blonde wig all evening then you can deal with a little mask."

"It's not the same." I take hold of the cauldron of candy we have prepared for the neighborhood children in my white-gloved hands and stand next to Carl's tank. "Did I tell you that you look lovely?"

"Only about a million times," Anne laughs. "But I love hearing it each time."

"Good. Because I love saying it. What panties are you wearing under that tiny blue skirt, by the way? So that I can at least think about tearing them off while I do this terrible chore."

"You're a pervert. Did you know that?" She scoffs.

"Yes. Now answer the question."

"The white ones with the ruffles." She bites her lip and runs her gloved hand down my white vest. She knows very well that those are my favorite.

"I'm going to take those off with my teeth, you tease," I growl, clutching the cauldron tightly.

"It'll have to wait until I get my treat. I plan on sucking on my candy as soon as we're back inside." She walks past me to the door, stroking my cheek as she goes.

"Tease. Horrible woman."

"You'll just have to punish me for it later then, won't you?" she asks as she opens the door, walking out with an extra sway to her full hips, the red bow at the back of her skirt shaking with each step.

"I certainly will," I whisper, following her out the door and locking it behind us.

Passing out the candy is...fine. I mostly sit on the stairs and hold the cauldron. Anne a couple steps above me, waving and talking to anyone that says anything to us. I admit that some of the children are...cute. I even decide that I don't dislike *all* children. Anne tells me she feels the same, though she still does not want them to touch her. They're too *sticky* and full of *germs* she says. Seeing all the leaky noses come past I can't say she's wrong.

When the stream of children comes to an end Anne stretches out her arms and her white-booted legs with a long yawn.

"I think it's finally time to go in and take a long shower. I did pretty well though, didn't I?" She smiles proudly.

"Yes, you did, darling. You did wonderfully. I'm ready to go home as well." I smile as sweetly as I can, hiding how ready I am to ravish her as soon as our door closes.

And I do. I toss the cauldron down, creating a loud clatter that startles Anne. Wide-eyed she looks at me, searching for something wrong, a reason why I would have tossed it so suddenly. There's nothing wrong at all.

"On your knees," I command. I fling the horrid mask across the room and untie the cape that has been annoying me all night as well, letting it fall to the floor. "We're going to have to take that wig off darling, there's no way it's going to withstand this."

"What's all this about?" Anne asks, eyes wide, hand on her chest, appearing to be shocked at my demands. Of course, I can tell she's only playing at being surprised. I love my naughty little actress oh so much.

"I told you I'd punish you, my love."

"In the name of the moon?" she asks with a cheeky grin as she points to her costume.

I roll my eyes with a huff. "We can do this the hard way if you like."

Stroking her cheek with the back of my hand allows me the privilege of watching her eyes flutter closed in an uncharacteristically angelic way. When her lips turn up in a softly relaxed smile, I take my moment to strike, lifting her over my shoulder and carrying her to the kitchen.

"Hey! What are you doing?" she laughs.

"Punishing a brat."

I lay her back first on the kitchen table and spin her toward me, so that her head hangs over the edge, looking up at me. When she tries to sit up, I gently press her back down. As I begin to undo my pants, I can see her eyes widen again, this time in genuine surprise.

"Oh," she breathes out, "I see."

"Now, open very, very wide."

Licking her lips with a grin she lets out one breathy laugh before following my instructions. I slide my fabric cock into her soft, wet mouth with a sigh that speaks more words than I could say. The first bit of drool at the corner of her lips brings a dark chuckle from the depths of my cotton chest.

"That's my Anne. My naughty, darling Anne."

The wig very much does not withstand this.

Chapter Four

Anne

My yellow-blonde wig falls to the floor as Ori's wonderfully non-flesh cock pushes hard into the back of my throat, making me gag, before I relax and let him pass deeper. While he fucks my throat I reach between my legs and rub my clit in quick circles.

I love that Ori can be so commanding like this sometimes, but so sweet and giving others. He always seems to know what I want before I even do. I mean, I certainly didn't know I wanted to be face-fucked on the kitchen table tonight, that's for sure.

"You look so lovely with my cock in your mouth. You're taking me so well, Anne."

His words make me moan around the thickness of him and I rub myself faster. I love it when he talks like that while he's like this. And that's just the thing; he's never really cruel. The last three months we've done a lot, like *a lot,* of experimenting and discovered what we like. And so maybe I like just a little punishment mixed with all the praise he loves giving me, and maybe he's all too happy to oblige. It's just another way we're perfect for each other.

He thrusts into me faster and I can feel myself approaching climax already. My fingers are drenched and sliding around in firm, manic circles as I get closer and closer to my finish.

"Your punishment is nearly at an end. You're such a good girl." He's panting now and his hips are losing some of their rhythm. He's almost there.

My hips begin to raise, my thighs tightening. A strong orgasm finally crashes through me at the same time as Ori pulls out of my mouth. My pussy is still fluttering as I hear the sloppy wetness of my saliva on him as he pumps himself once, twice, and groans.

Feathers fall over my face and chest. I sneeze as they tickle my nose and sputter as I try to spit one out that's stuck to my tongue. Ori helps me sit up, brushing feathers off of me as he does so.

"You did so well, my love. Thank you."

"Yeah, well, you have to clean up the feathers."

"I always do." He kisses the side of my head and takes my hands in his. "Now, I know you want to take your shower, so why don't you do that, and I'll clean up and make dinner."

"You're a wonderful househusband, you know that?" I ask with a laugh.

"Only an alpha providing sustenance for my omega." He gently slaps me on the ass as I walk away.

"You're so weird," I shout behind me as I walk to the bathroom.

"I'm literally a pillow. What do you expect?"

"He's right, I guess," I laugh to myself.

My shower is hot and brief but sufficient. I put on clean, soft pajamas and find Ori already at the stove making me a grilled cheese and tomato soup.

"Sorry for the simple fare. It's quite late and I didn't want to make something that took all night. I know you have a meeting in the morning."

"Oh, Ori. It's wonderful."

How many guys would be as considerate and sweet as he is? Yeah, okay, he's only cleaning the house, making dinner, and remembering my work schedule. But that's on top of all the other little things he does every day. And I know he would do *anything* for me. I'm so lucky to have him. I doubt there could ever be a second guy as good as Ori on the entire planet.

We eat dinner, well I eat, and Ori tells me about a game he played while I was at work, and then make plans for our trip to the mall. I'm excited for Ori to get to explore more of the world than he has so far but I admit I'm not particularly excited about leaving the house myself. I've had bad luck with people in my life so far and I have no reason to believe any time will be any better than any other. But, if Ori will do anything for me, I'll do anything for him.

"Oh, we can't forget to feed Carl," I say as we're about to head off to bed.

"Oh dear, I almost did forget in my excitement. Apologies, my friend."

Ori and I grab some blood worms for Carl in honor of the spooky holiday and drop them into his tank.

"Goodnight Carl," we say together before heading off to bed.

Time to get some sleep. I have a busy day tomorrow and then the day after that is my adventure with the best man in the world.

Chapter Five

Ori

Ugh. *The bus.* I shield Anne with my jacket the whole ride to the mall. She's taken the day off of work so that we may go at a time of day when it won't be busy. So smart, she is. My darling Anne.

Ding

The bus arrives at our stop, and we wait for the last person to exit before we do. Thankfully we avoid getting shoved or otherwise jostled about. It would be a shame to start this trip off with Anne in a panic. As it is, she's already rubbing her fingertips together in the way she does when she's nervous or stressed. I take her hand in mine and smile down at her.

"It will be alright. Now, show me the mall. I need to understand this important cultural gathering space. Perhaps then I'll learn enough about social skills to be able to get a job."

"Important cultural gathering space? If you say so." She squeezes my hand and smiles up at me. "Okay. Let's go. I want a soft pretzel and a smoothie."

"What good will *you* getting food teach *me*?" I gripe as she tugs me along behind her.

"It will teach you the difference between a hangry Anne and a happy Anne."

"Oh, I know that one already. I was pretty sure you were going to take a bite out of my arm last Tuesday when we were waiting for the pizza to be delivered." I chuckle at the memory.

"I wasn't far off. Okay, here we are. The mall!" Anne opens the glass doors, and we walk into a larger building than I could have imagined.

Of course, I've seen massive structures on the television and such but to be *inside* one is entirely different. In fact, it's overwhelming and I take a step toward the walls to ground myself.

"Ori, are you ok? You don't look so good," Anne asks with pinched brows.

"I'm fine," I stammer out. "It's just so...a lot."

Anne looks around us, taking in everything before returning her attention to me. "Yep. I guess. It's not really that big of a mall. I've been to the biggest mall in the country before and that one is like *really* overwhelming. It even has a rollercoaster inside it!"

"I will not be riding a rollercoaster. I don't know what would happen to me," I insist.

"Don't worry, there's no rollercoaster here. This mall is barely big enough to have a movie theater next to it. It's fine."

"Alright. Lead me to your pretzel then." I hold out my hand and this time she's the one in front when we start walking.

The pretzel stand is near the entrance, and it takes only a moment waiting in line. I proudly pay the man at the register like I learned how to do on our trip to the lingerie store, though of course

I must use Anne's money to do so. The smoothie bar is next to the pretzel stand and ordering there goes just as smoothly, though the sound of the blender aggravates Anne's anxiety.

We sit on a bench and Anne smothers her hands in hand sanitizer several times before she eats. I'm proud of her for eating in a place where she's unable to properly wash her hands, even if it means she goes a touch overboard with the precautions. She's taking big steps today.

I watch her quietly as she eats. Smiling, she chews and looks around at the shops near us and all the things in the windows. There are few people here at this time of day to upset her. I've never seen her out like this and it's a wonderful sight. If I could, I would kiss her right here, make love to her on this bench in the wide-open space of this community landmark. But that will have to wait.

She finishes her smoothie and looks over at my silent face. "What? You're being so quiet."

"You're just so perfect. I didn't want to interrupt."

"Oh jeez. You're so sweet. Okay, let's get up. Where should we go first? I say not the fancy candle store." We both look at the scented candle store across from us and the thought of flames on fabric crosses my mind, making me shudder.

"No candles."

"We already had food so let's avoid any restaurants or treat shops for now. You already make your own clothes. Hmm. Let's just get up and walk around, see what looks fun."

Strolling along the long halls of the mall with Anne's hand in mine fills me with pride. The people passing by feel like my subjects and I their king when I have such a majestic queen as her on my arm. The air is fragrant with so many scents, such as the terrifying candle shop, a cinnamon roll stand Anne says we should stop at later, a perfume kiosk. The colors and lights are bright and vibrant, and I don't know where to settle my eyes. A glowing red sign for the exit, a bright yellow sign above a shoe store, red for a doll crafting business.

Wait. This doll crafting place. "Make-A-Friend", it's called. I pause in front of it and stare into the large glass front of the store, watching the employees do their work.

"Anne," I say, completely mesmerized by the sight before me. "We must go inside."

My Anne furrows her brow as she peers into the window, then turns back to me. "You want to make a stuffed animal?"

"Absolutely."

"Are you sure? They're kind of expensive so if you don't really want one-"

"I want one."

"Okay then. Make-A-Friend it is."

The store is mostly empty at this time of day, with the children who would normally be occupying it at school and their parents at work. The lighting is bright, the atmosphere cheerful, every employee with a smile on their face. Sighing with happiness, I walk to one employee who greets me with equal joy.

"Welcome to Make-A-Friend! Will you be making a friend today?"

The employee looks around as if to make sure we don't have a child with us, but I nod enthusiastically, nonetheless.

"Oh yes. And I'm very excited to do so."

I don't get to talk to many people, and I suddenly become hyper aware of my words. I squeeze Anne's hand for comfort and when she squeezes back it gives me the strength to continue on.

"I know exactly which one I'd like. Please."

"Well let's begin then. Which friend will you be taking home today?" the smiling woman asks as she leads us to an area with dolls and unfilled polyester animal pelts in boxes below them.

I make a beeline to the bright orange display animal that caught my attention from outside and take the matching empty pelt from the bin underneath it.

"This one. This one is perfect."

Anne's eyebrows raise as she lets out a loud giggle. "That is perfect for you, Ori."

"Let's continue," the woman says, leading the way to a large, brightly colored machine.

In front of the machine are little things shaped like brains. I look at them curiously, wondering whatever they could be for.

"Would you like to add a memory for your friend?" the woman asks.

"No," Anne replies at the same time I reply "Yes."

When I look at her questioningly, she says "They cost extra."

"My friend needs a memory, Anne," I insist.

With a sigh she nods to the employee. "Alright. Memory it is. I can't say no to that face."

"Now, what I need you to do," the employee begins, "is hold this mind carefully in your hands and make a wish."

I take the mind and gently cup it in my palms. With my eyes closed I think of the most important thing I could ever think of. *I wish Anne and Carl would live forever and be the happiest people ever.* I open my eyes and tell the employee "All done," before it occurs to me, I referred to Carl as a person. Ah well, I refer to myself as a man and I'm a pillow.

"Next, I want you to give the mind a good pinch until you hear a click. When you do, say a very quick message. When you're done, click it again. From that point on, whenever you click the button, you'll hear the message you recorded."

I wrack my brain for the perfect thing to say but there's only one thing I'd ever want to repeat over and over forever that I know I'll always mean.

Click "I love you, Anne." I click the button again, then hand it to the employee.

"Wonderful." She puts the mind inside the head of the orange pelt, and we walk to the large machine. "Now, I'm going to place this on this tube right here and you're going to press this big, blue button. That's going to fill your friend all up with stuffing. Are you ready?"

"Absolutely!" I declare.

Anne smiles at my excitement, her initial grumpiness finally worn off.

"You're so cute, Ori."

"And don't I know it," I say with a wink that makes her giggle.

The employee places the item on the end of a tube and after a countdown I press the blue button. A happy jingle plays as the stuffing fills the pelt, turning it from flat, orange, fur, to my stuffed friend. She tugs the filled animal off the tube and smiles.

"Now we just need to sew your friend up. It will only take a moment. While I'm doing that, please head up to the register and fill out its birth certificate."

As she walks away Anne and I grin at one another and clasp hands once again. I choose the name Luffy for the stuffed animal after a character in a show Anne likes. She finds it quite amusing.

At the counter Anne pays an admittedly preposterous amount for my new friend and she fills out the birth certificate, as I unfortunately can't write yet. Type, yes. Watching Anne use the internet for years taught me to read, and I learned to type in no time at all but writing with pen and paper is still a challenge.

When we get my new stuffed animal and leave the shop Anne stops me outside of it and turns to me.

"Ori, what made you want a stuffed goldfish so badly any-way?"

"It reminded me of you and Carl. You because you created me and brought me to life. And Carl is my only friend. I know it might seem silly to be a grown man with a stuffed animal but...I think I needed that entire experience."

"I guess I understand the first part but I'm not really sure I understand the last part."

"That's alright. I don't think a human could. No one but me could, actually. It's a bit lonely, being the only one who's like this sometimes. But I wouldn't trade it for anything. Just please know I love you very much."

"Oh, Ori." Her hand softly caresses my jaw as she slips a gentle kiss upon my lips. "Never change."

"Never."

Chapter Six

Anne

We wander around a bit more, stopping at a bed and bath store where Ori scoffs at the "inferior pillows" and then ending up at a store known for their novelty items and adult goods. There are a lot of tasteless or silly things here, like a t-shirt that says, "Boobies for Bros," pipes for smoking less than legal substances, and edible panties. It reminds me of being a teenager and I only go in there to show Ori how weird we all were when we were kids who thought we were so cool. I didn't expect to find anything he liked.

Of course, being the strange being he is, he finds things he likes. At first, he finds a lava lamp and is absolutely mesmerized. Bright blue blobs float up and down in the light while Ori stares wide-eyed.

"We need one, Anne," he says.

"We do not need one, Ori," I reply. If I wasn't kind of broke, I'd be up for buying him whatever he wanted but work is cutting back hours lately. "Just wait until December at least. Maybe it can be a gift."

He turns to me and smiles with his perfectly white teeth and I already know he's going to say something adorably sweet before he does. "You're the only gift I need Anne."

But then his eyes flit up to something on a shelf behind me and his head tilts. He walks past me with a determined expression, and I can't help but be very curious as to what would make him stop so suddenly. When I turn around and see what he's looking at I slap my hand over my eyes. *Please don't let him make a scene.*

"Anne," he begins at what I rationally know is a perfectly normal volume but feels like yelling in my head. "Have you ever tried one of these gadgets? Anne? You're covering your eyes. It's called a vibrator. This one appears to have some sort of suction bit on the outside. Would you like that? Anne? Why are you so red?"

Oh god. Kill me now.

"Oh, you're afraid someone will hear, aren't you. No need to be shy. I want the whole world to know that you're mine. But I suppose if you're not comfortable with the world knowing I'm yours then that's alright."

I uncover my eyes and see that he looks like a kicked puppy. "That's not what that means! I just don't like anyone hearing about my...preferences. Except you, of course. Let's get out of here."

I take Ori by the hand and as we're almost out the door he turns to me and asks, "Are you sure you didn't want the t-shirt that said, "World's Horniest Dad?"

"I'm extremely positive," I can barely say as I laugh. Ori joins me in my laughter as well and we begin our walk back toward the exit.

"I think this was a good excursion, darling. We really should go out into the world more often," he suggests as he wraps his lean arm around my shoulder.

"I agree. It was a lot of fun spending time with you, and I was only afraid a few times. I can really see this sort of thing being beneficial to my therapy, not to mention just being good for life for the both of us in general."

"There's only one other place we need to stop."

"The cinnamon roll place, I almost forgot. Thanks for reminding me!"

Ori guides me toward a dim hallway that says, "employees only" and I look at him, puzzled. "Two places then."

"Uh…this isn't a place for shoppers, honey."

"I know. I checked the mall map online several times before we came to prepare myself for our visit and noticed an odd area that didn't seem to be used for much of anything. All of the storage areas behind shops are used, obviously, and there are general mall use ones for cleaning, storage, security, but this one didn't appear to have a purpose."

We pause in front of an unmarked door. Ori jiggles the handle and finds it locked. "No matter," he says with a mischievous grin before turning one finger into a long point and shoving it into the lock.

After a second there's a click and the door pops open. After flipping the switch, we can see it's clear that this room is meant to be storage for one of the few empty shops in the mall. Though this mall is fairly popular, it's still the age of online shopping and that means a few empty storefronts here and there.

"Perfect," he whispers as he closes the door behind us.

"Ori, this is an empty room," I say with a raised eyebrow.

"Not quite. Have a seat."

He guides me to a stack of boxes on the floor where he immediately leans in for a kiss. I hesitate for only a second before meeting that kiss; he's impossible to resist even in these strange circumstances. His satin tongue glides against mine and I moan at the perfection. It's an almost painful sense of loss when he pulls away.

"I'm going to remove your pants now. Don't argue. I know you'll try to."

He's right, I would have tried to, but when he gets frisky and controlling, I can't help but comply. He tugs off everything below my waist and kneels down, spreading my legs before him.

"Fantastic. I imagine I'll never tire of this sight," he rasps out.

I run a hand through his silky, black hair and brace the other on the cardboard behind me. Ori pounces on me suddenly, face planted between my thighs, filthy, wet sounds filling the empty room.

"Oh, yes," I moan as I raise my hips to press against him. "Thank you."

It doesn't take long for him to bring me to a climax. Bringing me pleasure is Ori's favorite activity and he's an absolute expert. He pulls himself away and offers me a cocky look. The man knows he's done well. His elegant fingers slip up and down through my wet slit as he gives me my next command.

"Now bend over, my love. We're going to make this rough and fast. We can't have the security catching us, can we?"

I gulp and shake my head. "Nope, can't have that."

I turn around and bend over the boxes, ass in the air, waiting for Ori to give me what is sure to be a good time.

"Oh yes," he growls out. "Fast and rough it is."

Chapter Seven

Ori

My darling Anne presents herself to me like an offering, a sacrifice, a gift I may use to take my pleasure. When she's like this I feel raw, animalistic. I need to take her *hard*.

"Oh, Anne. How wonderfully I've been made for you." I slide slowly at first into her wet center, letting her adjust to me until I'm fitted inside her like a glove.

She whimpers when I push my hips forward, pressing against her deepest parts in a way I know is sensitive but a pain she enjoys. As a pillow I wouldn't have guessed pain was a thing that could be enjoyed and even now I don't like it myself but Anne...a little bit here and there has proven to be pleasurable for her.

"Are you going to be good for me, Anne? Can you handle what I give you? Can you take *more*?"

She knows I will push her limits sometimes but I'll always, always stop if she seems to not enjoy something. We've had the conversations many times and now we can trust one another.

My cock grows inside her, stretching her wide. She whines and writhes against me as I rock in and out, gradually increasing my pace.

"Yes," she barely forces out as I grow even thicker and pulse in opposite rhythm to her heartbeat for extra sensation.

I take a clump of her hair in my hands and pull her closer to me as I lean over her.

"You're a very good girl. You deserve a treat."

From the area below my cock, I branch out a tentacle, but this one is a little different. I model this one after a flower-shaped device I saw in the novelty store and add a sucking bit that fits perfectly around Anne's adorable bud of a clit. When it latches on and begins to suck, writhing in quick circles against her as it does so, she shouts out nonsense words and begins to tense up immediately.

"A treat for my sweet," I laugh as I hold onto her hips and thrust hard and fast, taking my pleasure from her glorious cunt while I offer it equally to her sweet clit.

She comes before I do and she does so hard around me, with a shout of my name. The hard squeeze of her sends me over the edge and at the last second, I pull out, feathers flying out of my cock and over her back, her ass, and in the air.

I brush the down off of her as best as I can and hold her to me as we stand together.

"I love you." I tell her with every bit of truth inside me.

"I love you too, Ori. Now I need my pants, and we need to get out of here before we get arrested." She gets dressed and, giggling together, we exit the storage room.

Only problem is, we run into two angry security guards.

"Step back into the room, please," the shorter, bald one with the big mustache commands.

"Oh, we were on our way out actually," I say in a faux cheerful voice.

"Don't fuck around. It's listen to us or we call the cops. Your choice."

"Okay. We're listening," Anne says shakily, taking my hand and tugging me backward with her.

The security guards follow us into the room and the second one locks the door behind him. *Oh dear. That's not a good sign.*

"What were you two doing in here, huh?" asks the short one with the gray buzzcut.

"Just exploring," Anne replies.

"Yeah right," says the short one with a scoff. "We know what people do here. Now, what we want is a little show. That's all. Just take off your clothes and show us all the good things you did while you were alone. When you're done, you can go free. Easy as pie." Spit flies out from his mouth with every letter s, barely missing us.

"No," I growl. "No one forces my Anne to do anything she doesn't want to."

"Oh, it's Anne then? Well, hey Anne. Maybe if your boyfriend doesn't want to put on a show you can put it on with us? Would you like that better?" The bald, wrinkly guy laughs as he strokes her cheek with one tobacco-stained finger.

They threatened her.

They propositioned her.

They sexually harassed her.

*He **touched** her.*

Any bit of calm I have is gone, replaced entirely by the need to protect Anne. She is *mine* and she is mine to protect. I feel something surge inside me I've never felt before. Flashes of every time Anne has come home crying. Of Todd trying to harm her in her home. Men touching her at the bus stop. A goose being taken to slaughter.

"Don't touch her," I spit out. "Never again."

My arm snaps out, my hand wrapping around the throat of the bald man. My eyes widen and the corners of my lips curl in a feral grin as his thick, brown mustache turns gray.

But I don't stop there. I keep draining him. When his skin turns thin, and his eyes grow sunken I don't stop. When his heart stops, I continue to *take* from every cell, every bacterium in and on him. I take everything until there's nothing but dust at my feet and a bit of hair in the shape of a mustache.

The man with the buzzcut pulls something off of his belt as I finish sucking the life from that piece of rubbish. He points the object at my chest and presses on it. Wires fly out of the little gun-like contraption and latch onto my chest. For a moment there is an expression of victory on the man's greasy face, as if something should be happening to me. But nothing does.

I pull the hook-ended wires from my body. A few feathers fly out in a puff from the tears, but they're quickly repaired, as I'm filled to the brim with energy at the moment.

I'm contemplating how to burn off some energy so that I can take him down without gaining too much flesh, when he snatches Anne and holds her in his arms. Rage blinds me and I move without further thought.

"You fucking fool," I roar as I graze his hand with mine. That's all it takes for him to still and me to get a stronger hold on him. His life force is draining quickly as I look to Anne and tell her "Get away. I've got this."

Anne runs off somewhere and I'm laughing as I fill with more power than I can handle, feeling overstuffed, nearly over-whelmed but also so strong. Then the loudest noise I've ever heard rings out and a burning goes through my chest. I drop the man, he's nearly empty anyway, and raise my hands to the inflamed area.

There is a hole. Through my chest. When I turn my eyes to the man, I see him holding a gun. *Oh, that won't do.* I seal the hole in myself within seconds. Somehow even in his frail state he shoots again but I seal the wound. I shoot out a tentacle and grab the gun, ripping it away. Finally, I take hold of his throat and look into his eyes. I say nothing as I watch the life force drain from him until he's nothing but dust.

When I drop him, I'm panting and I bend over, feeling a pain in my side. *Pain. That's odd.* I straighten up and look around to find Anne.

"Darling? It's alright. You can come out now," I shout.

Anne peeks out from around some crates at the back of the room before running toward me and embracing me. She sobs as I run my hands over her smooth hair.

"Your glasses are all foggy, dear. Let me wipe them clean for you." I tell her gently. She hates when they get dirty.

When she hands me her glasses, I go to wipe them on my softest fabric but they only smudge. My brow furrows as I try a different area, but they only smudge worse. Confused, I hand them back to her.

"I must have gotten all dirty while fighting. Apologies."

"Thanks anyway, Ori. I've got it," she says with a sniffle as she rubs her glasses clean on the end of her shirt.

When she puts them on and looks into my face I smile at her, happy to see she's safe and sound after all of that trouble. She begins to smile back but her look changes to one of confusion, then one of fright as she screams.

"Anne! What's wrong?" I ask in a panic.

"Your face," she cries before backing away, covering her mouth with her hands, eyes wide.

"What's wrong? Am I flattened again?"

She shakes her head quickly from side to side. "No. You're...you..."

"Anne, what is it? Please," I beg.

"You're made of flesh."

Chapter Eight

Anne

O ri runs his hands along his cheeks, his nose, his neck.

"No. Oh no, no, no, I didn't mean to do this." Ori panics. He looks at me and clasps his hands together in front of himself. "Please don't leave me, Anne. I'll fix it somehow. Please."

I rear back in shock. "Leave you? Why would I leave you?"

"Because I have skin now. You won't want to touch me." A tear falls from his eye, and he wipes it away in frustration.

"Don't be silly. I love *you* Ori, no matter what."

I wrap my arms around him, and he returns my embrace enthusiastically, holding me on the edge of too tightly before letting me go.

"We have to get out of here before someone comes in and sees us, darling."

"We're in deep trouble, aren't we?" I realize. "You...you *killed* those security guards."

"I don't think we will be. It's not as if there's a body. But it's better to not be caught at the scene of what I admit to being a crime and we're not supposed to be in this room anyway. So, come along. Our chariot awaits."

We take the bus home and I barely register time passing as we do. Everything is just a fog until we get home and Ori walks me into the shower to clean up.

This time when Ori joins me in the shower, he doesn't get all messed up. He's totally fine, though he says he doesn't like the water as hot as I do. There is no romantic funny business, just cleaning off until my mind is clear, and I feel like I can function again. We both get out and wrap ourselves in the fluffiest towels I have and cuddle on the sofa.

"I don't have any clean clothes," Ori realizes. "Should have bought some at the mall I suppose."

"That Horny Dad t-shirt could have been yours."

We both laugh until I begin to cry, all my worry coming out at once. I'm so afraid for him and he barely seems worried at all.

"Aren't you scared, Ori? You've barely said anything?"

He sighs as he pets my hair. "Absolutely terrified. I don't know if I'll be able to return to myself or not. I'm so far gone. I don't want to be human. It's terrible. No offense."

"None taken," I reply as I stand and stretch. "I wouldn't want to be either. Personally, not a fan of humans, as you know."

A rumbling sound comes from below me and my eyebrows raise. Ori puts his arms over his stomach and looks at me with concern.

"My stomach hurts and is making all sorts of sounds. What's going on?"

"You're hungry. Let's go get you some food." I hold out my hand and he takes it, standing up to follow me.

"I don't like this one bit. Eating means I'll have to use the restroom. The *toilet,* Anne. I won't do it. Being *Human.* Disgusting. I can't do it."

"You'll be fine," I laugh. "I promise we'll figure this out together. Hey! You can finally try pizza! Maybe we can do pineapple."

"Anne, there are tiny hairs on my arms now and when you said that they all stood up."

As we walk past Carl's tank, I hear a ripping sound and feel the catch of my towel on the side of the table. My arms spin as I fall forward, then over correct and begin to fall backward toward the glass of the tank walls.

Before I can crash into it and cut myself to ribbons, Ori slides to my side, catching me in his strong arms. His hip, however, slams into the table, pushing it over just enough to upset the aquarium.

Carl's tank slides off the table, slamming into the floor with a mighty crash. The glass cracks then breaks apart, water flooding the living room floor. It goes flowing over our feet, as do shards of glass and aquarium rocks.

"Carl. Oh no. Carl!" Ori screams at the top of his lungs.

Ori sets me away from the glass then scrambles to his knees, glass cutting into them, and begins to frantically search the floor for his fishy friend. It takes him a moment to locate the goldfish, and when he finds it, it's out of the water, flopping helplessly in the air.

"Carl, no, please," Ori pleads.

Tears stream down his face as he looks around for somewhere with deep enough water for Carl. There is nowhere.

"Carl. You're supposed to live forever. You're my only friend. I love you. Please." Ori stands and holds a still Carl to his bare chest as he closes his eyes and sniffles. "Why do I have too much life and you have none? It's not fair."

Ori's eyes snap open and he takes a sharp inhale. He takes another breath. Then another. I watch, confused, as he holds Carl in front of him and grins. Ori gets down on one knee, still holding the unmoving fish in his hands.

"Ori. Are you okay honey?" I carefully ask. I'm concerned he's having some kind of nervous breakdown.

"Oh, I'm wonderful. We're going to get our beta, my little omega."

"What are you talking about?" He's clearly having a breakdown. *Fuck.*

Then the fish starts shaking. Stretching. Pulsing. Growing.

What the fuck?

Chapter Nine

Ori

I can feel the life force draining out of me and the relief of it is one of the best things I've ever felt. When it leaves me, I can see Carl changing as it flows into him. I was afraid it wouldn't work but it is, *it is* working. Carl is becoming *more*. He's *alive*.

"Come on Carl. Just a touch more," I encourage him.

His body is having a difficult time accepting the amount of life I'm attempting to give it, the form I'm attempting to put it into. The little fish wants to *stay* a fish but that won't do any longer. If I want to stop having so much *flesh*, I have to get rid of a good lot of this human life force and Carl is the perfect receptacle since he needs to be revived. He needs to *live*. I won't let my only friend go. He's *mine*.

I push a little harder and finally it takes. I set him on the ground and step away until I meet Anne, wrapping an arm around her waist to watch Carl as he shifts into his new form.

"Ori, what's happening? Please give me a straight answer," Anne asks.

"Anne. Look at me."

She turns to look and when she does, she gasps. She raises her hand to stroke my woven face, my shoulders, my chest.

"You're fabric again. How?" she asks, wonder in her voice.

"I gave my humanity to Carl. Well, much of it. I still need to be part man after all. He'll be mostly man. Still a little bit aquatic though."

"He'll be what?" Anne gasps and turns her stunned gaze back to Carl.

"A little bit fish. I hope it's not too visible a bit. Though I suppose we could always take down another security guard and fix him if it was."

"Ori! That's not funny!"

"I'm only being practical." I notice a large change in Carl and my excitement grows. "Oh look! He's growing so fast!"

Carl is changing much faster than I did. I'm so proud of him. He's already nearly Anne's size. He isn't in human form yet by any means. He's more the form of...an overfilled bag of trash. But it's something. And he's changing every second. Becoming *more*.

"This is so freaky."

"Please don't faint." I panic and grab hold of her, remembering what happened when she saw me mid-change. I don't want that to happen again.

"I think I've seen enough weird stuff to prevent the fainting now. But wow, this looks gross." Her nose scrunches up at the sight and I have to admit she's correct.

Carl's scales, gills, eyes, and fins are swirling around in a mass of orange and white flesh. The throbbing blob is only barely beginning to form into a shape that could almost be described as human.

"Give him a moment. I gave his form an excellent description of what to look like. Hopefully it works."

"You could tell him what to look like? What? What did you tell him to look like?"

I smirk. "You'll see."

We watch as the mass before us takes form slowly. Height much shorter than mine but taller than Anne, slender but with a fair amount of toned muscle, light golden skin with a healthier glow than I, pale hair, ice blue eyes, softly freckled cheeks. He also has a slight red-gold sheen all over his fit body, and he's certainly *not* made of fabric.

Anne squints when Carl is finished changing. The man is standing still, panting and flexing his hands, staring off with a glazed expression.

"He's practically your opposite." Anne crouches to the floor, keeping her eyes on Carl the entire time. She stays silent for a moment longer before turning her head to me. "What now?"

"I suppose he's done, and I should help him. He's had an entirely different experience growing than I did. Honestly, I don't know what to expect. But here we go."

When I get to Carl he's still staring off into space, as if entirely unaware I'm there. With a shaking hand I brush back his flaxen hair and get close to his ear, before announcing my presence.

"Carl. It's me, Ori. Are you alright?"

Carl blinks slowly and turns his head to meet mine. His glazed gaze clears and focuses on my face as he sighs, his shoulders relaxing. A soft smile lifts his lips and crinkles the corners of his eyes before he speaks in a low voice.

"There you are, Ori."

"Here I am, Carl. How are you feeling?"

"Confused. What happened to me? How can you understand me? Wait, how do I know how to talk anyway? Where's Anne?"

"You know of Anne?" I shake my head. *Of course he knows Anne.* "She's here too, Carl. Let's all sit down and talk."

I lead Carl to the sofa where we sit next to each other. I toss a blanket over the both of us, as I haven't had time to make my clothes and we're both nude at this point; Anne is skittish about these things. Anne comes over then and sits next to me, burying her head against my side so that I'll toss my arm around her, which I do of course. I'd do anything my Anne wanted. Then I begin to tell Carl his story.

"Carl, let me tell you how you came to be a man."

Chapter Ten

Anne

After explaining everything to Carl about how Ori brought him to life, and then having to backtrack and answer about a billion questions about Ori's origin, we all finally fall silent so that Carl can take a moment to process things. There will be so many more questions coming up in the days, or even years, ahead, from Carl. There's no need to rush things for the poor guy. I breathe in Ori's scent but don't find it there; instead, I find he still smells like antibacterial soap. For the first time ever, I don't want something to smell like soap.

"Will I be able to stay here?" Carl asks quietly.

I sit up so fast I nearly smack Ori's jaw with my head. "What? Of course you can! You're part of our family."

With a smile, Carl blushes and lowers his head. "Thank you. I promise I'll be a useful part of this family. I'll learn all the things people do to find food and fight off predators and of course if you need a male for mating, I offer my services."

Air seems to stop running through my body properly and I choke out a cough at the same time Ori barks out a laugh.

"You have many things to learn, Carl. We must discuss the concept of money. I'll take care of predators for the most part. As for the mating...we'll have to have a talk, man to man." Ori slaps a hand down onto Carl's shoulder, probably a little firmer than necessary.

"You're a good male, Ori. You saved my life and now you're helping me live it right." Carl smiles and it's the biggest boy next door grin you could ever imagine. This guy really is the opposite of Ori.

"Now, let us prepare some food for the two of you. Thankfully I was interrupted before I needed to partake in that particular ritual." Ori shudders and I roll my eyes.

"Are we having those pellets?" Carl asks. "Ooh, or those little brine shrimps? Or- "

"Carl," I interrupt, "people eat different things from fish."

"Oh. Yeah. Sorry." Carl ducks his head shyly and it makes me feel guilty for correcting him, even though it needed to happen.

"Oh Carl, no, don't be sorry," I soothe him, giving him a tight hug. He's so new to being human there's no way he could be sick, so touching him doesn't bother me, I guess. "You're just learning. You'll catch on soon."

"Thanks, Anne. Okay, I'm ready to try anything."

Before we head to dinner, I grab Carl something to wear. He gets some gray sweatpants that are super baggy on me but barely loose on him, and a white t-shirt that says "Best Baby Girl" that my mom bought me, and I can't seem to get rid of even though I will never, ever wear it. I know it's ridiculous on him but it's the only thing that fits over his firm shoulders and biceps. The man isn't quite as tall as Ori but he's incredibly fit and solid...and I really shouldn't have given him gray sweatpants because I should *not* be looking at him the way I am.

We take him to the kitchen, and Ori and I decide just to make some salads. As a fish he ate the occasional vegetable and salads are something he'd be used to, with the dressing and croutons and stuff being new things to try. Plus, I'm kind of stressed and don't really want anything heavy anyway.

Ori prepares the food while I get on my phone and hop onto a shopping website that is known for having fast delivery for its members. Some items can be delivered even overnight so I look to see what men's clothes can be sent as quickly as possible that fit Carl and that we can afford. I manage to find some cute, basic things for him and hit buy. He didn't really know what he liked so it was basically me picking it out, but I figure in time he'll develop his own style. For now, this will have to do.

Ori sets our plates down and takes a seat. "Anne, I believe I have an idea for a job. While I was putting together dinner, I remembered this part of a fanfic I read where-"

"Ori. I really don't want to talk about fan fiction now. It's been a long day. What we need is to eat dinner and go to bed."

"Alright, my love. It can wait. Anyway, given a choice, I'll always choose to be in bed with you."

Chapter Eleven

Carl

It was much easier swimming in the tank. I knew what to do and how to do it. Now I have to learn so many new things.

The salad before me has some recognizable things in it. Well, sort of recognizable anyway. Basically, they're green and leafy looking and that's about it. I'll try the leaves first. I grab the fork in my hand and prepare to stab the leaf, but Anne reaches out her soft hand and places it over mine.

"Not like that. You don't hold the fork like you're going to stab it. It's more of a poke-scoop. Like this."

The warmth of her hand when it wraps around mine sends a shock through my body that heats me all the way through. I manage to pay attention to her lesson enough to catch on to how to use the fork properly but most of my mind was occupied by the feeling of her skin on mine.

"Your skin feels really interesting," Anne comments. "It's textured almost like snakeskin."

"I was pondering that, and I think it's the remnants of scales," Ori guesses. "As if they've left an imprint on him."

"I think you're right," I say, running a finger along my own arm now.

It does feel different from Anne's skin. I hope she doesn't think I'm gross. I frown and get back to eating my dinner, trying not to let the talk of the difference in my body from theirs upset me. I poke the leaf and bring it to my mouth for a bite. It tastes like I remember nibbling it in the water, only this time there is a strange liquid drizzled on top of it that I'm not sure I like.

"What do you think?" Ori asks.

"It's great," I reply and take another bite.

I'm not going to criticize anything tonight. They could give me aquarium gravel and I'd gladly eat it. I eat the entire thing and manage to *mostly* enjoy it, as long as I discreetly wipe off the drizzled stuff. Anne is yawning by the time we're done, and I admit to feeling tuckered out as well. Ori cleaned all the broken glass and mopped the water while we ate so thankfully everything in the house is covered for now.

"I hope it's ok that you have to sleep on the sofa, Carl. Ori and I already take up the bed."

"Well, this is the first time I'm really sleeping like a human, so I won't know the difference between a bed and a sofa anyway." I smile.

"Still. I want you to be comfortable."

"You may have the best pillow in the house to make up for it. The best pillow that's not me of course," Ori offers, presenting me with a large, fluffy pillow. "Only the best for my best friend."

My heart warms at that. I've only been human a handful of hours and I've already got a best friend and a wonderful family. This is a scary transition, but I think I've got the best two people in the whole world to make it with.

"Thank you, Ori." I lunge forward and wrap my arms around him. He and Anne both laugh and hug me back. I'm so glad to have them.

When we're all tucked in for the night, I try to fall asleep but can't seem to, even though I'm very tired. My mind is just racing with so many thoughts and questions. There are so many it's like I can't even focus on one thought at a time. Until I hear Ori and Anne.

It's a sound I've heard before many times. Not to mention the fact that I've witnessed the actions that create those sounds happen in this very room before.

They're mating. Now there's *definitely* no way I'm going to fall asleep.

When I was a fish, I didn't really think much of it, obviously. It was just the two animals who kept me safe mating. I had a special fondness for those two animals due to them saving me from that scary place that mistreated us fish, but they were just big animals, nonetheless. I wasn't sexually attracted to them.

When I became human everything instantly changed. All my biological instincts are all mixed up now. I still feel like a goldfish in some ways but in my loins...wow, everything is different. My mating drive now sees Anne as more than an animal. Much more.

Anne is the one who told the man in the shop he was an asshole for keeping me in that tiny bowl. Who held me in the plastic bag on the way home and assured me that I'd be in a real aquarium. Who spoke to me like I was someone that mattered even when I was a fish. Her hair is so shiny. And she smells *amazing.*

My hormones are going wild. And also, it feels weird to say, but what my eyes are attracted to is different now. I see her large breasts bouncing underneath her t-shirt and her thick rump flexing under her cotton pants and I feel a rush to my groin that makes me grit my teeth. I would never have found those things beautiful before but now they're so attractive I *ache.*

Hearing them mating is bringing back all the times I saw them mate out here in the living room but wasn't fazed by it. I'm seeing those memories with these new eyes now and...*fuck.* I shift so that I'm lying on my back and when I look forward, I notice there is a tented area in my blanket. After a moment of confusion, I realize it's...my cock. I've never had a cock before so it's no wonder I was confused. This whole human mating thing is confusing really.

I slip my hand under the blanket, softly gliding my hand along my stiffened member. Right then a particularly loud moan comes from Anne's room, making me flinch back. *That touch felt really good.* I sit still for a moment, wondering if I should do it again. When another loud moan comes from the other end of the apartment, I decide that yes, I would like to continue stroking it.

At first, I just try different types of touches, nervously stopping and starting, afraid of being caught. I'm not sure whether or not it would be frowned upon to do this but I have an instinct telling me it's meant to be private. Soon though I find a rhythm and way of squeezing I enjoy, memories of Anne bouncing on Ori's cock on this very couch running through my mind, and I keep at it until I feel a strange but good build up and a pull in the new balls I have. I move faster and my jaw tenses, my hips lift. A powerful feeling pulses through me, making me want to cry out with pleasure. I barely manage to stay silent.

If this feeling is why they are always mating, then *wow* do I understand it. I was already willing to help fertilize Anne's eggs if she needed it but now, I'm *very* eager to.

Ori had a brief talk with me earlier, when Anne was washing up for bed, and said that humans reproduce differently from fish, that they put their penis inside the other one's "vagina" to make babies. He didn't say where the eggs come into play but maybe that's different from person to person.

He did also say that sometimes humans do mating things with each other just for fun and not for reproduction too, so that's interesting. I *did* get the desire for Ori to chase me, and chasing is a mating behavior. Mating between two males obviously wouldn't create offspring, so I guess there is something to the "mating for fun" thing.

These thoughts are silly. Ori and Anne are my friends, and I shouldn't be worrying over this stuff. What I should be doing is resting so that I can be useful to the household tomorrow. I will do anything to be a good member of this family and if that means a good night's sleep then so be it. Now I just need to figure out how to make my eyes stay closed. *Sigh.*

Chapter Twelve

Ori

"Carl. Wake up." Gently, I shake my friend by the shoulder. His pale blue eyes flutter open, and he smiles his boyish grin when he sees me standing above him.

"I did it, Ori. I fell asleep," he croaks out in a sleepy voice. "It wasn't easy, that's for sure."

"I'm proud of you. Now, cover up. Anne will be out of the shower soon and she doesn't need to see your erect prick staring at her." I point to said prick and watch as his cheeks turn red.

Rising in a panic, Carl hurriedly pulls the blankets back over himself. "Ah, I'm sorry. I'm not used to this."

After a brief moment of semi-awkward silence, Carl speaks again.

"So, for sleeping, I don't know. I miss the heaviness of water. I feel like if I'm going to relax, what I have covering me has to be something heavy. Something with pressure. Otherwise, it just feels...wrong."

"I have a weighted blanket I tried but wasn't fond of that you can try out," Anne says from behind me, drying her hair on a towel. "And good morning by the way. Did Ori give you the clothes yet? Thankfully they were delivered early. Gotta thank the giant corporate overlords on occasions like this I guess."

I have no idea what she's talking about when it comes to these powerful beings she refers to, but I pretend as if I do regardless. I'll figure it out in time, I'm certain. I haven't taken the time to study politics but perhaps Carl and I can study them together and we can find out who our overlords are.

"He didn't, he just woke me up right before you came in," Carl says, hunched forward in his seated position on the couch.

"Oh okay, well let's have you try them on! I'm excited to see you all dressed up! They're not the coolest clothes ever but they're comfortable, I hope, and you'll blend in with a crowd."

"Blending in, *hmph*," I scoff as I brush the front of the black suit jacket I'm wearing. The suit is much simpler than the one I normally wear but it still looks fantastic on me.

"Yes, blending in. He already has golden skin with a scale pattern that we're going to have to worry about. And you made him very handsome, frankly, which will always draw looks. We can't risk him standing out any other way. He's going to have to look like just a regular boy next door in his clothes," Anne replies.

The smile on Carl's face is so wide it nearly splits it in half. "You think I'm handsome?"

Anne rolls her eyes and crosses her arms under her bosom. "I said what I said. You know Ori wouldn't make you ugly, it's just a fact. Now let's get you in your new clothes already!"

I locate the packages for Carl and show him how to open everything. He needs a little assistance dressing, as zippers and buttons are not things that come easily to someone only a day old. He has the intellect but not the practice. It will come with time.

"There you are." With a proud smile I step back and watch as he zips his hooded sweatshirt himself. "You've got it."

"Only took about ten tries," he replies with a bemused smile.

"And next time it will take fewer."

I wrap my arm around his shoulder and gaze at the closed door, on the other side of which waits my darling Anne.

"My love did a wonderful job of figuring out what would fit you. Isn't she amazing?"

"She's really great, yeah. You've already asked me that a bunch of times, you know that, right?"

I turn my head and grin at him. "Oh, I know. I simply cannot resist any chance to show her off."

"Clearly," Carl replies with a laugh. With a quickness he ducks out from under my arm and stands in front of me. He's fidgeting with his hands in front of himself and looking everywhere but at me when he says, "Would you chase me?"

My eyebrows pinch in confusion. "Would I what?"

Carl turns away and opens the door. "Never mind. It's stupid. Let's go show Anne the clothes."

The frown won't leave my face as he models his denim pants, white t-shirt, and black hooded sweatshirt for Anne. The sneakers she got him are even a perfect fit.

But I'm not pleased that he wouldn't open up to me about whatever it was he wanted to ask in the bedroom when he was changing. He asked me about *chasing* him. That seems rather odd. I wish he would have elaborated. I'm going to have to approach him about it. Not now when he's clearly not willing to talk but in a moment when he seems relaxed. There should be no secrets between best friends.

Chapter Thirteen

Anne

I'm the worst person alive. I have the most amazing partner that has ever existed, who is perfect for me, who has like literally killed for me, and yet I'm thinking naughty thoughts about his best friend. What the fuck? Prison. I deserve prison.

"So, you're sure this looks alright?" Carl asks yet again. "You're not just saying that to be nice?"

"Believe me, I wouldn't say something just to be nice. You look really good. Great, actually. You're definitely pulling off the boy next door vibe I was going for. As long as you keep the sweater and t-shirt pulled up to hide your shimmer when we're in public you'll be fine. You don't have to hide it here though, don't worry. I think it's cool."

"You're not disgusted by it?" Carl's eyes open wide.

"What? Of course not! It's just a shimmery texture. Whoop-de-doo. Big deal." I shake my hands in front of me in an exaggerated motion. "Plus, it doesn't feel like human skin and, believe me, that's a huge bonus in this house."

Carl's face lights up with his signature wide grin and I can't help but match it. This guy is such a ray of sunshine and I'm so happy he's in our lives. He makes Ori so happy, and it will be nice for me to have someone else here who needs to do mortal body stuff to relate to and...his eyes are so pretty, his hair looks so soft, his lips look so full, he-

UGH STOP. Prison: I deserve it!

"Ah, I'm so happy, you don't even know. I hope everything I learn goes as smoothly as this."

"Me too! I want you to enjoy being human." We smile at one another for a moment before I pat the seat next to me on the sofa and wait until he sits down to speak.

"Are you having any troubles so far that you want to talk about? Anything we can do to make life better?"

He sighs and looks down at his fidgeting hands. "Well, there's the pressure thing. It feels so odd to move through the air. I can handle it throughout the day when I'm busy and not thinking about it, but it was hard to sleep when my mind wasn't occupied."

"We'll get you that weighted blanket right away, okay? Don't worry. And maybe we can see about getting you some time in the water to relax. Anything else?"

"I'm afraid to leave the house. Ori says we have to, that we can't stay locked up all the time, but I'm really nervous. I'm not that smart and I don't want to mess something up and get hurt or something." He runs his fingers through that feathery blonde hair, messing it up and leaving it in disarray.

"Why do you think you're not smart?" I'm surprised by that statement. The man was a fish less than a day ago and he's already sitting here having emotional conversations with me in perfect English. I wouldn't say he's lacking in intelligence.

"I don't know, I mean I can't read. I don't know anything about most of what you two talk about. Anything that I couldn't learn from just swimming around you two the last few months, or was transferred through Ori's life force thing, isn't there." He drops his head into his hand and blows out a long breath.

"Oh, sweetie, it's okay. No one learns everything about the world in a day. Ori and I will both be here to help you and you'll catch on in like no time flat. There are things Ori still needs to learn you both can work on together. Shoot, there are things I'm sure I could learn too."

"You?" He lifts his head and turns to look at me. "I doubt you have to work very hard. You're super smart."

"Oh, thanks." I blush at the compliment.

"And talented. I saw all the beautiful drawings you'd bring home from work and even when I was still a fish I could appreciate them."

"Really? That's so sweet of you to say, thank you." My blush gets deeper now. I can't help it; being noticed by a handsome man will do that to a girl.

"And you smell amazing. It makes me want to follow you everywhere. If I could be pressed up against you all day, breathing you in, feeling your warmth, I would be." His eyes are wild now, his breathing quick.

Well, now my face is just about on fire. "Oh. Well. I don't think that's really appropriate to say, Carl. That's very intimate and I'm only physically close with Ori."

A look of horror comes over Carl's sweet face and he covers his mouth with his hand. "I'm so sorry. I got carried away. I don't know how to control these...I don't know. I need to talk to Ori. I'm sorry, Anne."

Carl stands up and begins to march toward the bathroom.

"Carl, it's fine. I'm not upset."

"I just need to talk to Ori when I'm done in here," is all he says before he enters the bathroom and locks the door behind him.

Ori, I know, is in our bedroom using the computer to do something that has to do with getting a job. At dinner last night he began to tell me what his idea was, but I cut him off. I realize now I've been doing that a lot lately and that's really shitty of me. Just because I'm tired or in a bad mood or something doesn't mean I shouldn't respect his needs. He never complains and so I never know when I've upset him. I really don't deserve someone that sweet.

I don't want to go talk to Ori now when I know that Carl plans on it, so I need to kill some time. Guess I'll just open those damn fan fiction sites and read more about the omegaverse.

Chapter Fourteen

Carl

I'm so dumb.

The water splashing on my face helps to calm me a little. Water always does. Giving myself a moment to relax before talking to Ori will help, I think. I don't want to go in there all emotional.

Having all of these emotions is new to me anyway. I had some basic ones as a goldfish but none of these complicated ones. Navigating them is way too hard.

Alright. I dry my face off and head out of the bathroom. There's no sign of Anne so I go to the bedroom and find Ori sitting at the computer watching Anne's favorite anime, a look of deep concentration on his face and his phone in his hands.

"Hey Ori. Can I talk to you?"

His serious look turns to a smile at the sight of me, which warms me inside. "But of course. Have a seat."

Ori pats the bed beside him, and I sit down on it. I fidget a bit while thinking of exactly how to say what I need to without making him mad. Fidgeting seems to be something that has come naturally to me, I'm not really sure why other than having hands is still pretty weird.

"I think I'm having trouble with my hormones or something. I know we talked about mating a bit but it's just on my mind a lot. And I...I said something to Anne I maybe shouldn't have."

Ori's eyes snap to mine, a flame in them. Mine widen in fear briefly before his settle.

"You didn't threaten her, I know you know better," he says with a relieved sigh.

"Of course not! I would never! But I said something sort of sexual, I guess? Not crude but definitely more than friendly. It's because my hormones are going crazy, and I don't know how to control them." I tug on my hair in frustration.

Ori looks away in thought for a while before turning back to me. "I believe we need to take a walk. To relieve some stress. Anne and I take our Sunday walks to a quiet little park. You and I can go there alone, work off some energy, get you out of the house. Sound alright?"

I nod vigorously. "Whatever you think would work."

"Good. We'll go in the morning." Ori pats my knee and I sigh contentedly now that we have a plan. Then Ori speaks again. "And Carl. Whatever happens with Anne, remember this: she is *mine*."

My mouth goes dry as I nod my agreement. When I was still a fish, I saw what Ori did to that landlord and I wouldn't want that to be me, that's for sure.

"So, anyway," I desperately try to change the subject, "what are you doing?"

"Research. Sit and enjoy, it's an excellent program." He smiles at me, and I can't resist agreeing. There's something about Ori that makes it hard to say no.

Chapter Fifteen

Ori

It takes some convincing, but Anne agrees that Carl and I walking to the park while she's at work is a fine idea. She's so very worried for us and I understand why. Neither of us has ever been anywhere alone, and our social skills are lacking to say the least. But I'm confident. And there's something important that needs to be done today, between Carl and I alone.

Carl wonders at every sight along the way to the park. It's only a few blocks away, a straight walk, but to him it must seem like an incredible adventure. I would know how he feels. Only a few months ago I was in the same position.

"I haven't seen so many people since I was at the pet shop. And most of those people weren't very nice. They'd tap on my bowl and scare me. But these people just walk right past and don't do anything. Some even smile at us!"

"Something Anne isn't particularly fond of. She's had some unfortunate experiences with people so I can't entirely blame her for it." My darling Anne. So troubled and yet she carries on each day without having murdered anyone.

"I wish we could help her."

"Just being her friend does."

"Wow, look at all the leaves! Are they the kind we can eat? Is this where they come from?" Carl stops near a tree at the edge of the park and strokes a leaf on a low branch.

"No, no. Anne buys the groceries on her phone, and they get delivered to the house. The delivery people don't wear the same outfits as the overlord's servants, so I think they're just from a normal store."

"The overlords?" Carl tilts his head questioningly.

"Hmm, yes. I'm not well informed on them. I've decided we can learn about politics together. But for now, let's walk toward that wooded area farther into the park." I signal to a path that leads down into a forested area that's been kept wild at the edge of the city. This will be perfect for what I need to do.

"Okay! What are we doing down here? Wow, there's so many types of plants down here. We don't eat any of them? Oh! I think I saw a bird! Is it going to hurt us? Birds frighten me."

"You don't have to worry about birds, Carl."

On the path we pass by two young women. They're both clearly beautiful, though I have no interest in them. Anne is the only woman I'll ever have eyes for. Carl glances their way and I have a thought. When they are out of earshot, I ask Carl my question.

"Carl, how did your hormones react to those women?"

"Oh. Not really at all, actually. I mean, they were pretty, but I didn't feel anything."

"Did you feel any pull toward anyone on the walk here?"

"Nope. Must be too distracted or something I guess." He shrugs and keeps walking.

I watch the back of his head as he goes. He's so carefree, not aware he's being stalked by a predator. When he hits the end of the path, the beginning of the tree line, he stops and turns to me.

"Okay, what now?" he asks with a grin.

"Keep walking," I reply, no grin on my face.

"Into the trees? Isn't that dangerous?"

"I'll be with you."

"Oh. Okay." Carl nervously fidgets as he begins to walk into the forest.

The day is bright and light streams through the branches above. The trees here are not thick enough to shut out the light entirely, only most of it. As Carl walks further in he looks back at me every few seconds as if making sure I'm still there. After we've gone in deep enough to not be heard by those on the path, I stop him.

"You asked me something yesterday and refused to elaborate when I asked you to repeat yourself. But I heard you, Carl. You want me to chase you. Now I will."

Carl sucks in a surprised breath but before he can say anything I hold up a hand.

"I understand that this is something goldfish do when they are attempting to catch a mate. It is my hope that this will relieve some of your distress. As your alpha it is my duty to ensure my pack is well satisfied."

There is a breath of silence in which Carl's face screws up in confusion, his head tilting to the side, before he haltingly asks, "Alpha? What are you talking about?"

A smirk lifts my lips and my eyes laser focus onto his. "It means swim, little fishy, as fast as you can. Go."

Carl's face blanches before he turns around, stumbling briefly over a tree root, and takes off in a run. It's a terribly awkward run; the man has barely had time to learn how to use legs, after all. But it's quick enough to make the game fun.

Laughing, I put my hands around my mouth to amplify my voice as I shout after him, "I'm almost ready to come after you. If I catch you, I'll nibble on your fins, beta."

Researching goldfish habits while everyone was asleep last night was quite enlightening. There are so many things we could get up to if he truly has retained many of his instincts. But for now, we run.

"Here I come!" And with that, I'm off.

I'm not the world's fastest runner, I'll admit it. I'm not *made* for it. But I'm determined, I have long legs, I've had more practice with my legs than Carl, and I won't run out of breath. I'll catch up with him in no time.

And I do. It doesn't take long to find Carl in a small clearing, hands on his knees, panting. His back is to me as I silently creep from between the trees toward him. He takes no notice of me at all before I pounce.

I take him down easily in his current position and though he struggles, he still ends up belly down on the ground. I lay my body flat on top of his and slam his hands on the ground above his head, pinning him in place. With a dark, low laugh I drop my head toward his neck and lean in.

"Okay Ori I got it now. You-" Carl begins but I cut him off with a short snap of my teeth on his earlobe.

"Got you now. Nibble, nibble, little fish."

Carl groans as I nip his ear one more time, just barely, and grind my pelvis against his ass, pushing him hard into the ground.

"Ori, I get it. You're the dominant one. I know that. Okay?" Carl pants out. "But if you keep doing that I'm going to-"

I grind into him again, ensuring that he understands my strength, how easily I could take him down. My cock is hard and thick against him, and I make sure he feels how huge it is between us.

"Do you feel how strong I am, Carl? Even with what I'm made of?" I growl next to his ear.

"Yes, Ori," he replies, still panting.

"Do you feel the size of my cock? You could never pleasure Anne the way I could. But you want her, don't you? You want to stick your cock into her perfect cunt. Taste her impeccable flavor. Don't you?" I free one of my hands, clasping both of his in one of mine. I tug his hair back with my loose hand so that I can see his eyes when he answers.

"Yes. I'm sorry. I want to mate with her. She smells so good, and I want to give her my milt and I bet she has a really lovely ass and...Ori please stop pushing me against the ground because it feels-"

Straddling his hips, I grind against him over and over, forcing his groin into the dirt. Unexpectedly, moans of pleasure are reluctantly wrenched from Carl as he finally stiffens and shudders underneath me.

Perhaps I've gone too far.

"Ori," he *whimpers*, "I...you know."

"Hmm. Well." How awkward. I clear my throat and sit up some. "You won't be touching Anne without my permission. You understand?"

"Yes, Ori. I'll wait for permission to touch her."

"That's not really what I meant but...you know, good enough. Let's go home."

Chapter Sixteen

Carl

I'm so confused.

Ori and I walked home after that, neither of us speaking at all most of the way. The fronts of my pants and sweatshirt were filthy, as were Ori's knees, and we got a few strange looks from passersby. Ori ignored them all, acting as if they didn't even exist, except once when he stopped a woman to ask where she had purchased her backpack.

The bag was decorated in soft pastel colors and featured characters from a classic anime that Anne loves. I guess he wants to buy one for her. The woman he spoke to stumbled over her words, blushing and unable to look him in the eye as she told him where to find it. Her behavior was strange, as prior to Ori speaking to her she had seemed quite reserved. When we were done talking to the woman and were nearly home, I asked Ori about her change in demeanor.

"Why did that lady act so weird when she was talking to you?"

"She was attracted to me," he states matter of factly.

"How do you know that? You've already learned all the human social queues?" People seem really complicated and I can't imagine ever being able to figure them out.

"No. I learned some from watching television for the years I was still Anne's pillow, you know. Now I learn things online when they confuse me. But in regard to that particular situation, the one you just witnessed, I've had personal experience more than once. Anne created me to look like a passably human anime character. It's a look that some find attractive and often they react the way that woman did around me. Anne had to point it out on one of our Sunday walks."

We reach the apartment building and head inside. *Am I attractive?* The thought appears in my head as soon as we step through the threshold, and I can't get it out.

Ori walks into the bathroom, and I hear the water turn on briefly. I can smell the food Anne is cooking now that she's home from work. It's a scent I don't recognize, and I don't look forward to another night of eating something new. But eating with her, that I'll do.

Am I attractive?

Anne is beautiful, though she tries hard to hide it. Ori is handsome and not afraid to flaunt it. But am I good looking? Anne said I was handsome but what if she was just saying that so I wouldn't feel bad?

Now I'm feeling a little panicked. My stomach hurts, my lips feel numb, and my heart is racing. *What if Anne and Ori think I'm hideous?* Sweat beads on my forehead and I feel like everything is too close, it's going to crash into me, crush me. *What if Ori never gives me permission to touch Anne?* I sink to the floor and curl up, feeling like I can't breathe. *What if they don't want me around at all?*

"Carl? Hey, what's going on?" I hear a voice that sounds like it's coming from far away even as the speaker's hand lands gently on my shoulder. "Carl, sweetie, can you talk to me? What happened?"

"What happened to the man? I only stepped into the restroom to cleanse my hands and legs. Is he hurt?"

"I don't know, he won't say anything. He's just curled up and shaking. Hey, Carl, please say something."

It takes all my willpower, but with a shaky breath I manage to speak. "Please don't leave me."

Suddenly, a soft body is wrapped around mine, holding me tightly. I can smell Anne's intoxicating scent caressing me. My breathing and my heart rate slow; I feel instantly calmer.

"Why would we leave you? You're our best friend. Why would you even think we'd do that?" Anne says against my shoulder.

"Because I'm not beautiful like you. There's no room for me. You two are inseparable and you'll get tired of having the golden freak of a friend taking up what little space you have. I don't have anything to contribute, and I'm not even allowed to touch you without permission. By the way, I hope Ori sees that this touching isn't my fault."

"Noted." He replies haughtily.

"What the hell are you two talking about? Permission? I'm not an object you can lend out. You're both lucky I can stand your touches anyway. But whatever. That's not the point of this. What matters is that you know we won't ever stop caring about you, Carl. This is your home too now. And yeah, we'll probably need a bigger one but, on my paycheck, we can't afford much right now. We'll do our best to make things comfortable with what we have. And the attractive thing? Have you seen yourself? You're gorgeous. You look like you should be part of a fairytale, rescuing me from danger and taking me to your magical ocean kingdom."

Anne inhales deeply against my shoulder and it strikes me that she's inhaling my scent. I wonder what she'll find.

"You smell like the forest. Did something bad happen to you two there? Is that why you're acting this way?"

"No. It was fine. Ori and I talked. He told me I'm the beta and he's the alpha. I don't really know what that means but I think I got the point. Ori is in charge here."

Anne scoffs. "He thinks he's in charge."

"Anne," Ori speaks up. "I've been trying to speak to you about the Omegaverse."

"Is this really the time?" Anne says in frustration, gently releasing me from her hold then sitting up, tugging me along with her.

"I know the things I like are silly to you, Anne, but they've helped me get through days that would have been otherwise torturously dull. Yes, I may be still and patient but only because I have a lively imagination. Only because I've heard or seen or read fantastic things to feed into my well of creativity. I could sit as a pillow for years entertained on nothing but the memory of a few stories and my darling Anne. Now I only desire to share some of what's inside me. That's all. And in this case, I believe it could help."

Anne stands and wraps her arms around Ori. I tug my knees to my chest and set my chin on them, watching the two lovers embrace.

"Ori, I'm sorry I've been so dismissive and stubborn and, well, rude. I've taken my frustrations with work and bills and all that and let it mess up my head and it should not be affecting the way I treat you, ever. I love you. Tell me everything. I want to hear it. Carl too, right?" Anne turns to me and offers me a smile that I can't resist returning. *She didn't forget to include me.*

"Yeah, I want to hear too."

"Alright. First off, a warning. The plan includes Carl mating you."

Chapter Seventeen

Anne

"What?" Carl chokes out. "I thought we weren't supposed to do that."

"Excuse me?" I ask, incredibly shocked.

"Yes. Alright so, the Omega-"

"I'm explaining. You said you'd listen. So here I go. The
Omegaverse is a trope in fiction. There's a lot to it, I can
provide some examples of stories if you'd like, but for our
situation I'd like to simplify it. Keep it more specific to our
situation."

I listen to him as patiently as I can without interrupting.
Omegaverse is a pretty well-known trope among people who
read the types of things I do so I don't really need a primer. I
just need to know why he's trying to *mate me* to Carl.

"Initially there were only the two of us, Anne would be
the omega, which is the submissive member of the pack who
generally gets bred by a strong mate, and I would be the alpha,
the one in charge who generally does the breeding. We didn't

have a beta and I thought that would be fine enough, as betas are complicated in omegaverse lore anyway."

Ori paces the hall with his hands clasped behind his back as he tells us his fucked-up plan. I contemplate whether or not he should have access to the internet.

"But then we were blessed with Carl. I created him physically to be someone I believed you would find attractive, Anne. A fairytale prince, a light to my darkness. Impossible for you to resist. As he was generated using my life force, there was no chance he wouldn't have at least *some* attraction to you in return. My entire being is dedicated to my love for you, Anne. Carl inherited some of that. As it turns out, Carl, being a young fish-man in his prime, is filled to the brim with mating hormones. He also has a specific desire for you, Anne, beyond what I gave him. He didn't glance once at any of the beautiful people we passed today but whenever you're around he lights up like a match.

"Carl is also submissive to me. I proved it today, in fact. This is a necessary characteristic for our ideal beta. Today during our outing, I also found out that Carl does, in fact, ejaculate a kind of fluid. This is also beneficial as I do not. If we are roleplaying, we need someone to stuff you with cum."

"Ori!" I shriek.

I turn to look at Carl only to find him covering his face with his hands. It's then that I take in his dirty clothes and start to wonder what exactly happened in those woods and how Ori knows about Carl's jizz.

"Ori, you're talking about this like it's all real-life stuff, but you also know it's actually roleplaying. So, what is it? This all sounds insane." I fling my arms out in frustration, nearly smacking Carl. "Sorry, sweetie."

"Of course it's not real. But we're real. And we have real desires. I know you desire me; you've shown me nearly every day for months. And, Anne, I know you desire Carl."

"Ori, stop right now. You know I love you and I would never be unfaithful to you."

Ori grabs me in a big hug and snuggles his face into my hair before pulling away.

"Of course I know that. You're mine. Whatever develops between the two of you will be its own relationship, as will the one that develops between all three of us. Neither will change the one between you and me. That's ours."

I sit on the floor next to Carl again and lean my head on his shoulder. This time Ori joins us on the floor, his long legs crossed in front of him.

"Carl. The world is brand new to you. You're flooded with hormones. You shouldn't be getting involved in a triad. I do like you though. He's not wrong. So eventually...I mean, honestly, I don't even know what this omegaverse thing had to do really with this whole discussion when we could have just talked about it in a normal way. Why is he so weird?" I grumble.

Carl snickers. "You made him, you tell me."

"Oh no, I'm not taking responsibility for that. The personality was fully intact when I found him."

The both of us start laughing until we fall backwards, facing the ceiling, tears in the corners of our eyes. Ori just watches, shaking his head. When the two of us finally calm down I turn my head to Carl's only inches away from mine now.

"But really. It's too soon for you to be getting involved in an intimate relationship."

"You were intimate with Ori the first day you met him."

"That was different! Things were really weird. I was a different person then."

"What if we took things a little slow then? Because I know what I want, Anne. At this point it's you who needs to be comfortable. I'm fine." He smiles that fairytale smile and I want to kiss him right there.

So, glancing at Ori first to make sure it's okay and seeing him nod, I do. I place a soft kiss on Carl's plush lips, pull back several inches, and wait.

Carl's pupils grow massive in his ice blue eyes. He blows out a long breath, staring at the ceiling. I wonder if I should give up on him but right then he sits up and places one golden hand on the back of my neck, drawing my mouth toward his.

This kiss is a little sloppy, the skill a little lacking, but it's fantastic, nonetheless. He's going to be an amazing kisser once he gets used to his body. I return his attempt at hormonally frantic kisses with gentle guidance, using show rather than tell to teach him how to use his mouth. He takes to it *very* quickly and soon I'm whimpering and pressing my chest against his.

I thought I wouldn't be able to touch someone made of flesh like this, but Carl is different. When I stroke his cheek, I can feel that wonderful texture like snakeskin, not human skin. He doesn't smell like a human, he barely smells like anything, and the scent he does give off is fresh and bright. And his taste is like water. Not like distilled water, but like spring water. Slightly tinged with minerals but clean and almost refreshing. Nothing about him makes me feel anxious or disgusted or afraid. He's wonderful.

After several moments of passionate kissing, Carl pulls away with what I can tell is some reluctance. "Anne. If we don't stop now, I won't be able to stop at all."

Realizing I feel the same way, I just nod my head against his cheek. We lay there, breathing one another in, a world of possible futures between us.

Too many futures. So many possibilities. So much could go wrong. I don't want to hurt this sweet man. This man who has never caused any harm to anyone. Why would I ever choose to hurt him?

And then the scent of earth finally hits me.

"Oh. Oh no. You need to change now, and I need a shower. *Ugh.*" I stand up and scurry toward the shower, hands held to either side of me. There are bits of dirt stuck to the front of my clothes, and I can't help but think that it's on my hands or in my mouth or eyes. It's going to make me sick; it's going to make Ori and Carl sick. I just know it. I need to wash *now*.

"Fuck fuck fuck," I chant as I run the water in the shower, making sure it's as hot as I can handle. I strip off my clothes, placing them into the plastic bag-lined hamper, and get under the steaming stream.

The near blistering heat begins to soothe my anxiety almost immediately and when I begin to scrub with my antibacterial soap it's as if I can feel it physically run down the drain with the suds. They don't understand that I'm doing this to protect us. That we need to be clean. No one understands. I scrub harder.

Chapter Eighteen

Carl

I find some clean clothes and head to the kitchen right away. My stomach had begun rumbling and there can be no discussing feelings while hungry. I'm pretty sure Anne is going to want to discuss some stuff when she gets out of the shower because she was acting pretty weird. So, food.

When I get to the kitchen, however, I realize I have no idea how to cook. Or what anything even is. It's overwhelming. After trying, and failing, to figure out what is inside some of the boxes in the cabinets, I sit at the table and lay my head in my arms in defeat.

"You hungry?" Anne asks from behind me.

I nod my head as I raise it. "Very hungry. I don't know how to find food yet. I'm sorry that I can't provide food for us. I'm a failure."

"A failure? You haven't even had a chance to try. How could you fail?" Ori asks from behind Anne.

"You knew how to do so much more stuff than I do by the time you'd been around two days, Ori."

"Well, not really. I mean, I knew a lot of information and the general concepts behind things by watching Anne but *doing* them is an entirely different matter. Anne and I didn't do much more than lay around and have sex for several days after I was made, frankly." Ori takes a seat next to me and Anne sits next to him.

"Oh. If you learned so much stuff from watching Anne, how did I learn all this stuff? I know a lot that I don't remember learning at the pet shop or while I was here."

"You learned it through my life force, I suppose. I'm not entirely sure but I think so anyway. I have a feeling we're in territory that hasn't been well explored so the answers may not be easy to come by. This is all new to me, too."

"To all of us," Anne says with a bemused expression.

"I didn't think about it that way. What should we do now?" I look back and forth between the two of them, hoping one of them has the answer, but the way they're looking at each other it doesn't appear that they do.

Finally, Anne clears her throat. "Maybe, we just...live. Like, you two really need to learn how to be people with full and joyful lives outside of the apartment. And I need to get back on track with getting over my fears. I had a panic attack again tonight like I haven't for a while, and I can't do that anymore. So, let's just be individuals. Learn. Grow. See what happens."

Everything is silent for a moment except the soft, dry sound of Anne's fingertips rubbing together underneath the table. Suddenly, Ori stands up so fast from the table his chair is knocked backward.

"Are you breaking up with me?" he asks in a panicked voice.

"Oh god no," Anne replies, grabbing his arm in comfort. "Never. Never, ever. I just think you should get a job and maybe a hobby. Wow. I really need to do a better job of explaining things."

"A job? Me too?" I ask as I watch the two of them snuggle together in Ori's relief.

"Yeah, you too. Though, of course we won't expect anything right away." Anne assures me. "But...well, this is harder to say, but I think there shouldn't be anything romantic going on between us. You really need to discover who you are as a person. If I could do things over with Ori, I would let him discover who he was too. It's too late for that now, obviously, but it's not too late for you, Carl."

I sit back in my chair in a slump. There's no point in arguing; a no is a no. But I *will* find a way to win her over.

A job and a hobby. I have no skills. I can't even read. What the heck am I going to do?

Chapter Nineteen

Carl

Anne wanted to wait, so I waited. For months. Now I'm standing near someone else.

She has long, red hair that flows over the front of her perky breasts, which are barely covered by a yellow bikini top. Her skin is fair, freckled, and flawless. When she walks her hips sway from side to side and everyone has to stop and stare, it's so hypnotizing. She's smart as a whip, funny, and she swims faster than all the other girls. Her name is *Emma,* and everyone wants to mate with her.

"Heya Carl. Your shift almost over?" she asks in her adorably raspy voice, bouncing on her toes at my side.

"You know it is, Emma. You ask every day." I gently shove her on the shoulder in a playful way. She *does* ask me every day. And she asks the same follow up question too.

"Well, then, maybe would you like to go out after? With me, I mean." She twists her hands shyly in front of her in that sweet way that drives a certain type of man mad.

Giving another look around the pool to make sure everything is alright before shooting a quick glance at Emma, I shake my head and sigh. "No, thank you. I'm busy. And here's Josh, that's my cue to go."

Everyone wants to mate with her except for me, that is.

"Okay fine," Emma pouts as Josh comes up to me and takes over.

I've been working as a lifeguard at this indoor pool these last few weeks, which should turn into an outdoor job once the weather warms up. It took a little bit for me to get this job, but I think it's obviously pretty good for someone who was very recently a fish. Going through all the trouble to get set up with all the "legal" documents needed to apply was worth it.

First, Anne had to come up with fake identities for Ori and me, which is apparently not easy at this time in history when everything can be verified online. But she managed to do it with time and money and the help of this really sketchy guy. We all decided to take Anne's last name so now we're Carl, Ori, and Anne Athans.

Then I had to learn to read and write enough to pass the lifeguard classes and...boy, that was tough. I worked on it day and night though and I actually took to it a lot faster than I thought I would. I think it was probably because of Ori's force-thing-whatever but Anne likes to say it's just because I'm smart. I'll let her think that if it makes her like me more.

Once I could fumble through the reading and writing I took the necessary classes. I passed those with flying colors. Turns out, I'm a really good student! Maybe someday I'll go to school for even more stuff. Ori wants to learn about politics and geography for some reason so maybe we can do that together.

Once I got through my training it wasn't too hard to find a job. I'm pretty likable apparently, and I can swim better than just about anyone. The only thing that was tough to deal with at first was my golden, shimmery skin. People were pretty curious. I would kind of clam up when they asked about it. Now I'm good at answering in a natural manner. I just say it was a cosmetic procedure I got done overseas, sort of a new kind of tattooing, and people believe it.

So yeah, I really like this job. It's nice when I actually get to be in the water and not just standing or sitting around especially. I miss Ori and Anne, but I know they have their own things going on during the day anyway and I'll get to see them when my shift is over.

Today the locker room is hot and grimy as usual. I make sure to keep my sandals on like Anne told me to when I'm in here because apparently there are creatures or something lurking on the floor waiting to stick to people's feet. Yuck. When I go to grab my bag out of my locker it gets stuck and, try as I might, I can't seem to get it out.

"Hey, let me help," a smooth, rich voice offers.

A pair of deep brown, muscular arms reach over me and easily pull my bag from the locker. Ahead of me is a set of glorious pecs, glistening with sweat from the heat of this steamy room. I raise my head and look into a pair of beautiful brown eyes, framed by curling black lashes.

"Thanks, James," I say. "I don't want to be late for my ride again."

James is a swimming instructor here and he's a really cool guy. Everyone likes him and I have lunch with him sometimes.

"No problem, Carl." James smiles a perfect model-bright grin as he nervously scratches behind his ear. "I just, uh, if you got one sec can I ask you something?"

"Sure! I managed to get rid of Emma fast today for once," I laugh with a roll of my eyes as we both chuckle.

"Yeah, so, I was wondering if maybe Emma isn't your type, you know..." He rubs the back of his neck and raises a brow with a knowing look I'm not seeming to catch onto.

"Well, no. She's not. Which is part of the reason I keep turning her down, obviously."

"So maybe your type might be less of an Emma and more of an...Ernest? If you feel me?"

I scratch my head with the hand not holding my bag and look at how James is acting. He seems a little different than usual. Then it hits me. He reminds me a little of that time Ori asked that lady about her backpack. *James is attracted to me.*

"James, you're very handsome. If my heart wasn't already spoken for, I would like to mate with you in several ways that could not possibly produce offspring. But I'm taken. I hope we can continue to be friends."

"That was a strange rejection speech, I'm not gonna lie, Carl, but I'll accept it. And yeah, of course we can be friends." He holds out his hand and I shake it like Ori taught me to do.

We say goodbye and I head outside into the cold to catch my ride. Anne is outside in our car waiting for me in the parking lot already when I get there. Now with three incomes we're able to afford a car, and no one has to take the bus anymore. Which is great because the bus sucks a lot. I understand that it's better for the environment but when one of you is terrified of germs, and two of you are not human, the ride is kind of scary.

"Hi Anne!" I say as I hop into the front seat. "Where's Ori?" He's usually with her when she comes to pick me up.

"Oh, he decided to do a special birthday show for one of his clients. She was paying extra, and you know he's been saving up to take us all on that mystery trip he's always talking about. He should be done by the time we get back home."

It turns out he's not done when we get home, I can tell because the red light outside of their closed bedroom door is on. After she takes a quick shower, Anne and I split some reheated veggie lo mein. I've gotten used to human food the last few months, I even like a bunch of stuff, though some things I still can't stand. I'll just never eat beef or maple syrup again and no one can make me.

As we're cleaning up our dishes, I see the color coming from the hall switch from red back to its normal white color.

"Hey Anne, Ori's done." We finish our cleaning and head to their room to see my best friend.

When Anne opens the door, I find Ori sitting in front of his computer monitor in the fancy chair they have set in front of a Victorian wallpaper style backdrop. Our new apartment is much bigger than our last one and their bedroom is big enough to fit this small filming area for Ori's work. When he needs more room, he'll sometimes set up in the living room or something but usually where he's at is fine.

"Hi Ori! How was your day?" I ask as I sit on the end of their big, soft bed.

"It was fine. She paid quite a lot. We'll be taking that trip very soon." Ori grins charmingly, his hair slightly mussed, and his cheeks flushed. He must have just finished his assignment before we came in.

Ori zips his pants, buttons up his shirt, takes the time to straighten his clothing. I like to watch him put himself back together like this. He could, frankly, just snap himself into a new outfit entirely if he wanted to. After some experimenting, we've learned that his clothes seem to be shed in the way humans might shed hair or nails. When they're on him they grow from him like part of his body and when they're detached, they're inanimate, pretty much. There's a lot to learn about the way Ori and I work but little by little we're figuring it out.

"Alright, all better. Now, how was your day, my love?" Ori asks Anne.

"Fine. I submitted the final designs for the characters. I'm really nervous but I think I've got this. Chandra is such a good supervisor; I really think she'll see the potential."

Anne started working at a new indie game company that is a lot more gender diverse and she seems way happier. Her health insurance covers much more in the way of mental health services and she's been doing really well in therapy. I'm so proud of her. The art she's been putting out lately has been fantastic and she's doing so much of it too now that she's not so anxious all the time. Ori and I picked out some fancy painting stuff for her Christmas gift and she's been doing a ton of awesome pieces. Our apartment is like a gallery. It's beautiful.

"If she doesn't see how wonderful you are then she's blind," Ori says before kissing the top of Anne's head. "Now, how was your day, Carl?"

"Me?" I perk up. "It was great, as usual. Except I had to turn down Emma *again* and today James of all people tried to ask me out. That's so weird, isn't it? I never knew James thought of me that way. Mrs. Phillips also tried to offer me fifty dollars to give me a blowjob but I said no, obviously."

Anne makes a choking sound and nearly falls off her side of the bed. "Mrs. Phillips? Reverend Phillips's wife? She's like seventy years old!"

"Well, you're never too old to suck c-" Ori begins before Anne slaps her hands over his mouth.

"That's enough." Anne sighs before releasing Ori, who has a naughty smile on his face that tells me he will be showing Anne all about age and blowjobs later. "Anyway, why do you keep turning everyone down? I mean, Mrs. Philips I get, but Emma and James are great catches. Every day some absolute gem tries to bag you, and you turn them down. Why?"

"I don't feel a connection." I shrug. "Unless I feel something, I'm not interested so why would I waste their time pretending to be?"

"If you've never felt a connection, how would you know though? Maybe you just need to spend some time around them before it clicks or something." Anne insists.

"No," Ori softly interjects. "He's already felt a connection, Anne. Stop pretending you don't know it."

Ori places his hand over hers and gently rubs them together before intertwining their fingers. She looks into his eyes for several long seconds before letting out a long breath.

"I know," she whispers before laying her head on his shoulder and closing her eyes.

I get up and walk out, to go to my bedroom to be alone.

Chapter Twenty

Ori

My Anne. My darling Anne. She's perfect in every way. Every way, that is, aside from her stubbornness.

"Anne, you're still rejecting him?"

I know why. She thinks I won't love her if she accepts both of us. And she worries for Carl, that he's too sweet, he needs someone of his own to be happy. She's wrong about it all.

"Leave it, Ori," she mumbles against my shoulder.

"Fine, for now. But only because I missed you." I turn and lift her face to mine.

"I was only gone for the workday," she laughs. "That's the same as always."

"It felt like forever. I could barely hold back during my shows due to thinking about you. I've been edging myself all day. It's been torture."

Special effects, we've had to come up with them to replace the feathers. The people who watch my performances want to see me...finish...and I can't very well show them the real thing.

"Well, we'll have to do something about that then won't we?" Anne smiles up at me with her eyes blinking sweetly behind her glasses.

"Yes, we will. Undress for me, quickly. I can't stand waiting a moment longer, my darling. I want what is *mine.*"

Growling the last word hungrily, I tear off my own clothes without care. I don't seem to need to worry about the energy to replace things anymore. Ever since I...well, *killed* those fucking pig security guards I've seemed to have an endless well of energy.

Biting her lip, Anne begins to remove her clothing, only pausing when she's down to her little blue cotton panties. I groan at the sight of them. She knows they're special to me, as they're the ones she wore the first time we were together. She lies back on the bed, heavy breasts waiting for my kisses, and spreads her legs, revealing a river of blue cotton between her thighs.

"Come on, Ori. Let's have fun."

"Oh, I believe we will."

Several hours later, after much fun was had, Anne is busy playing some visual novel while I'm on my phone using social media to watch hamsters run on wheels on a live feed. *Is this really what I need to be doing?* I scroll up to find a live feed of a strange old man dancing instead. *No thank you.* With a frown I toss the phone onto the mattress and lay back, stretching out.

"Anne, I'm bored. Come play with me," I whine.

When I reach out to rub her side, I accidentally nudge her mouse hand. I hear a click followed by a groan. Anne's head flops backward and she spins toward me in her chair.

"You made me click the rude dialogue option on accident right before it auto saved. I hate clicking the rude dialogue option. Now he's going to hate me," she grouses.

"It's a cartoon. It can't hate you. Perhaps it will be fun to see what will happen when you aren't always nice to the characters for once. Besides, you should take a break, you've been playing for ages, and I miss you."

"Ori, it's been like maybe twenty minutes max," Anne laughs as she crawls next to me.

"As I said, ages. You need some sleep, don't you darling? You have to work in the morning."

"*Argh* when did you become the responsible one? Fine. Let me use the restroom and I'll be right back."

Anne gives me a kiss on the cotton cheek and yawns before leaving the room. My darling Anne. How I do love to watch her backside jiggle and flex as she walks away. I will never tire of it. My goal, though she doesn't know it, is to find a way to get her and Carl to live forever. I'll succeed, I know it. If I turned from a pillow to a man, I could do anything.

But that's a problem for later. For now, I need Anne and Carl to finally get frisky. They don't understand. Their joining needs to happen.

When I made Carl, he was made from *my* life force. That means he inherited the thing that made me who I am. And that thing is my love for Anne. That means he will, naturally, have love for her. As he is my best friend, I will not let him suffer without her.

And I know he's perfect for her. I made him that way. He's everything I'm not. Where I'm dark he's light. Where I'm selfish he's generous. Where I would hurt, he would heal. She *needs* him and I will *always* give Anne what she needs. She is *mine* and I won't let what is mine have anything less than everything.

Besides, an alpha needs a beta, doesn't he?

Chapter Twenty-One

Anne

Ori's right, I really do need to go to bed. My new job is so great, but it does start early. It's a lot more demanding than my last one but it's also much more fulfilling. Going home each day, I really feel satisfied with the work I've done, and I feel appreciated by my coworkers and superiors. Getting up a little earlier or occasionally staying a little late is no big deal.

The bathroom light is on, but the door is halfway open so I'm guessing whoever used it last just forgot to turn the light off. When I open the door all the way I see that I've guessed wrong.

We have a pretty big bathtub in our new place. It's something Carl really wanted because he likes to take long baths. And that's what he's doing right now. This time he's fallen asleep in the water. I always warn him not to do that because I'm super paranoid he'll drown or something, but he just laughs and tells me not to worry. I can't help worrying, that's like a huge part of who I am. But I have to admit he looks super peaceful right now.

I've seen him naked before when he was transformed but things were more than chaotic and strange at the time so I couldn't really process it. Looking at him now, I see that Ori made him *very* well. I've figured out by now that Ori tried to go for a soft, fairytale sweetheart-type and he succeeded. Yes, Carl is covered in those golden almost-scales, but underneath is a strong body, perfect for rescuing damsels in distress. That soft, innocent face, with this built body, and a big...well, he's got a great combination going on. Really, really, great.

I shouldn't be staring like this but I'm having a hard time tearing my eyes away. He's so beautiful in the water. My eyes drag over every part of him, stopping specifically to wonder at the strength of his legs. He's taken up running as a hobby. Mixed with swimming as his other pleasure, his body is...wow. When I bring my eyes back to his face, I see his eyes are open, watching me watching him.

"Oh! I'm so sorry. The door was open, and I didn't realize you were in here." I stumble over my words, trying to explain myself as quickly as possible.

Carl smiles and sits, all those perfect muscles flexing as he does. "It's my fault. I thought I closed it. Sorry. I'll be out in a minute so you can use the bathroom. I just drifted off. Don't kill me."

He raises his hands in a defensive posture, and I can't help but laugh at him.

"I won't this time but you're on thin ice, buddy."

"I'll be sure to watch myself," he nods. Then he raises an eyebrow as he looks me up and down. "Though, I think you've watched me enough for both of us."

"Oh my god," I squeak out before rushing out of the bathroom back into my bedroom.

Ori is laying on his back, nude, twirling his cock into a corkscrew shape. When I give him a shocked look, he shrugs.

"I'm only testing something. I think you'll like it." He snaps back into shape and tosses the blanket over himself, patting the spot on the bed next to him. "Get your pajamas on now and come to bed."

"Oh, I still have to use the restroom. Carl was in the bath. But I suppose I can get dressed and then go."

"Hmm. You walked in on him?" Ori raises an eyebrow.

"Don't start," I warn as I take off my shirt and begin the search for pajamas.

"Was he simply lying in the water? Was he touching himself?" Ori asks with a mischievous grin.

"Ori, stop being a brat."

"Was he stroking his cock in the water? Thinking about you? Did you watch him, Anne? Did he cum?"

I slip on a cotton nightgown with a picture of an orange cartoon cat wearing a cowboy hat on the front of it. Ori does not deserve my sexy satin numbers tonight.

"No. Not that it was any of your business. He was just bathing."

I bite the side of my thumbnail to keep from rubbing my fingers together. This conversation is making me anxious. The truth is the idea of walking in on Carl and seeing him doing something like that is flooding me between the legs and Ori messing with me about it is stressful. I know he wants Carl and I to be together, but I don't want to hurt Carl. He's so sweet and innocent. Ori and I are so close, and we will *never* part. Introducing someone else into that dynamic is a big fucking deal and I'm worried that Ori is treating it like a game. Or that Carl doesn't understand the stakes. Because when it comes down to it, I'll never leave Ori and if I really care about Carl, I won't put him into a relationship where he could be pushed out by Ori. I know how territorial Ori is and if one day Ori decides he's tired of Carl what then? *Ugh.*

"Anne," Ori says much more softly, seriously. "I shouldn't have made fun."

"No, you shouldn't have. You know this is a sore subject. But thank you for recognizing that." I crawl into bed next to him and lay my head in the crook of his shoulder.

"Give him a chance, Anne."

"Goodnight, Ori."

Chapter Twenty-Two

Carl

After work I go outside and see Anne isn't there, so I check my phone and find she sent a message. She says she has to work late so I need to take the bus. *Bleh.* I hate the bus.

It's cold, my hair is still wet, and I'm feeling a little crabby today so waiting for the bus just feels like it takes a lot longer than usual. Last night after I got out of the bath and went to my room, I couldn't stop thinking about Anne looking at me. I jacked off several times because I couldn't freaking sleep. She wouldn't get out of my head. Now I'm tired, I miss her, and I want to go home already.

Finally, the bus pulls up and I pay the fare. It's pretty empty thankfully so I take a big seat in the back and relax. The next block over a lady gets on who looks like she maybe hasn't slept in a lot longer than me. Unfortunately, she sits right next to me, despite most of the other seats being empty.

"Hey cutie, where you going to?" she slurs out in a breath that smells like menthol and bacon. She leans so close to me that a greasy lock of her yellow blonde hair brushes against my cheek, making me flinch.

"Home," I reply curtly. Maybe if I keep it short, she'll get bored and go away.

"You want some company at home, sweetie?" Another brush of her bleached hair against my face makes me press back against the cold glass of the bus window.

Her calling me "sweetie" makes me angry. That's what Anne calls me. No one else can.

"No. I'm not your *sweetie*. Please leave me alone now." I don't like being mean, it makes my stomach hurt. I just have a feeling this lady isn't going to take nice for a no.

"I can be your sweetie. You're too cute to go home alone." She brushes my cheek with one long, blue, dirty fingernail and I nearly gag.

"I said no. And don't touch me. Go sit somewhere else." There. Clear as day. There's no way she can misinterpret that.

And she doesn't. She starts crying. *Fuck.*

"You guys are all the same. Won't give a girl a chance," she blubbers while green snot leaks down her face. "You think you're too good for me."

I look around for an escape route, but her big nylon duffel bag is blocking the aisle. I'll have to hop over it.

"It's not you, I, uh, I'm taken," I mumble as I stand.

"Yeah right," she suddenly screeches.

Okay, time to get the heck out of here.

"Fuck you, liar," she screams as she lifts a knee and trips me as I attempt to hop over her bag.

I manage to catch myself on the handlebars so that I don't smash my face into the floor, but I don't prevent myself from slamming my knees into the ground and my hip into the side of a bench. *Fuck that hurt.* When I pull myself up the woman shoves me so that my chest slams into the top of a bench. *Ouch.*

"Go home to your mama, asshole," she shouts as the bus pulls up to the next exit.

The woman gets off the bus and runs away as I plop myself into a seat. I think about whether or not to report the incident but decide against it. That woman clearly has some major problems to deal with and I just want to go home to my Anne and Ori. I'm hurting and I need their comfort more than anything.

A few stops later I limp home to our apartment and find Ori in the kitchen making snacks for Anne and me. He looks so handsome in the early evening light, his dark hair falling over his brow, his grin that always looks like he is about to cause some trouble, his long, pale limbs that move so perfectly gracefully. He stops what he's doing and looks up at me when he hears me enter the room.

"Hello there, my friend. I've got a little treat for you before dinner, coming right up." He raises the platter to show me the charcuterie board he's working on. A look of concern crosses his face as he notices my expression. He sets down the tray. "What happened?"

"I got attacked by some crazy woman on the bus. Not hurt bad or anything, more just made me feel sad is all. Stupid bus." I wash my hands at the kitchen sink and dry them on a paper towel while Ori looks me over with a frown. "It's not a huge deal, really. I'm just bummed out."

"Perhaps you need some water time, followed by a video game?" Ori smiles as he gently lays a hand on my shoulder.

I perk up at the game suggestion. We haven't gamed together as a household in a while, and it could be fun. I could use a silly time dropping banana peels and shells on Ori for a while. But first he's definitely right about needing some water time. That always makes me feel better.

"You're right, as usual," I lay my head on his hand before I hear the front door open and close.

We both turn toward the sound. *Anne's home.* It's just instinct for both of us to go to her as soon as she enters. We always want to be where Anne is. But when we see her, she holds up a hand and drops her purse and coat on the polished wood floor.

"Not now. Bad day. I've gotta get into the shower right away." She rushes past the both of us and into the bathroom, slamming the door behind her.

Ori and I look at each other with frowns on our faces. "There goes my water time," I grumble.

"Not necessarily. I'm sure if you explained what happened she'd be willing to share her time," Ori says, his smile growing wider and his eyes shimmering with mischief.

"Ori. You're going to get me into trouble."

"No. I'm going to get you the girl. Go. If it doesn't work then blame me, she can't stay mad at me long."

Well, he's right about that. "You think she'll be okay with it?"

"If you act pathetic enough, yes."

"Oh. Well. That sure sounds great," I mumble.

With some hesitation I head toward the bathroom door. I can hear the shower running. My throat tightens up. *Is this okay?* With a racing heart and a determined set to my jaw I decide *fuck it* and turn the handle.

Today I get the girl.

Chapter Twenty-Three

Anne

*F*uck, work sucked. I mean, I love work, it's just that we had a meeting about doing a joint project with my old company and I wasn't aware of it until like right beforehand. It was super awkward, and I nearly passed out from the anxiety. My boss was disappointed in my performance in the meeting but what the fuck was I supposed to do? My brain was in total panic mode the whole time. I just hope she doesn't hold it against me too much.

The water runs extra hot against my tense muscles, soothing them, and loosening the tightness that has built up throughout the day.

Then the curtain opens. Carl blinks at me with those impossibly blue eyes as I startle at his sudden appearance.

"Sorry for scaring you. I thought I could join you in the shower," he explains while his eyes are very much locked above my neck. "And maybe help you if you need it."

"I don't need any help to shower, Carl. And for the record it's rude to just open the curtain when someone's showering." His face falls and he looks as if he's going to turn away. But that's not what I want. I have to admit it to myself. So, I keep talking. "Why did you think to come in here today?"

"Honestly," he pauses and looks at me with a genuine look of sadness, "I've had a pretty bad day and could use some water time."

"Oh. Well. Of course you can join me then, I guess."

Okay it's weird that we're showering together, right? But we're friends and we both need the shower so it's okay. Right?

"You want to talk about it, Carl?" I ask once he's in and we're both awkwardly positioned so that there's some water spraying both of us.

"Not really. I just want to enjoy this time."

"Okay."

We face each other and I stand there looking at the tiles because I don't know what else to do. Then he speaks and everything changes.

"Can I look at you?" Carl asks and his cheeks have turned red with nervousness.

My eyebrows shoot up in surprise. "You mean, like, my body?"

"Yeah. I've only seen you naked through the tank, as a fish. I'd like to see you as a human. I've never seen a woman naked as a human."

"Oh. Um. Wow. That's...sure." *Wow, that's a lot of responsibility.*

I stand with my arms at my sides, feeling more than a little awkward as his eyes graze up and down my body. They pause at my breasts and my pubic area longer than the rest of me, which is unsurprising. When I feel a soft tap at my navel, Carl steps backward and I realize his cock has hardened and decided to say hello.

"Sorry," he whispers.

"That's fine. To be expected," I whisper back.

"You're beautiful. I didn't know what to expect but this is better than whatever I could have imagined."

"Well, I'm the only woman you've ever seen naked when you've had human hormones. There are much better-looking ones out there. But I appreciate the compliment nonetheless."

"Don't put yourself down. Why would I care what other people look like when what I have in front of me is already perfect? Already makes me feel like my heart is going to explode just from being near it?" His voice is starting to get louder, faster, and I can feel myself grow slippery between my legs. Not the wetness of water but the satin texture that comes with desire.

"You're so sweet. So incredibly sweet." I'm lost for words. Nothing I can think of can fit how I'm feeling right now for this man.

"I wonder how sweet you are. Ori says women enjoy being kissed between their legs. I've seen him do it to you before. Would you let me try? We've already kissed; would it be different?"

His eyes have gone half lidded and he steps closer to me, his hard cock pushing against my stomach in the most delightful way. Is this really happening? Am I letting this happen?

"It's definitely different. And what if you don't like it? I'm-" *I'm afraid you won't like me.*

"The chances of me not liking anything to do with you are zero. But if I don't like it, I promise I'll tell you. Okay?" He steps so close there is no more possible room between us. "We have to make this water a little less hot though, if possible, I feel like I'm going to boil."

"Oh," I laugh. "I suppose that's fine. Just for you, sweetie."

Chapter Twenty-Four

Carl

*S*he's so beautiful.

I knew what she looked like, but it was only in memories and those were my fish memories. It's like looking back through a slightly cloudy mirror. I can see it but not the details. Seeing her up close, in all her glory, is beyond words. I'll never forget this moment. And now she's going to let me touch her. *Taste her.* Has anyone ever been so lucky?

Well, Ori. But I'm not thinking about him right now.

Anne turns to lower the temperature of the water and as she bends over, I drop to my knees and pull her hips toward me. She yelps and tries to stand but I keep a firm grip on one hip and hold her back down with the other.

"Stay. I like this view. Can you spread your legs a little wider please?" I ask.

"Carl! This is not how you do it!" She protests.

"I've seen Ori do it this way. Actually, can you put one foot up on the side of the tub please?"

"I mean...okay." She does as I say, and I can't help but slide my hand up and down my stiff cock a few times when I see what's before me.

Now *this* I've never seen. They've always been too far away to catch this much detail. I've been missing out on something very, very, good.

"Are you going to just stare all day?" Anne asks with a nervous giggle.

I shake my head, realizing I've been staring at her perfect entrances for what must have been far too long. But how could I not? I can see *everything* like this. Her tiny asshole, those spread lips surrounding her treasures, the pink wetness I know is waiting hungrily for a cock to fill it, the little bud that Ori says is solely for pleasure. All of that and more is revealed before me, waiting for my mouth. *Fuck, I'm so lucky.*

"Oh, I'm going to do much more than stare. Hold on, pretty girl, tell me if I'm doing this right because you deserve nothing less than perfection. Okay?" I run my hands along the outside of her hips, her thighs, and I can feel her skin grow goosebumps.

"Okay," she says in a squeaky voice.

"Wow," slips reverently past my lips when I slide one finger through the slippery liquid along her entrance. I bring that finger to my lips and my eyes close as I delight in the taste of her.

I can see her legs shaking and I don't know if it's from strain or nerves or what, so I grab hold of her hips to make sure she's supported. Then, unable to resist any longer, I lick a long line up the center of the most beautiful woman in the world.

Anne moans and pushes back against my face, making me so happy. If she wants closer that must mean she liked what I did, so I do it again, but this time with more pressure so that she doesn't need to push against me. By the sounds she makes and the way the entrance to her cunt seems to clench up I think she enjoys that, so I keep going.

It seems she really, really likes when I focus on the clit area, so I make sure to pay that special attention. She cocks her hips to make it easier for me to access and soon I find myself directing my focus almost entirely on it.

When Anne starts making these really fantastic groaning noises, I decide to take one hand off her hip and slip a couple fingers inside of her to see what happens. It turns out that when I do that while gently sucking on her little bud she really, *really*, likes that. In fact, she likes it so much her legs start shaking and she starts shouting things.

"Oh fuck, yes Carl, yes," she's shouting as her insides begin to clamp around my fingers. "Just like that. Don't stop."

I certainly don't plan to stop, not when it's getting this sort of reaction. She clamps so hard around my fingers I can barely move them, and I can feel liquid inside her leaking all around. It's so silky and slippery, I imagine it all around my cock and moan against her clit.

"Okay, stop, it's too much, I can't take anymore," Anne pants.

I reluctantly pull away and help her into a sitting position, on my lap. I turn us around so that the water is splashing the back of my head and not her face.

"That was really fun," I say, realizing even as I say it how dumb it sounds.

Anne giggles and drops her head onto my chest. "Yeah, it was, wasn't it?"

We're both silent for a good minute at least, just enjoying the warmth and comfort of the water and each other's bodies. Soon, Anne lifts her head and places a hand on my cheek.

"Let's get out of here. I think we've got some things to talk about," she says before placing a gentle kiss on my lips.

I could stay in the water forever with her, but I nod anyway. I know we need to talk about this with Ori when things aren't all emotional. It's just...I'm not great with handling feelings yet and there have been a lot of them already. So many. Do people always have these many feelings?

Chapter Twenty-Five

Anne

I want to throw up. I'm about to open the door to my bedroom and tell Ori what just happened. I rationally know he'll be okay with it; he's been trying to get it to happen for months, but I'm just like...*ugh*. So worried. What if he changed his mind all of a sudden? I can't lose him. I just can't. The knob is cold in my hand, and I wonder if I can somehow psychically freeze it in place so that I have an excuse not to turn it. Stranger things have happened to me, after all. But, alas, when I turn my wrist, the knob turns with it and the door opens.

"Hey honey. We've got to talk about something," I say right off the bat. When he turns to look at me with those bright eyes and that charming smile, however, I clam up.

"What is it, darling? Do you have some exciting news to share?" he asks with a knowing grin.

Ah. He already guessed somehow. I should have known. *Ugh.*

"I kissed her vagina in the shower and made her have an orgasm," Carl states proudly.

"Carl! Oh my god!" I flop onto the bed and cover my face with a pillow.

"Well, to be exact, it wasn't just her vagina. It was her clitoris and her-"

"Carl, shut up!" I shout as I throw the pillow at him. He catches it easily with a smile.

"I'm just letting him know what happened so that there aren't any secrets between us."

"You could be slightly vaguer, I think that would be alright," I grumble.

"Oh, no, I don't mind the details at all. Please continue." Ori's smile widens as he sits all the way back in his chair, hands on his lap.

"Anyway," I interrupt with a clearing of my throat. "I thought we should let you know that Carl and I were intimate. I think, and I think Carl agrees– I hope or else I'm going to feel really stupid– that we would like to try whatever this three-way thing would be. I'm having a really hard time accepting it though because I don't want to lose you, Ori. And I don't want to lose Carl. He's become a necessary part of our lives. I don't want to destroy what we have just because Carl and I add romantic feelings into the mix. I'm all messed up in the head over this, you know? *Ugh.* Please tell me it will be okay, Ori?"

Ori stands up and crawls onto the bed to sit next to me, wrapping an arm around my waist. Carl hesitates for a second but after a look from Ori joins us on the bed on my other side, propping his head on my shoulder.

"It will be more than okay, my love. If it was anyone other than Carl, I would tear them to ribbons before turning them to dust for even attempting to court you. I'm sure you know that," Ori says before tickling my side and making me giggle.

"Yeah, I know that. You're pretty creepy sometimes," I chuckle.

"Creepy in love. But with Carl, no violence is necessary. I know he would never cause you harm and he would never do anything I didn't approve of. He's the best of men because he is, like me, not really a man."

I laugh at that. "And that's why I love you. No human stuff getting in the way."

"And probably the amazing sex as well." Ori shrugs.

"That certainly doesn't hurt." I kiss his cheek, and Carl buries the top of his head against my neck.

"I have an idea," Ori says as he leans back on the bed, crossing his long legs in front of him. "Why don't you and Carl go on a date? Have a day out. Then we can meet back at home and spend time together as our little pack."

"Our little pack?" I ask suspiciously.

"Yes. What about it?"

"I'd like to go on a date," Carl speaks up, raising his head. "I think I even know where we could go."

I turn my attention away from Ori's clearly mischievous plans and focus on Carl.

"Oh yeah? What have you got in mind, sweetie?"

"Well, when you drive us home you pointed out the cat café and said how you want to go there but can't because Ori and cats don't mix. We could go if it's just you and me," he smiles boyishly, and I can't help but return the grin. He's such a ray of sunshine.

"That is such a great idea, Carl. I can't believe you remembered that!" I hug him and breathe in that light, clean scent he has.

"I remember everything about you, Anne. You're the most important thing in the world to me." Carl brushes the hair back from my brow and I can feel tears pricking the corners of my eyes.

How the hell did I get *two* incredible guys? I'm really ripping off some chick out there who has lost the guy lottery and now has no one, it has to be. I swallow my feelings back and blink my eyes a few times before speaking.

"Cat café it is. Tomorrow morning. I'll drive."

Chapter Twenty-Six

Ori

The duo went to the café this morning and I've gone out to take care of some private business. I don't like keeping secrets from them, but I don't want to let them down if what I'm trying to do doesn't work out. If it does, however, the temporary withholding of information will be easily forgiven.

I had to take the *bus* to get here, which was as disgusting as always, but thankfully, I wasn't bothered by any miscreants or perverts. Now, I'm walking through the automatic doors of a department store, the same one that delivers our groceries each week in fact. This is the second time I've been here alone. The first was when I was looking for a gift for Anne. I knew they had an exclusive set of the little anime monster toys she collects here, and I wanted to surprise her with them. I didn't want to risk her finding them in the mail, so I needed to get them in person. I found them, thankfully, but I also found Marlon.

Marlon. *My brother.*

A woman in a red shirt and a green apron offers me a sample cup of some sort of cookie as I walk past her little table. I shudder, thinking of when I was briefly human enough to almost have to eat. I shake my head no and walk faster.

The whole grocery area is useless to me, so I walk away from that third of the store and head toward home goods. When I see some of the anime monster trading cards on the way there, I consider stopping to get some for Anne but decide against it. If I get them, she'll know I went out and I'm trying to hide that.

Once at the home goods area, I look around near the bedding and it doesn't take long to spot him. Stocking the sheets and blankets is a tall, thin man with a shock of ginger hair, wearing the red shirt all the employees wear. He looks normal from far away, but I know if I get close enough to him, he'll look slightly off, just as I do.

"Hello, Marlon," I call out as I walk toward him.

When he looks up to see me, he smiles widely, his gap-toothed grin making him look friendly and approachable.

"Hi there, Ori! How's life?"

"Fantastic. Would be even better if I had the item you promised me, of course."

Marlon sighs and puts his freckled hands on his hips. "Straight to business then. No time to catch up with your only brother."

"Only brother that we know of, anyway."

It turns out I wasn't the only feather that fell off when the phoenix died. We think it was only two. Him, who ended up in a down comforter, and I. But we can't be sure.

"Oh, you. Well, I do have what you need. But you know as well as I do that it might very well be just garbage."

"I know that, brother. But I'll take any lead I can follow until I reach my destination. Don't worry about me."

"I have a feeling you can take care of yourself just fine," Marlon nods. "I'll be right back."

I wait for a few minutes, inspecting the low-quality pillows in this section, before Marlon returns.

"Here you are. One map. I hope you can decipher the directions." He hands me a folded piece of paper that I take gladly.

"Thank you, Marlon. If this proves to be the real thing I'll bathe you in riches, I promise." I shake his hand with a laugh.

"I don't need riches. I'm just happy to have found a brother. Come back and see me any time, Ori."

"Of course."

Only if my plan succeeds, of course.

Chapter Twenty-Seven

Carl

I'm so excited! I've never seen a cat up close, only through windows or on the internet. They look really soft and cute. Anne loves cats so I'm happy she'll get time to play with them too. And of course, I'm excited just to be on a date. My very first date.

The café is bright and cheerful with art all over the walls depicting cartoon cats in all kinds of silly poses. There are shelves full of knick knacks for sale and more artwork on display. I pause on the way to the counter to inspect a particularly adorable statue of an orange kitten curled up on a big, white pillow. I'm going to have to bring that home to Ori for sure.

"Come on, silly goose. We can shop later. Let's get our drinks." Anne tugs my arm impatiently in the direction of the counter.

"Okay, okay." I laugh.

When we get to the counter, a smiling young person in a bright blue apron and matching blue hair greets us from behind the register.

"Hello, I'm Jamie. What can I get for you today?" They are incredibly peppy, and I have to wonder if everyone here is as upbeat as Jamie, if maybe working with cats is just that fun. Their colorful "they/them" name tag catches my eye, along with all of their flashy buttons. There is a smiley face button, one with a cute grumpy-faced cat, one supporting an ocean clean-up initiative, and more. I think I could be friends with Jamie.

"I'd like a matcha latte with soy, please. Oh, and one of those cupcakes shaped like a ball of yarn." Anne points inside a glass case containing various treats and I see a purple cupcake that has indeed been covered in tons of frosting strings made to appear as if it's a ball of yarn.

"I'll have, um..." I pause nervously.

I'm not very good at reading fast yet and some of these words on the menu I don't know. I start to feel really bad about myself. I've tried so hard to learn and I've done really well- I know I have. But some of these words are confusing. I don't want to seem stupid in front of a nice person. I know I'm not stupid, I'm just still learning. It's just hard to remember in times like this. Maybe I'll just order water, at least I know that.

"He'll have a green tea, unsweetened," Anne says.

I breathe a sigh of relief and smile at her, mouthing "thank you," when the server looks down to type in the order. I don't think I've ever had a green tea but if she says I'll like it I trust her. She's only truly led me wrong on beef and maple syrup. *Yuck.*

"Do you two have an appointment with the cats today?" Jamie asks.

We give them our appointment details and stand at the opposite end of the counter to wait for our goodies. It doesn't take long; Jamie seems to be very good at their job. We thank them and walk back to our table with the assurance that we'll be told when it's our time to visit with the kitties.

"Mmm, this is a good latte." Anne sips her drink with her eyes closed, clearly enjoying it. "We need to get out more."

I take a drink of my tea and flinch. "Ow! Hot!"

The tea was about a thousand degrees. I have no idea how Anne seems to be able to handle heat so well. She pats my hand while I blow on my tea and very carefully take another sip.

"Not so bad now that I can actually taste it." It's just some kind of plant water and that's fine with me.

"See? I knew you'd like it. Want to try some of my cupcake?"

"Yes, but I'll pass on the baked goods," I reply over the rim of my cup before taking another sip.

Anne nearly spits out her drink when she laughs at my innuendo. "Carl! Did you just flirt? And in a like perverted way?"

"It's not perverted. Oral sex is a very common practice between loving partners, Anne. Making a silly joke about wanting to lick your pu-"

"Oh my god, Carl, please stop," Anne begs as she sinks down in her seat, cheeks flaming red.

"I don't know why you're being weird but whatever, I'll stop. You should finish your treats because I think it'll be our time soon."

I was right. In only a few minutes we get called to go to the special room where the cats are. We're both finished so we walk in empty handed and ready for petting.

The room is cozy, with sofas, cat trees, and the like set up all around. There are toys all over to play with and I can't decide if I should grab one or just try to get a cat to play with me without one. Turns out I don't need to try to lure a cat to me, one just comes right over as soon as we take a seat on a big, gray sofa near the door.

"Hi kitty!" I whisper nervously when a large, black cat jumps onto my lap.

I'm afraid to touch it at first because I don't want to hurt it. It looks so small and fragile compared to me. But I take a chance, lower my hand to its sleek fur, and give it a long stroke. The cat crawls closer to me and butts its head against my chest, twirling around on my lap, then seeking out my hand again. What a strange creature. I pet it again and it begins to purr. I can't help but to grin so wide I feel like my face is going to split open when I hear that sound. *It's happy. I made it happy.*

"Oh, look at you! It likes you!" Anne squeals. "That's the most adorable thing I've ever seen."

The cat sniffs my hand and makes a sound like *mrow* before licking it. I laugh at the strange feeling. Its tongue is all bristly and weird and catches on the texture of my skin. It pauses to make that same sound again, then increases the pace of its licking.

A second cat hops onto the sofa and butts its head into my other hand. Anne, who is without cat, raises an eyebrow at me.

"Don't be jealous, I'm sure there will be one coming for you soon," I tease.

The second cat starts licking my hand even more aggressively than the first one as a third cat begins to sniff my pant leg. A fourth jumps onto my lap, standing on its back legs to attempt to lick my neck. The one on the floor pushes its head under the hem of my pants and finds a sliver of bare leg where it begins to lick.

"Um, Anne, this is weird," I point out.

"Yeah, I don't think that's supposed to happen," she slowly replies as yet another cat joins the one on the floor in attempting to find leg skin.

Then, the one licking my neck takes a bite.

"Oh, fuck," I shout trying to push the cat away.

Unfortunately, the cats licking my hands grab tightly onto me with their paws and dig into my arms with their teeth. Anne screeches and attempts to help me, but they hiss and claw at her when she tries to get them off. Another cat jumps onto the back of my neck, digging its nails into my hair as it licks at me.

"Fuck fuck fuck," I repeat, trying to shake cats off of me.

"What the hell is going on?" comes a voice from the open door.

Jamie has stomped into the room with a confused and unhappy look on their face. I much preferred the happy one.

"Get these cats off of me please," I plead.

"Why are they doing that? What did you do?" they bark at me accusingly.

"Nothing, I swear!"

"Bullshit. They only act this way when they get their Fishy Treats from the vet." They carefully pull a cat from my arm and walk it to a crate where they lock it safely inside. "The kind with the irresistible flavor, so they'll go where he wants them to. This is what you get for messing with them."

"I swear I didn't," I insist as Jamie continues to yank cats away from me and put them into crates.

"He really didn't," Anne chimes in.

"Whatever." Jamie really doesn't seem like they'll want to be my friend after this.

Anne just stays quiet, biting her lip, and rubbing my back soothingly while the whole ordeal ends. We're told not to come back and shown the door.

When we get outside, Anne looks at me with a grim expression as we walk to the car. Once we get inside, however, she bursts out in hysterical laughter.

"What?" I ask, confused. "That was not at all funny."

"It was. Don't you get what happened?" She continues to laugh so hard tears stream down her face.

"No. All I know is some cats decided to attack me."

"No. They decided you were a snack. I'm going to call you my Fishy Treat from now on." She breaks out in another round of laughter, and it finally hits me.

I guess you can't hide a fish from a cat.

Chapter Twenty-Eight

Anne

I only need a quick shower after our trip and then I'm right back with Carl, alone in our apartment. Ori sent a text earlier that he'd be out for a bit so it's just us, and there's a feeling of anticipation as soon as I walk into the living room and see him standing in front of the window, bathed in afternoon sunlight. He turns to me, and I see the deep yellow sun reflected in his bright blue eyes, a perfect ocean day. His golden skin shimmers and shines. His pale hair is wild from our misadventure at the café. When he smiles at me, his perfect white teeth flashing, he looks so youthful and healthy. I love this man. I *love* this man.

"Hey Carl. Doing okay?" is all my pea brain can think to say.

"Better than ever now that you're back. What do you want to do now?" His hands are behind his back and though he looks straight at me in a confident pose there's something in the way his throat bobs and the pace of his breath increases that tells me he's as nervous as I am.

"Have a seat, Carl." I gesture toward the sofa.

"Uh, okay." He sits on the sofa with his hands at his sides, his posture perfectly straight.

Without hesitation I slink to the sofa as smoothly as I can, making sure to sway my hips along the way. I'm thankful I decided to wear a dress today. Normally I'm a practical pants type of woman, but I figured I'd stay dressed up for our date even after my shower. It's nice because when I get to Carl, I can hike my skirt up and straddle his thighs. The look on his face is absolutely priceless.

When I wrap my arms around his neck and settle myself on his lap, I see his eyes go wide, his mouth slightly open in awe. His cheeks have turned pink along with the tips of his ears.

"We have the place to ourselves, Carl. Let's take advantage of that," I purr.

"I think that sounds good," he shakily replies. "Can I touch you and stuff?"

"Absolutely. In fact, that's what I'm hoping for."

"Okay. Good."

There's a sudden change from shy boy to hungry man when his hands fly from his sides to my thighs, sliding up my dress to my hips and under the band of my underwear. He lifts his hips as he pulls me against him, forcing me to feel how hard he is for me. One hand slips back out and up behind my head pulling me toward him, joining us in a rough kiss that almost hurts my lips but more than anything feels so fucking good.

I roll my hips against him and moan into his mouth as he continues to kiss me deeply, passionately, gripping my hip, tugging at my hair. *Where has this Carl been?* He pulls my head away from his and looks into my eyes for a moment, breathing heavily, before speaking.

"Anne, I'm going to be forward with you. I would like to mate with you now. Would that be alright?"

He grips my hip tighter as if he can keep me with him no matter my answer. His peculiar wording might make me laugh in another situation but right now it only makes me ache between my thighs.

"Yes, fuck yes. Mate with me, Carl. Take me, please," I beg.

His eyes are wild as he swings his arm under my ass and stands in one smooth motion. I yelp in surprise at the sudden change of position but quickly calm as we head toward his bedroom.

Carl's bedroom is different from Ori's and mine. Where mine is filled on one side with all of Ori's business stuff and our gaming setup and anime collectibles on the other, Carl's is simple and the décor sparse. The only furniture is a bed, a side table with a lamp next to a soft chair he sits at to practice reading, and a dresser with a mirror and a photo of Ori and me on top of it. His possessions are all tucked away neatly and the only things on the walls are a couple pieces of my artwork. Everything is clean and dusted and he even makes his bed every day. *Such a good boy.*

With one hand Carl pulls aside the sheets and weighted blanket, then lays me on the bed. He stands over me, appraising, before placing a hand on either side of me and leaning down until his face is only inches from mine.

"I'm going to undress you now and then I'd like to taste you again. I'd appreciate it if you didn't try to stop me by acting all shy and stuff. Okay?"

I have to admit he's got me pegged. *Damn.* He really does pay too close attention to me, for real.

I nod. "Okay."

Carl nods back as he lifts my stretchy, sleeveless, yellow dress over my head. He tosses the dress on the floor and doesn't pause before sliding off my purple panties.

"Take off your bra, please," he requests as he stands to remove his own shirt.

I follow his directions and toss my bra to the side as I watch him remove his shirt, rippling muscles appearing in front of me. *Fuck,* he looks amazing from all that swimming and running. As he unbuckles his belt his eyes flick up and down my body, dark with lust.

"Spread your legs," he commands, forgetting the please this time, apparently, as he unzips his pants.

I almost get too shy to do as he says but remember his request from before and just swallow my awkwardness. I open my legs and hear the sharp intake of breath coming from him when his eyes meet my center. I take a few extra deep breaths of my own when he lowers his boxer briefs to reveal his thick, shimmering cock.

"You're very good at following directions, Anne. Normally you're so stubborn." He laughs softly as he climbs onto the bed.

"What can I say? I'm hypnotized by lust."

"By lust? Hmm." He fits his shoulders between my legs, reaching a hand down and swiping a finger along my pussy. When he pulls his hand back, I can see the glisten of my juices there. "Definitely lust."

His head cocks to the side as he looks me in the eye for a moment. "Anne, when I'm desiring you and grow hard for a long time I feel an ache, sometimes it can feel almost really painful if I don't relieve it. Do you have that too? Do you ever desire me that way, when you become wet like this? Is it the same as when I get hard?"

"This is a weird time for a question like that, but if you're asking if women get the equivalent of blue balls, then kind of? Yes, we can get so worked up that we can feel an ache where our clit is sort of and feel a sense of frustration. And yes, I've felt that way because of you before." My cheeks feel like they're going to burst into flames. "Why?"

"I'm just letting you know you can tell me any time, and I'll relieve your discomfort. Okay. That's all."

With that terrible segue, he drops down and lifts my ass at the same time. When his mouth meets my clit, his tongue swiping hard against it, I let out an embarrassingly loud moan of relief. My hands go to his hair, and I direct him to all the places that need his tongue, his lips, his fingers.

He perfectly remembers every spot I've told him I like being touched, every movement, every type of pressure. "Memory of a goldfish" is clearly the most bullshit expression on the planet. It doesn't surprise me how very little time it takes for me to peak, shouting his name in pleasure.

He raises his head from between my legs, face wet and proud, and places a short kiss to my thigh.

"Thank you for that. I'm ready now," he says, surprising me.

"You're thanking *me?* I...okay. I'm not going to try to understand that one. Just come here."

I hold out my arms and when he meets me chest-to-chest it doesn't surprise me that our racing heartbeats beat in time with one another. Everything about us together, in this moment, is perfect.

"Mate with me, little fish," I whisper as our brows press together. "I need you inside me."

His breath quickens, his light hair tickles me, his pupils blacken the blue of his eyes. I'll remember every detail of this. I can feel the oh-so-slightly scaled texture of his cock, velvety soft in that place, as he rubs it up and down my wet slit, preparing to enter me.

"You'll take my seed then, Anne? You really want me? You're sure? I promise I'll be careful. I'll-"

"Carl," I stop him before he can go into a panic, "just fuck me."

"Oh. Sure."

He starts slowly, pushing in gradually, a half an inch at a time. He keeps his eyes locked on mine the whole while and I can see a world of wonder in them. His eyelids flutter and his mouth pops open halfway through. When he's fully sheathed inside me, he groans, laying his head on my shoulder and letting out a long breath.

"Give me one second, Anne. Just one moment."

I can't help but giggle a little and pat him on the back. The only other person I've been with is Ori and he's not made of flesh, so it was much different. Oh, Ori. I hope he's alright. I hope-

"Oh, *fuck,* that feels good," I can't help but exclaim when Carl starts to slowly slide out of me. The texture on him, even though it's so light, somehow catches on my insides *just right.* "Holy fuck, Carl."

I wrap my legs around him when he is almost all the way out of me and shove him back inside. Needing more force from him. The muscles in Carl's strong arms shake then.

"Alright. That's how it will be then," he grits out between his teeth before pulling out of me and beginning to pound relentlessly back in and out again and again.

The drag of the texture on him through my insides at this speed and pressure is nearly unbearable. When he shifts so that my legs are pressed against my shoulders and he's grinding against my clit with every thrust I explode in an orgasm so hard

I think I see sparks, though I realize in my post-orgasm fog it's just the shimmer of his skin.

"Anne," he pants out, head dropping down to my neck, "I'm sorry, but I won't last much longer."

"That's okay, sweetie. I already came, and it feels so good. We can do it again as much as you want."

"I'm glad but...oh *fuck,* that feels so good. It's just that I don't know where your eggs are."

My brow furrows in confusion. "What?"

"Your eggs. Where did you put them so I can fertilize them? I don't think I can last much longer, you have to tell me. Oh my god. Anne, you feel amazing."

It hits me then that Ori did a terrible job of explaining human procreation to Carl and that even if he explained it to him that Carl doesn't know I'm on birth control. Holy fuck, this is a disaster. I'll just say...*shit,* what do I say? I'll make it easy, I guess.

"They're inside me, sweetie. That's how people do it."

"Oh. I like that then." Carl looks me in the eyes with a huge grin as his pace increases.

He leans down and kisses me hard, the kiss going wet, frantic, and so hard I think my lips will bruise until he shudders and slows, then stills. When he breaks the kiss and nuzzles his nose against mine that perfect feeling of connection returns for just a moment. I wipe the damp hair from his brow. He kisses down my neck as he lays next to me, arms around me, holding me tightly.

Then we hear the front door open, and the moment is lost.

Chapter Twenty-Nine

Ori

Home sweet home. I do hope my two had a lovely day. As I ride the elevator to our apartment, I wonder if they're home from the feline facility yet. The return visit on the bus took longer than I expected due to an incident involving a deviant in a trench coat harassing the driver and the police being called. Someday I will move my family out of this god forsaken city to somewhere more private. Somewhere with no *buses*.

When I enter the apartment, I can see the door to Carl's bedroom is open and the light is on. Both Carl and Anne are quite particular about turning off the light when they're not home so surely, they must be here. Seeing as it is the *only* light on, they must be in there together. *Success.*

Well, open doors in this house mean anyone can enter. I shove my hands in my pockets, trying and failing to reduce the width of my grin, and enter Carl's bedroom.

"Oh, hello there. And what have you two been up to? Here I thought you were out visiting a pussy café. Didn't know you'd decided for home brewed instead." The looks on their faces are priceless as I crack my admittedly crude joke. I'm not sorry, it was too easy.

"Ori, I'm going to kill you," Anne growls with a genuine look of frustration, or possibly even anger, on her face.

"It was only a joke. I'm fine with you fucking. Happy about it even. Congrats, by the way, Carl," I nod to the man who is blushing dark red.

Carl buries himself farther under the sheet they've both covered themselves with and Anne's eyebrows form into an angry V. *What did I do?*

"I need to talk to you, Ori," Anne growls as she tosses off her half of the sheet. She picks up a yellow dress from the floor and a pair of purple panties, a pair I quite like, and jerks them on. "In the other room."

Still confused, I nod, and we head toward our bedroom. Anne stomps the whole way. When we get there, she shuts the doors so hard it could nearly be classified as a slam.

"Ori, I thought you told me you explained human reproduction to Carl. You encouraged me to be with him and when I was, he was missing crucial information."

"I explained to him how sex works and babies are made. You put the penis in the vagina. To make a baby a sperm fertilizes an egg. I even explained oral sex, anal sex, where the clitoris is, all about my tentacles, what knotting is, what-"

"First off," I interrupt, "I don't know what knotting has to do with human reproduction. Second, and more important, you didn't tell him that the eggs aren't like fish eggs. That they aren't *outside*. And you know what? He didn't know anything about birth control. *Nothing*. Did you even explain safe sex to him? What if he'd have had sex with someone outside of this household and gotten a disease or gotten someone pregnant?"

A growl rises from my chest at the thought of Carl fucking anyone else. I bare my teeth as I snarl.

"Carl is *mine*. He would never take a lover outside of this house. *None* of us will. We will be together forever. Don't you understand, Anne? I will *never* let you go."

Anne's eyes widen and she backs away from me until the backs of her knees hit the bed. She stumbles backward and falls flat on her back. I lurch forward, planting my hands on either side of her face, my nose barely an inch from hers.

"Tell me you understand, Anne. My darling Anne." It's a plea and a command both.

"You're scaring me," she whispers. But I can see her nipples harden under that dress. I can see how she licks her lips and squeezes her thighs.

"Tell me you know you belong to me, Anne. I've told you already I'm yours forever. I'll do anything for you, *be* anything for you. I live for and because of you. I could not have existed without you and now I *will not* exist without you. So, tell me you know. Say it. Say you're mine."

"I'm yours," she says in a voice that sounds like a whine and sigh at once, something reluctantly admitted but done with relief, nonetheless. "Forever."

I drop my nose the last inch to hers and sigh as the knock on the door breaks the tension.

"And so is Carl," I whisper before standing up. "Just...a little differently."

"Sorry, we had a disagreement, but everything is fine," I say as cheerily as possible when I open the door and see Carl's distressed visage behind it. "Do come in."

Carl enters the room wearing his favorite gray sweatpants and white tank top, looking like a fitness god compared to my long body in my black suit. We really are opposites, and I'm pleased with my decision to make him so, though I wonder if he wouldn't have ended up with this build anyway. With his love of running and swimming he would be bound to end up somewhere in this direction at least.

And I know he would have loved Anne whether he received my feelings in my life force or not because his love is different from mine. I do see occasional glimpses of the possessive, rough, worshiping love I bring shine through, but his own love, the love at the front of it all, is all its own. Carl's love is quiet, curious, reverential. In the great series of luck I've had, he's one more four-leaf clover.

"Did I do something wrong?" he asks nervously, looking between Anne and me.

"Oh no. No, no. Here, sit with us," Anne says, patting the bed next to her. "I just was frustrated with Ori for not telling you about the eggs. And also, well, for not telling you that I can't get pregnant. At least not now anyway. Are you upset?"

Carl heaves out a great sigh of relief and wraps his arms around the both of us as best he can in a hug before pulling away. There's a smile on his face that I'm quite happy to see.

"No way. I don't think I was ready for babies, but I was going to go for it anyway for you guys. And I'm glad about the egg thing because, wow, that felt really nice doing that inside of you, Anne." His cheeks go pink again and I can't resist poking at him. I just can't.

"That? You mean coming inside her? Filling her cunt with your hot-"

"Ori, stop!" Anne groans.

Carl looks away and I see him trying to slyly place a pillow over his lap, where an erection has become *very* obvious. I think now is the perfect time to bring up my ultimate plan.

"Speaking of filling my love with cum," I start.

"What a segue!" Anne throws her hands up in the air. I clear my throat.

"*Ahem.* You see, I can't. I can only produce feathers. It is a great tragedy. You, Carl, can. Now, as I am the alpha, it is my position to knot our omega. I've explained to you about knotting, yes?" I nod to Carl who nods back.

"Yes. The alpha expands at the base of his penis to create a firm hold inside the omega's vagina or anus and then the omega is pumped full of semen." Carl answers proudly.

"I'm going to die," Anne says, laying on her back with a pillow over her face. "We're discussing Omegaverse as if it's high school sex ed."

"Correct, Anne. You and I only moments ago had a discussion on the importance of proper education so I'm simply making sure we're all on the same page. Now, back to the topic. I can easily create a knot with my abilities. That's beyond simple for me. Anne can take it, she's a champ."

"Thanks," she grumbles.

"You're welcome. What we're missing is the cum. That's where you come in, Carl."

"*Uuuuggggggghhhh,*" Anne lets out a long, frustrated sound from under her pathetic pillow. I choose to ignore her at this moment.

"Quite literally *cum* in. You see, as my beta, you'll need to provide me with any assistance I require. In this case, I require your cock. We'll enter Anne together. We'll need to be careful of timing, of course, but you're good about following my directions so I trust you'll be able to wait until I'm ready."

I pat Carl on the shoulder, and I receive an awkward, confused grin in return.

"*Uuuuugggggghhhhhhh.*" Anne again.

"We'll need a good amount of lubrication, and we'll need to take it slow. When I begin the knot, you'll be unable to move aside from perhaps the shallowest of thrusts, Carl, so you'll need to cum right before it's too late. The timing must be impeccable. Are we together on this?"

"Um. I'll do anything for you guys. And I liked sex a lot when Anne and I tried it. So, I guess whatever you guys want," Carl replies, scratching the back of his neck and looking back and forth between the two of us.

"You're weird, Ori," Anne grouses, still under that unimpressive pillow.

"So that's a yes from all of us. Excellent! What a wonderful pack I have! Now we only need our omega to go into heat."

"People don't have heats." Anne sits up while rolling her beautiful eyes at me.

"We'll just have to make you beg for us then."

"I'm not going to beg to be double penetrated," she snorts.

"We'll see."

Chapter Thirty

Carl

The awkwardness of that talk was a bit of a, uh, boner killer. So, Anne and I left the room pretty quickly to get something to eat. The filling tacos we made hit the spot pretty well after the wild day. I had my first date, pet a cat, got attacked by a group of cats, got banned from a café, lost my virginity, officially entered a relationship, and got chosen to be part of a three-way omegaverse sex thing. I'm not sure anyone has ever had quite a strange and busy day. Well, maybe Ori and Anne.

"Hand me your plate so I can put it in the dishwasher," Anne requests from behind me.

I've been done eating for a bit, but my mind has been wandering. As I raise my head to turn toward Anne with my plate in hand, I see Ori watching me closely over tented fingers across the table. *He's definitely plotting something.*

"Would you all like to watch a film?" He asks. *Here it goes.*

"Sure. What were you thinking?" Anne asks from near the sink.

"Oh, whatever you like darling. I would just enjoy some quality relaxation time with our little family. You've had such an exciting day."

"Sounds good. Hmm. There's this movie from like the eighties I think about a mermaid who gets legs and goes to New York to find a man she loves. Sometimes I think about Carl as a weird kind of merman. I mean, he's not, but with the whole scale-skin thing and being formerly a fish, you get the connection." She laughs. "It's a pretty funny and romantic movie so maybe we could watch that."

"I'd like that." I like that she thought of me when she thought of what movie to watch and it's kind of fun to be thought of as a merman as opposed to a weird fish-guy.

When we're all done in the kitchen, we head to our living room where we have a pretty nice setup. Our blue sofa is big and cozy. Ori doesn't really tolerate anything that isn't comfortable. We have all the streaming services and stuff because of Anne's anime addiction so we're able to find the movie she's searching for eventually. Anne sits to my left and Ori sits to my right and we start up the film.

It's kind of weird to have both Ori and Anne sitting next to me. Ori always sits next to Anne so I'm never in the middle. It feels weird at first like this, but then it feels nice. I feel safe and cared for. A weird fish-guy could get used to this.

The movie is really good, and a few times Ori and I even chime in on how we can relate to some things, like the fear of getting caught as a non-human, or how strange it is getting used to things humans are already so used to. When the bad guys catch the mermaid though it makes me feel kind of nervous. It hits a little too close to home. I'm always afraid that someday someone will discover Ori or I and take us away and hurt us.

"You seem tense, Carl," Ori observes.

"A little," I reply quietly, trying not to disturb Anne, who is super engrossed in the movie.

"Let me rub your shoulders then," he offers.

"Sure, that sounds nice." It does sound great. With all the swimming and stress and excitement, my muscles are pretty tight.

I angle my body to give Ori better access, and he begins to rub, doing it just how I like: slow and hard.

"Does that feel alright, Carl?" Ori asks quietly.

"Definitely." I sigh, letting some of the stress go.

"Here, let me get some lotion and you can take off your shirt. It will be even better, hmm?" Ori purrs next to my ear.

Hmm. Now he seems suspicious. But...*massage.* I can't resist.

"Okay," I reply as I lift off my shirt and tuck it next to me on the sofa.

A few seconds later, I feel hands slathering my skin with lotion before they return to rubbing away my stress. Where he got the lotion in the living room, I have no idea, but I don't take the time to wonder. Instead, I close my eyes and let out a grateful moan as I feel a knot in my muscles come loose.

A sharp inhale of breath from in front of me makes me open my eyes. Anne is watching us, eyes focused where Ori's fingers are sliding over my skin. When she briefly looks up at my face and notices me watching her, she snaps back toward the screen without a word.

"Let me get a little on your lower back. You look a bit tight there as well," Ori says.

"Yeah, sounds good," I whisper back, eyes on Anne to see if she reacts.

When Ori begins to work a sore spot near my hip, I can't help but release a groan. Anne's eyes flit to the side to watch again, but she looks away once more as if guilty of something.

When I let out a strained "Fuck," at Ori's manipulation near my spine her eyes linger longer. Her little pink tongue darts out to lick her lips and I can't help but start to grow hard in my sweatpants. *Damn, I hope Ori doesn't get weirded out by that.*

Ori is very much *not* weirded out by that.

"Oh, how tense you are. Perhaps we can alleviate this discomfort as well?" Slowly he slides a hand around my hip, across my pelvis, and under the waistband of my pants.

I hiss and jerk my hips in surprise as his fingertips make contact with my stiff cock. This, of course, gets the attention of Anne, whose jaw drops all the way when she sees what's going on. She freezes in place, silent, and stays that way as Ori continues.

"So incredibly tense that even the softest touch makes you jump. *Tsk.* How poorly we've taken care of you these past months." Ori drags a lotioned palm down the length of my cock and then cups my balls, squeezing them gently. "You need a release, beta."

When I try to reply all that comes out is heavy breathing. *This is so weird.* When Ori wraps his hand around my shaft and starts to stroke me, I can't help but to thrust my pelvis along with him. The texture of his hand is so strange and the way it runs against the semi-scaled texture of mine, slippery with whatever he's using as lotion, is maddening.

"Please," Anne breaks her silence.

"What's that, Anne?" Ori asks before giving my cock this incredible twisting-squeeze-twirl motion that has me groaning loudly. He snaps his teeth against my earlobe. "Ssh, dear, Anne has something to say to us."

"Please. I give in. The fucking. I'll beg. This is just too much." Her voice is breathy and quick, as if she can't get the words out fast enough.

"Say 'Please fuck me at the same time. I want both of your cocks inside my cunt.'" Ori's words and his stroking are almost too much for me, but I have a feeling I'm not supposed to cum now. *Damn it.*

"Please fuck me with both your cocks in my pussy at once or whatever you said. Oh my god, just hurry," Anne whines.

Ori *cackles* and releases me from his grip. I let out a deep sigh and slump forward. *Here we go.* This day just keeps getting weirder.

Chapter Thirty-One

Ori

I knew it would work. There are few anime fans who like the things Anne does who can resist the allure of two exceptionally handsome men at once. I've seen the hentai she watches. I've read the manga and the fan fiction she reads. If she thinks I don't know what will please her, then she's forgotten the most important thing about me: that I will do *anything* to make her happy.

And now I'll do whatever it takes to make Carl happy as well. If someone had asked only half a year ago if I'd ever care for anyone even half as much as Anne, I'd have torn the life from them for even suggesting such a thing. How quickly things can change.

Of course, Anne will always be my first priority. She is part of me. The first flickers of my life were given to me by her. I would not exist without her, and I exist for her. But now it's only...I have someone else to live for as well. Someone else I look forward to seeing every day. Someone I...well, *love*, in the way that I'm able to. How strange life is.

I carry Anne to our bedroom bridal style and lay her on our bed. She's let her hair grow out a little in the last few months. Not much, of course; she still hates attention and lovely hair like hers would surely draw looks were it to grow long. Right now, it spreads around her in a golden-brown halo on the bedspread, framing her face, so full of lust.

The corner of my lip lifts in a taunt. "My sweet Anne, so full of desire, with such an empty cunt. It will only be but a moment, my love. Do not despair."

Anne spreads her legs and slips a hand into her panties, beginning to fondle herself. "Hurry, Ori. I need you."

I panic momentarily. When my Anne says she needs me I react instinctually. My head swivels to the doorway where thankfully I find Carl waiting, leaning against the doorframe, arms crossed over his well-built chest.

The bulge in Carl's pants is exceptional and impossible to ignore, but I tear my eyes away. His pants fall low on his hips, showcasing his Adonis belt, the V-shaped line running from his hip bones to under said pants. His abdominal muscles are well-defined, his shoulders and arms strong. The light hits on the angles of his face, making the scales on the high parts of his cheekbones shimmer. Despite the sharp jawline and his deeply masculine appearance, he still looks youthful, curious, sweet. Perfect for Anne. And I wonder if somehow, I didn't subconsciously make him a little bit for me as well. Or perhaps that developed over time. Maybe it's nothing and I'm just overthinking things at the moment.

I could tear my hair out thinking of all of this...*emotional* business, but I have important things to focus on. Things such as Anne and the orgasms we're all about to have. Good. That will get my mind off of things.

"Come on now, Carl. You heard the woman. She needs us."
I snap.

"I don't know," he drawls, inspecting his nails. "She said she needs you. She didn't say anything about me."

Damn it.

Anne shoots up and turns to face Carl. "I need you both. Now. Please." she whines.

Carl breaks out in that boyish grin of his and leaps onto the bed, tackling Anne. They both break out into raucous laughter. *Perfect.*

"What a silly omega and beta I have," I purr as I begin to remove my clothes. "If you want to play together, then why don't you race to see who can undress the fastest."

Anne wins by a mile.

"Totally not fair. Pants are harder to take off than dresses," Carl complains as he lays on the bed, nude, one arm behind his head, one leg up.

"You snooze, you lose." Anne snarks from next to him. She's laying on her side, facing me, head propped on her hand.

Looking at the two of them laying there in their fully naked glory I could nearly feather myself by the time I'm undressed. Damn all these layers of clothes I wear.

Finally, I'm down to nothing but my fabric skin. I slink onto the bed to meet my mates, wrapping an arm around the both of them, pressing my body against Anne's.

"Are you in heat, my omega? Do you need my knot to fill you?"

"Yes. Yes, alpha," she replies from right next to my ear. I growl. *Finally,* she's playing along.

"First, I need you to cum. Get on Carl's face," I bark out an order.

Carl shakes his head in confusion at the same time Anne pulls away.

"I can't do that! I'll suffocate him!" Anne squeals.

"I'll hold you up. I'd never let Carl die. Now, Carl? You're ready?"

"Absolutely," he grins. I know him too well.

Anne bites a lip nervously but straddles his face, nonetheless. I hold her hips gently, ready for if she needs me, and smile as she lowers herself onto him.

She doesn't stay shy for long and I don't have to hold her hips. Carl grabs onto her ass like it's the only thing keeping him from drowning in a sea of pussy and presses her harder against him rather than keeping her farther away. Anne certainly doesn't try to be gentle with him. The way she grinds on him reminds me of when she flattened my face and I have to let out a quiet laugh as I stroke myself alongside them.

Then I sneakily laugh again as I decide to stroke Carl as well. He nearly bucks the two of them off the bed in surprise, but to his credit, doesn't stop feeding on her cunt like he does it for a living. In fact, I think the extra motion finally sets her off and she cums against him, squeezing her thighs around his head. Finally when she's panting and done, she rolls off of him. He lets out a gasp for air and I let go of his cock.

"There we are. We're all ready then." I reach over to the side table and grab the bottle of lubricant. "Time to play."

Chapter Thirty-Two

Anne

Easy enough for these two to be relaxed about this, but they aren't the ones about to be double stuffed. Well, as nervous as I am, *fuck* I want it bad.

I turn back to Carl and place my hand on his cheek, bringing his face to mine for a deep kiss as I swing my leg over him. I've thought about the logistics of this...a lot...and I think this position will be the best. So, when Carl holds my ass and drags my soaking wet slit along his cock, I reach down and line it up with my cunt. Sinking down onto his textured skin feels nice but raising up on it feels just as weird and amazing as it did earlier. I'm seriously the luckiest woman on the planet, hands down.

"Lean forward a bit more, darling," a raspy request comes from Ori. I obey his command, and a hiss comes from behind me. "Look at you two. My naughty darlings joined together. Perfect."

The sound of a cap popping open, followed by a good amount of liquid being sloshed around, joins the sound of Carl and I making love. Soon, some of that liquid is rubbed onto and into me by Ori's soft hands. I can feel him rub some onto Carl and hear him slather it onto himself.

Ori takes hold of my hips as he drops a leg over both of Carl's. "Be still for a moment. Breathe and keep your muscles relaxed. I'll start small."

Ori keeps his promise and doesn't enter me too large, though his ego prevents him from going too small. The stretch of him entering me with Carl already inside burns at first but Ori is slow, checking in to make sure I'm okay with every little bit. I keep my eyes focused on Carl, who has his hands on my hair, stroking it and alternating kisses with sweet words.

"You're doing so good, Anne. That feels crazy, right?" Carl smiles and nudges his nose against mine. "You're such a crazy girl. I love you so much."

A tear forms at the corner of my eye. *How dare he tell me he loves me when I'm being double penetrated.* But yet it's still somehow perfect.

"I love you too," I force out as Ori sinks another inch inside me.

Carl's smile is so wide I don't know how I'll ever manage to kiss all of it, but I do. The kiss is wonderful. The fresh, clean taste of his tongue, the texture of his face that's become so familiar to me against my hand, the brush of soft hair against my cheek, it's all perfect. Even the moans we let into each other's mouths when Ori finally fits fully inside me and begins to rock in and out are perfect.

I break the kiss and toss my head back to let out a long groan of pleasure. Now that the initial stretch is over everything feels so, so good. I feel full like I've never felt before and I know the feeling is only going to increase when Ori really starts his little game.

Carl starts to find his groove opposite Ori and I'm too overwhelmed to say anything or do anything other than just be fucked. I'm completely at their mercy and for once I don't mind losing control a little.

Ori pulls me against his chest and both men adjust their positions to accommodate. Dark hair brushes my cheek as he nips my ear. "Look at my Anne, fucked by two men at once. Pathetically mewling and desperate on our cocks. Do you want to be knotted, my desperate little omega? Do you want to be stuffed with cum until it leaks down your thighs, drenches the sheets? Answer yes and maybe I'll even let you cum too."

A sob is wrenched from my chest. I don't know if I can speak right now, I'm so overwhelmed. But I'll try. A high-pitched noise comes out, that's it. I try again.

"Yes," I breathe out. "Knot me. Fill me."

Another sob is all I can manage after that, but it seems good enough for Ori. I feel him begin to grow inside me, larger all around but even larger still at the base.

"Faster Carl. It's time," he snaps as he bends me.

Carl sits up more so that we're all close to one another in every way. He begins thrusting up into me rapidly, leaning in to kiss me wet and messy. Ori continues to slowly grow until both Carl and I pull away from one another, gritting our teeth.

"I can't...I can't last any longer," Carl looks over my shoulder at Ori. Whatever look Ori gives Carl has him nodding and going as fast as he can against Ori's increasing size.

He keeps his eyes on Ori and, to my surprise, when he comes, he reaches a strong hand out and pulls Ori's face to his, trapping him in a brutal kiss. *Well, hello.*

Chapter Thirty-Three

Carl

Ori's tongue feels strange. Not like Anne's. But I like it. All of Ori feels different. I like that we're all different. We're all special. It makes things twice as fun.

And *holy shit, I'm kissing Ori. What am I doing?*

As the last drops of cum are spurting out of me, the base of his cock swells so thick I can't move anymore. It kind of makes me want to panic, because who wouldn't panic when their cock was trapped, but I trust him. He gave me life, after all.

I break the kiss and look into his eyes, desperate for an answer to my unspoken question: *"Was that okay?"*

Ori's eyebrows are raised in surprise and his wet mouth is open in shock. My hand is still on the back of his head, and I can't help but to give his scalp a soothing scratch. His bright eyes flutter closed, and his face relaxes. He tips his head to mine until our foreheads touch, giving me my answer: *"Yes, it was."*

"Fuck!" Anne shouts from between us and my attention snaps back to her.

"Are you okay, pretty girl?" I ask.

"I'm so stretched out. I don't know if I can take it any longer." She grips my biceps and bites down on my shoulder when Ori shifts his hips. Her blunt teeth and gentle bite don't hurt but I worry she's not having a good time, and I want to stop if she's not.

"Anne, we've practiced with my tentacles. You've got this." Ori swipes her hair across her shoulder and kisses her cheek. "The fun is really just beginning."

"Oh, wasn't that the end?" I ask with a cock of my head.

"Oh no. We have to *fill her* with cum. Once isn't enough." Ori pats me on the cheek then returns to holding Anne steady. "And don't worry about the next round. I've got you."

"What does that mean?" I'm very genuinely confused now as Anne breathes a laugh against my chest.

"We love surprise tentacles in this house," she giggles. "Say no if you're opposed though."

"I...don't think I am?" I guess I'll say no if I figure out what the hell they're talking about and don't like it.

"Excellent." Ori scrapes his teeth over Anne's shoulder causing her to moan against my chest.

Just then I feel something tickle against me as Anne moans more and more. With us sandwiched together like this I can't see what's going on down there but whatever it is Anne sure seems to like it.

"What's going on?" I brush her hair behind her ear and moan softly myself as she ripples inside around Ori and me.

"Tentacles." Ori laughs darkly as he places a finger under my chin, lifting my face to his. "Surprise."

It's then that I feel them begin to squirm around me. They slither from Ori, squeezing along my shaft while it's still trapped inside Anne, wrapping around my sac, and sliding along the passage that leads to my rear entrance. My cheeks turn hot, and I tense up when I realize what he's planning on doing.

"It's thin and lubricated and if you relax it won't hurt you. Quite the opposite. Just ask Anne." Ori nips her earlobe, and she groans, but in delight.

"Oh, fuck yes. Kiss me, Carl." Anne begs and I can't resist her, I can't resist anything Anne asks of me.

Anne presses her mouth hard against me, licking and sucking on my lips desperately. The wet tentacles around my balls start massaging in the strangest ways, rippling, squeezing, pulsing. It shouldn't feel as good as it does but combined with the way Anne is clenching inside and the little bit I can thrust it's fucking glorious. And then when I relax, the tentacle breaches my asshole, swells just slightly, and hits a pleasurable spot I never knew existed, I'm panting right along with Anne.

The tentacles that are working on Anne begin to move faster and soon she's crying out and shaking in an orgasm. *Fuck, she's so beautiful.* She's sweating and her hair is stuck to her face, but she looks like she's in ecstasy.

All the slippery tentacles on and in me work faster, their strange motions confusing and exciting me and I don't even care what they're doing, I just know it feels fucking fantastic. My hips thrust faster in the shallow movements I'm able to make and everything is so warm, so wet. Anne's head is on my shoulder, her lips softly caressing my neck. Ori's eyes are locked on mine as I come again.

When I'm done and feel like I'll scream if I'm touched anymore, Ori suddenly retracts all the tentacles, except for the one behind me, which he removes more slowly.

"Anne, Carl, lie back. I need to see this." His voice is rough and desperate, and I remember that tone from when I was in the tank. *He's close.*

Anne and I lie back as Ori begins to shrink inside her, watching the point where we're all joined with complete focus. When he's back to a normal human size, and Anne is bent over, he slides out of her. I can feel both our combined liquids rush out of her and over my legs. Ori's eyes open wide, and his grin goes manic as he takes in the sight.

"Yes, that's it. That's what I wanted to see. You did so well, both of you."

Anne and I both just lie there and pant as Ori spouts feathers onto the cum, making it a three-person mess.

"I need a bath," Anne mumbles from beside my ear.

I can't help but laugh as I agree that I need the same.

"I'll start the water," Ori offers as he hops up and off to the bathroom.

"Come on, Anne. I've got you," I say once I'm sure my legs will be steady.

I pick her up and carry her to the bathroom where Ori has started the water just like he said he would. When I sit in it with her in front of me, she sighs.

"Exactly what I needed. I think I'm going to be sore for a week. At least." She snuggles back against me and I wrap my arms tightly around her.

Ori sits on a stool next to the tub with a pile of clean towels on his lap. Somehow in the last minute he got himself cleaned up and I have no idea how.

"Ori, how did you just get clean so fast?"

"It's private."

"What? Why?"

"Everyone needs a secret, even if it's a little one."

"Boo," Anne says sleepily with a thumbs down.

I laugh. "Agreed. Boo."

"Boo or not, I have your towels and I'm going to sit here and relax until you're done. I have to make sure the people I love don't fall asleep in the bathtub and drown."

"The people you love, huh?" I try to ask lightly but my throat feels like it's closing up. This feels like a big deal, and I need to hear it again.

"Yes. I love you both." He turns away and inspects his nails, putting an arrogant look on his face. "So, you're quite lucky of course. Having someone so loyal, dedicated, handsome, tentacled, no wonder you love me so much."

His eyes shoot to the side and there is a hint of vulnerability there.

"It's no wonder we love you indeed," I assure him.

"The tentacles really seal the deal," Anne mumbles.

We all laugh. The rest of the night is spent in relaxation until finally I'm able to get some sleep. What a weird day that was.

The next morning at breakfast Ori sits at the end of the table watching the two of us eat our cereal.

"So," he says, crossing his arms primly in front of him. "Now that we did omegaverse and that's over with-"

"That's over with already?" Anne asks with a raised eyebrow.

"Yes, of course. As I was saying, now that that's over with, what shall we try next? Anne, any ideas? Carl?" He looks back and forth between Anne and I as the two of us just look confused. "Come on now, there are masses of things to play. Some are more difficult. 'Mpreg' or 'why choose?' wouldn't be possible for our dynamic, for example."

"Ori. No more fan fiction." Anne drops her head to the table, making a loud thump.

"We'll see. We could always find ways to set up a pretend alternate universe. I could temporarily gender swap, I think anyway. Alternate setting trope. Unexpected baby. Damsel in distress. Partner-"

"Ori. Let's just be normal for a little bit, okay? Carl hasn't even had a single day of being in a normal relationship. We should just have no surprises, no games, no fanfic."

"How long do I have to be normal?"

"What?" Anne asks incredulously. "You want a specific date?"

"Yes. When can I surprise you?"

"Well, I guess Christmas is the closest date where surprises are expected." Anne chuckles. "You better not 'unexpected pregnancy' me though. Hard limit."

"Oh, I have something else in mind."

Chapter Thirty-Four

Anne

A few months after that heaping helping of stuffing we've settled into our routine. We work, we relax, we even leave the house sometimes. We just tend to avoid the mall and cat cafes. Everything is wonderful.

Today is Christmas and we're settled in front of our little tree opening gifts. I'm not great at picking out gifts, and we told each other we wouldn't get anything expensive, so I didn't get them anything super big. I just hope they like what I got them anyway.

Ori tears into the perfectly wrapped gift I know is from me with total glee in his eyes. He pulls out a thick book and a sheet of paper.

"Oh, Anne, I love it! I'm going to learn all about the over-lords. We'll have power soon, you'll see."

I scrunch my brow. Overlords? *What's he talking about?* I know he's been talking about wanting to learn about politics, but not knowing where to begin, so I got him signed up for a community education introduction to American politics class. I also got him a book on the history of America as told from a variety of ethnic and immigration viewpoints. I figure once he gets all that down, he can move onto world politics. This overlord stuff is weird though. Then again, it's Ori. Who knows with him? I just smile and look at Carl, who is opening his package from me.

"Whoa, look at all these!" he exclaims when he sees what's in the package I got him.

He has been super dedicated to learning to read, and he's great at it now. Reading is basically his favorite hobby. I tried to get him to read the manga I like, and Ori tried to get him to read fanfic, but he wasn't interested. So, I thought I'd try giving him something I'm pretty sure he'll be into. And, if not, at least it's silly enough for him to smile.

"Okay, what's this one?" He picks up the first book and reads the blurb on the back. "This is about a...sentient *door*? And it's a romance?"

"What can I say, I got you some books that reminded me of you two. I think you'll like them." I bite my lip to keep myself from laughing.

He picks up the next one. "This is a swamp creature romance? And this next one is a living gingerbread man? A scary house that comes alive! Anne!"

Carl stares at me with the books in his hands. *Uh-oh.* Maybe I made a mistake, and he hates them.

"I love them!" He grins and looks at all the covers again, running his hands over them, rereading the blurbs.

"Let me know what you think of them."

"My turn, my turn," Ori interrupts. "I can't wait. I've waited months for this surprise."

I sigh and cross my arms. *Here we go.* As long as it's not a surprise pregnancy we should be fine. Ori hands us each an envelope and steps back, bouncing on his toes in excitement.

"Okay. Here we go." I look at Carl as we both open our envelopes.

At the same time, we each pull out...a map. *Huh?* I hold the map in front of me looking for any sign of what it might mean or where the map even leads but can't figure it out.

"So, what is this?" Carl asks.

"Glad you asked," Ori says as he steeples his hands under his chin. "For the past half a year or so I've been researching the most important topic in the world. I'm sorry that I've had to hide what I've been doing but if my plan had failed I didn't want to disappoint you. Thankfully, I have not failed.

"Not only did I accidentally discover a way to permanently renew myself when we offed those security guards, I also found out I have a brother, and I discovered the natural habitat of the phoenix, which is what is marked on your map.

Most importantly, I discovered what is almost surely the solution to the problem we have."

"We have a problem?" I ask.

"Yes, a very big one."

"And what's that?"

"You and Carl will die, and I will not."

"Well, that's morbid," I grumble.

"And you can't really fix that," Carl chimes in.

"No, Carl. Humans can't fix that. *I* can."

Carl and I give each other another confused look as Ori gets down on one knee in front of us, pulling a small box from his front pocket.

"Anne. Carl. We have an adventure to go on."

With a nervous clearing of his throat, he opens the box to reveal a tiny flame.

"That is, if you want to live forever."

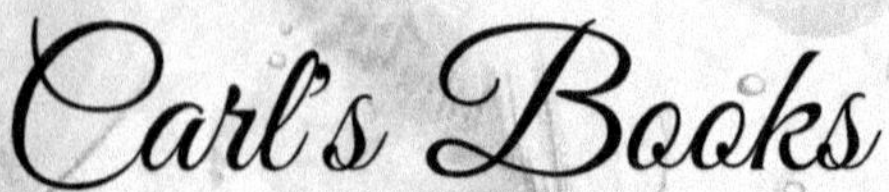

Carl's Books

One more thing! In the story Carl receives a gift of books from Anne. I based those descriptions on real books you might enjoy if you liked this one. Here they are:

Unhinged by Vera Valentine (the door book)

Seduced By the Swamp Creature by Ivanna Schloppykoch (the swamp creature book)

Cookies and Cream by Latrexa Nova (the gingerbread man book)

They Came from the Walls by S.R. Griffith (the house book)

Marlon

by Sylvia Morrow

Content Warnings

This story contains one brief occurrence of the *unsuccessful* assault of a sleeping child. The mention occurs in chapter **Two-***Marlon*.

At the end of the content warnings, I will post a spoiler warning and then do a (very) brief summary of what happens in chapter two so that you can skip that if you want to.

The remaining content warnings:

Murder, stabbing, poverty conditions, needing to seek false identities, orphanage, kidnapping a child from abusers, non-human creature that looks and acts human, mention of car accident death, mention of parent death, multiple sexual activities, home school, shoulder wound, tentacle, light religious mentions, mentions of bugs and rodents.

Spoiler for **Two-***Marlon*:

Charlie attacks a sketchy orphanage employee to protect Imani and ends up stabbing the man in the shoulder. Marlon finishes the man off with the death-suck. All three go to an off-grid cabin Charlie knows of to hide out. Marlon starts to feel weird from all the extra power in his blanket body.

Spoiler over.

Chapter One

Charlie

"Come on, baby. Hurry up. We can't slow down here."

I tug Imani's little hand harder than I intend to. Urgency turns my normally soft touch rough. It's not an ideal start to a life together.

But neither was the murder.

"I'm scared, Mr. Charlie. It's dark. We're not supposed to go outside when it's dark," Imani says in her scratchy little voice.

"This is a special exception, little one. You get to go to a home of your own. With me. And I decided to take you at night, so the other kids don't get jealous. Makes sense, right?" Hopefully she buys the excuse, at least for now. I had to get her away from the orphanage as fast as possible. There was no time for an explanation when I was getting her out the door. How could I explain that her teacher is now a killer, a kidnapper, and on the run. *Please forgive me.*

"I'm gonna live with you?" There's a hint of suspicion and a lot of hope in her voice. "Really?"

"Really. No more Saint Simeon's House. No more of those people ever again." My jaw clenches at the last words. *Those people.* The people who hurt her. The ones we're running from.

"I didn't like those guys," Imani says, the quiet darkness in her voice bringing tears to the corners of my eyes. *If only I had known sooner.*

"Neither did I. Here's my car. Let's get in. You have to sit in the backseat. I'm sorry I don't have a booster seat for you yet. This happened very quickly. I'll get one though. For now, just buckle up really well. Let's get you out of the rain." I help her into the car, though she's hesitant at first. Her parents died in an accident from what I've heard, though it happened when she was too small to remember. She'd been in that hellhole ever since. "It's okay. I'm a wonderful driver."

"Okay, Mr. Charlie." She's such a resilient little girl, letting me lift her into the car even with her fear. I buckle her in and force a smile as I pat her on the head. Her braids are matted, and most have lost their barrettes long ago. I'm going to fix her hair as soon as I can. "Can I have Marlon?"

"Of course, sweetie." I hand her the orange comforter which she named after a cartoon fish. She wouldn't leave the building without it. It's her prized possession. Before closing the door, I tuck it around her lap. Quickly, I make my way through the light rain to the other side.

"Alright, here we go." When I start the car, I drive away from the life I've lived for thirty years.

After what happened I can't take us to my home. Hell, I don't even know what happened really. It's all a blur. All I know is someone is dead, I'm decently sure I did it, and since I was the only one there, I'm in deep shit. *Pardon the language.*

The sin that comes with murder is too heavy a weight on my soul to save myself, but I still must save the child.

I drive aimlessly until a thought strikes me. *The cabin. That's it.* My ex is a survivalist and has a cabin on his land that isn't technically supposed to exist. He isn't there most of the year. I'll drain my bank account of as much money as I can and head there. Hopefully this isn't the time of year he decides to vacation.

So that's what I'll do. Money. Cabin. We'll stay there and hope no one finds us. *We'll find a way out of this.* I'd do anything for Imani.

Chapter Two

Marlon

*O*ops. I didn't expect that to happen, but that man was going to hurt Charlie and Imani. What the heck else was I supposed to do? I would *never* let anyone hurt Imani.

But I feel weird now, all mixed up. When I drain living things, I sometimes get new emotions, or small abilities. I don't know how it works. When I touch things, I can just sort of suck the life from them, and it gives me a little boost. But this doesn't really feel like that. Maybe there was something in that man that's making me sick, darn it. He was a sick man, after all.

Imani was in her bed, sleeping quietly, and this awful man, who was meant to watch over her at night, took me off of her. She shivered but didn't wake up. I got real mad that he was making her cold, but there wasn't anything I could do. And then he got this look on his face like he wanted to *really* hurt her. I couldn't do anything to stop him since I couldn't exactly walk over there and grab him. Charlie could though.

He wasn't even supposed to be there. Charlie works in the afternoons teaching the kids. Sometimes he comes in at nights when there's an emergency since he's got some kind of training. I don't understand it, I only know what I overhear when I'm with Imani. But tonight, I think he was just coming to get something he forgot. Darn lucky he was there too.

Charlie came in, saw what was happening, and grabbed that man. They started fighting. Really fighting! Like on the television Imani isn't supposed to watch, but the big kids put on sometimes anyway. There was kicking and punching and everything.

The bad man even took out a knife and was going to hurt Charlie with it. They both fell on the floor where the man had tossed me, right on top of me, and they were rolling around. Charlie and the man both had their hands on the knife. I got so darn mad I took all the energy I had from the dang bugs and mice in this nasty place and just grabbed hold of that man with my corners.

Charlie was too busy struggling to really notice I had hold of the creep. He took the knife easily when the man got surprised by me and he stabbed into the man's shoulder. The man was bleeding all over and shouting, trying to get up, but I held him down. I was still so darn mad I started sucking in the man's life force just like a cockroach.

He started shriveling up. Charlie jumped up all scared. I was pretty scared too, but I didn't stop. That man would hurt my friends if he got back up and I had to make sure he didn't. There was fear, panic, in Charlie's eyes, and he kept shaking the bad man, but I still didn't stop.

Pretty soon the man stopped moving. Charlie paced back and forth a bit before running his hands over his closely cropped hair. Soon he was waking up Imani and trying to get her to leave, but she wouldn't leave without me. Blood was all over me, but I shook off the stains and made myself clean. He looked surprised, but Charlie took me from under the shriveled up man anyway, and they both ran out of the building. Then we were in the car. Then eventually we got to the cabin.

And now I feel weird. I feel...*more*. I feel like I can't stop something changing in me and there's just no stopping it.

Chapter Three

Charlie

"I don't wanna go to bed," Imani says with a yawn. "I ain't even tired."

"You should say 'I'm *not* even tired' because school will start in less than a year and they'll want you to speak a certain way. Schools are strict like that." I brush her golden-brown cheek with my thumb as her eyes flutter closed.

She's laying in the only bed here, where we were sitting and talking about her favorite topic, tropical fish, but I don't want to move her. If I try to transfer her to the sofa where she's meant to sleep, she'll just wake up. I'll sleep on the sofa tonight.

"I don't want school. Wanna be with you," she whispers before finally settling into a light snore. I sit for a moment more to make sure she's fully asleep before heading to the living room.

The cabin is old, dusty, filled with cobwebs and mildew. But it's safe. At least for now. I can relax for a moment on the green plaid sofa. Relax as much as I can after I've watched a man shrivel nearly to dust in front of my eyes. *What have I done?* I drop my head into my hands and breathe deeply. There is nothing I can do now except sit. Sleep. Wait for a new day. With a sigh, I raise my head and flop backward on the sofa.

Some documentary on a red-haired former prince from a country I don't even live in is playing on the television. I start to switch it off but stop. May as well finish watching it. I need something to help me fall asleep.

I wrap Marlon, Imani's down comforter, around my shoulders. It's rare she would leave it anywhere. I contemplate bringing it into the room for her, but my comfort overpowers my kindness when I start to get warm.

As I continue to watch, I grow sleepier and sleepier. The blanket grows warmer and snugger around me. Snugger and snugger. Tight like a hug. A– What?

Groggily my eyes open and I awake fully to find myself cocooned in Marlon. *What the hell?* I struggle to move my arms, but they're held tight.

"Let go!" I shout but it's muffled by the fabric and feathers. "Let me out."

Suddenly, it does let me go. The blanket falls to the floor between the television and me. And it begins to...*pulse. Throb. Stretch.*

It's alive.

Chapter Four

Marlon

I feel like...I need to move. Something in me is changing and I don't think I can stop it anymore. When I'm feeling almost like I'm on the edge of a cliff, Charlie wraps me around him.

Charlie. He's so sweet. Lately I've started thinking about Charlie differently. I've noticed things about him I didn't used to. How nice his arms look when they flex. How full his lips are. How his skin is so beautifully dark that in some lights it almost looks blue. He's kind to all children. His voice is deep. He always tucks me in and never lets me fall on the floor. When I think about him, I feel good. *Really* good. I like Charlie.

When he falls asleep, I take my opportunity to hug him. I like to hug my people sometimes when they sleep, when they won't notice I act different from the other blankets, not that other blankets do any kind of acting. He feels *so darn good* that I can't help but squeeze him a little harder. But this time

I can't stop. Even when he wakes up, I can't stop. Whatever is pushing me toward that cliff is starting to shove me off.

And then I fall.

I let go of Charlie, just barely, and fall to the floor, just in time to begin my change. Something happens to me, and I don't know what it is but it's big. In fact, as my fabric stretches, and feelings like lightning and acid run through me, I realize I'm not gonna be a blanket anymore.

I get this feeling like...like I have a choice to make. *What do I wanna be now?* And I think I have to make it fast. There's just too much power in me from draining that man.

A thought floats through the chaos in my mind. I wonder how much power would have been in him if Charlie hadn't stabbed him first? I shudder at the thought even as I pulse and stretch.

What do I wanna be? I wanna be with Charlie and Imani. But how?

I think I have to be a person, so I have to build a body. Oh boy. I'm glad I watched all those educational programs with Imani about anatomy.

Focusing hard, I begin to form arms and legs. *It's happening. I can feel them.* A torso. A head. There's still so much power.

Charlie is staring at me with his jaw dropped. He's not moving but he sure does look terrified. I think about how I must look. A person shaped blanket. That's not great. Must be real scary to look at.

On the television the red-haired man tells a story. Before I can stop myself, I begin to change, imitating the man on the screen. My arms and legs thin out, become more flesh-like. A suit and tie grow from my new body like leaves from a tree. I can feel my face changing, developing human-like features. *Oh gosh.*

When I feel everything stop moving around, I look Charlie right in the eyes. They're wide open, the deep, brown color nearly black with how big his pupils have grown.

"Well. I guess I'm not a blanket anymore. Can I still stay here?" I ask in a voice that sounds like a toy accordion filled with applesauce.

Charlie makes a garbled noise, then, eyes rolling backward, passes out.

Chapter Five

Charlie

What a wild dream. I must have–

"You're awake," a strained, scratchy voice says from a chair next to the sofa where I'm now laying. Someone must have laid me out here.

"Who the hell are you?" I ask as I sit bolt upright.

"No need for rude language now. It's just me, Marlon. Same as always," the familiar, handsome man in front of me says. Familiar from the television, not from real life, I realize.

"Same as always, my ass. I saw you do...something. What are you? An alien? A monster? A demon? Begone demon!" I form my fingers into the shape of a cross, but the man just frowns at me.

"I'm a blanket. Well, a man now. I think I used to be a bird. That's about it. What ya see is what ya get. Anyway, sorry about killing that man. I didn't mean to make you have to move away. He was gonna hurt Imani though so I'm not sorry I stopped him."

This is too much to take in at once. I drop my head into my hands and take several deep breaths. Finally, I focus on one point. My head snaps up, and I'm fully alert.

"You killed him? Not me?" I ask.

"Yep. Sucked the life right out of him. That's how I had the power to do this." He gestures to his new face and body. "It's like draining his battery and giving me the juice."

"That means I didn't do it. My soul is safe." I breathe a sigh of relief and sit back. "Still, no one would believe the story. If I tell them a blanket killed the man they'll only commit me to an institution and return Imani to Saint Simeon's. No, I cannot let her go back."

"Can't you just go somewhere else? Pretend to be someone else?" He scratches his head in thought.

What the blanket man said gives me an idea. Not a particularly legal idea, but an idea, nonetheless.

"Well, demon, we may have to do just that."

Chapter Six

Marlon

It's been a few months since the cabin.

Charlie has mostly gotten over the fact that I'm a blanket. Feather. Bird. Whatever. He still calls me a demon sometimes, but I think it's a joke. I hope. It was probably easier for him to accept what happened because he saw it go down. If I had just shown up when he wasn't looking, he'd probably have thought I was a regular human intruder or something, and things would have been a lot different. I'm glad it worked out though because we've been getting along swell.

Imani was disappointed to lose her blanket, but when she was told that I used to be said blanket she pretty much believed it right away. I don't know if she's just easy to convince or if it's because my skin is still made of fabric. Either way, she's fine with it. I think she's mostly just happy to have two people who care about her around.

It took a little time, but Charlie did manage to find someone to make new identities for him and Imani, and a first one for me. Boy, was that guy sketchy. They just called him "Cadillac Dan" and we weren't allowed to talk to him. Just go, listen, leave. Got the job done though.

We had to stay in some pretty awful places and do some not-so-great things to get enough money for our first apartment, but we did it. We kept Imani safe and away from anything and anyone dangerous. I would never let her get hurt and I know Charlie wouldn't either.

I've had to learn more about life than just what was on kid's television pretty fast. I kind of miss seeing the world the old way.

All of the rough situations made us have to really learn to trust each other and we've really all grown pretty darn close. We're a real family now, even if we don't have blood connecting us.

When we finally settled down, Charlie decided to stay home with Imani and do her first couple years of school as home school, since we can't afford daycare, and after looking at finances it really was the best option out of some pretty terrible ones. So, I'm the one who has to work. I got a job at a big retailer stocking shelves, mostly in the home goods and bedding area. It's not so bad.

We don't have a lot, but we have each other at least. Someday we'll have more. Hopefully. Because our apartment could use some help. The appliances barely work, the hallways always smell like garbage, our lights flicker randomly, the hot water is a joke, the noise level outside is atrocious, and that's only the start. But I'm working hard to pay the rent anyway, and I'm happy we have a place to live at all.

Today I got home from work, and I was pretty tired. I don't get really physically exhausted unless I haven't taken sips of power from people in a while. I don't like taking sips from nice people, so I just stick to really rude customers. There's no shortage of those generally, but business has been a bit slow.

The springs on the old sofa squeal as I sit down and wrap my arms around my knees. I lay my head back against the cushions and close my eyes, just thinking about ways I can maybe make some more money for the household. I think about that a lot since I really want Imani to get the new scooter she talks about.

"Thinking about money again, demon?" Charlie asks from behind me in his deep, rich voice.

"You caught me. I'm thinking about maybe taking overtime in the café."

"No. You can't get wet. Your fabric will get all soggy." He shakes my arm reminding me of when I tried to do the dishes. It didn't go so well. Feather-stuffed fabric and water don't mix.

"You're right. As usual." I smile at him, showing the gap in my teeth he likes to joke about. "I just feel like things will never get better sometimes."

"Where I come from, they say 'Lu metti yàggul te ku muñ muuñ.' Whatever is painful does not last, and whoever perseveres smiles." He sits down, wraps one of his strong arms around me. When he mentions anything involving Senegal, the place he was born, I know he's comfortable, that he trusts me. I feel a warmth run through me that's more than just comfort. "We'll get through this. I swear it."

"Alright." I drop my head on his shoulder. He smells like shea butter lotion, crayons, and baby powder deodorant. His specific mix of scent always soothes me. "Want me to make you dinner?"

"I absolutely do not. You still cannot cook worth a damn. When Imani gets out of the bathroom you can play with her while I cook. You're much better at that."

"I'm gonna get better at cooking, I swear it. You're gonna want me cooking for you every day," I say with a determined grin.

"I'm happy to have you around every day either way."

Charlie's eyes soften, and for a moment I feel something pass between us. Something I don't really understand, but I'd like to.

"Marlon! You're home!" A voice squeals from the bathroom door.

"Flush the toilet!" I shout.

"Wash your hands!" Charlie shouts.

We both lean our heads back over the sofa and sigh.

Chapter Seven

Charlie

Things have gotten a little better. I've been able to take some work from home hours when not helping Imani, and Marlon has gotten a raise. We're careful with every dime and one day things will be great, I have faith.

Aside from money, life is wonderful. Imani is so smart, so sweet. We take her to the park and library as often as she wants so she can be with other children. The parents there assume Marlon and I are a romantic couple, and we let them think that. It's an easier explanation than the truth.

The truth...well, part of the truth is that I think there might be something developing between Marlon and me. I won't push it, however, because I don't know anything about what a blanket man feels romantically. Does he feel anything of the sort at all? I know *I* feel something.

He works so hard. A good work ethic has always been something important to me in a partner. No lazy layabouts for me. He smiles easily and genuinely. When I'm feeling down, I know his gapped teeth will lift me up. And he is very handsome, though in a strange way. If you would have told me I'd be attracted to a freckled man with demon-red hair a few years back I'd have laughed. Not even beginning to mention that there is a fabric texture to him that was shocking at first but that I've grown used to. It's part of him. And I think I'd like whatever he is. Whatever he looked like, or felt like, he'd still be Marlon.

"Hey there Charlie! You taking Imani to the pool today?" Marlon asks as he sees me exit the bedroom.

"No. She wants to go to the playground. More dirt and sand to clean from her shoes. I'm so joyful."

Marlon laughs with a shake of his head. "Tonight, when Imani goes to bed can I please try to cook for you again? I'm trying my darndest, I swear."

"Trying to poison me, demon? Well, you know I'm too strong for your potions. Bring it on." I laugh.

"Excellent! I swear it's gonna be great this time!" He's practically bouncing in his seat now. For his sake I hope it is good. I will not lie to him, and I don't want to hurt his feelings.

"Some strange person at work gave me a map, by the way. Do you know anything about this?" He hands me a much-folded piece of paper with an unlabeled map on it.

"I don't know. Somewhere in Bolivia. Perhaps Argentina. It's hard to tell from the way this is drawn. Who gave it to you?"

"They were really weird, but they said it was important. I should probably just toss it but, I don't know, I have a feeling I should keep it." His brow crinkles in thought.

"Then keep it. Don't overthink it. We have better things to do." I could think of many things I'd like to do with Marlon that would be a lot of fun.

Today at the playground we sit together on the bench and watch the children play. The parents all know us and wave hello as they pass. It's a beautiful day.

"Hey you two!" A blonde lady we see often named Maggie comes up to us waving. "How are you?"

"We're fine and dandy! And yourself?" Marlon replies.

"I'm great! We're just leaving but I had to say hi to y'all first. You're the absolute cutest couple I know, and you always make me smile. So gosh darn cute. Well, y'all have a nice day now. Bye!" She waves and turns back to her gaggle of children and muscular husband.

After a beat Marlon turns to me and asks, grin wide and blue eyes sparkling, "Do you think we'd make a cute couple, Charlie?"

I cough at the unexpected question, but I take the words as seriously as the feelings. "Yes, I suppose I do."

"Me too."

Things are very quiet between us the rest of the trip to the playground.

Chapter Eight

Marlon

"And here ya go. Steak, mashed potatoes, and green beans. I know it's not a fancy recipe but I tried to make something basic so I could really get the technique down. Anyway, I hope you like it," I say as I set the plates down in front of Charlie.

I wring my hands as I sit in my own seat across the table. Cooking has not been a talent of mine. Since I can't really taste anything, and the thought of eating honestly kind of disgusts me, it's hard to guess whether or not something will taste alright. I try to follow recipes but somehow, they always turn out wrong, darn it.

This time I tried really, really hard. I even recalibrated the junky old stove to make sure the temperature would be correct for baking the apple pie. Now Imani's in bed and I can finally give Charlie the food I've been working on. Gosh, I hope he likes it.

Charlie smiles wide and shimmies in his seat. None of our dining table chairs match but that's alright. A place to sit's a place to sit.

"It certainly is pleasing to the eye, Marlon. I want you to know that whether it tastes fine or not, I appreciate your efforts."

"Oh, just try it already. I'm on the edge of my seat."

Charlie barks out a laugh before picking up his knife and fork and cutting into the steak. The inside looks pink and tender. He nods as he lifts the meat to his mouth for a bite. When he begins to chew, his eyes close and a smile forms on his lips. He swallows, opens his eyes.

"You've done it. It's perfect." He rushes to take another bite as I stand, pumping my fist in the air.

"Woo!" I shout. "Finally!"

I start to head toward the kitchen, walking past Charlie as I go. He reaches out and grabs my elbow as I start to pass him.

"Stop. Where are you going?" he asks.

"To do the dishes. Then when you're done, I'll bring out dessert," I say matter of factly. It should be obvious to him. Doing the dishes is a chore I do often. It's fine as long as I wear the dish gloves. The time I forgot wasn't great. Soggy, floppy hands. Ugh.

"Please, sit while I eat. The dishes can wait. We have so little time to talk these days. I miss it." His brown eyes seek my blue ones and when they find them, they don't let go.

"Well, alright. But if they get all dry and crusty then you're doing them," I mumble.

"I don't mind." He laughs.

I sit and watch as he takes a bite of the potatoes with a smile, clearly enjoying them. My chest puffs with pride at my success.

"Has anything new happened lately, Marlon?"

"No, same old nothing. How about you?"

"Nothing here either."

There's quiet between us. Our silence has never been awkward before, but somehow it is right now. I speak again just to fill it.

"Imani got gum on that weird map earlier and tore a piece already. I swear I can't be trusted to take care of anything." I huff and shake my head.

"You've taken great care of our daughter. She knows she is loved and protected. Nothing is more important than that." There's a fierceness in Charlie's eyes, though his words are soft. He takes another bite and sits back further into his chair.

"That still sounds so strange to me. 'Our daughter.' Like we're a couple." I laugh softly but when I look at Charlie he isn't laughing. There is silence again but this time it isn't awkward, it's heavy. It's waiting. He sets his silverware down, leans forward.

"We could be a couple, Marlon. Could we not?" he asks quietly.

I pause to consider my answer carefully. It's not as if I haven't thought about this. I've thought he was beautiful since I was a blanket, for goodness' sake. And there's a clear connection between us. But there's a kid involved here. Things aren't easy.

"I mean...what if it doesn't work? I don't want to lose you and Imani."

"I would never take you away from Imani. She loves you too much. Even if I grew to hate you, I could never take you from her. Trust that." Charlie leans forward farther to grasp my hand over the table. He rubs his thumb along the back of my hand, and I feel secure as I'm caressed.

I think on it for a moment before nodding. I do trust that he'd never take her from me. I do trust *him*.

"But do you really want to be with *me*, or are you just bored and lonely?" I ask as the thought creeps into my mind. He could just want me out of desperation, a desire for romance he can't fulfill any other way. But I want to be truly wanted by him. It's important to make this distinction. I know that we've been stuck together a while, and I want to make sure he doesn't want me only because we're the last two stranded on our island. I can't help wanting a one true love when I was raised on cartoon romances, I suppose.

"Marlon. I do not make decisions lightly. When I do things, I do them with all my heart. I would not ask you to be mine if I did not want specifically you. *You,* Marlon. I want to feel your strange fabric skin against my own. If that is not something you want as well, then I will not offer again. I promise to leave you be and to return to how we were if you do not want me. But I must let you know now that you are what I want."

My mouth opens and closes several times silently before finally shutting. I nod my head rapidly.

"Yes. Yes, I want that. Us. I want us," I say, my words fumbled and awkward but understandable at least. I know they're understandable anyway because Charlie springs from his seat and walks toward me the few steps it takes to cross the distance between us. He drops to one knee, holds me on either side of my face, presses his mouth to my ear.

"Thank you, demon. I am blessed to have you."

And then he kisses me. My first kiss.

At first, it's just a press of his soft lips against my fabric ones. A shiver runs through my feather-filled body. I think *this is perfect* but then his warm, wet tongue glides across the seam of my closed lips and I know it's about to get even better.

I open my mouth a little and his tongue pushes in, forcing me to open even further. I moan at the feeling of being breached, being entered by someone. This is new, this is wonderful. I want *more*. I want *everything*.

I wrap my arms around Charlie's sides, pulling him closer to me as our kiss grows deeper, wilder. His hands explore my hair, running his fingers through the soft layers, gently tugging in a way that makes my eyes roll back under the lids. When I go to pull up the bottom of his sweater, he pulls away from me, takes the sides of my face again.

"That's far enough for tonight. We'll sleep and then tomorrow see if we feel the same, before we go further. Yes?" He looks me over, inspecting me for any doubt. I have none but appreciate his concern.

"I know I'll feel the same but if it makes you more comfortable then I'll wait. I'd wait for you forever, Charlie."

He presses his forehead against mine for a moment before pulling back, planting a kiss in the center of it, then standing up.

"I have dinner and apparently dessert to finish. Delicious too. I'm sure it's gotten cold by now, but the flavor will still be there." He smiles. I can't help but smile back.

We're a couple now.

Chapter Nine

Charlie

S leep was difficult. I offered to sleep next to one another, but Marlon insisted on sleeping on the sofa like he normally does. He said he would not be able to rest if he were next to me. I agreed but it turns out I can't rest anyway.

The kiss between us has changed everything. It was truly magical. His tongue was so strange, but I didn't mind it. He could have been made of wood and I wouldn't have minded, because it's *him*. I've got it bad, as they say.

This morning, he left for work as usual, and I taught Imani. We are so lucky to have her, so I hope she is alright with Marlon and I being a couple, and not only friends, if she even understands the difference. Perhaps I should find out.

"Imani. Do you know the difference between a boyfriend and a friend that is a boy? Or a girlfriend and a friend that is a girl?" I ask as we play with stacking blocks during her recess time.

She purses her lips in thought before answering. "One is kisses and one is no kisses. Can I have the blue block? I want to make a tornado."

"A blue tornado? That's pretty creative there, little one. I can't wait to see it!" I hand her the brick as I smile. I suppose kisses and no kisses is good enough for now.

When Marlon gets home, we head to the park. We sit closer on the bench than ever as we talk.

"Anything new happen at work today?" I ask.

"Yes, actually. I'm pretty excited about it. I was going to wait until we were at home to tell you but it doesn't look like anyone can hear us, so I'll tell you now." Marlon looks around, I'm assuming to double check that no one is within hearing distance, then turns back to me. He says softly, "I have a brother. I met him today."

My eyebrows shoot up in surprise. *A brother?*

"I thought you were the only one! There are more? Is every feather on the bird going to be a man?"

"Whoa whoa." He holds his hands up in a stop gesture. "Slow down. I don't really know much other than we were two feathers that dropped. We *think* we're the only two from that bird. We talked a little on my break and he was very interested in that map from that weird guy. I'm gonna lend it to him. Gosh, can you believe it? A brother."

Before I can even comprehend the implications of such a thing, Imani skips up to us, braids bouncing as she goes.

"I wanna go home now. I'm hungry. Can we have pancakes?" she asks.

"Sure, little one. But I think Marlon should cook. Don't you think so, Marlon?" I raise my eyebrow at him teasingly, smiling at his frightened expression.

"I don't know if I can handle pancakes yet. Maybe I'll just cut up some fruit and pour the juice. Charlie can do the pancakes." If he was human, he'd be sweating right about now.

I grin widely and wrap my arm around his shoulder. "We can work together then."

I cook the pancakes while Marlon makes a fruit salad on the counter next to the stove. It's a small kitchen so we're very close to one another. I don't mind one bit.

"Look at this grape! It's perfect." Marlon holds up a particularly impressive looking purple grape.

"Ah, you should give it to Imani." I flip a pancake and offer him a smile.

"Nope. It's for you. Open wide." Marlon points the grape in my direction as I scoff.

"Don't feed me fruit, demon. We know what happens when your kind feed humans fruit." I love to joke with him about this sort of thing. He really doesn't even understand the references but plays along anyway. Such a good sport.

"Oh come on now, put it in your mouth," he says.

I feel my cheeks grow hot and it's not from the stove.

"Are we still talking about grapes, Marlon?" I ask with a raised brow.

Marlon looks confused for a second before his eyes grow wide. He turns back to cutting fruit silently. I laugh quietly to myself.

After dinner and bath time Imani heads to bed. The apartment is quiet, aside from the normal street noise and sirens in our less than desirable neighborhood. Marlon is putting away the last of the dishes when I walk behind him and put my hands on his waist. I gently press my body against his, run my nose along the back of his neck. He shivers and lets out a soft breath.

"Marlon. Come to bed with me tonight."

"I'd just keep you awake," he replies, his voice breathier than usual.

"I don't plan on sleeping with you there, demon. Not if I get my way." I slide my hand from his waist to his hairless stomach, down to the waistband of his corduroy pants. A snap breaks the silence when I pop the button there. "Do you understand?"

"Y–yes," he stutters. "I just–I don't know what I'm doing. I don't even know if my, uh, parts will be acceptable to you."

"I'll teach you. I care for you. We'll figure things out together. Come now, to the bedroom." I take his hand and softly tug in the direction of my room. A second passes before Marlon turns and nods.

"Alright," he says shakily. "Just don't blame me if things get weird."

Chapter Ten

Marlon

As soon as Charlie closes the door behind us, he wraps his strong arms around me and gives me the deepest kiss yet. The cock I built myself recently swells in excitement and I groan at the feeling. I don't know why I waited so long to make myself one. I experimented with it last night and *wow* does it feel nice. But with how just being like this with Charlie feels so good already I can tell it's going to get even better than it was alone.

Charlie backs me into the bed until I'm lying on it with my legs off and tugs off my old t-shirt. With great anticipation of the feeling of his skin on mine, I watch as he removes his own. When he leans down to kiss me, and we press together, that feeling is just as good as I imagined.

Next, he takes off his pants and undergarments. My eyes grow wide at the sight before me. He's beautiful. All lean muscles and dark, glistening skin, with the slightest roundness to his belly. He strokes his cock and a bead of pre-cum appears on the tip of it. A shaky breath escapes me. Charlie lurches forward suddenly and with one smooth motion tugs my pants to my ankles, revealing the cock I've made for myself.

His eyebrows raise when he sees what I've made. I'm nervous. Clearly, he hates it. I'll have to change it. It's horrible. It's–

"Fucking hell, it's huge," Charlie mumbles.

"Oh," I reply while he strokes himself, looking me up and down with heat in his eyes. "Is it alright? Should I change it?"

"It's fine, demon. Touch yourself. I want to see you stroke your cock for me."

I swallow the lump in my throat and do as he says. His breathing increases to a rapid pace as he watches me intently. His eyes are focused so strongly on me it makes me nervous, but also makes me feel attractive, more confident somehow at the same time.

"You look so fucking good with your big, fat cock in your hand. Lay down on the pillows," Charlie commands. I would do anything he tells me to do.

I lay flat on my back and Charlie lays his body on top of me, kissing me hard and grinding his hips against mine. It feels so good and so right to be with him. I don't know why it's taken us so long.

"Your mouth is wonderful, Marlon. So strange with your satin tongue. I wonder how it would feel wrapped around my cock?" he practically purrs in my ear. It's a statement but also a suggestion, a request.

"Maybe we could find out," I reply in a whisper. "I don't know what I'm doing though. So just...cut me some slack if I fuck up."

"There's no fucking up," Charlie laughs, "unless you use teeth. Don't use teeth."

"I won't." I laugh in return. *No teeth. Got it.*

Charlie flips over onto his back and I crawl until I'm on my hands and knees over his body. *Oh gosh am I nervous.* I move down until I'm in the right position and take hold of his beautiful brown cock. *Alright. Here we go.*

The first taste surprises me. It's sort of salty and bitter at the same time. Now, I don't really taste much, and what little I do I don't generally like, but I kind of like this. What it says about me that the only flavor I like is human, I don't know, but it can only be something creepy. So, I don't think about it too long.

I lick along the head, the shaft, getting used to the feeling in my mouth before I wrap my lips around it. The way I begin to move seems to be okay if I'm judging by the noises Charlie is making. He's hissing and sighing delightfully. I want to impress him, make him feel better than he's ever felt, so I decide to do something crazy.

I decide to use my abilities. My ability to change my form that is. I know it's risky, but I think it will pay off. So, I look him dead in the eyes and as I'm moving up and down, licking and sucking, I stretch my tongue out longer and longer until it's wrapped around his cock several times. I swirl it around, squeezing, finding every movement that makes him groan and repeating it until he's shouting and shooting loads of hot cum onto the back of my throat.

When he finishes, I retract my tongue to its normal size and sit up with a smile. Charlie lays there, panting, with a confused look on his face.

"What just happened?" he pants out.

"I can choose my shape, remember?" I say with a wide grin. "I just happened to decide on a little longer tongue than normal."

"A little?" He lets out one incredulous laugh. A moment passes while he stares at me in awe before he speaks again. "We're going to have a lot of fun."

Chapter Eleven

Charlie

"So, you can do any part?" I ask in shock.

I feel a tickle on my stomach, like a snake slithering around. I look down to see what was a beautiful cock is now a long, pointed tentacle. I jump with a startle, but still, I reach for it, stroking along the smooth, PVC-like texture.

"Well, that's certainly new."

"Yeah." He laughs. "This is kind of fun."

"Feel free to experiment all you like. What's mine is yours to explore," I softly chuckle.

The tentacle returns to the original shape. "I think I just want to try things the old-fashioned way tonight if that's okay. We can continue getting weird another time."

"Fine with me." I brush some ginger hair back from his pale brow. "Get on your back again. We'll come together this time."

As he does what I say I open the side table drawer and grab the bottle of lube. My cock is already hard again as I hover over him, spreading the lube on both our cocks. His eyelids flutter beautifully as I stroke him. I lay my body down onto his and kiss him, softly and deeply.

I hold both our cocks and begin to pump into my hands, stroking us, encouraging Marlon to move his hips as well with mine.

"Don't come until I tell you it's alright. We have to come together this time. Got it?"

"Okay. I think." His voice is strained but I can tell he's trying his best to agree.

"Good boy," I say against his lips, and he moans right as I sink my tongue into his mouth. Guess he liked that.

Soon we're frantically moving, and I can feel my orgasm approaching. The desperate look on Marlon's face says he can't hold back much longer.

"Alright. You can let go," I say, my forehead pressed against his.

I lose it first. A spray of sticky cum coats our hands and Marlon's chest, his stomach. I'm barely finished when Marlon's hips raise, a loud groan escapes him, and he stiffens. Then, something highly unusual happens.

I bark out a laugh of surprise as a shower of soft, white, feathers float down in front of my face. Most of the time I don't think about the fact that Marlon started off as a comforter, but I suppose I must be reminded sometimes. I fall forward in laughter and kiss him over and over. He soon joins in, and we're wrapped in each other's arms, smiling and laughing for long minutes before we stop in sighs.

"I forgot to warn you about that," Marlon says with a sheepish look on his face.

"I think it's better you didn't. It was a great surprise." I lay my head on top of his and pull the blanket over us. "I can clean up the mess. Then I'll shower. You...do whatever it is you do to get clean."

"Oh, I insist on cleaning up the feathers. It's my mess."

"We can take turns then. There will be many opportunities in the future. I hope." I stroke my thumb along his cheek.

"I hope so too."

A knock comes at the door and Marlon and I look at each other in panic before it opens wide. Imani is standing there in her little pink nightgown, looking sleepy.

"I heard laughing." She looks at both of us appraisingly. "Were you kissing? Are you boyfriends now?"

"Well, you see, Marlon and I love each other very much," I say. I'm nervous as hell and have no idea where to go from here.

"Okay. You can be boyfriends. Don't wake me up though that's rude." She yawns and closes the door.

I hear her tiny feet slapping against the floor on the way back to her room and when it goes quiet, I let out a long breath and fall back down to the mattress.

"We love each other?" Marlon asks, laying his head on my chest. The beat of my heart must be so loud now I'll be surprised if he keeps his hearing.

"Do we not?" I ask back, a nervous shake to my words.

"Yeah, we do."

"Good." My heart slows, relaxing with the knowledge of my perfect destiny. "I have defeated the demon with the power of love. How predictable."

Chapter Twelve

Marlon

"Yep, my brother invited us to dinner. It's exciting! I've only met him a few times and it was always brief. He's an odd fellow, really. Kind of creepy, if I say so. But I think he's harmless. And he's my brother so we have to go! We're going to meet his family. I'm so excited! I can't wait!"

I'm practically bouncing on my toes as I tell Charlie the news. My brother Ori came into my work today to ask me to dinner to meet his family. Apparently, he's told them all about me and they're excited to meet me. I can't believe it! For a bit there I thought he was only using me for that darn map, and I'd never talk to him again.

"Are you sure about this? He's not going to turn us into the police or harm Imani or anything? We have to be careful, you know." Charlie is always worried. I understand. I also would do anything to protect Imani.

"As far as I know he doesn't know anything about what happened at the orphanage. And I really don't think he'll hurt us. He's just weird. Like, sort of dramatic. It'll be fine. We can go, right?" I put on my best puppy dog eyes and hope it works. It does.

"Fine. But if things seem off, we leave."

"Of course! You got it!"

"What's he got?" Imani asks, looking up from her book. She's still so little but she's reading way ahead for her age. Such a smart girl.

"Oh, he agreed to let us meet your uncle. My brother. His name's Ori. He's a little weird but he's got a family and we're gonna get along, I just know it."

Imani perks up. "Does he got kids?"

"Does he *have* kids," Charlie corrects. Imani and I both ignore him.

"I don't think so. Sorry, little buddy. But I think he's got a wife or girlfriend or something so at least it won't be all boys around for once."

"Well, that's good at least I guess." She goes back to reading her book and I turn back to Charlie.

"So, dinner with Ori then?" I ask.

He sighs and crosses his arms.

"I guess we're having dinner with Ori."

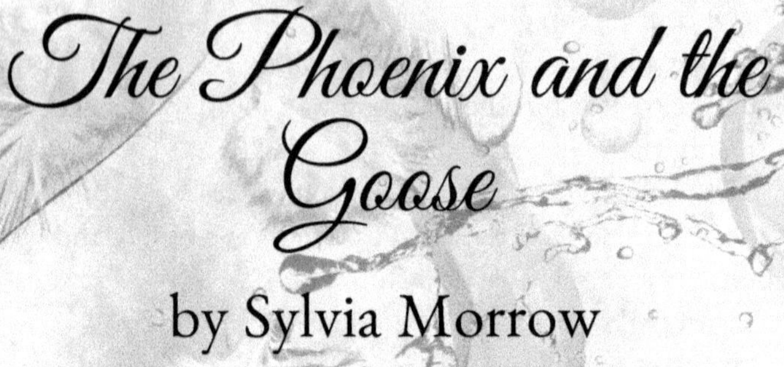

The Phoenix and the Goose

by Sylvia Morrow

Please Read

THIS IS NOT A ROMANCE. THERE IS NO HAP-PILY EVER AFTER.

I need to make it clear that this story is a **TRAGEDY**, not a romance. It will end with the death of both main characters. This is not a spoiler, as the basic plot has already been explained in "Stuffed." However, **you must know the basic characters and summary of this story to best enjoy the final "Stuffed" story, "Stuffed Up."** I will post a page that contains an **entire summary** of the story for those that want to know what happens in the story, but do not want to read it because of the content warnings. This way you can be caught up for the remaining stories.

The story also contains parts that require major content warnings. You may not want to read this story if you only want to read uplifting stories where the main characters have happy endings, no animals are harmed, and no one is a liar or a cheat.

Content Warnings

Cheating, pet harmed, animal (not pet, not on page) death, death of main characters, no happily ever after, main character gets badly injured, awful death, sex, kidnapping, murder, burned alive, loved one being eaten, description of how an animal is butchered.

Spoilers

Entire Plot Spoiler For Those That Want to Skip

This is for people who want to skip this novella due to triggers but want to continue with this series.

Do not read if you want to read this story. It contains FULL spoilers of the ENTIRE Phoenix and the Goose novella.

Again, **if you don't want spoilers, skip this** and go to Chapter One.

Summary:

Luke is a phoenix shifter. Phoenix shifters all come from Greece, but most moved to Texas. Some phoenixes have strong abilities to change their own and others' physical attributes, even into entirely different species. Luke has a fiancée named **Iris** who has that ability.

Luke did not choose to become engaged to Iris. The people in charge of the phoenixes—the Council—forced Luke and Iris together because of their strong bloodlines. Iris is a cruel person, who is determined to be on the Council, and Luke doesn't like her.

Luke meets a human named Lara. Despite knowing he shouldn't do it, he goes on a date with her. When he kisses her, he realizes she's his fated mate. Luke goes to the Council and tells them that he has to break his engagement with Iris because he has found his True Love.

The Council warns Luke that Iris is powerful and could react poorly to the breakup. The Council insists he must be certain that Lara is his True Love before they will agree to the breakup and gives him one week to think things through, during which he cannot tell Iris. Luke agrees.

After the meeting, Luke has a date with Lara where she really falls for him. They make love. The next day when she is working Luke comes into her job, not knowing that is her shop. She says she misses him after their date and calls him a "silly goose." She doesn't notice Iris there with him.

Upon discovering Luke has been cheating, Iris turns Lara into a goose and traps Luke in his phoenix form. Iris kidnaps them. Lara escapes out of Iris's car window but is injured when she lands on the highway. A goose farmer finds Lara and takes her to use for feathers and meat.

Luke escapes the car a while after Lara and searches for her. By the time he finds her, she's too injured to walk or fly away. Men on the farm capture Luke. While he is tied up, they kill and eat Lara.

Luke decides he cannot live without Lara and burns himself up, deciding not to be reborn out of the ashes. Before he burns up, two of his feathers get snagged on a rusty pole and float toward the barn where Lara's feathers are. The feathers are mixed with those of geese and made into a pillow and blanket.

Chapter One

Lara

Goosebumps travel up my bare arms as I stroll past the glass doors of the frozen foods aisle. It's cold in the freezer section. Hot as the blazes of hell outside, though. That's summer in Texas for you.

"Grab some pizzas, girly. I don't feel like dealing with delivery and all that tonight," my cousin says as she starts to walk away back to the beginning of the aisle. "Let me get some of those little cinnamon bread things."

"You got it, Vera."

Shivering, I open a door and grab a couple of pizzas as fast as I can, toss them in the cart, and hurry along. This is the last of the frozen food aisles, and then we just have to grab a few things I forgot earlier, like beans. Can't leave the beans behind. When I speed around the corner, however, my trip to the legumes is delayed when I slam into an unexpected barrier.

"Oof."

A man clutches his stomach at the far end of my cart, his basket and its contents clattering to the floor.

"Oh! I'm so sorry! Are you alright? Let me help you with that."

I hurry to the side of the poor man I've just charged straight into and drop to the ground to pick up his goods. He crouches down to join me.

"It's okay, you don't have to. I'm sure it was an accident. Wait, was it an accident? If not, you should definitely help because that would be really mean, crashing into someone on purpose."

I pause with my hand halfway to picking up a bag of habanero peppers, checking his expression to make sure he's kidding. The sparkle in his strangely copper-colored eyes and the twitch to his full lips give him away.

"Yeah, I should help, then. I really have it out for cute blond guys. My apologies."

He really is cute. And I'm a flirt. Always have been.

I can tell by the way his lips roll in and his cheeks turn pink that he's trying not to laugh as he picks up a large jar of cinnamon sticks.

"Well, it's only mean to crash into the cute ones. The ugly ones are fair game," he says in an overly serious tone.

"Oh, of course, of course." I pick up a bag of what has to be nearly two pounds of fresh ginger root. "You have some very interesting groceries, Blondie."

"You went with Blondie? Damn. Was hoping for Cutie."

This time, he can't keep his laugh in once mine escapes.

"Alright, Cutie it is."

"What can I call you?" he asks, cheeks now turning even pinker against his fair skin.

Aww, he's shy.

"You think you're the only one who likes being called cute?" I give him a wink that has him shaking his head and smiling broadly. "But my name is Lara."

"Okay, Cute Lara. Nice to meet you. My name is Luke."

"Nice to meet you, Luke."

We shake hands, which seems awkwardly formal. It feels like I've known this guy forever, not just met him.

"You sure you're okay? I hit you pretty hard. I feel terrible." I cringe.

"It's alright, really. It was just a bump. Accidents happen."

He smiles so brightly and my heart flutters around the room, cartoon-style. After having been in so many relationships with people who wanted to hold every mistake over my head forever, '*Accidents happen*' is a really nice thing to hear.

"I have to run, but do you...do you want to talk again sometime? Not at the grocery store?" he asks as we stand.

I have to admit, I'm caught off guard. It's not like I've never been asked out before, but this blushing sweetie didn't seem like the type to make the first move. I'm certainly intrigued.

"Yeah, that would be great! Here, take my number."

We take our phones out, and I tell him mine; he tells me his. There's a lot of nervous tucking my hair behind my ear on my end, despite being so brave just a moment before. I discover his nervous tic is rubbing the back of his neck. Despite the nerves, our smiles show how excited we both are.

"I look forward to seeing you soon, Lara."

"Same, Cutie."

And with that, we part ways. I'm off to check out the beans and he's off to the registers.

"Cutie, huh?" A moment later Vera meets me. She drops the frozen cinnamon bread in my cart. "Don't tell me you're gonna go out with that guy."

"Eh, I might."

Vera snatches the beans out of my hands and looks me in the eye. "You're supposed to be taking time off of dating."

"Don't worry. This one seems sweet. And I promise, I'll be gone at the first sign of trouble."

Chapter Two

Luke

"Luke? Hello? Earth to Luke!"

My sister tosses a balled-up napkin that hits me square in the forehead, interrupting my spinning thoughts about Lara. It's for the best. I *really* shouldn't be thinking about her. Not that I can stop. She's been the only thing on my mind since she slammed into me with her shopping cart.

But I really shouldn't have asked her out like I did. We can't have a future together, and it's crazy to even imagine one after one meeting. I shake my head, try to clear my thoughts.

"What's going on?"

"I asked why you're zoning out today."

I don't know, Emily, maybe because I met the girl of my dreams at the grocery store and I can't stop thinking about her even though I have a fiancée.

"Just tired. Eat your food, Emily."

My eyes flick to her plate, mostly empty compared to mine. Normally, I'd gobble up the meal, a classic phoenix dish made from ginger, cinnamon, ghost pepper, anise, and horseradish. The kind of stuff that would leave most humans panting.

"Well, wake up. Iris is coming over tonight and I'm not going to entertain her for you. She gives me the creeps."

Inside, I groan. I'd forgotten about that. She wanted to come over and discuss wedding colors. As if I care what our wedding decor looks like. I don't even want to marry her in the first place.

Iris is from a wealthy, healthy phoenix family. I'm considered lucky to be paired off with her—my family is middle class at best. There are only so many acceptable matches with how few phoenixes are left in the world, so to be paired off at all is a blessing. The leaders decided she and I would make good offspring, so we're getting married. That's that. I will do my duty for my species—even if I really don't want to.

"Make sure to keep your dog in your room," I grumble.

Iris hates dogs. *Really* hates dogs. I'm a fan of animals, but I don't think we'll be having pets when Iris and I are married. I saw what she did to a street cat who scratched her once and it wasn't pretty. Not willing to take a risk by putting an animal in a house with her.

There are a lot of reasons I wouldn't have chosen Iris as a wife on my own and that's one of them. But what the Council says goes. They want another healthy generation of phoenixes, and they want Iris and me to be their breeding pair. It's depressing if I think about it too much, so I just kind of...don't.

I suppose the "not thinking" is what got me in trouble with Lara. Then again, maybe it was too much thinking. Because I just *cannot* get her out of my head.

I finish eating my dinner and head to the shower. My mind wanders back to the woman at the grocery store today. When I saw her, it was as if everyone else was in shadow but she lit up like a Christmas tree. All of that deep, tan skin showed off in her tiny shorts. Big, brown eyes, wrinkled at the edges with mischief. Crayon-red curls with tiny braids mixed throughout, falling down her back, perfectly highlighting the curvature of her waist as she walked away. Even the little gap in her front teeth was sexy to me.

Lara.

Fuck. I know I only spoke to her briefly, but I've never met someone so beautiful, someone who shone so bright. Everything else seems so dull since I left that store. Even my flame, the very magic that grants me eternal life, seems like nothing compared to her. I imagine her as pure light wrapped around me, running through my veins. It's overwhelming. I don't know where these feelings are coming from, but I don't want them to stop.

Lara, my darling Lara.

I rest my head against the wall of the shower and let the water beat against my skin uninterrupted. In my mind, however, I'm still with *her*, with *Lara*, for a few more minutes.

Then I have to face my fiancée.

Chapter Three

Lara

My eyes flick up, scanning the aisles of footwear to make sure no one needs me. I shouldn't have my phone out when I'm at the register, but I'll be damned if I'm gonna stand here for eight hours staring at shoes. Working in a shoe store ain't the most exciting job on the planet, but a job's a job. Discount's nice too.

As I'm scrolling through my apps looking for something to give me a hit of dopamine, I get a notification. *Luke.* I can't help but squeal as I open the text with a quickness.

Luke: Hi, Lara. Injure anyone today?

I wrinkle my nose at his sense of humor. *Dork.*

Me: Hey there, Cutie. That's a way to start a conversation, I guess. But no, not today. How's your tummy? Not too bruised, I hope?

Luke: No lol

Luke: Not bruised.

Me: That's good to know. You won't be too injured to take me out then.

Luke: Guess I won't be. Would you like to? Go out?

Me: I think it was implied that I would, wasn't it?

Luke: I suppose it was. How foolish of me to even ask.

Me: Foolish, Blondie. Clownery, even.

Luke: Hey, what happened to Cutie?

Me: Cute? Are you? I'm starting to forget...I think I need a reminder...

A moment later, a notification arrives with a picture attached. A smiling blonde man in a white button-up shirt. *Damn.* He's even more adorable than I remember. I take in every detail of the photo before I reply, and I only stop looking because my cheeks are starting to hurt from how wide I'm smiling.

Me: Yeah, you're pretty alright. I'd be fine with your company.

Luke: High praise!

Luke: How about Friday? Seven? I could pick you up and we could get dinner.

Me: Why don't we meet somewhere instead. Tomorrow, six, early dinner at Eve's Fig downtown?

Luke: I'll see if I can get reservations.

Me: I'll get them squared away. Don't you worry your pretty head.

Luke: Well, alright then. I'll just focus on staying pretty and arriving on time. Let me know if plans change. I can't wait to see you.

Lara: Tomorrow at six.

I know I took control of the whole date thing a little more than I would have in my past relationships, but I wanted to see if it would scare him off. The last guy I dated just wanted a woman he could push around, and he treated me like shit every time I stood up for myself. He was a lying, cheating bastard who made me feel small and weak.

I promised myself never to be with someone like that again. I'm only dating honest sweethearts from now on. Luke seems like a really nice guy so far. Hopefully, I'm getting better at avoiding shady guys than I used to be. I think another broken heart would kill me.

Chapter Four

Luke

"**N**o, Iris, you're already beautiful. You don't need to change anything else. I swear."

I'm exasperated. She's been transforming her appearance little by little for hours now. A freckle here, a half shade lighter hair color there, ever so slightly trimmer around the waist...it's exhausting watching it. She said she wants to make sure she looks perfect, but the fact is, I don't care what she looks like. She could be the Venus de Milo and it wouldn't matter.

She even tried to get me to let *her* transform *me* tonight. Fuck that. I told her if I wanted to change, I'd do it myself. All phoenixes have the ability to use our life generation powers to alter material at will, including ourselves. I'm strong enough to alter my looks if I want—to a pretty decent extent. I can even change other people a little, and animals a lot.

Some of us have much stronger abilities than others. Iris, for example, is ridiculously powerful. She's as strong as any Council member, I'd guess. If she wanted to change something about me, I couldn't stop her, and I couldn't do anything to change it back. Thankfully, she just sighs and whines when I don't listen to her and doesn't force me to comply. She's pissed that I won't fix the cowlick in my hair but screw her. I think all the little imperfections are what make people unique and beautiful.

She can get as *flawless* as she wants, but I don't know if she'll ever truly be beautiful to me. She'll always be an obligation, and as much as I want to do right by my people, as much as I never plan on letting Iris feel like I don't care about her, it's exactly that—there's no feelings. All the things that would attract me to someone—kindness, a sense of humor, generosity, uniqueness—are missing from her.

My sister's chihuahua yaps at Iris from the other side of my bedroom door. *Fuck.* Emily knows better than to let her dog out when Iris is here.

"Shut that dog up, Luke," Iris tosses over her shoulder.

"Emily, come get Louie!" I shout as I pick up the poor little guy. She found him wandering in an alley eating garbage a couple years back. He's ugly as sin, smells terrible, and yaps constantly, but he's sweet. Loves to cuddle. "Hurry up!"

"I should go one shade lighter blonde—my brother is going darker blonde this season and I hate twinning with him. My eyelashes could be longer, maybe. What about my ass? Is it too big, do you think?" She turns around in front of the mirror and pouts.

I sigh. It doesn't matter what I say, nothing is ever good enough for her. Still, I have to say something. I turn to her and smile. The dog grunts.

"You know I think you always look great, but of course, I'm biased."

Iris curls her lip in disgust at the dog briefly before looking back at the mirror. She tucks her hair behind her ear, pouts her lips at her reflection, then turns back to me. "I know I look great, but how can I look even better?"

Louie growls at Iris. He never growls at anyone else. *Bad choice, doggie.* I have to take this dog out of here before things go south.

"I'll be right back," I say as I attempt to wrestle the now wriggling dog close to my body.

And then, the damn thing bites me. I unfortunately loosen my hold just enough for him to jump to the floor.

"What the hell is that rat doing?" Iris spits out.

I attempt to catch him, but he swoops under the bed. Next thing I know, he's coming around the other side. By the time I stumble around to the other side, he's managed to jump up onto the desk chair and from the desk chair to my desk. The damn thing is usually whining with arthritis and begging to be picked up, but chooses this moment to miraculously heal himself and learn to jump. Great.

"Luke, what the hell? Get him!" Iris snarls.

The chihuahua sniffs the objects on the desk with great interest. I sigh and reach for him. As if in slow motion, I watch as Louie does the unthinkable—he pees on Iris's wedding planning notebook.

"Well," Iris says as she takes a deep breath, "I think that's enough of that."

Emily walks in just as Iris lifts the barking dog in one perfectly manicured hand.

"Iris, what are you doing? Give him to me. I'm sorry he got away for a minute. I'll take him back now. Please," Emily begs.

Iris scoffs. "You look like I'm going to kill the disgusting thing. Is that what you think of me? That I'm a murderer?"

Emily shakes her head. "Of course not."

Ah, fuck. This is bad.

"Iris, Emily can take him—"

"I'm only going to make it more enjoyable for everyone. Something pretty. Quiet." Iris smiles as Emily's eyes grow wide in anticipation of whatever awful thing is coming. "I suggest you get a bowl, little sister. Fast."

Louie lets out a sharp cry as he begins to change his shape. Resigned, I lay back against the wall and let out a long breath. This shit is incredibly fucked up, but we're at the point of no return now. Nothing left to do but see what happens, then try to fix it—if we can.

"A big bowl. Lots of water." Iris looks Emily up and down with a mix of curiosity and frustration. "Why are you standing there?"

Emily bolts out of the room and into the kitchen. I can hear water running in the distance as I watch the horror taking place in Iris's hand. By the time Emily gets back, the transformation is complete. Iris is holding on with both hands, laughing as a koi fish flops wildly between them.

"Much better," Iris says as she places the fish gently into the bowl. "You'll have to get an appropriate habitat for it, of course."

Iris smiles as if she's genuinely done Emily a favor—as if this really is a happy ending. I suppose for Iris it is.

The water in the bowl sloshes from Emily's hands shaking, but she says nothing. She stares, white-faced, into the bowl as she turns and exits the room, closing the door behind her. *Fuck.* My poor sister.

"She's not going to talk about it to anyone, I assume?" Iris snaps her neck in my direction and locks eyes with me. There's a definite threat in those eyes, despite her flat expression.

What she did to the dog isn't entirely forbidden in our culture, but it's frowned upon. Transforming without consent is *always* taboo, however, and Iris desperately wants to be on the Council someday. If they have definitive proof that she's going around transforming people's pets without their permission, that's going to be a strike against her for sure. Emily's not so stupid that she'd snitch on Iris and risk getting on her bad side, that I know. *No one* wants to be on Iris's bad side.

"She's not gonna say anything, Iris, believe me."

"Good. Anyway," Iris says as she wipes her palms on my bedspread. "We were talking about my eyelashes."

This continues for another hour—her making tiny adjustments, while I wonder things like *"How am I going to raise children with someone like this?"* Every time the thought of her taking care of our future kids crosses my mind I feel like I'm going to throw up. Do we really need more people like her in the world? Could I raise them well enough to counteract her influence? The whole thing is giving me a headache. I'm *very* thankful when she finally packs up and gets ready to go.

As I'm happily escorting her to the front door, she turns around and holds up a manicured finger.

"Hold on. Don't forget next weekend we're picking out my shoes."

Ugh. Phoenixes all originally come from Greece, and even though we've been gone for a long time, we still practice the traditions. One is that the groom chooses the bride's wedding shoes. Even tradition cannot escape Iris and her obsessive, controlling ways, so while I may be buying, she's picking them out.

"Of course. See you then."

And then she's out the door.

Iris stayed far too late. And now I need to spend time with my obviously distraught sister to convince her that Iris will fix her dog. Eventually. Probably.

In the past, when she's done fucked up stuff like this, she's fixed it. Even the cat, sort of. Once Iris flexes her power and makes sure everyone gets her point, it just takes a little begging and adoration to put things to rights. I know what I have to do, especially because Emily is too angry and distraught to deal with Iris. And if it doesn't work...it's a really pretty fish, I guess.

Chapter Five

Luke

I barely get any sleep because of the shit with Iris. It's not difficult to get out of bed, however, as I'm looking forward to my date night with Lara. I haven't been as excited about a date in—well, I've never been this excited about a date. I'm also more than a little anxious, considering thoughts of Iris turning Lara into a fish keep running through my mind, but I try to brush those off whenever they pop up.

My day goes painfully slowly because of how much I want it to end. But I leave early and rush home. I shower faster than I've ever showered and dress in the clothes I prepared yesterday. I know I've cut it close on time, but I didn't want to tell her no. She could have said she wanted to meet any time, and I would have found a way to get there.

I pull up to Eve's Fig with one minute to spare. I use the valet parking so that I'm not more than a single minute late. When I get inside, it isn't hard to spot her, considering she's the brightest thing in the restaurant. She's the brightest thing everywhere I've seen her so far.

She's seated already. Her hair is pulled up in a way that lets her high cheekbones shine. The candlelight dances in her dark eyes and it makes me think about having my light inside of her. I almost groan at the thought before pushing it aside. *Not the time for thoughts like that.*

"Lara, I'm so sorry I'm late," I apologize as I take my seat at the table.

"You're one minute late, I think I'll survive. But I appreciate the apology nonetheless." She adjusts the strap of her sundress—the red color of it matches her hair—and smiles.

"Your beneficence will not be forgotten."

We don't have time for further pleasantries before the waiter is upon us. Lara orders red wine, but I get sparkling water. My kind avoids alcohol. Our species enjoys an alcoholic drink called Mastika so much that we can become heavily dependent on it very easily. We're warned away from all alcohol as it can trigger a desire for it in us. Just a weird phoenix thing.

"I have to admit I was pleasantly surprised when you suggested Eve's Fig. It's not easy to find a fellow vegetarian in this part of Texas. Or at least I assume you're one if you're eating here."

Eve's Fig is a strictly vegan restaurant. While people with every diet can and do eat plant-based food, most people don't go out of their way to eat somewhere specifically vegan. Eve's Fig, however, is always busy regardless of its status because of how fantastic the food is.

...Not to mention the high population of animal shifters that live in the area. Most shifters tend to be at least vegetarian, since it's weird for us to eat animals. When your friend might turn into a cow, it's hard to eat beef.

Phoenixes are considered shifters, despite our animal not existing anywhere in the wild. Unicorns and griffins are the same—they don't exist separate from their human half. Griffins eat meat, though. *A lot* of it. And from what the rumors say, it's, uh, not *animal* meat. *Ugh.*

"That I am. I had a feeling you wouldn't be opposed to eating somewhere outside of a steakhouse after seeing the contents of your grocery basket. What were you making, anyway?"

I take a big gulp of my water. Lying isn't fun. Fudging the truth isn't much better. Have to do a lot more of that than I'd like with Lara.

"We just enjoy our food well-spiced in our house. Very well-spiced."

"I get that." She cocks her head. "Who's we?"

"I live with my younger sister. She's currently out of work, so I'm letting her stay with me until she gets a new job. Won't be long."

Not *entirely* a lie. That's why she's staying there now. But I'm supposed to be handing over the house when I marry Iris, as I'm meant to move into hers. It's *much* bigger and we wouldn't need mine anymore. However, if I can somehow get out of this marriage, I won't need to leave and I won't be lying at all. Getting out of a marriage contract that the Council arranged is nearly impossible, however. So, that's a tiny problem. Not going through with the marriage would mean complete isolation from my people, including my family, banishment from the territory of Texas and all other phoenix settlements, and Iris would be able to choose another punishment she saw fit, up to and including a total rebirth. Finding a way out of the contract without those consequences would be nice.

"Well, that's nice of you. I live alone, but my cousin, Vera, comes over to hang out a couple times a week. Speaking of jobs, what kind of work do you do?"

"I'm a dermatologist. I have a clinic in El Paso that just opened recently. And you?"

Lara cringes before taking a drink of her wine. She looks sheepish when she finally answers.

"Well, nothing nearly that exciting. I work retail." She laughs. "I sell overpriced accessories to ladies with too much money."

"Someone has to give them something to do with their money. Better than buying Dalmatian puppies to make coats or whatever else they might do."

"Oh, yes, good point." She nods. "Can't believe I didn't think of it that way."

"Where do you work? Maybe I'll stop by and get some accessories for my sister."

"Oh, lord. You don't want to spend the kind of money those things cost without a discount. But the place I work at is called—"

The waiter interrupts her when he returns to take our order. I'll have to ask her some other time.

We decide to share an order of fried artichoke hearts to start. They're no fun for me to eat due to the lack of spice, but I take a few bites to seem normal. Lara, however, notices my lack of enthusiasm and slides the bottle of Frank's Red Hot toward me.

"Any good vegetarian restaurant has hot sauce at the ready. There's always at least one in any group that needs everything spicy, I swear." Lara laughs.

"She's not wrong," the waiter laughs as he refills my water.

For our main courses she orders lemongrass tofu tacos, and I get a spicy kimchi BLT (the "B" being tempura tempeh) with a double side of their house extra hot sauce. When the waiter walks away, Lara looks at me with a raised eyebrow.

"What?" I wipe my face to make sure nothing is there.

"You really *do* like it spicy, huh?"

"Oh. That. Yeah. Uh, runs in the family."

"I expected you to make some smarmy comeback about how the dining room isn't the only place you like it spicy or something," she teases.

"Oh, well, sorry. I like it bland in the bedroom. It's like skim milk in there. I just turn off the lights, get in the missionary position, and think of the sexiest woman in history, Margaret Thatcher."

"I almost hope you're not kidding because the Thatcher role play would be something else."

Lara's laugh is infectious. For much of the dinner, my cheeks are sore from how wide I'm smiling. I just can't stop. No one has ever made me feel this way.

"Would you like to see the dessert menu?" the waiter asks when our plates are approaching empty.

I'm full to the brim, can't fathom eating another bite. Then I think of having to end the conversation with Lara for the evening.

And maybe never getting to see her again until I figure things out with Iris. *If* I figure things out.

"Absolutely," I say, "Let's see it."

Chapter Six

Lara

I really like this guy.

"Well, considering the waitstaff has been giving us dirty looks for a while now, I suppose it's time to go," Luke says, "Would you like me to give you a ride home?"

I consider using an app for my ride. It's the practical thing to do on a first date. But I just don't want my time with Luke to end. Not yet.

"Sure. Thanks. It's not too far."

"That's too bad. I wouldn't mind a long drive. More time with you sounds good." He holds out his arm to help me out of my seat. Goosebumps form on my skin at his touch.

"I suppose I wouldn't mind either."

The ride isn't nearly long enough. Far too much of it is spent with me giving directions or commenting on traffic. There's no place to park in front of my apartment, so I expect him to stop in the street and wait for me to get out. He doesn't, though.

"Are you gonna kidnap me? Just wanted to give me a last vision of home before driving me to your spooky dungeon?"

"Yep, you caught me." He laughs as he pulls into a parking spot at the far end of my block. "No, there's no dungeon. Just thought I'd walk you to your door, that's all."

"Well, aren't you a gentleman," I say as he comes around the car to help me out.

"It's what Margaret Thatcher would want."

"Oh, lord."

We stop on the stairs, and I take out my keys. Nervously, I wring my hands as we face one another.

"I hope you don't expect to come in. No offense, I just don't let men into my home on the first date."

He smiles sheepishly, pushing back the light hair from his brow.

"I didn't expect it, no. Of course, if you did, I would happily accept, but no, no expectations. I just had to walk you to the door so I could spend every last second possible with you." He chuckles softly, his copper eyes glinting in the yellow light from above the landing. He rubs the back of his neck. *Nervous, ain't ya?*

I admit, I'm nervous too. My heart is racing nearly as fast as my thoughts as I take two steps closer to him. We're nearly pressed together, and I slide my hand through his hair where his hand had been just a moment before.

"That doesn't mean I won't be thinking about what would happen if you did join me tonight," I say.

His throat bobs. *There, I've got him.* He'll be thinking of me all night. I internally brush my shoulders off. *Still got it.*

"I, uh, I'll certainly be thinking of you, Lara."

Leaning forward just slightly, raised on the tips of my toes, I wait.

He takes the hint, crosses the distance.

Our kiss is soft, sweet. The hand he lays on my cheek is warm—hot even. His lips are smooth and just as warm. My hands shake as they run along the back of his neck, but only from excitement. He tastes like cinnamon and peppers. There is no clumsiness to our first connection. It's a perfect kiss.

"Lara," he whispers against my lips as we gently pull apart. It sounds like a vow, though he says nothing else.

There's silence between us as we stand, foreheads pressed together, his hands cupping my face. I didn't expect that kiss. I expected a quick goodnight peck, or maybe even some tongue action. What I didn't expect were *feelings.* Something bubbling up from inside telling me *it's him. He's the one.* After *one* kiss!

The way he looks at me makes me hope he's feeling the same thing.

"Luke I–"

"I should go," he says as he suddenly pulls away.

I feel a sense of whiplash at the change in mood. Did I do something wrong?

"See you," he says as he waves.

"Oh, okay. Text me?"

"Of course. Tomorrow. Thank you, Lara."

And then he's walking away, and I'm left standing on the stairs, wondering what the hell just happened.

Chapter Seven

Luke

That kiss sealed it.

It wasn't easy getting an appointment with the Council of Phoenixes the same day I called them, but I managed to use a favor the secretary owed me. This can't wait. *Lara* can't wait.

In the old times, the Council would have met in some grand temple with Corinthian columns. Today they meet in a tall office building with big, glass windows. I'm sitting nervously in a gray waiting room for my turn to talk to them. The last time I was here was when they gave me the order to marry Iris. It was not a pleasant day for me. Hopefully, today I'll leave here with better news.

"Mr. Onassis? It's time for your appointment," the secretary announces.

Alright. Here we go. I smooth down the front of my jacket and adjust my tie as I stand. Nothing should be out of place when meeting with these people.

The heavy door thumps solidly behind me as I enter the large space. At the opposite end of the room, four people—three men and one woman—sit behind a desk of highly polished wood. They're all dressed in fine clothes, well-groomed. Each of them gives off an air of power that makes me feel a little sick and *very* weak. Any one of these people could turn me into an ant and crush me with a flick of their finger.

"Take a seat, Mr. Onassis," the woman, Janet Alexopoulou, says. All of them watch as I follow her instructions, sitting in the chair in front of their desk. "What brings you here today?"

"Thank you for seeing me, Ms. Alexopoulou. And, um, everyone. My problem is with my impending marriage. I'd like to request permission to cancel the engagement."

"Your marriage? The one *we* assigned? The one to whom is probably the most desirable, wealthy phoenix woman available?" the man on the far right asks.

The incredulous look on his face tells me it might be harder to convince him to let me out of this than I'd hoped it would be. I slow my breathing and keep my posture straight. I can do this.

"I'm sure you can see many reasons why this would be a less-than-ideal decision, Mr. Onassis," Ms. Alexopoulou replies with a single lifted eyebrow. "And we don't particularly appreciate this gift being rejected, I must admit."

"And I'm sure you're very aware of the consequences of not following through with this contract, should we decide not to change our minds, correct?" the man on the far right asks, the look on his face making it clear he doesn't expect to change his mind.

"Yes, I am *very* aware. I know this was a careful decision by the Council of Phoenixes. Please don't get me wrong, I appreciate the opportunity, and I did plan to follow through, I really did. The thing is, I've found love. *True Love.* It's new but it's real. I have to follow it, and therefore I must end things with Iris."

Sweat runs down the back of my neck as I watch the four of them exchange glances. Whatever decision they're about to make passes silently between them. They've known one another for hundreds of years. The need to speak passed by long ago.

A third man, Mr. Atlas, sets his elbow on the desk then settles his chin on his hands.

"Mr. Onassis, you know True Love is not taken lightly by our people," Mr. Atlas says. "It is the *only* thing that can break your contract without fault. However, if your feelings are as untried as you are implying, then we would like you to take another week to ensure you are *certain* of them before the contract is broken. Simple infatuation is no excuse to break the contract—it must be *Fated Love* and nothing else. If you are still certain after one week, then you may return and your request will be granted."

It's not exactly what I wanted, but it's better than nothing. I know my feelings for Lara won't change. I felt it in that kiss and the signs have been there since I first saw her. She's my True Love. The Council's answer is as good as a yes. The pressure in my chest relaxes by half.

"Thank you, Mr. Atlas. Thank you, everyone."

"We need you to understand, however," Mr. Atlas interrupts, "Iris is very powerful. Frankly, we don't know how she's going to handle the news. You know how she is, I'm sure. Always had a temper, that one. If she doesn't react well, things could go to shit."

"We are also fully aware that she intends to try for a seat on the Council. She may see this broken contract as bad for her public image. Tread carefully," Ms. Alexopoulou says, long nails tapping on the desk in front of her. "Love and politics don't mix."

I swallow hard at their words. I've never heard a member of the Council speak so bluntly about another phoenix. They're right, though. Iris's transformation skills are some of the strongest among the phoenixes. Emily's dog can attest to that. She might be as strong as any of the Council members, even. If she does something to me, I won't be able to fight back. I'll be relying on her being a sane person and not reacting to the news with violence. Let's hope that's the case.

"I'm sure everything will be fine. It's True Love, after all." Judging by the somber looks on their faces, the confident smile I attempt does not have the intended reassuring effect.

"You don't know what can happen when a vain, powerful woman is publicly embarrassed," Ms. Alexopoulou replies.

There's a moment of heavy silence before Mr. Atlas slaps a hand on the desk.

"Well, if things go as you expect, we'll see you in a week. If not, then we'll see you at the wedding. Have a good afternoon, Mr. Onassis."

When I exit the building, I lean against the glass for a minute and sigh. *As good as a yes.* I just have to fake it with Iris for a week, make her think everything is okay, and act like everything is normal. Then, I'm free.

Smiling as I walk to my car, absorbing the energizing sun, I text Lara, something I was afraid I may never get to do again. My fingers buzz merrily across the screen as I text her. My True Love.

Me: Hey there. What are you up to today?

I make it to my car and get inside, put on my seatbelt, then feel the buzz of my phone. *Yes!*

Lara: Not much, Blondie. About to go get a coffee. I'm tired. Stayed up too late thinking last night.

Me: Thinking? About what?

Lara: A certain someone.

The grin on my face is so wide it hurts.

Me: Who would that be?

Lara: Well, he's smart, handsome, sweet...

Me: Hmm. He sounds great. I don't know if I have a chance against someone like that.

Lara: Well, maybe he's not that smart.

Me: Then it sounds like I do have a chance. Do you want some company for that coffee?

Lara: If you don't mind seeing me looking like a hot mess.

Me: I don't think it's possible for you to look anything other than beautiful.

Lara: Maybe you are pretty smart after all.

Me: Tell me where to meet you, beautiful.

Chapter Eight

Lara

"Why am I not surprised you're drinking a hot, cinnamon beverage when it's nearly a hundred degrees out? You got a furnace in there or something?" I shake my head at Luke when he walks to the table with his cup of hot cinnamon tea.

"You are what you eat and all that. Can't help that I'm hot stuff." He shrugs and takes a long drink of the boiling hot beverage.

"Oh hell no." I can't help but laugh. The man has the corniest personality. For some reason, I'm a sucker for it. "Anyway, what are you up to today?"

"I have a late shift at the clinic. There is a kids' charity that comes in every month, and we do some free work for them. We keep the clinic open later so we can get as many patients in as possible. After that, I'll probably just grab some food and sleep. How about you?"

"Well, I ain't doing charity work for kids, so whatever I say next will be a let down." We both laugh. "I'll just be working the closing shift. Trying to get those commission sales. Doing the real humanitarian work, saving spotted puppies one sale at a time."

"See, making a difference in the world." He raises his cup. I tap mine to it. "What are you doing tomorrow? It's Saturday. I have it off if you're interested in getting together."

"Well, at least one weekend shift tends to be mandatory in retail. Mine is Sunday this week, so, yeah! If you want to get together tomorrow, I can. I don't know if that's too many days in a row together for you or—"

"Nope, it's perfect," he jumps in. "Did you have a preference for what you'd like to do? Or I could plan something?"

"Hmm. There's this theater near me that plays older films on Saturday evenings. They're playing one this week that's a guilty favorite of mine, but I never got a chance to see it on the big screen when it was first released. It's this video game movie, kind of a spooky one, about this little girl who's sleepwalking and talking about this town. So, her parents take her there to try to figure out what's going on. And—"

He holds his hands up and smiles in a cheeky way that I already know means he's gonna say something goofy.

"Say no more. You want to take me to a spooky movie so that you can pretend to be scared and cling on to my arm. I'll protect you and all of that. You don't have to ask twice."

Yep, goofy.

"Mhm. Sure. Whatever makes you happy, Blondie." I roll my eyes as I take a drink of my iced latte.

"Oof, *Blondie.* That's twice today." He clutches his chest. "I'll have to work hard at the movie tomorrow to earn back my title."

"Wouldn't hurt." I check the time on my phone and see that it's getting uncomfortably close to time for work. "Damn. I got to go. Text me later and I'll give you the details on the theater."

"That I will. You have a wonderful day." He takes hold of my hand as we stand and kisses the back of it. "Until tomorrow."

We part ways, me heading to work a little early so I can toss on some makeup in the office before my shift starts. I don't bother going full glam or anything, but I try to look presentable enough. Our customers can be judgy about that type of thing.

Before I hit the time clock, my phone shakes in my back pocket. I'm not supposed to take it out on the floor, but no one listens to that rule. When there are cute new guys that may text, I certainly ain't gonna follow it. And text he does.

Luke: Are you sure you won't be too scared tomorrow? I don't want you to get nightmares.

Me: Nightmares? Really?

Luke: Yep. You might faint from fright.

Me: Boy, bye.

Luke: Okay, okay. You'll have to make sure to let me know if you need me to stay over and keep you company.

Luke: Because of the nightmares, of course. Just in case.

Me: Uh huh.

Me: You are too goofy. I'm going to work now. See you soon.

Luke: Enjoy your day!

I put away the phone and shake my head. He definitely likes me. No guy texts this much unless they're actually into someone. I'm pretty sure I'm into him too. *Hmm.* Maybe there's a chance he will come over after the movie tomorrow. I won't be having any nightmares, though.

Chapter Nine

Luke

"Perfect seats. Yes!" Lara sits her plump behind down into the cushy red seat in the upper center of the theater. She shoves a handful of salty popcorn into her mouth and chews happily, a rogue piece falling past the cleavage showing in her pale-yellow halter top. "I love movies. Sorry if I get ultra enthusiastic. It's just something I really enjoy, and I don't get to go nearly often enough lately."

"You can be as openly enthusiastic as you want. You being excited makes me feel excited. Seriously." I take a handful of sadly bland popcorn and munch it, barely holding back the huge grin trying to break free.

Her leg shakes with barely contained excitement as she watches the ads play on the big screen. Red licorice snaps loudly as she bites off a chunk of it. Classic candy choice.

"We can go whenever you want," I promise. "I'd be happy to go with you."

"Yeah?" She peels her gaze away from the big screen and locks it to mine. "You like movies, too?"

"Yeah, I like going to the movies." *With you.*

She grins widely. "That's awesome. We should go to the next one of these re-releases. Next week."

"That would be great." Especially since I'll be free from Iris by then. No guilt.

Just then, the lights dim and the previews for the next movies start. I love the previews. I'm locked in. We barely talk or interact at all for the entire movie. Turns out, it's now going to be a guilty pleasure of mine, too.

When it's over, we walk outside with the crowd and once we hit the outdoors, we move to the side of the exit. We stand pressed against the brick front of the building where no one is streaming past.

"Alright, you have to admit the guy with the pyramid on his head was kind of hot," Lara says.

I blink at her quietly a few times before responding.

"He was a murderer, Lara."

She shrugs. "Everyone has a few issues."

I rub my forehead as I laugh.

"Okay, what would you like to do now, Mrs. Pyramid Lady?"

"I don't know. I took a cab here. We either walk somewhere or you drive."

"It's kind of casual, but there's a hot dog stand a couple of blocks away."

"Yeah, I know it. But I don't eat meat."

"I know, neither do I. But they have these loaded cheese fries that you can order vegetarian. They're so good. It's a top veggie secret." I must look so proud of myself, but it's alright, I feel like peacocking about this incredible find.

"Alright, let's go."

We walk the two short blocks to get the fries, and they're made really quick. They're *so good.* We gobble them up in no time flat, despite the portions being huge.

"What the hell was in these?" She asks through the last mouthful of her fries. "I almost want to eat the container to get more of the taste."

I can feel my eyelids grow heavy as my gaze heats. I think back to my lips on hers.

"That's how I felt after kissing you. Craving your taste. Wanting more and more."

She sets down the fry container and watches me closely.

"Then why did you leave so abruptly? Until you texted me again, I wasn't sure you were even into me. Thought maybe I was a terrible kisser and didn't know it." She huffs out a soft laugh.

"That's definitely not the case." I reach across the table and take her hand in both of mine. "It's just that I felt...I don't know how to say it. It was something *big.* My mind was whirling, and I needed to process it. I'm sorry. The last thing I wanted to do was upset you."

"That's some heavy talk for two and a half dates, Cutie," she says with a nervous, breathy chuckle.

"Well, I'm back to Cutie, so you can't be totally frightened off. Right?" I turn over her hand and massage her palm, my eyes watching the motion to avoid looking into hers. "I'm not too scary, I promise. I'm just a guy who happens to have found someone he really, really likes. A lot. And I don't need to pretend I don't know how I feel just because we haven't known each other very long. I'll save the games for wherever your sexy pyramid-headed guy comes from."

I look up and give her the most charming smile I can in my vulnerable state. She's looking at me with her brow furrowed, as if she can't figure out what to make of me. Things are tense between us for a moment until she shakes her head and slaps the table with the hand I'm not holding.

"I told you he was sexy," she says with a laugh. I join her in merriment until we have tears in our eyes, letting the tension of the moment leak out. She sighs. "No, you're not too scary. I don't know, though—I still might have nightmares. Might need someone to stay the night and comfort me. Not certain what I should do about that."

"Well, I know a guy who's free tonight. He's nearby. Tall, handsome, doctor. Not afraid of the dark even a little bit."

He's also supposed to go shopping with Iris tomorrow, but we'll ignore that nagging in my gut for the moment. Ugh.

"Sounds perfect. He's gonna need to be able to stay up in bed for a long time. To watch for the nightmares and all. You think he can?" She leans forward, her breasts pressing against the wooden picnic table.

"He's got no problem staying up in bed. I can tell you right now you've already kept him up enough."

She smirks as she stands, hikes her purse strap onto her shoulder, and walks back toward the theater. She turns her head toward me over her shoulder and says, "Come on, let's see how long you can stay up."

I stumble rushing out of my seat to go after her, but thankfully manage not to fall. She's turned around and doesn't notice. Good.

My palms are sweating. I can feel the light inside me blazing. She's my *True Love,* and she just invited me to spend the night with her. I can't fuck this up.

A girl walks past with a chihuahua. My mind snaps to Iris, a fish flopping in her hands as she laughs. My stomach twists for a moment when I look up at Lara, guilt simmering in my guts.

She turns around when she realizes I'm walking behind her at a snail's pace. "You coming or what?"

"Yeah, sorry," I say as I increase my speed, negative thoughts replaced by her glow, "Was just distracted by a fantastic view."

She wiggles her rear end and sticks out her tongue before slapping me on the bicep.

"There's plenty of time to admire the goodies later. Let's get to your car. It's hot as hell out here." She waves a hand in front of her glistening face.

I barely notice the heat. My people come from fire, after all. But if she's overheated and wants to get somewhere cooler, then she's getting what she wants.

"Then let's get you inside. We've got some staying up to do, anyway."

Chapter Ten

Lara

I didn't plan on letting this man into my apartment so soon, but *the best laid plans of mice and men* and all that. Thankfully, I keep the place tidy. I'm also thankful that I shaved and wore damn cute panties. Can never be too prepared.

"I like your apartment. It's very colorful," Luke says as he turns around in the center of my living room, looking at my décor.

It is colorful, he's right. My parents were a little bit of the wannabe hippie type. They loved tie-dye, old Psychedelic poster art, stuff like that. I took after them in that area and my wall art and furnishings definitely show it.

"Let me guess, your house is a lot of beige, right? Maybe some white here and there?" I smirk as I sit on the sofa, draping my arm across the back.

"Hey now!" He drops next to me, mouth open in indignation, "I have a lot of blue in my house. And brown. We have plants too!"

"Plants? My lord, I might faint."

"Lara, are you insinuating I'm boring? Bland?" Luke slaps a hand over his heart.

"I don't think the man who had a basket full of hot peppers when I met him is bland. Are you boring? *Hmm.*" I tap my chin and lean toward him until we're only a few inches apart. "Why don't you show me you know how to have a good time?"

A sudden heat washes over me as Luke leans into my space. Arms on either side of my body, he prowls slowly forward, nose against mine. I'm flat against the sofa and he's looming over me. The heat increases as his breathing grows more rapid. *Is he feverish?* The copper of his eyes seems to almost glow, like coals in a fire. *Maybe I've made a mistake.*

But then he's kissing me, his lips are soft, and it feels like we're breathing from the same lungs. I wrap a leg around his hip, and he moans into the crook of my neck, rubs his clothed erection against the seam of my shorts. He kisses and licks my neck, behind my ear, nips at my earlobe. Our hearts are beating at the same pace.

"Luke. Take me to the bedroom," I whisper.

"Anything, Lara."

I point the way, and he carries me to my room. When he sets me on the bed, I don't stay down—I stand straight up and begin to undress. Luke watches me for a moment before he joins me. His eyes stay on my body as he removes his clothes, and mine stay on his. I like what I see. A lot. He's fit and has an incredible cock.

The best part is the unexpected tattoos. Loads of fiery feathers all up and down his body. Makes the little goldfish I have on my hip seem like nothing, that's for sure.

"Well, hot damn. Didn't expect that," I say as I finish undressing.

I walk over to him and set my hand against his chest, look up into his eyes. Luke wraps his arms around me and looks at me with a smirk.

"You're exactly what I expected," he says.

"Yeah? What's that?"

"Fucking perfection," he growls as he lifts me, then lays us in the bed.

Everything is a whirl of feelings then as we go from a frantic tangling of tongues, to him licking my neck and chest, to kissing up my thighs. Things begin to come into focus again the first time his tongue touches my clit.

Hot. Fire. Burning.

I pull back from his spicy tongue. *What the fuck was that?* He pulls me back toward him. He softly kisses along my center, relaxing me again. Slowly, he slips a couple fingers inside me, curling just right. Then, as I'm sighing in pleasure, his tongue is back on me.

Spicy!

I start to pull away but he *yoinks* me again.

"Just go with it," he rasps out. "Give it a minute."

"But—"

"Trust me."

Alright, coochie. We're giving this man about ten seconds. If he's still got a jalapeño tongue at that point, we're tapping out!

He restarts from relaxing kisses, then moves on to sigh-inducing inner motions. Once again, he lightly grazes me with his tongue. It's that burning tingle again. I flinch but don't pull away. His tongue makes a second pass, this time lingering a little longer and pressing a little firmer. The burn moves further up my body, like fire creeping up my veins. He kisses, licks, and sucks on my clit for I don't even know how long but in my haze feels like a lifetime.

The burn runs through my entire body. When exactly the feeling turns from unwanted to incredible, I'm unable to place. All I know is that now everything is perfect. *Luke* is perfect. I am a fire only he can feed. He's the oxygen I need to burn.

One more moment and I cry out, my back bowed, hands gripping his pale hair. In the white ceiling, I see visions of flames and feathers before my heart begins to slow down, my blood cools, and the ceiling is nothing more than paint and spackle.

Luke kisses my stomach, my chest, my neck. His hard cock presses into my hip, leaking hot fluid onto my skin. He whispers against my cheek, "Are you alright?"

"I'm more than alright. Confused about what just happened. But very good, thank you," I say, my eyes still on the ceiling. "Did you see the—actually, never mind."

"I'm glad you feel good."

Thankfully, he accepts my odd response without question because I couldn't really explain it if he did question it. Instead, he repositions himself so that he's on all fours, his body caging mine in.

One hand goes to the back of my neck so that he can redirect my attention to him. He kisses me until I'm focused again. When I'm moaning and pushing my hips against him, he pulls his lips away from mine, just until we're far enough apart for him to get words out.

"Shall we then?" he says, barely loud enough for me to hear.

"Yes," I sigh back.

And then we're making love.

Chapter Eleven

Luke

"Yes," she answers me on the slightest of breaths.

A soft shudder of anticipation rolls through me as we arrange our hips, eye contact never breaking. I swallow hard as I line the head of my cock up with the sopping-wet entrance of her cunt. Watching her come on my tongue was nearly enough to have me bursting into flames. I'll certainly have to be careful.

"Oh, Luke. Yes." Lara grabs my hips and uses the leverage to push herself forward. My cock enters her several inches in one thrust. "Yes, yes. Fuck."

Very careful. Human woman. Don't start a fire.

It is, in fact, very easy for two phoenixes to start a fire during sex. Even one, when in True Love with a human, can start a fire if they let go of themselves too quickly.

"Slow down, darling," I force out between clenched teeth.

"You don't want to burst yet, huh?" She giggles.

I huff a laugh. *You have no idea.* "Something like that."

Sliding into her achingly slowly, I manage not to set the room ablaze. When I'm fully seated inside her, I take a moment to stop and appreciate the feeling of the two of us, connected. I gaze deeply into her dark brown eyes, wondering how many generations before her had the same eyes—as many as share mine? More? I run my thumb across the wavy baby hair over her forehead, the smooth skin on the flat bridge of her nose, her lips still wet from kisses.

Lara's fingertips dig into my hips as she writhes underneath me. "Come on, lover boy, show me that good time you promised."

"Well," I kiss her as I slowly pull nearly all the way out, "if I promised."

Our next kiss leads to another and another as I glide smoothly in and out of her, gradually building up the light between us. *Don't start a fire*, yes, but the light—that's different.

"Oh fuck, you feel so good," Lara moans. She looks between us, at the point where we connect, and her brow furrows. I distract her with a kiss.

Don't look. I know there's a very soft glow there right now. Barely noticeable. I have to get her mind distracted, so she won't notice it, like I did before with my tongue. I roll us so that we're on our sides, face to face, kissing wildly, while slyly maneuvering myself behind her. Soon enough, she's facing the headboard and I'm entering her beautiful cunt from the back. I stroke her long neck with one hand, keeping her from looking between us, while I circle her clit with the other.

Fuck. It's pat your head and rub your tummy time, for fuck's sake, but I manage to keep my dick inside her, nonetheless.

The light between us begins to shine brighter. It branches off throughout our bodies as it grows into our veins. Lara is now in the place in her mind where she can accept the light, the heat, so I let go of her neck. She whips her body backward, slamming into me with a loud moan. Her cunt is like a vise around my cock as she comes, each pulse squeezing me tighter. The light travels farther up our veins.

When her grip on me softens and her body sags, I let her fall softly to the bed, but I don't stop our session. My desire only increases. Seeing the light through her like marble, feeling my heat in her skin, pushes me nearly to the breaking point. I grab her hips and fuck into her hard, fast.

"Luke, there's a bird," Lara whimpers just before she comes again with a shout.

This time I join her. Releasing inside of her is like nothing I've felt before. It's not about the sex itself—though, of course that's enjoyable—it's the joining of our destiny.

As my seed spills into her soft, warm insides, I get images of feathers. Soft, white feathers, and fire. I don't know what it means. Visions are strange and rarely straightforward. But fire must be good for phoenixes. And, of course, Lara and I are fated lovers so whatever else it means could only be positive, I'm sure.

When the light begins to fade, I wrap my arms around Lara and turn her around with me so that we can cuddle face-to-face. She looks bewildered but pleased. I'll have to explain the phoenix thing soon, I suppose.

First, I need to get rid of Iris. One thing at a time.

"That was really—wow," Lara says with a soft laugh.

"A good time?" I smirk.

"Yeah, pretty decent." She smiles.

"Oh, okay. Good to know I have room for improvement."

"You can show me how much you've improved next week, if you like." She raises an eyebrow in question.

"Ah, a second chance. I would like that very much."

"If I didn't have to work tomorrow, I'd be up for giving you chances all night, but—bills don't pay themselves."

"Well, I'll figure out a way to wait. Somehow." I kiss her hand. "We have all the time in the world ahead of us."

Chapter Twelve

Lara

"That'll be five hundred and forty-two dollars, please," I tell the lady at the register. She attempts to tap her card on the machine about seven times before giving up and swiping it. I smile awkwardly when she angrily snatches the receipt from my hand. "Have a fine day now!"

As the aggravated woman nears the exit, the door opens for her. A man's arm holds it as she leaves. Once she's gone, he enters. It's a man I'm beginning to know well. Everything else in the store seems to fade away, leaving only him in my sights. My face lights up with a grin as I dash out from behind the counter and toward the front door.

"Hey there, silly goose!" I shout and wrap my arms around Luke as he makes it all the way into the store. I plant a kiss on his cheek with a giggle I know makes me sound like a schoolgirl, but I just can't help. "I missed you as soon as you left this morning, Cutie."

"Silly goose?" a woman's voice asks. "Silly goose? My fiancé Luke? Ah, yes. What a *silly goose* he is."

I feel then how frozen stiff Luke is. When I step away from him, I catch his eyes. All I see in them is shock and sorrow. Behind him is a woman I hadn't seen enter because of how blinded by excitement I was. She's beautiful. And *furious.* There's a smile on her face but it's all *teeth*. Her gold eyes are filled with so much rage they look like they could burst into flames.

I look back at Luke and his face is begging for forgiveness. Copper eyes already half flooded with tears.

I close my expression entirely. No man will ever make me cry in public. Especially not a cheating one. *Fuck that.*

"How do you know my Luke?" the woman asks.

"I don't think I know him at all," I reply, my tone flat, "Clearly, I made a huge mistake."

"Clearly," she replies. "I'm Iris. What's your name?"

She holds out one pale delicate, hand. My stomach sinks. She looks like a perfect doll. Nothing to be afraid of. But something is *screaming* at me not to touch her.

"You look like you're afraid of me." She laughs, so gently, like little bells. "You silly goose."

She's right. I'm just being silly.

"I'm Lara. Nice to—" My hand connects with hers, and the next thing I know is *pain.*

"Silly, silly goose," the woman, Iris, says in a sing-song voice as she squeezes my hand so hard I feel as if my bones will shatter.

"Iris, what are you doing? Stop!" Luke shouts.

My bones *do* shatter then. At least some of them do. Not sure which ones. I can't tell exactly what's happening because *all* of me hurts, but I can *hear* the crack of the bones.

"It's not like I'm going to kill her, Luke," Iris says calmly, her voice full of mirth.

"Stop whatever you're doing. She didn't do anything wrong!" Luke says as he grabs her arm.

Iris shoves him off of her with her other hand. He crashes into a display of heels, knocking everything to the floor. I scream when I see my arm shriveling up in front of me. The sound comes out as a hideous cross between a hiss and a wail.

"Don't stop me, Luke. *You* did this. What were you going to do? Keep a whore on the side during our marriage? Or try to call it off and make me an embarrassment to our people? Ruin my chance at a Council seat? What makes you think you could do that to *me?*" She shrieks out the last word so shrilly I'm surprised our glass displays don't shatter.

My skin itches like it's being pricked with a million pins, and I find myself unable to form words to shout anything at all.

"Iris, please, she's innocent," Luke sobs.

"Just a sweet, innocent thing," Iris says mockingly. She holds me to her chest. "Just a silly little goose."

She's holding me to her chest. My feet can't touch the floor. Oh fuck, oh fuck.

I try my best to get away from her but whatever hold she has on me is as strong as before. The best I can do is wiggle around a lot and flap my arms. My—

I don't have arms. *I don't have arms.*

"Please change her back. I'll never talk to her again. I swear. I'm so sorry," Luke sobs, begging on his knees before Iris.

Wings. I have wings. Not arms.

"You aren't convincing me. Sort of just seems like you're sorry you got caught," she snaps.

"Please—" he pulls on the hem of her dress.

"I'm tired of you," she says calmly as she sets her free hand on Luke's forehead.

His eyes grow wide as he tries to pull away, but it's too late. In a flash of smoke, what was my handsome lover boy is now a majestic copper-colored bird.

The bird is unlike anything I've ever seen. The animal itself stands maybe four feet tall from head to toe, but its tail is at least an additional six feet long. Its feathers are a mix of various shades of orange, red, and yellow, all coated in a metallic copper glaze and tipped in gold. Its eyes are the exact same copper as Luke's. When it opens its mouth to cry mournfully, I see it has a tongue made of flame, real flame. With each cry, I see the shaky haze of heat warp its body.

"Oh, quiet," Iris snaps. "I'll turn you back when I'm done. You'll be fine."

The bird—Luke, I suppose—cries out again.

"I said 'quiet!' I'm going home to think. I know very well I'm not *supposed to* transform fellow phoenixes against their will, but I'm sure they'll make an exception considering the circumstances. And like I said, I'll switch you back—eventually. Now, come on. Let's get out of here before someone sees you."

I try to wriggle free from the woman's grasp as we exit the building. She's pushing the Luke-bird along like a slow toddler while we get to her car. I do my best to make it as hard as possible for her to get me inside, but eventually she does, strapping me in with the seatbelt. I manage to make a honking noise during the commotion that, combined with the few physical and verbal clues I have, finally tells me what I am.

A freaking goose. Why couldn't I have called him a silly *lion* or something?

I'm too stunned to think of an escape plan while Iris is shoving a very loud Luke-bird into the trunk. *What will I do now that I'm a goose? Will I be this way forever? Could I be happy like this?* When it slams closed, I'm shocked out of my introspection. My struggle to get free begins anew when Iris gets into the car.

"Alright. Well, that's a no to shoe shopping, I guess. Another day. I'm going to call and see if there's a petting zoo in some shitty little town somewhere that wants a dirty bird," Iris says as she pulls out of the parking lot.

We get right onto the freeway, as it's pretty close to my work. I try to figure out how to get out of the seatbelt with my beak. Or is it my bill? Whatever a goose's mouth is called. Not having any teeth or fingers is a serious issue. I poke at the button from different angles, growing increasingly frustrated. *I will not be in a petting zoo. Argh.*

Suddenly, the back windows roll down and I can feel the wind ruffling my feathers.

"If you can get out of the seatbelt, you're welcome to try your luck through the windows. You'll have a damn hard time finding someone to change you back though, consider that. Who will you go to if you escape? But if you're in my car when we get to my house, I get to do whatever I want with you. I might do something terrible, or I might just change you back and set you free. Haven't decided. Either way, up to you. Go or stay. How about that? Give you a choice?" Iris asks, her eyes flashing like coins in the rear-view mirror. "Not much of one, I admit, but I am feeling generous."

I don't know what the fuck I'll do as a goose out in the wild, but I know I sure as shit don't want whatever happens to me to be left up to that bitch. Finding a fucking wizard or whatever the hell I need to change me back has to got to be the better option. I'll get to Vera and spell out words in the dirt or something. I don't know. I'll figure it out.

I stop my panic struggles and focus on what needs to be done. I just have to push the button, and the seatbelt will come undone. I can do this. It ain't that easy to aim my beak when my eyes are on the side of my head. The monocular vision thing geese have is meant for watching out for predators, not for escaping from luxury vehicles. It just so happens this vehicle is being operated by a maniac.

Ugh, I need to get out. Most of my movement so far has just been panicking, not exactly fine motor skills. But I can learn. I'm smart. I got this.

"You sure that's the best choice? You can stop struggling and relax," says the predator in the rear-view mirror.

Hell no. I try again.

Click.

The seatbelt buckle comes undone. *Yes!* I just barely stop myself from getting tangled in the belt in my hurry to escape. Instead, I wait for it to retract before I scramble to my feet.

Whoa. This feels weird. Big body. Wobbly neck. Skinny legs. Now that there ain't anything holding me down and I have to move on my own, I'm not so sure about this.

"Better get a move on if you want to go, goosey. I'll be home soon," Iris warns.

That's enough to make me sure. I jump onto the door handle and then up to the open window. Okay. Now I need to figure out how to fly. *Boy, the wind sure is moving fast. Pretty wobbly up—*

And then I'm flying. Well, no, I'm not. I'm sort of flapping in the wind in a mostly horizontal but ultimately downward direction. I manage to stay in the air probably about forty seconds, eventually crashing *hard* on the opposite side of the freeway. At least I made it into the grass side of the shoulder and not in the middle of traffic. That's nice. But I hurt my leg pretty bad. My wing too. And my head hurts. *Shit, I don't feel so good.*

"Hey, here's another one. I think that's about it though," a gruff voice says right before someone lifts me off the ground. *Aww damn, not more lifting.*

"Wow, it got tossed all the way over there? Who knew one little fender bender could have a truck full of geese spread across the highway that far? Wild," an older man says. "Put it in with the others and let's get home before your woman has a shit fit."

"She's gonna already considering all the geese that got hit. You know how she is about profit margins," the younger man says as he opens the back door of a truck. Inside it are cages and cages of geese. He's about to open one of them when he pauses, looks closely at my face, and steps away from the truck. "Hey, Jim! This goose ain't one of ours."

The man pokes his head out of the driver's side of the truck. "How do you know that? Looks like ours."

"We mark ours dumb ass, since they're special and organic or whatever Mazie markets them as. If they aren't marked, she can't do her little marketing videos about them, so they aren't useful to her. Except maybe, I don't know," he looks me over as I try not to pass out from the pain I'm in, "I suppose she could use the feathers. Maybe we could eat it."

"Hell yeah, we could eat it. Get your ass in the truck and let's get back in time to butcher it."

Butcher it. Eat it.

Fucking cheating Luke.

I think at some point, women have to wonder if dating is really worth all the trouble.

Chapter Thirteen

Luke

"**L**ET ME GO YOU FUCKING BITCH!"

She can't understand me *exactly* when we're in different forms, but Iris gets the point well enough, I'm sure. It'll sound like a cawing bird to anyone else but her and I are both phoenixes—she knows I'm *pissed*.

More than anything though, I'm terrified. I need to get to Lara. When I'm in my bird form, my primal senses are stronger. I can *feel* Lara's essence near me because she's my True Love. We're connected. She probably doesn't believe it at the moment—probably hates me, actually—but it's still true. I can feel her, and I know that a moment ago she left the car. I don't know how, seeing as we haven't stopped moving. But she's growing farther and farther away every second.

I have to get to her before she gets hurt. Anything could happen. We're in open country and at the moment she's a fucking farm animal. Some kind of wild animal or huge stray dog could be out there waiting to maul her to death. *Oh fuck.*

"FUCKING LET ME OUT!"

When I shift my position further back I notice something glowing on the trunk door. My heart starts racing. I saw this in a video about how to escape a kidnapping. It's the trunk's emergency release! I never thought I'd use this information, but I guess it pays to scroll the Internet aimlessly for hours in the middle of the night.

Okay. Good. I angle my body so that I can grab it with my talons and beak, making sure I've got a good hold on it, and then *tug.*

POP!

The trunk flies open and my shiny ass is airborne. It's not every day you see an Ancient Greek phoenix flying above a Texas Highway, but for a couple of very confused travelers, today is that day. The Council will not be happy to hear about that, but I think they'll forgive me considering the circumstances.

I get high above the road, making sure to keep in the sunlight so that anyone looking will have to avert their eyes. I take a deep breath and let myself feel for Lara. Just Lara. *Where are you, my Darling?*

I feel her. She's gotten so far away. But I'm fast. I fly with no regard for secrecy. Fuck trying to hide. No one is paying attention to me anyway. People are dealing with their own bullshit.

It takes a while, but I feel her getting close, really close. I land in a tree outside of a little farm with a sign out front that says "Mazie & Co. Organic, Free Range, All Natural Geese." *What the fuck does that mean? I guess Lara doesn't belong here then, because she's certainly an unnatural goose.* I feel a twinge in my chest that tells me not only is Lara close, but that something's wrong. *Fuck.*

This close to a group of people, I don't want to be too conspicuous. It's one thing to fly around high up above the freeway—people can always assume it was a trick of the light and not an actual shiny, golden bird—but when you're right next to them, things get dicey. That's when they start to freak out. Having to fight for my life would really make it harder to save Lara. So, I'll be careful.

I stick to the shadows as best I can, moving slowly, following the feel of Lara in my chest. The place is nice as far as farms go, I guess. The animals seem like they're taken care of at least. Well, things are nice until I get to the area with the geese. Then it's a shit show.

Two men are letting geese out of crates into a large barn, inspecting them as they're let out. Some of them look all beat up. There's a woman with them yelling and fussing. I can't understand what's going on, so I creep along the side of the truck to get a listen and to better see the geese.

"There better not be a single scratch on any of the last few. I can't believe you. Got ten of my best geese run over," the woman says.

Run over? I almost start to panic before remembering that I can still feel Lara. It wasn't her. If I can feel her, she's alive.

One of the men takes out another crate and dumps two geese out and declares them fine. A final crate comes out, but he doesn't open it right away, his hand pausing on the latch.

"Now, hon, this isn't one of yours. We found this one out wandering. It's a little bit beat up but looks otherwise healthy. I think it might have gotten hit or something. We were thinking if you can't use it for the business, we could use it for the home."

"I don't know how I feel about road goose," the woman replies. "Let me see it."

"Sure thing," the man says as he opens the crate and tugs a goose out by the neck.

This one does look a little pitiful. One of its legs is bent wrong, and it doesn't look like there's as much strength in its wing as there should be. But the thing most noticeable about it to me is the way it makes my heart race. Even as a goose, she's just *brighter* than everything else.

That's my Lara.

Oh no. Oh no no. *That* is Lara. Shit.

The woman looks Lara up and down. She crosses her arms and nods. "That's fine. I can use the feathers. I don't think I can eat roadkill, though."

"Hey, it ain't roadkill if it ain't dead!" the second man says with a laugh.

"Whatever you want to call it. Just save me the feathers." She kisses the man holding Lara on the cheek and walks away.

"Alright, Mazie," the man says as he shoves my love back into the crate. He turns to the other man. "Do you happen to know how to cook a goose?"

The men both laugh.

"You know I do! Let's go have a smoke and then get that bird cleaned."

I'm frozen. What is someone even supposed to do in this situation? If I could get to another phoenix, I could ask for help. I don't know if I'd have enough time to get back before...I just need to think of something else.

The men walk toward a different building, one of them carrying the crate. I scurry after, lingering behind a bush in front of the entryway. They talk for just a moment inside, but then they're out, stepping around to the side of the building. I take my chance and dart into the open door.

The room inside is as bad as I'd feared. The smell of death permeates the floors. The essence of fear from so many lost lives is so strong I feel like I'm choking on it. In the center of the room sits the crate holding Lara. Above her is a metal funnel of sorts—a killing cone, it's called. I need to get her out of here before she's in that thing. *Oh god. I can't believe this is happening.*

I tap the crate with my beak to get Lara's attention. She raises her head as much as she can in the cramped space to look at me before turning her long neck away. I may not be able to understand her in words but I get the point—she wants nothing to do with me. Rightfully so. I should have been honest. I should have done so many things differently. I wish I could change everything.

I search for the latch on her cage, but when I find it, I'm forced to pause. There's no fucking way I can undo that type of latch without hands. At my age, I've gotten good with my talons, but I'm gonna need something else. *Shit. I could heat up the metal, but I'd hurt Lara in the process.* I look around frantically for anything that could help, but nothing comes to mind. I need more time.

Footsteps have my head swinging toward the side of the building. *Okay. I'll just have to wait until they open the cage. Then I'll surprise them. It's my last shot, but it'll work. It has to.*

I tuck myself into the corner on top of a barrel, under a shelf, and wait. The two men come in shortly after, laughing about who knows what. One of them leans against a table, grinning, as if they aren't planning to murder the love of my life. The other goes right for the cage where they're keeping her. I slowly shuffle forward as he opens the latch. His dry, cracked hand reaches in and pulls out my beloved. She barely fights him. My heart is breaking for her, but my spirit stays strong, as I launch myself from my hiding spot toward the man holding her.

LET GO OF HER!

I snatch at his head with my talons until I see blood. I release a high-pitched screech from the fiery blazes of my throat that I know very well hurts their ears. He drops Lara. As I beat my wings against the man's face, she attempts to stand, but she falls when she puts weight on the broken leg. *Fuck.*

"Goddamnit, get this thing off of me!" the man shouts.

"Yeah, I got it," the other man replies.

Lara flaps her wings, but only one works properly. Still, she slowly pushes her way forward. *Come on. Somehow, we'll make it out.*

"Hurry it up!" the man shouts as I scratch his face.

Lara looks up at me, and for a moment, I almost feel as if I hear her. As if she's saying *Goodbye.*

But that can't be right. Romances don't have sad endings. Especially not ours. Especially not when I love her so much. Not when I haven't said I'm sorry. How can—

And then there's a loud, electric buzz against the back of my head, and everything goes dark.

.

.

.

.

This is the worst headache I've ever had.

The light slowly returns. My body feels stiff—no, restrained. My thoughts become clearer as I wiggle around, realizing I'm tied up. Then I remember what I'm supposed to be doing.

Lara.

I concentrate until my body is hot enough to burn through the ropes wrapped around me. The cages, I guess, weren't big enough for me. Speaking of cages, I look around the room, back to where Lara was, and discover that the cage is gone. The scene in the room is entirely different. I feel as if I'm going to be sick.

Below the killing cone is a large cup that contains what can only be one thing—blood. That's how they work. You put the goose in the cone upside down so just their head and neck poke out of the cone. You electrocute them. Slit their throat. Then bleed them out. Clean meat and feathers and they can't make a fuss.

I look to the opposite side of the room and sure enough there are the feathers. *Her* feathers. I look away but see the area where they—well, no one should have to see those parts of the person they love.

I hurry out of the building before I faint. There's no way I want them to capture me. They can't have us both. As soon as I get out of the doorway, I take flight, but as I pass by the farmhouse, I stall in midair, falling to the ground from pure horror.

I knew they were going to do it, but seeing it, really seeing it, is too much.

In front of the setting sun, the two men and the woman are sitting at a wooden table, carving into a roasted goose. The love of my life, my reason for living, served with potatoes.

I stumble away from the gruesome sight, not sure where I'm even going. It doesn't matter anyway. Nothing matters. Life doesn't matter without Lara.

I end up back where I was, facing the building where they butchered her, where her beautiful feathers still lie. I hop up on top of a rusty post that must have been from an old fence. Two of my feathers get snagged on a jagged bit of metal and come free. They float away, heading toward the building. We're supposed to destroy any of our feathers that come loose—leave no proof for humans and all that. But fuck it. I'm not leaving this spot. I'm done.

I'm so sorry, Lara. I wish I could take it back. You deserved so much better.

I'd do anything, be anything, to give you a happily ever after.

Lara, my darling Lara.

Let my last thoughts be of you.

And with that, I start my fire. I will not protect myself from the heat. I will become ash. When my body tries one last time to be reborn from the ashes, I will resist and scatter into the wind. This is my death. May I find my way to her so that I may beg for forgiveness.

May I find my way to Lara.

Later

A Department Store, Sometime Later

"Are the feathers in this pillow ethically sourced? Like, were the geese harmed?" the young woman asks the sales associate.

"Uh, yeah, totally ethical," replies the sales associate, who is not trained to work in the bedding department. "Happy geese."

"Well, that's good. I'll buy it then. It's perfect."

The sales associate gladly scans the pillow and watches the woman tap her credit card against the machine to pay. The sooner the woman leaves, the sooner he can go back to his favorite section: footwear.

"Here's your receipt," he says and holds it close to her hand.

The woman recoils as if he were covered in poison.

"I don't need it, thank you," she says before hurrying toward the exit, pausing at the hand sanitizer station on her way.

Some people sure are strange, he thinks as he makes his way to the footwear section. He sighs when he sees an orange comforter hanging crookedly off a display. He feels obligated to adjust it as he passes by.

There, nice and tidy, waiting for just the right customer.

Thank You, Apologies, Justice For the Dog

Thank you to those who took a risk and alpha read my first non-romance story.

I apologize to anyone I made sad. People wanted the back-story, so here it is. I don't know why my brain is the way it is.

I promise the dog will be okay. I'll prove it in the final book in the series!

Texas is for Michaela.

Stuffed Up

by Sylvia Morrow

Discussions about death, worrying about life after death, gender swap, spicy sex, police encounter, talking about bed bugs, fear of germs, representation of mental illness that includes a character participating in behavior that is harmful to themselves, seeing a cockroach, reckless driving, outdoor sex, tentacles, tics, implied sex work, chasing, mention of a character from The Phoenix and the Goose burning up, mention of depression at being rejected by a lover.

Chapter One

Anne

Things have changed since Christmas. For one, Ori informed us that the Athans family tree had a hidden branch.

"I can't believe you didn't tell me you had a brother. Of all the secrets to keep!" I shove my glasses up the bridge of my nose, into position. "You know family is important to me!"

"I simply had your best interests at heart, my love." Ori reaches for my hand, an apologetic look in his dark eyes, but I pull away. I'm too upset for hand-holding right now.

"We're not supposed to have secrets. This is really important to me. You broke my trust. You have *family*, Ori! A brother! You might even have other family members out there!" I slap my hands against the sides of my thighs in exasperation. How does he not understand what a big deal this is?

"Well, I do have other family, if you count his partner and daughter. But as for other feathers, I don't think–" Ori doesn't finish that sentence before my eyes nearly bulge out of my head.

"DAUGHTER!?" I shout. "He got someone pregnant? Does that mean I could get pregnant? Oh my God, I'm gonna faint. I'm on birth control, so I'm safe, right? You've never, you know, inside, because of the feathers. So, we're safe, right? But why didn't you tell me it was a possibility?!"

"Oh, calm down." He waves a hand dismissively.

My eyes squint in annoyance at the gesture. He's on thin ice right now.

"Don't tell me to calm down. This is my body. This—"

"She's adopted, darling. You know very well family doesn't have to be about blood. Right, Carl?"

"Uh, yeah. I'd like to stay out of this argument, though. Anne's pretty mad. I'm just gonna work on this map while you two sort this out, if that's alright." Carl turns away from the two of us. I don't blame him. I'd also rather not be having this argument.

Carl has taken up working out the map Ori got from his brother. Carl and I both got copies in our Christmas surprises that we thought were intentionally unlabeled, but it turns out even the original map is incomplete. So, we've had to do all kinds of searches to try to figure out where the heck it's supposed to show. Ori was confident we'd know where the map was supposed to actually be, but he was very wrong. So far, we think it's in South America. Maybe. Carl is trying super hard to figure it out, though.

"*Hmph.* You were barely shocked I kept the *phoenix fire* a secret, a *magic item*, but *this* of all things upsets you? He's only a blanket." Ori crosses his arms, a pout on his perfect lips.

"I could understand why you kept *that* such a big secret, though honestly, I was still kind of mad about it. And by the way, where did you get that? Actually, never mind. We can talk about that later. But you didn't have to keep *Marlon* a secret!"

I cross my arms and give him a stern look. "Ori, I want to meet him. AND his family."

"Even the child?" Ori's nose wrinkles in distaste.

"Even the child, Ori."

"Don't blame me when your belongings are sticky." He smooths the front of his jacket, sniffs, and sighs. "I'll need a ride to the store. You know I'd do anything for you, Anne, but if I must do this, I'd prefer not to have to take the bus during rush hour."

Cotton socks slipping a bit on the freshly polished wooden floors, I jog the half room to the door to grab my keys and purse. He may annoy the hell out of me sometimes, but I do always get my way when it's most important. He's stubborn, but he knows when to give up. I'm still mad at him, but for now, I'll let things cool off.

I'm just way too excited about meeting this brother to stay actively angry. *I wonder if he's like Ori? I can't wait to find out.*

"You got it, you grump. We're going to the store, Carl. Need anything?"

"I'm fine. Ooh! We're out of eggs. You wanted to make that cake." He looks at me with his perfect little puppy dog grin. "Oh, and some laundry soap. By the way, I don't know where all my underwear keeps disappearing to, but I'm getting suspicious of the neighbor across the hall. I'm gonna keep an eye on him. No one touches my underwear but us."

I just want to pat him on the head and call him a good boy. In fact, I'll just have to show him what a good boy he is later. Shivers run down my body at the thought of it.

"Anne, you have goosebumps. Are you cold? I'll get you a sweater," Ori says, rubbing his hands up and down my arms.

I slide on my shoes, double-check for hand sanitizer, and take a few calming breaths. *Time to face the world, Anne.*

"Oh, I'm alright, Ori. Everything is alright."

Chapter Two

Ori

Everything is terrible. The store is loud and crowded. One would think that so soon after a gifting holiday, people would be done with their shopping, but it appears they are not. My plan to get in and out quickly dies on the vine the first time we get trapped in an aisle between two carts. I want to confront the rude customers taking their time perusing shampoo, but I can't. If I make a scene, it will only spell trouble.

"Ori, when we get out of this aisle, you go to Marlon, and I'll wait in the car. It'll be faster. This place is nuts today. As excited as I was to meet him, I don't think I can handle it." Anne wraps her arms tightly around herself, and I notice she's looking very pale.

"Alright darling," I say calmingly against her cheek as I embrace her. "Head out and I promise to meet you as soon as I can. I love you. You did wonderfully, by the way. You tried your best."

"Thank you, Ori." She exhales a shuddering breath into my shoulder. "Okay, they finally moved. I'll see you in a bit."

Anne stands on the toes of her sneakers and plants a quick peck on my cheek. I watch as she walks out the door at a brisk pace, rubbing her fingers against one another at her sides the entire way.

"Move, damn it," an old man in a flat cap barks from behind me. There is an entire half of an aisle empty next to us. Why he needs to be directly behind me, I have no clue.

I turn to face him, rage in my eyes. *No one tells me to look away from my Anne.* Nearly reaching for his wrinkled throat, I stop myself. *No,* I need to calm my temper. I retract my hand, straighten my collar, and head toward the bedding aisle. The man grumbles something behind me as I walk away, unaware of how lucky he is.

At first, I don't see Marlon in the bedding area. With a satisfied grin on my face, I turn around, ready to head to the doors.

"Ori? How's it going?" *Marlon.*

"Hello," I reply disappointedly.

"What can I do for you today?" He replies in his bright and sunny way.

"I would like to know if you'd want to—" I take a deep breath and prepare myself for what I know will be an annoying reaction, "—join my family and me for dinner. You could bring your family as well, of course."

"Wow, sure! A family dinner! That's a fantastic idea, Ori!" Marlon says as he *hugs* me.

I cringe as I stand there, arms straight to the side until he gets it out of his system. When he steps away, he's smiling wide, his gapped front teeth on full display.

"Yes. Anyway, Saturday. Seven. If that's alright. Here's my phone number. Text me and I'll give you the address." Reluctantly, I hand him a note with the number on it.

"That sounds fine! We'll be there! Gosh, a family dinner. This is great!"

"Alright, well, goodbye." I walk out quickly to meet my Anne.

"You asked him? He said yes?" Anne asks as soon as I sit in the car and begin to buckle in. The whole car reeks of her pineapple-scented hand sanitizer.

"Unfortunately, yes. Saturday at seven it is."

My phone dings as I receive a text. Normally, I only get texts from Anne or Carl, and Carl only texts if he really needs something. I hope he's alright. When I check my phone, I groan at what I see.

"Marlon," I grumble. "He's already texted. A whole paragraph about how excited he is to see us. Lovely."

I text him our address and nothing else.

"I don't know why you're so opposed to meeting up with him. Everything you've told us about him makes him seem like a nice guy." Anne drives toward our apartment, occasionally shooting the briefest of glances at me out of the side of her eye as we talk.

"He *is* nice. And the *idea* of having a brother is fine. But I don't want anyone else in our family. Just us. I don't want anyone else taking up your time."

"You're afraid I'll be friends with him? Really? Ori, you're ridiculous. I can have friends. You can too. And Carl. Don't be so possessive. *Ugh.*" Anne scrunches her nose in disgust at the word *possessive.* She has no idea what she's just done.

"Anne. I know you like to park on the street but pull into the parking garage today. Park in the darkest spot near the back," I request as we approach home.

"Why? It takes longer to walk from the garage, and it's spooky."

"There'll be something of mine there when we arrive. I need to take it."

"Oh, why are you leaving stuff in the garage? That's weird. Okay. Anyway, here we are." Anne pulls into the spot and turns off the car.

I can hardly get my seatbelt off fast enough, but she takes her time. Her seat is pushed quite far forward because of her height, so there's no way I'm going to be able to take her there. *Damn.*

"Get in the backseat. Now," I command, practically panicking. I didn't think this plan through.

"What?" Anne looks around, checking for some invisible threat. "What's going on?"

"Hurry," I say, scrambling out of my door and into the backseat myself.

Anne quickly follows, confusion on her face. As soon as her door closes, I reach over her shoulder and hit the lock. I tug her body under mine until she's trapped.

"Telling me not to be possessive is quite silly, Anne. From the very start, you've been *mine* and I've been yours." I hold her hair tightly in my fingers, tugging her head back to give me access to her throat. "Have I ever said anything different?"

"No," she whispers.

"Good. You *do* listen. Just to make sure, however, I need to remind you who you belong to." With my free hand, I tug down her leggings and panties, tossing one sneaker into the front seat. When I run my fingers along her center, I find her to be absolutely drenched. "No matter who you're with, where you are, you're *mine,* Anne."

I free my cock from my trousers and with a groan run the head of it along her wet slit. As I'm pressing against her entrance, Anne pushes her hands against my shoulders in a signal to stop. I immediately cease my actions.

"Ori. You forget the other half of that. I'm yours, but you're *mine.*"

Anne lunges forward and meets me in a rough kiss. She wraps her legs around my waist. With as much force as she can in her position, she pushes my shoulders back until I'm in a sitting position with her on top of me. I lift her up to allow her room to pierce herself upon my throbbing cock. We both moan in relief as she sinks slowly down.

"Mine, Ori. Forever." She rides me hard and fast in the back of the vehicle meant for our family.

I look up into her beautiful face as she moans in delight, her mouth partway open, eyes shut, cheeks flushed, and I make a promise.

"Forever."

Chapter Three

Ori

"**O**ri, stop pacing. You're driving me crazy," Anne says from behind her manhwa.

"I'm not pacing," I reply as I march back and forth in front of the door. *Perhaps I am pacing.*

Carl walks out of the kitchen. As he passes me by, a SMACK sounds, and I jump from the shock of my ass being slapped.

"Carl!" I shout incredulously.

"It's gonna be okay, Ori. No need to be nervous." He smiles.

"I'm not nervous. I just want to get this over with. By the way," I say as a thought comes to me, "you were humming that song earlier, the one you've been humming for days now. The one about the singing map."

Carl shakes his head in confusion.

"I was humming? Wait, the cartoon one—"

"Yes, yes, keep up."

"Oh boy." He rubs his face with the heels of his hands. "The kids at the pool have been singing it and I guess it got stuck. So embarrassing."

"As I was saying, you were humming the song, and I just couldn't help but wonder why the map was given to *Marlon* in particular when I'm the one who wants to use it."

Carl perks back up. "That's a good question, and it's one I've been thinking about, too. What if we need Marlon to figure it out? Maybe even all of us together. The map has a weird feeling to it. I don't know how to explain it. Do you know what I mean?"

"I think I do. Something that makes me want to touch it, almost."

"Yeah, like that. It makes me think that we can't figure it out the normal way. Maybe we can ask him at the dinner party. What do you think?"

"I'm more concerned with what you think."

Carl looks at me as if he's suspicious. *Rude.*

"You want to know what I think? Gosh. How come?"

"The map has been your pet project. It only makes sense you'd have the best idea of how to handle it. Besides, Anne says I have to stop doing everything alone. Or in secret." I brush a piece of lint from my black trousers.

"Oh. Are you going to tell us where you got the flame, then?"

Thankfully, at that moment, there's a knock on the door. I waste no time in getting it open and greeting our guests.

"Come in," I say brusquely.

"Ori, be polite," Anne sighs as she walks over to the group. "Hello, everyone. Welcome to our home. I'm Anne. It's nice to meet you."

I squint as Marlon reaches for Anne's hand. If I see any sign of him draining her life force, there'll be hell to pay.

"Hi there, Anne! I'm Marlon!" He says as he shakes her hand. No draining. Good. "This here is my partner Charlie and our daughter, Imani."

Marlon gestures to the smiling, handsome Black man next to him. I look the man over while he shakes Anne's hand. Anne retains her smile throughout the interaction, though I know she must be working hard to do so. She has been practicing for this, and it's going well so far. I'm proud of her.

Charlie turns to Carl next. They greet each other cheerfully, though I'm not surprised—everyone loves Carl. Charlie looks like a perfectly normal, even above average, man. Well-dressed, good-looking, well-mannered. Why would *he* be with *Marlon*? Strange.

Carl bows to the little girl, who curtsies back to him, the hem of her fluffy white skirt lifting daintily as she giggles. Children especially love Carl, and it appears Imani is no exception. He then turns and offers a princely bow to Anne, who blushes and waves him off with a laugh.

"Marlon, you know Ori. Ori, this is Charlie and Imani," Anne says. When they turn to me and can no longer see her, she points to them and silently mouths the words "*Say hello now!*"

"Hello. I'm glad *you're* the one who got Marlon," I say to Charlie as I shake his hand.

"Thanks," he says with a smile. That smile falters for a moment. "I think so, anyway."

I look down at their child. Her black hair is braided into perfect rows, the ends tied off with white bows. She looks up at me with big brown eyes. We both squint, each assessing the other.

"Hello, child. Please don't make a mess."

"I can't make any promises," she replies in a slightly raspy voice. At least she's honest. "You got any kids? Or pets?"

"No children. And the only pet is Carl, but I don't think he counts."

"Ori! Why would you say that?" Anne gasps.

"What? You think he *does* count as a pet? That would make some of the things we've done highly problematic, Anne."

"He's right, Anne, it would," Carl nods.

"What is my life?" Anne mumbles.

"Speaking of life," I pipe up, happy to find a decent segue. "Marlon, did you ever see that man again? The one who gave you the map?"

"No, I'm sorry Ori," Marlon says with a sad shake of his head. "I really wish I could help you out."

"Well, that's alright, I suppose. We—"

"First, everyone sit down. Let's serve the food before it gets cold. Some of us have digestive systems to tend to," Anne says.

"Oh, fine," I grumble as I wave everyone toward the dinner table.

We all get seated as Carl brings out the food. Those who can eat it *ooh* and *aah* over what a good job he did. Normally, I would be the one doing the cooking, but Carl insisted. He wanted to make a good impression. By the looks on our guests' faces, as the plates are filled, he has. *Good boy.*

I face Marlon, who's seated across from me, and clear my throat to get his attention.

"As I was saying, Carl and I were thinking it over and decided that we need to look at the map *with* you, Marlon. If there's something related to phoenix magic in it, and it was given specifically to you, perhaps you must be the one to unlock its secret." I turn to Carl, who is lifting a forkful of something green from his plate. "Carl, will you retrieve the map, please?"

Carl sets his fork down and scoots his chair back.

"Oh, sure. I'll be right back." Like the wonderfully obedient darling he is, he makes his way to his room.

"Ori, we're in the middle of dinner. Can't you wait?" Anne asks. My far less obedient darling.

"*You* are eating dinner. Marlon and I are not."

She rolls her eyes at my admittedly smug look.

"That's not what I meant. I want to get to know your family before we start on the other stuff."

"Before, after, it doesn't matter." I wave my hand. "Time will matter far less when you're living forever, my love."

Anne sighs and takes a bite of the green stuff just as Carl returns. He slides into his seat and opens the map.

"Here ya go. Oh boy, I'm excited!" he says with one of his charming grins. Everyone at the table smiles back at him. It's impossible not to.

Marlon reaches across the table to take the map Carl hands to him. As both of their hands are still on the map, I remember something I wanted to point out. I take hold of the third corner of it, the final corner that's not torn.

"Oh, before you take it, I wanted to show you that Carl excluded Bolivia earlier today based on—"

The lights overhead flicker rapidly.

"Ori," Marlon says quietly, "something weird's going on with the map."

All three of us still have our hands on it, as if we're afraid to move. In fact, everyone in the room has stilled. There's something strange in the air. An uneasy feeling. I look at the map—there is indeed something happening.

All the ink on the map is running toward the center, while the paper in the torn corner is growing back. We stand in silence as the ink meets to form one black dot. There is a sudden fiery burst from the dot of ink. Veins of fire burn through the paper, drawing a new map. It burns fast and hot and extinguishes as quickly as it is lit. The completed map is much easier to read than the old one.

"Well. It looks like we have our answer." The smile on my face must be a mile wide. *Finally.* "The key to infinite life is in El Paso, Texas."

A sudden chill blows through the room. A deep sense of dread hits like an axe. There's something very *wrong.* Again, the lights flicker.

The child crawls out of her seat and onto my brother's lap. She wraps her arms around his neck and holds him tightly. He looks to be just as relieved to be holding her as she is to be holding him. Anne slides her hand on top of mine and squeezes it.

"Ori, what's happening?" she asks quietly.

"I don't know."

"Daddy, I'm scared," the little girl whispers.

"It's alright, Imani," Charlie assures her. "I think there must be something wrong with the electricity is all. Right, Ori?"

I search the man's deep brown eyes and find encouragement there. I nod.

"Yes. Everyone relax. It's nothing." I smooth my hands down the front of my lapel and adjust the cuffs of my sleeves. "As I was saying, now that we have the location, we plan to extend Anne and Carl's life indefinitely."

The lights go out. Anne and the little girl shriek.

"Anne! Are you okay?" Carl asks, panicking beside me in the dark.

"I'm fine, hold my hand, Carl," she pleads.

"It's alright, honeybee," Marlon soothes the crying child.

Lightning zaps and thunder crashes—*Inside* my apartment.

Out of that lighting, comes a woman—sort of.

There's a glow that lights the dining room enough for us to see the newcomer, and each other, just barely. Where a sensible person would have a head, she has an oversized bird's skull—a crow, perhaps a raven. I'm no bird expert. The rest of her body looks human. She's voluptuous like my Anne, though this *person* is tall, taller than even I. She carries a scythe, which I admit is curious, yes, but mostly terrifying. The white dress she wears is wrapped in garlands of snow-covered pine needles and a matching crown is on her skull. Her very presence radiates a cold that cuts to the very soul.

I don't think I like her very much.

"Ori Athans," she says. Her voice is low and raspy, with a crackle that reminds me of fall leaves underfoot. I swallow hard and sit as straight as I can.

"Hello, yes, that's me. How may I help you?" I reply as quickly as possible. Anne squeezes my hand reassuringly.

"Marlon Sakho," the bird-woman says next.

"What? Me? Oh, boy." Marlon passes a crying Imani to Charlie. "What'd I do?"

"Ori and Marlon, despite my better judgment, since you've awakened, you've been allowed to run about doing whatever you please with life and death. I have, however, received a message that you're planning on acquiring eternal life for humans. I'm here to tell you I've had enough of this nonsense. You are no longer allowed to meddle in Death's affairs. This is your only warning. Any further action of the kind will receive punishment as I see fit, approved in advance by Death himself. Understood?"

"Yes ma'am," replies Marlon immediately.

Pushover. I'll not give up my quest to save my family so easily.

"What gives you the right to come into my home and tell me what to do to protect my family?" Far too upset to sit still, I stand with a slam of my hands against the table.

"Ori, I think maybe you should listen to—" Carl begins, but I don't want to listen.

I see the bird-woman, the supposed employee of *Death*, leaning on her scythe now. She's watching me as if I'm a toddler having a meltdown. It infuriates me even further.

"How dare you try to take away my chance to give everlasting life to my family? I will not comply." I cross my arms and lean against the table to mimic her.

An owl peeks from behind her and looks at me with a *hoot* before going back inside.

"Ori Athans, I *will* prevent that from happening if you insist on trying. You will not like what I have planned."

"You won't change my mind," I reply.

"It's not your mind I'm going to change." She stands straight and holds her scythe in both hands. With a boom that shakes the apartment, she slams the handle into the floor. "Apologies to the rest of you. I know you cared for him, but it had to be done."

With that, there's a sound of fluttering wings, and then she's gone. The lights return to normal, the room temperature is much more comfortable, and the feeling in the air far more pleasant. Anne and Carl are looking down at me with looks of horror on their faces. Both of them have turned white as ghosts. Suddenly, Anne breaks the silence with a near scream of a wail.

My Anne! I attempt to reach for her, but something's wrong—I can't move. Everyone is looking down at me with panic and fear on their faces. Even the child is crying at the sight of me. I want to ask what the hell is going on, but I can't make a sound. In fact, I can't feel my mouth at all.

"Oh Ori, no," Anne sobs as she clutches Carl.

"We'll fix him, Anne. Don't worry." Carl turns to me and smiles with the least believable smile I've ever seen. "We've got you, Ori. It'll be okay."

"But is he okay?" Imani asks her father between sobs.

Anne breaks away from Carl, then reaches for me. Finally, someone can help me figure out what's going on. She plants her face against me and cries, her tears seeping into the fabric of my—hmm. Come to think of it, I'm not sure what part of me she's crying against.

It becomes clear what happened, however, when she wraps her arms around me, holds me to her chest, and carries me to the sofa. My body has changed—a lot. Quite a lot.

In fact, I'm almost certain I'm a pillow.

Chapter Four

Anne

"No, no, bring him back. You have to bring him back. Please help," I beg Marlon. If anyone can help, it has to be him. "Ori saved Carl, right? So, you can save him, maybe."

"I don't know. I can try," he says as he takes a seat next to me.

"Let's hope the psychopomp doesn't come after you for helping him," Charlie says before walking toward the hall with Imani.

"A psycho what?" asks Carl.

"Psychopomp," he says over his shoulder as he pauses. "It's the term for those who work for Death in the physical world. At least, I assume that's what she is. It isn't as if I had time to ask her. Either way, I'd rather not make her mad."

"Understandable. I wish my freaking boyfriend had the same amount of sense, so we wouldn't be in this situation. But no, he always has to be so stubborn." I squeeze pillow-Ori hard as I sob into him. "Is he even in there? Or is it just a regular pillow?"

Marlon sets a hand against the pillow and closes his eyes. His freckled cheeks turn pink as he squeezes his eyes shut and clenches his jaw tightly. After a moment, he relaxes, releasing a long breath. There's a deep frown on his face that is in no way reassuring.

"Well, good news is he's in there. He's not dead, Anne. That's what matters most."

A bit of the tension in my chest loosens. It feels a bit easier to breathe. *He's alive.*

"The bad news, though," Marlon continues, "is that I can't switch him back. Can't even loosen a stitch. He's stuck real good."

My stomach drops. The room feels like it's spinning. *He's stuck.* I don't know what to say. I stare off into the hallway where I can see Imani and Charlie drawing with my Copic markers. *I hope they make sure to put the caps back on,* I think. Why, I don't know—it's not exactly important right now. Maybe I'm going insane.

"Is there anything else we can try? Do you have any ideas? Can he take some of my life or something?" Carl asks Marlon. He puts his arm around me and the warm strength of it brings my focus back to the task at hand.

"I'm as lost as you are. I tried to push some life into him, but nothing happened. But what if—okay, hear me out? What do you think about—and I know this is dangerous, so if it's out of the question I get it—but what if you went to Texas, anyway?" He holds up his hands to stop me when he sees the immediate look of protest on my face. "Not to get eternal life. I'm thinking if Ori and I have transformation abilities, maybe the phoenixes have even stronger or different ones. Maybe they can help bring him back."

I sniffle as I think about it. It's honestly not a bad idea. It might not work out, and it might even get us into trouble, but it's worth a shot. Anything is worth it for him.

"You really think it might work? I need him, Marlon. I love him so much." I can't help but to start crying again. *What am I going to do without him?*

"Well, there's something in Texas that's meant for me, Carl, and Ori. I know that because the map didn't change until all three of us touched it. So, take Ori there and find whatever it is. I have faith in you, Anne. You'll get him back."

"You're not coming with?"

"No, I'm sorry." His shoulders drop with his gaze. He looks at a button on his shirt, twisting it round and round, as he speaks. "I have a family to take care of. A kid. I can't take risks like that. It'd be different if I didn't have Imani. I just worry if something happened to me, that she'd have to go through losing a parent again. I couldn't do that to her."

I lunge for Marlon and give him a big hug, pillow-Ori squished between us. It's not hard to hug Marlon—he's fabric just like Ori, so his touch doesn't bother me much. Plus, he's just kind of a lovable doofus.

"It's okay, Marlon. I understand. Carl and I can take care of it."

"I've always wanted to go on a road trip," Carl says with a grin. "Too bad I can't drive."

"How come? I can teach you some time if you need someone," Marlon says.

"Oh. We're just always worried about my ID. Legal stuff. We got ones good enough to work for day-to-day stuff, but if I get pulled over and they search the system, it's a gamble." Carl scratches the back of his golden neck nervously. He always gets antsy about this stuff.

"You all just need to see Cadillac Dan. He's got the best stuff. The government will think you're fine and dandy in no time." Marlon and Carl exchange smiles that are equally wide and goofy.

"Oh, boy, that's great!" Carl says.

"Oh, I can't wait to call him up," Marlon says.

"Ori," I whisper to my pillow boyfriend, "I think you gave Carl the part of you that was related to Marlon."

A little while later, Marlon, Charlie, and Imani leave with the promise to send Carl information about this Dan guy. It sounds a little sketchy, but Carl is a grown man and allowed to make his own decisions.

"Hey, Anne, do you want anything to eat?" Carl asks on his way to the kitchen.

"No, I'm okay, thanks, sweetie. I'm just gonna take a shower, then go to bed. It's been a tough one." I squeeze Ori with a sigh.

"I get that. You sure you're okay? Do you wanna talk?"

"I'm fine, seriously. Go eat some food. You have a phenomenal figure to maintain, after all." I shake my behind at him on the way into the bedroom.

"Why, thank you!" he shouts. "I will make sure to show you my appreciation for your kind words by offering you a guided tour of my phenomenal figure, free of charge."

I set Ori on the bed and place a kiss on his cotton exterior.

"I love you, Ori. Be right back." I grab my robe off of the back of the door and walk back out into the hall. "Free of charge, Carl? That sounds like a pretty good deal."

"Yep. And it's a private viewing!" he shouts over the clang of pots and pans.

"My goodness! How could I resist?" I laugh as I step into the bathroom. "I'll be out of the shower in a bit."

"Okay, love you, Anne!"

I make the shower as hot as I can stand and undress. Tonight calls for my exfoliating gloves and my antibacterial soap. It's not like I'm fully over my issues with germs, I don't think I'll ever be, but I've improved a lot. These days I really only get worked up when I'm anxious or upset. Tonight, I'm both.

I work the soap into the gloves and begin to scrub myself in the near-scalding water. I'm going to try to act as normal as I can in front of Carl. If we're going to make the long drive to save Ori, we need to remain as calm as possible. I'll need to let these feelings out in private.

Tears run down my face, disappearing with the stream. I scrub myself so hard it hurts. If I can't save Ori, if I fail him, what will I do? How could I forgive myself?

"Hey Anne, are you okay? You've been in there a while," Carl shouts from the other side of the door.

"Yeah, I'm fine. Just got lost in my thoughts," I reply in as cheery a tone as I can muster.

"Oh okay! Just making sure!"

My skin is flaming red when I turn off the water. The lotion stings when I apply it. I don't know how I'll keep pretending I'm alright, but for Carl's sake and most importantly for Ori's sake, I'll keep smiling.

Chapter Five

Carl

It's hard to pretend I'm okay, but for Anne's sake, I've got to.

When Anne comes out of the bathroom, she's smiling, but I can tell she's not okay. Her eyes are bloodshot and the skin on her neck has been scrubbed so red and raw that parts of it even have pinpricks of blood. The parts of her legs peeking out from under her robe are almost as bad. I don't know if I've ever seen her like this. I'm having a hard time deciding if I should acknowledge it. I'm not sure if it would make her feel better or worse. Gosh, this emotional stuff is tough.

"So, uh, you still want to go to bed?" I ask.

"Yeah. We should spend time with Ori."

"He's probably so bored. No phone to scroll on," I huff a soft laugh.

Anne sighs and shakes her head. "I guess I'm happy to have a break from the fake conspiracy videos. His theories about alien politicians were getting old."

"Wait, those were fake?"

Anne blinks at me a few times. "Yes, Carl. We really need to work on you and Ori's media literacy."

We enter the bedroom where Ori is still lying. Not as if he could have gone anywhere else.

Anne hops onto the bed and pulls him to her chest with a tight squeeze. "There's my grumpy guy. I miss you so much already. I'm so sad, honey. I'm so sorry. We're gonna get you back, no matter what."

I pull the blanket back and get into bed next to them. I'll skip my second shower of the day—I can tell Anne needs me now more than I need water time. She leans her head on my shoulder as she gets under the blanket and puts Ori between us.

We sleep with regular Ori between us most of the time. He says he likes to be in the middle to make sure we're both okay. I don't know why he has to make sure we're okay while he's in bed. He doesn't even need to sleep if he doesn't want to. I have a feeling he just likes being snuggled. Not gonna say that to him, though. He'd never admit it.

"Yep, Ori. We have a plan. You're gonna be just fine."

I reach next to me and turn off the light. I can't fall asleep at first, but I fake it pretty well, I think. When I'm positive Anne's asleep—she snores, so it's not hard to tell—I let myself cry a little, quietly. Not gonna let her see it, but I gotta get the tears out. Ori saved my life and if I can't save him, I just don't know what I'll do with myself.

The next day I need to put in vacation time for our road trip. My boss isn't happy about the short notice *at all,* but I tell him it's a family emergency. Thankfully, he signs off on it. I would have had to quit if he hadn't.

Anne picks me up from work so I don't have to take the bus, thank goodness. Her work gave her a lot of trouble about taking time off too, but she got it. Now all we need to do is pack and set our route.

When we're getting out of the car, I get a text from Marlon. I check it out as we're walking to the door. I'm a little confused by it at first—other than what happened to Ori, everything from the dinner party had kind of fled my mind.

Marlon: Heya Carl! Cadillac Dan will be over soon. Hope you'll be home because he doesn't like to be kept waiting. Tried to tell him you might not be there, but he's not very good at replying.

Marlon: Don't look him directly in the eyes. Oh, and don't call him anything other than Cadillac Dan. Not Dan or Cadillac or anything else. And don't argue with him about anything. Actually, don't talk to him unless he talks to you. Seriously.

Marlon: Oh, and I already paid him for you. My apologies for not being able to go on the trip. I'm real sorry about Ori. We love you guys lots.

Marlon: Daddy let me get a fish! I named him Skipper!

Marlon: Sorry, that was Imani.

Wow, Ori was right; he does write long texts.

I tell Anne what the texts say. She frowns and mumbles something about needing a shower before heading to the bedroom. I take that as an okay and text Marlon back.

Me: Okey dokey. Thanks. I hope you got a good-sized tank for the fish.

I'm in the middle of eating a bowl of puffed rice cereal when there's a knock at the door. *Ah, dang.* Anne pokes her head out of the bedroom to watch me answer it. She's still a little wary when it comes to unexpected guests. I open the door and, remembering what Marlon said, lower my eyes when I see a man I don't recognize.

"Are you—"

"Yeah," he replies before I can finish. "Let's get this over with. I got shit to do."

He pulls a roll of blue fabric stuff out of a bag and hammers it into our wall. I'm too nervous to tell him to stop. The way Marlon talked about him makes me feel like I shouldn't get on his bad side.

"Stand there. Straight. Look at the camera."

I do as he says. I don't see his upper face, since it's behind the camera, but I get a better look at him than before. He's younger than I expected. If I had to guess, maybe in his thirties at most. He's thin, kind of short. Medium tan skin tone, dark hair. I'm pretty sure this guy could blend in with seventy percent of the world with no problems and no one would remember him.

Sure would be nice.

He grunts and lowers his camera. I flick my eyes down before he can catch me taking in his appearance.

"You're an unusual-looking motherfucker. Give me some time with this one. Be back about two weeks," he says as he starts tugging nails out of our walls.

"Oh, uh, thanks Cadillac Dan. Do you want my phone number or anything?"

He grunts again as he rolls up the fabric and shoves it into his bag. I'm not sure if that's a no or a yes. When he walks out the door and slams it shut behind him, I assume it's a no.

Anne pokes her head out again and when she sees me locking the door, she flip-flops out in her slippers and robe. She always looks so cute in her pajamas.

"Well, that was weird," she says with a raised eyebrow. She notices the holes in the wall then. "Ugh."

"Yeah, it was." I scratch my head in thought as I feel myself nervously blush. "Hey Anne, am I weird-looking?"

"Huh?" Her eyes snap from the wall to me. "What do you mean?"

"He said I looked unusual. Plus, I know I stand out."

"Yeah, you do. Because you're hot as fuck. You know that. There's the scale thing, but you've been able to pull it off as body art." She puts her hands on the side of my face and looks into my eyes with concern. "What's going on, sweetie? What are you really worried about?"

"Well, we're going on a trip to save Ori. What if someone notices that I'm different and they look too closely into my I.D.? It could mess everything up."

"I'm not going alone, if that's what you're thinking. So, suck it up, buttercup." She pokes my chest. "We're gonna drive safely and be upstanding citizens. It'll be fine. Okay?"

"Okay." I wrap my arms around her waist and kiss the top of her head. "Love you."

"Love you, too. Now, let's pack. We've got a pillow to rescue."

Chapter Six

Ori

D amn it.

They've put me in the backseat.

With all I've been through, you'd think I deserve the passenger seat. At the very least, I could be in someone's lap. Strapped into the backseat all by myself? Really? I can't even see out of the window. The indignity of it all.

We've been driving for hours. How many, I'm not exactly sure. We left at the break of dawn and now it's well past nightfall. Anne said something about looking for a hotel that had a high cleanliness rating on her apps this morning. The GPS has been blabbering about being close for a while now, so we should arrive shortly. Hopefully, they're kind enough not to leave me back here for the night.

"Ugh, I hate hotels," Anne whines.

"I know, you've said it about a million times today," Carl replies.

"But it's just—*ugh*. Sleeping in a public bed and using a public shower? Who knows who touched it last? Or *what* they did! And there could be bugs. *Blood-sucking* bugs that could have bit someone else before biting me, Carl!"

"Yeah, I know Anne. You told me about them." Carl sighs.

"You don't understand, Carl. Being in a hotel is like—it just makes me feel like I'm being touched. Unless I know it's spotless. It has to be spotless."

My poor Anne has been getting progressively more on edge the closer we get to the hotel. She has been doing so well lately with her touch aversion and fear of germs, but this is pushing her limits.

They thought about sleeping in the car but determined it was too risky. If a police officer were to bother them Carl could get in trouble. My poor, darling Anne will be forced to stay at a hotel.

"Turn right at two-point-five miles. Your destination will be on your right," the GPS announces.

They drive quietly the rest of the way, though I'm sure Anne's thoughts are loud and racing. If it were me in Carl's place I'd make sure to say something to distract Anne, even if it was something that annoyed her. *Especially* if it was something that annoyed her—those things distract her from her scary thoughts the best.

"Okay, here we are," she sighs.

"You check in, I'll grab the suitcase."

Anne heads into the lobby while Carl goes to get the suitcase out of the trunk. *Damn it, are they really leaving me out here? Impossible.*

Carl closes the trunk and walks around the car to open the side door. He unbuckles the belt around me and gives me a big squeeze before locking the door behind us.

"Don't worry, Ori, I wouldn't forget you."

Of course, I wasn't worried.

Inside the hotel room, Anne makes sure to set the suitcase inside a plastic bag, on top of the table that's near the door. After checking under the mattress for bed bugs, she pulls her travel blankets out of another plastic bag, lays those on top of the bed, then puts me on top of everything. It seems like a lot of work when, according to my research, there isn't a foolproof way to prevent them. But I know she's worried, so whatever makes her feel safe.

"Are you okay, Anne?" Carl asks.

"Ugh," is all she replies before stepping into the bathroom with her special bar of soap. I can hear her washing her hands. A few moments later, she comes out. "The shower looks okay. We'll just wear flip-flops and avoid touching the curtain, just in case. There are new rolls of toilet paper in here and the toilet looks okay too, I suppose."

"That's good. Now you can relax. You gotta get some sleep. Another long drive tomorrow."

They both get cleaned up and ready for bed while I lay there, uselessly watching some terrible television show; about terrible rich people investing in terrible products. It's surprisingly entertaining and I'm ashamed of myself for enjoying it.

"You know, the last time I had to stay at a hotel, this show was playing," Anne says to Carl as he comes out of the bathroom, drying off his flaxen locks. "I think it must be mandatory for all hotels to play it or something."

"I don't know what it is, but you know I'm not a big T.V. guy." Carl shrugs. He hops onto the bed next to Anne and grins, snatching the remote out of her hand.

"Hey!" she protests as she attempts to snatch it back.

"Nope. This is my first time in a hotel. I'm here with my incredibly gorgeous partner and I think I should have some fun." Carl pats me and nods. "And my other partner too, of course."

Of course. If I had eyes, I'd roll them.

"What kind of fun did you have in mind, Carl? It's kind of weird doing stuff when Ori's like...that." Anne frowns.

"Yeah." Carl frowns in return. After a beat, however, his face lights up. "Well, you used to do stuff when he was a pillow. Why can't you do it again?"

Anne's cheeks turn bright red.

"Well, I mean, I didn't know he was in there."

"He liked it, though. And you know Ori would never in a million years turn you down, Anne."

Damn right.

"I don't know." Anne bites her lip nervously. It makes me want to absolutely ravish her.

With one hand placed on the center of her chest, Carl pushes Anne to the bed. Her hips are lined up with me. All the wonderful things I *could* be doing with them now race through my mind. If I ever get my hands on that bird-woman there'll be hell to pay.

Carl leans over Anne and kisses her softly on the lips, behind the ear, on her neck. He slides his hands into her tank top and pulls her breasts over the top of it. Something about that looks obscene to me and he knows very well how much I love it. Carl is putting on a show for me. *What a good little fishy.*

"Carl, what do you want me to do?" Anne says softly.

She's so easy to convince sometimes. My sweet, moldable, plaything. I love it when she resists, I do, but I love it just as much when she submits.

"Take off your pants, beautiful."

"Okay," she says breathlessly as she slides them off, leaving her little panties on. *Good girl.* "Now what?"

"I want you to show me how you used Ori."

"But it's embarrassing," she whines and looks away.

Carl takes her face in his hands and forces her to look back at him. "Show me, Anne."

Hmm. This dominating side of Carl is new. Not sure what to think of it.

"Okay...okay."

If I had lungs, my breath would stop as Anne straddles me. Carl kneels in front of us and lifts her chin so that she's facing him. He gets close enough to her that their noses nearly touch.

"Watch me as you do it," he says before backing away just a bit.

Anne nods, grabs hold of me and begins to grind against me. It's just like the old days. She's already so very, very wet. It appears she's fond of this dominating Carl. Good to know. I try to make myself as firm as I can without being able to absorb any life force, so that I may best please Anne.

"Good. I like that. Keep fucking Ori for me." Carl grabs hold of Anne's hips and presses her harder against me as she grinds.

"Yes, like that," Anne moans before meeting Carl in a kiss that doesn't stop until she's coming against me.

She breaks away from the kiss to cry out an expletive as Carl continues to move her hips back and forth. When her breathing begins to slow, he pulls her forward, off of me, onto his lap, where they continue kissing, even more passionately than before.

Damn.

"Oh fuck, Carl, that was awesome," Anne laughs against his lips.

"Yeah? You ready for more? Why don't you take those off and I'll hold Ori so he can have a nice view while you ride *me* this time, alright? Let him see that pretty pussy get nice and stuffed, so he knows you're being taken care of."

No one can fill her like I can, but I appreciate the sentiment.

"Yes, yes, I want that," Anne pants as she rushes to slide her panties off.

Anne hands me to Carl, who holds me under one arm, thereby allowing us both an excellent view of the goings-on. Carl hisses in pleasure as Anne slides the tip of his golden cock along her glistening slit. I'm feeling murderous with jealousy, but if anyone is in what's rightfully my place at this moment, I'd rather it be Carl than anyone else.

"That's good Anne. Such a nice, wet cunt. Now fuck me, pretty girl," Carl says as he takes hold of her plump ass, keeping me tucked in tight against him.

I think I'm enjoying this side of Carl. I'll enjoy taming it out of him if he tries it on me. That would be lovely.

Anne sinks onto Carl as they both make delicious sounds. The sight of her impaled on him makes me jealous in the most delightful way. I want to push her farther down upon him and pull her off of him, in equal measure. When he opens his mouth to moan in delight, I can't help but to imagine grabbing him by the hair and forcing my cock into it. Watching those blue eyes look up at me, desperate to please me as he chokes me down? That will never grow old.

I'm going to do the most terrible things to these two when I'm out of this predicament. Such a fantastic time we'll have.

"Carl, I'm gonna come," Anne moans as she fucks herself harder.

"That's it. Just like that," Carl encourages as he rubs her clit with his thumb and guides her with his other hand.

He's gotten good at that. I suppose I haven't been paying attention when it's just the two of them.

Anne comes around him as Carl begins to pant, his stomach muscles flexing beautifully as he pumps up into her. Soon he's coming, pounding hard into her with each thrust, his cum coating his cock in the final pushes. I still find cum fascinating.

It's most attractive when it's inside Anne. Especially knowing she won't get pregnant from it, of course. Yet another reason I'm glad we ended up with Carl.

"Thanks, Carl. I needed that," Anne says as she curls up next to me, laying her arms across me and setting her hand on Carl's chest.

"No problemo. I'll be here anytime you need the fish stick!"

"Did you just say *fish stick*?" Anne asks.

Carl just laughs.

"I can't. Goodnight," Anne says as she buries her face against me.

Goodnight, darlings.

Chapter Seven

Anne

There isn't any snow on the ground now, so we're definitely getting closer to El Paso. Which is awesome because I'm sick and tired of driving and staying in hotels. Especially hotels. The second one was not as clean as the first. It wasn't filthy or anything, but there was hair on the sink and a candy wrapper under the bed. If the cleaner missed two things, then who knows what else they skipped?

"Uh, Anne, you're swerving all over again," Carl says, a light panic in his voice.

I snap out of my thoughts of the dirty hotel room and refocus my attention on the road. *Ugh.* My head is all messed up. Worrying about Ori is triggering every ounce of paranoia I have. Earlier today, I even found myself flinching when *Carl* tried to touch me. I've made so much progress and it's all been wiped away. I'm—

"Anne!"

I turn the wheel hard in time to avoid slamming into a road sign. Thank fuck it wasn't another car.

"Hey, maybe we should pull over for a bit or something. That was a really close call, Anne."

"Yeah, maybe."

And then, lights. And sirens.

Of course. It wouldn't be my life if I didn't get tangled up in trouble. It's probably best Ori isn't here to try and save me this time. Taking out a bunch of mall security guards is one thing, but taking out a cop would be a whole other deal.

"Oh no, what are we gonna do? They'll put me in a research facility, and I'll never get out." Carl slaps his hands on his thighs and looks forward, jaw set determinedly. "Alright, I've decided. I'll give myself up without a struggle. That way, they won't search and find Ori. You go on and save him."

I scoff as I put the car in park on the side of the highway. "You will not give yourself up, because nothing is going to happen. We'll figure this out. If they arrest you, don't say anything except that you want a lawyer."

Carl and I both take out our I.D.s and wait for the cop to come to the car. When he finally walks up, I lower my window.

"Hello, officer," I say nervously.

"You want to tell me why you almost hit the sign back there?" he asks. Straight to the point, I guess.

"It's just been a long drive, officer. We're almost at our destination and I suppose I'm getting distracted. I'm sorry."

"And that destination would be where?" he asks.

The cop slowly leans toward my open window so close that his face is just slightly inside. He takes a sharp sniff.

"Uh, El Paso."

He moves maybe an inch further inside and sniffs again.

"You. In the passenger seat. What are you?" he asks, voice alarmingly deeper than before.

Carl startles, looking back and forth before pointing to his chest. "Me? What do you mean, *what* am I?"

"Don't play dumb. What are you?" The cop lowers his sunglasses down the bridge of his nose, revealing widely spaced eyes, yellow but with dark brown circles around the irises.

"I don't know—"

"Fuck it," the cop spits before he grabs me by the neck and tugs me toward his mouth. A mouth that has begun to stretch out into a point filled with really big teeth. Sharp ones. "I'm hungry, kid. As I'm sure you know, there's nothing griffins like more than the fresh meat of sweet girls."

"I did not know that officer," Carl says, his voice shaking. "I don't even know what a griffin is. If you don't eat my girlfriend, I can go get you whatever you want though, I don't mind."

"Just fucking tell me what you are, and you can go. No harm, no foul. I won't even take a single nibble." His teeth drip thick, foul-smelling saliva onto my Hatsune Miku tee. I got it at a concert and can never replace it, but it's going into the trash after this.

"Okay, okay. It's kind of complicated," Carl starts. "I used to just be a regular guy. A human one. And then this man with, uh, yellow eyes came to my work and gave me a map. To Texas. And, uh, I got attacked and I don't know who did it, but they did something weird and it transformed me kind of into a, uh, fish...person? Yeah. And then they ran away. But I saw they also had yellow eyes! So, I thought I should go to Texas and see if someone there could fix me. And that's the truth."

No one would believe that story. *Yikes, Carl.*

After a pause, the cop's grip on my neck loosens slightly.

"Yellow like my eyes or different?"

"Uh," Carl pauses here. I know he's thinking of the guy who gave Marlon the map in that bullshit story he just made up, but the problem is Marlon never described that guy's eyes in detail. *Shit.* Carl takes a guess. "Different."

The griffin's hold loosens further. That must've been the right answer. I should have given Carl's storytelling skills more credit.

"And you say you're going to El Paso, huh?"

"Yes, officer."

A long, wheezing breath shoots out of me when the cop lets me go. He steps back from the car, pushes his sunglasses back up his nose, and places his hands on his belt. His mouth—and teeth—smooth back to their original shape. Unfortunately, I still have his nasty, slimy spit on me.

"God damn phoenixes did you dirty, is what it looks like. They're always in someone's business. Those pretentious fuckers are the reason why everyone thinks griffins eat people, you know that?" He shakes his head but then holds out his hands with a smile. "Rumor comes in handy occasionally though, gotta admit. Anyway, you go find 'em and you give 'em hell. They give you any trouble, you call me up and I'll have my cousin pay 'em a visit."

He digs a business card out of his shirt pocket and hands it to me. There's nothing on it but a simple black ink image of a griffin, a phone number, and the name Leonidas.

"Oh, wow," I stutter as I put the card in my wallet.

"Thanks, officer," says Carl.

"Call me Leo," he says as he slaps the roof of our car. "You kids get a move on. El Paso isn't much farther. Don't be running into any signs."

"You got it," I reply as my shaking hand barely manages to fit the key into the ignition. "Thanks again."

As we begin back down the highway toward El Paso, I am quite sure that I will not be running into signs anytime soon.

The amount of adrenaline coursing through my veins is going to keep me going for a while.

"Hey, Anne?" Carl turns to me, and I can see from the corner of my eye that his golden scaled skin looks mighty pale right about now.

"Yes, sweetie?"

"I think I liked it better before we knew other stuff existed. Like when we thought me and Ori were the only different kind of people. These griffins and death-bird-ladies and stuff? I don't think I like it." Carl wraps his arms across his chest and leans his head against the window. "I just want things like they used to be. Gosh, I think—and I feel kind of bad saying this because of what happened to him—but I'm mad at Ori."

"Why are you mad at Ori?" I turn to the side quickly to give him a questioning glance. "He's just a pillow. He didn't do anything."

"Not because of anything he did *now*, but before this. I've just been thinking about like how he decided we were gonna do the eternal life thing without asking us. He sassed that bird-woman, that obviously should not have been sassed, which put everyone in danger. He's now at risk of being a pillow forever unless we drive to Texas, a drive that has put me at risk. He didn't tell us anything about where he got the flame, and Marlon didn't know anything about the map, so we've ended up in some sketchy situation, going in totally blind to begin with. If he actually had listened to us and just been rational with the bird-lady or even listened to what we wanted about the life thing from the start, this wouldn't be happening. So, yeah, I'm mad."

Color has returned to Carl's face, only now his cheeks are pretty red. It's clear he's frustrated. It's not easy to make him mad either. But he's got a point. This *is* Ori's fault. And, honestly, Ori has been kind of an ass lately.

"I understand where you're coming from, Carl."

He perks up and turns to me.

"You do? You don't think I'm overreacting?"

"No. Ori needs to really get better about recognizing that this is a three-way relationship, not a dictatorship. I do think the whole growly, protective brat thing is cute on him—whatever the hell that says about me, I don't know—but sometimes I do let him take it too far. It's only healthy to set boundaries. We're in a grown-up relationship and we need to act like grown-ups." I nod my head to mark my final decision.

"Yes! We're going to be so much better about communication. This is great, Anne." He smiles as he watches out the front window. After a moment, he turns to me again. "Hey, since we're being open and stuff, I wanna admit something."

"Oh, no," I mumble. My stomach sinks. *What did I do wrong?*

"You've talked to me about the anime character you said Ori looks like before, well the whole show actually, a whole bunch of times. I mean, a million times. I've always nodded along and pretended like I understood, but the fact is I don't know what you're talking about. Honestly, I don't get most of the references you make. Ori does, because he was just sitting there as a pillow while you watched the shows and played the games and read the mangas, but I wasn't there. When I was a fish, I was in the living room. So, I just pretend like I know because I don't want to feel left out. Sometimes I feel dumb for not knowing normal life stuff already, and I don't want to feel dumb with you guys too." Carl shrugs. The color on his face now is the bright pink of embarrassment.

"Carl, first of all, I've never thought you were dumb. Not knowing something right away just means there's a chance for you to learn. You've done so well with learning to read, cook, do math, you did all that crazy government stuff with Ori—"

"He was so mad when he found out that the grocery delivery people weren't the government 'overlords'," Carl laughs.

"That was funny," I can't help but smile back. "But my point is, you're a smart cookie. You don't have to pretend to know something. I know if you really don't know it, and you want to, you eventually will. You've got tenacity, baby."

I give him a quick wink and get one of his signature handsome, goofy grins in return.

"I am totally making you watch all my shows though. You're not gonna escape, I hope you know that. I don't know how you've missed them so far."

"I think I've been doing other stuff, is all." He shrugs.

"Well, too bad. No more excuses. You, me, and our boyfriend are going to marathon some demonic Victorian butler anime. Then we're gonna get freaky afterwards. Just as soon as we get back from this damned road trip."

Chapter Eight

Ori

They're mad at me. I can't believe it. All I wanted to do was give them eternal life and *they're mad about it.* I'm the one stuck as bedding! This is preposterous.

We've been driving quite a while and all I've been able to do is sit back here and think about the conversation they had earlier. *Mad at me. Hmph!* The GPS says we're nearly to El Paso, which is good because if I have to sit here staring at the back of Carl's seat any longer, I think I'll go insane.

"Your destination is on the left."

Oh good. We're at the motel. Apparently, we're staying here tonight and then in the morning we're going to begin looking for whoever, wherever, or whatever will fix me. We don't have much to go on, so we must have an early start.

"Come on, Ori, let's go," Carl says as he lifts me into his arms. Good thing for him I can't bite him. *Mad at me.*

"Looks like we're supposed to check in out here. Seems kind of, I don't know, shady," Anne says quietly as we approach some sort of fast-food style window. She brings her fist up to knock on the glass. Upon seeing the filth on it, she lowers her hand and looks back at Carl. "Maybe you could. Also, it smells like burnt plastic and acetone over here. Makes my nose feel weird."

"Oh. Huh. That's different." Carl knocks on the glass. Then we wait.

A moment later, a wrinkled face presses against the window. Carl and Anne both jump back in shock before settling.

"Who's that? What do you want? Don't keep cash on the premises. Go on now, git." The person behind the window starts to step away before Carl interrupts.

"I'm sorry, ma'am, we have a reservation."

"A reservation? Here? Doubt it." She looks at Anne. "How many hours you and handsome need?"

"Hours? Uh, all of the night ones, I guess?" Carl replies as he scratches his head, confused.

I, too, am confused. What kind of motel rents by the hour?

"Um, what would you say your cleanliness score is?" Anne asks. Her voice sounds suspiciously shrill. "I thought I reserved you through my app, but I can't seem to find the reservation all of a sudden. Not sure what's going on."

"Cleanliness score?" The woman opens the window and looks at Anne thoughtfully. "Sugar, I think you made a mistake. As much as I want your money, I'll tell you right now, ain't no way *you* meant to come *here*. I can see that clear as day. Can also tell you with the game and the convention going on at the same time, you ain't gonna find anywhere else to stay tonight. Now, I'll give you the best room I got, but it ain't the Ritz. So, here's some new towels." The lady holds one skeletal hand out past the window. "That'll be sixty dollars."

"Oh." Anne pats her purse in a slow, zombie-like way.

Carl puts his hand over hers to stop her, then reaches for his own wallet. He hands sixty dollars to the woman at the window, then takes the towels and room key from her. Holding me and the suitcase in one arm, Anne's arm and everything else in the other, he escorts us to our room.

Carl adjusts everything in his hold so that he can get the key in position to unlock the door. When he's just about to insert the key, a bug skitters out from inside of the lock. Anne and Carl both jump backwards, Anne screeching in surprise.

"Oh no, Carl, that was a *roach*. I'm done. We're getting in the car."

Anne jogs briskly back toward our vehicle. I don't blame her. The last thing we need is an infestation. Carl sighs and walks after her.

"Well, two out of three motels isn't bad, I guess," Carl mumbles.

I disagree. I believe more than two-thirds of motels should be roach-free. If I had my phone, I would check the statistics. If I were to guess, purely on instinct, I would say at least three-quarters of motels in the country would be roach-free. It would—

"Um, could you move, please?" Anne asks a man leaning against the driver's side door of our car. "This is my car."

Carl moves quickly to reach Anne, stepping in between her and the man.

"It's our car. So, you'll have to move now," he says firmly. *Good work.*

"I'm aware it's yours," the man says, golden-yellow eyes glinting in the moonlight. "That's why I'm here."

What is happening with these yellow eyes? I've never seen them once before this trip and now I've seen two pairs. Plus, there are the ones Marlon told me about. I don't think I'm a fan.

"Okay, well, that's weird, considering we just got here, and we've never met you before. You'll have to excuse me if I don't have time for whatever bullshit scam you're running. I'm tired and want to get in my car. So, move," Anne spits out.

Well, then. Someone found an attitude along the highway. Good girl.

"I promise it's not a scam. I'm only assuming you'd want help with the map now that you're in town. I'm told it doesn't give exact directions." The man crosses his arms and smiles in a cheeky, sideways way that says *got 'em now.*

"The map?" Carl asks, body tense now, voice breathy with interest. "How did you know we have the map?"

"My sister can track the feathers, to an extent. I visited one of you to give you the map. Where is he, anyway? You were both supposed to come."

Feathers? Oh! Right. *Me.*

"Marlon? Oh, he—he had something important to take care of. You don't think I'm one of the feathers, do you? I'm just—" Carl starts, but Anne elbows him gently in the side. She shakes her head *no.*

"I don't think we want to tell you anything, no offense. We don't know you," Anne says.

The man puts his hands in his pockets and shrugs. "None taken. But I really would like you to meet my sister. She's gone to a lot of trouble to get you to El Paso, whoever you are."

Carl and Anne look at each other for a moment, making a silent decision, before Anne turns back to the man. "Alright. What's her address and is she awake? We've got nothing else going on."

"She'll be awake."

He takes a card out of his pocket and holds it out to Anne. Carl takes it from him, then reads the address to her.

"Well, enjoy your evening," the man says as he tips his head to Anne and Carl. "Just, uh, do me a favor. Give her a chance, alright?"

"Huh?" Carl and Anne each look confused.

The man gets into the car next to ours without saying anything else. Anne and Carl wait until he drives away before getting inside.

"That was so weird. Are we really going to go to that address, Carl?" Anne asks.

"I think we have to. We don't have any other clues. What else did we come here for?"

"You're right." Anne blows out a long breath, then puts the address into the phone's GPS and starts the car. "We're doing this for Ori."

Carl looks back at me, in my pathetic position in the backseat, and smiles. "For Ori."

We follow the GPS a bit along the highway. It doesn't take very long to get there, thankfully.

"Wow, okay. This is like a really nice place," Anne says.

"Yeah, gosh. I feel weird that I'm wearing shorts."

"I get that. I'm glad I changed out of the griffin-slobber shirt for more than one reason now, but I still feel underdressed."

What are they going on about?

They exit the vehicle, and Carl comes around the side to fetch me. Immediately upon exiting, I see what the fuss is about. The home is massive. The marble, columns, and lush gardens that are out of place for the climate give the illusion that we're about to step onto the estate of an Ancient Greek deity. It's truly beautiful. But it doesn't inspire a feeling of wonderment in me; in fact, it's quite the opposite.

This place seems frighteningly familiar. I know I've never been here, of course, but I can't help but feel as if I know it. As Anne and Carl walk toward the entrance, I want to scream at them to turn away. Run. There's something inside they should fear. I struggle to do anything I can to warn them, but it's useless. I'm simply a pillow.

Carl rings the bell at the massive wood doors. They're carved with intricate designs of birds and young women frolicking in fountains. They'd be beautiful if I wasn't fearing for the lives of my loved ones.

The door handle turns. With a loud creak, the heavy door opens, revealing a tall, blond woman with golden-yellow eyes to match the man from earlier. With one delicate hand, she gestures inside the building.

Don't go in!

"Hello. Welcome to my home. Please, come in." She shakes her head. "Oh, you must be wondering who I am. So sorry.

My name is Iris."

Chapter Nine

Anne

"Um, hello. I'm Anne and this is Carl." Carl takes my hand on the side of his that's not holding Ori and gives it a squeeze. I give him a squeeze back. "Well, let's do this."

We enter the dimly lit building and follow the woman as she makes her way down a long series of halls. She doesn't say much. The whole thing is quiet and awkward. Eventually we end up in a kind of sunroom. It's dark, so moon room now, I suppose. She gestures for us to sit on chairs around a glass table, her to Carl's right and me to his left.

As she settles into her seat, the moon highlights the delicate bones of her face. I can see how incredibly beautiful she must be when there's actually enough light to see her. At the same time, there's something *off* about her. She looks...drained. Yeah, that's it. Kind of like when Ori *takes* from someone, except she doesn't look old, she just looks like she's *missing* something. It's an odd thing to witness and I think if I hadn't seen what Ori could do, I might not have even noticed, might have just thought she looked a little tired or sick. But no, there's something off about her.

"Thank you for coming. I know you came a long way from what my brother told me. I'm sorry I wasn't more upfront with my instructions. Things are a bit tricky when dealing with magical items. Ridiculous rules." She waves a hand as if magical rules are some sort of common annoyance. Maybe for her they are. I'm just going with the flow at this point.

"It's okay. We got here fine. Had some trouble at the start." I shoot a glance at Carl. Not sure when, or if, we should mention Ori. We have to be careful. I suppose we just feel it out. "So, what made you invite us all the way here?"

Her eyes suddenly look as if they're seeing something far, far away. She folds her hands together and clears her throat.

"I need to make amends."

Carl and I glance at each other before he asks, "For what? We've never met."

"No, we haven't. Not really. But there's a part of—" She holds a hand up and looks back and forth between Carl and me. "I'm sorry, but which of you is the feather? I thought I'd be able to tell, but I guess not."

I reach over the space between our chairs and take Carl's hand. I need to be brave.

"Neither of us. But *the feather* is not doing well. We're here to get him help. If we tell you where he is, do you promise to help him?" My heart races as I wait for an answer. I don't even know if this lady *can* help him, but I need to try.

"Yes, of course," Iris leans forward, and I see sincerity in her eyes. "I swear I'll do whatever I can."

Even though I feel like I'm gonna barf, I give Carl's hand a squeeze and I nod to him. "Alright, Carl. Let's introduce her to Ori."

"So, uh, Iris, this is Ori," Carl lets go of my hand and wraps both arms around the pillow. "He had a little problem with a psycho-something—*psychopomp*, that's what she was. He's stuck as a pillow. If you could turn him back into how he was, that would be great. Thank you."

"Oh." Iris looks at Ori, brow furrowed, for a long moment before looking back to Carl. "Can he hear me? Is he alive?"

"We think so," I reply. "He was a pillow before, when I first met him. It's a long story."

"Has he ever mentioned me? Or anything of life before he was a...pillow?"

"He says he doesn't remember anything clearly, only a few foggy moments. He says that he remembers loving a goose and that the goose got cooked. He also remembers feathers falling off and choosing to die. But that's it. And those memories are all sort of dream-like. He never mentioned you. But you knew him? Really? What was he like?" I tuck my legs under me and get comfortable. *This is fascinating.*

"Well, you must understand first that it wasn't *him*, not really. Your Ori is more akin to his child than anything else. Not even that, exactly. Luke left behind two tiny fragments of infinite life as he chose to take his own. There was a bit of magic in that. It's only happened a few times in all of history. Ori and Marlon are special."

"Luke? That was his—the phoenix's name?" Carl asks.

"Yes. And as to what he was like, well, he was normal. Middle class. Good-looking. He didn't have any particularly unusual habits or interests. An all-around decent fellow, for the most part." She sits back heavily in her seat. "He was my fiancé."

"Considering you don't look like a goose—which is a part of the story that needs explanation, by the way—I'm going to assume there's some drama there." I ask carefully.

"To say the least." Iris sighs. "The *goose* was his True Love. She was a human. He intended to leave me for her. I took it...poorly, and, yes, transformed her into a goose. It was cruel and reckless. Now, I truly did intend to turn her back into a human once I thought they'd both suffered enough, but I was too late. Some farmers found her and ate her. Luke was devastated. You know the rest."

Holy shit. All along, I guess I just kind of thought Ori was actually just a bird or something. Now I find out he came from this horrible tragedy. And that the woman in front of me is responsible for it. *Yikes.*

"So, if you could transform that lady into a goose, then you can fix Ori, right?" Carl asks. *Good job, sweetie, staying on task.*

"There's a slight problem." Iris cringes. "You see, after I discovered what happened, I was, of course, upset. I didn't always have *the best* conscience, but I had one nonetheless. Then when other people found out I was responsible for what happened, I was ostracized. I lost any chance at the position in our people's government that I had dreamed of my entire life. It was awful. Still, I managed. I felt that even though what happened to the woman was terrible, it wasn't my fault that *Luke* chose to die. He could have moved on, eventually. After all, I was never going to be on the Council, and I had to move on. I wasn't going around dying of sadness."

Iris gazes out at the stars while Carl and I exchange confused glances.

"But then, I met Marco." Iris looks back at us. The devastation on her face is unlike anything I've seen before. "He was a unicorn, of all things, that had just moved to El Paso. He was my True Love. His light was brighter than anything else. Seeing him and how pure he was highlighted how sad and dark I had become. He made me want to be better. We had been together for two weeks when we went to the Council to arrange a marriage. Not enough time for gossip to spread to him. When the Council officials went to make the contract, there was a slight snag. My marriage contract with Luke wasn't fully broken. It was fixable, of course—he was well and truly dead. But it did bring up questions about why there were lingering traces of him. Gossamer strands of life still connected to the world. Not so easily ignored, however. It led to Marco asking things about Luke that I'd been avoiding. When he found out what happened, he left me right there in the Council office. Just left. Told me I didn't deserve love. It broke me. I understood Luke then. My heart was being torn to shreds. I truly wanted to die. It was then I promised that no matter what it took, I would find a way to fix something, somehow. The traces from the contract—I'd start there, see what I could find. I found the feathers."

"How does this have to do with why you can't help Ori?" Carl asks, frustration in his voice. *I get it, Carl. This tea is hot, but we've got business.*

"Well, it's how I found you all and brought you here that's the problem. I couldn't find Marlon and Ori. I sought all sorts of magical help, but the most information I got was that there were two feathers. I did, finally, find one vendor who promised me a map that would lead me to the feathers and would, in turn, lead the feathers to me. But he demanded a steep price. Seeing as it was my last resort, I paid it. The price was my flame. And now, here I am, a phoenix with no fire."

She looks at the two of us with her hands upturned like: *and there you have it.* Problem is, I don't have it.

"What does that mean?" Carl asks before I can.

"Oh, I suppose you don't know much about phoenixes. My flame is what gives me my abilities. What lets me live over and over. What lets me transform. I traded mine away. Without it, I can't return Ori to his previous form."

"No, no. We came so far. We were so close." I wrap my arms around my stomach. "What are we supposed to do now? Is there anyone else that can help?"

"No one around here has that type of power. Perhaps a member of the Council, but they may frown upon the feather even existing and demand he be exterminated. Could go either way."

"Oh my god, this can't be happening." *I feel like I'm gonna faint.*

"You said your flame? A phoenix flame?" Carl asks.

"Yes," Iris says.

"Like this?" Carl unzips a pocket on the side of his jean shorts and pulls out the box that Ori presented to us on Christmas. He pops open the lid, revealing the beautiful flame inside. "Ori said it was a phoenix flame."

"You kept it in your *jorts*?" I shout. "Carl!"

"What? I didn't want to just leave it in the car."

"That's it. That's *my* flame," Iris exclaims as she stands up. "How did you get it? I know I didn't trade it to you."

"I don't know, Ori won't tell us," I say. "Does this mean you can help him?"

"Yes," Iris says as she reaches for the box. The light from the flame brings out the gold in her yellow eyes. She looks like a dragon, hungry for treasure. "But if I use it on him, on such a huge task, it will eat up much of the life source. I won't be as strong as I was before afterward."

Carl pulls the box against his chest, out of her reach. "You *will* use it to help him, though?"

Iris blinks, shakes her head, and it's as if a fog has cleared. "Of course. Let me help."

Carl closes his eyes, gives pillow-Ori a kiss, then hands the box to Iris.

Iris inhales the flame in one long breath. Her body gives off a shocking burst of light before settling down to a subtle fading glow. The look she had before, the *drained* look, is gone.

"Alright," she says. "Tell me what he looked like."

Chapter Ten

Ori

"I'm a bit out of practice, so if he doesn't turn out right the first time, you'll have to give me a moment to recharge and I'll fix him," Iris says as she looms over me.

They've got me plopped on the floor, waiting for her to get this over with. I can feel the dirt getting between my fibers. *Terrible.*

"Just try to make him human, I guess," Anne awkwardly laughs.

"I'll try my best." Iris doesn't laugh. *Not reassuring.* "Here we go."

She puts her hands on either side of me. I can feel energy begin to flow throughout my fabric and my feathers. It feels odd, ticklish almost. There's an unexpectedly feminine energy to it, I decide. I wonder if my energy feels masculine. I shall ask Carl. He's been on the end of my transformation.

Hmm. What if he says I have feminine energy? It's possible. I'm not *really* a man, am I? The form I took was only to please my darling. I could be a woman or anything else any day if I wanted to be. How would Anne react? Carl's a good sport. He'd be fine either way. But Anne? Would she still feel the same for me? I wonder...

"Goodness. This one's really stubborn," Iris says. "I've got him started, though. I think I can step away. He's going to go through the whole process now."

I can feel myself stretching. I'm sure I look awful. Carl's face squishes up as he watches me, looking as if he's just been forced to eat maple candy. I suppose that proves me correct.

"Well, that's certainly...something," Iris says, a look of confusion on her face. "I've seen a lot of transformations, but nothing quite like that."

"Don't suppose you've transformed a lot of people made out of fabric, though, have you?" Anne says.

"No, I suppose not."

The process of becoming a person goes much, much faster than the first time. It's not long before I'm in human form. I color myself in with markers Anne sets aside for me from her bag. I make myself a brand-new outfit. I can't see myself, but I'm sure I look fantastic, better than ever.

The others watch in complete silence as I'm perfecting myself, looks of shock on their faces. It could be because of how nice I look. Well, I suppose it's more likely because I'm—

"Ori, why are you a girl?" Carl asks.

"Why not?" I reply, twirling in my pleated black skirt. "Thought I might try something different for a few days."

"Is that—Ori, I have an outfit exactly like that. You can't dress the same as me. It's weird," Anne says.

I huff as I tug at the buttons on the cardigan I copied from Anne. "Fine. I'll try a different style tomorrow. I'm too worn out to change. Now, is that all you're going to say?"

"No, of course not. I'm happy you're back. Obviously I'm shocked though."

"I did try to make him like the pictures you showed me. I don't know what happened." Iris raises her hands defensively, palms in front of her.

"Oh, I was just thinking about what it might be like to be a woman for a bit. It wasn't your doing." I step to Anne, nearly as close as I can get and look down at her. Obviously, I'm still taller than her—I decided to stay the same height as before—because I wouldn't have such a wonderful view of her if I were any shorter. I tuck a lock of hair behind her ear and watch as her cheeks turn red. "I'm certain it'll be fun to experiment. You'll show me how to be a woman, right, darling?"

"Uh-huh. Yep." Anne nods vigorously up at me.

"Wonderful."

A skittering and clinking sound comes from the hallway. I turn to check the floor for some sort of vermin. I want to get rid of it before it scares Anne. Instead of a rat, I find some sort of small, elderly dog entering the room.

"Oh, you'll have to excuse Louie. I'm pet-sitting and he's become needy in his old age," Iris says.

The ugly little dog makes a beeline for Carl and sits at his feet, staring up at him. Carl looks uncomfortably down at the dog and then to Anne.

"Uh, this isn't going to be like the cat café thing, is it?" he asks.

"He seems to like you. Perhaps it's your tattoos. He has a...history with fish." Iris taps on her lap and Louie scurries over to her. "Come on now, you old coot. Leave the guests alone. Took me the last year to get him to trust me, but we've made it."

"Well, thank you for helping me. We'll be going now," I say.

"Ori don't be rude," Anne says. "Thank you so much for your help. It was really interesting getting to know all about the history of the phoenix Ori came from."

"Thank you for letting me help you. I know I'll never be able to change the past, but if there's anything I can do to make things better now, I'll do my best."

"You don't happen to have any sway at any hotels, do you?" Carl asks. "Booking is full everywhere and the place we were going to stay fell through."

"I don't. But I do happen to have a very large home with many bedrooms, each with their own bathroom. If you'd like to stay here tonight, you're more than welcome. I promise Louie and I will not disturb you."

"You know, that would actually be amazing. I'm so exhausted," Anne says.

"Wonderful! Let me lead you up then!" Iris leads the way through the place up to the second floor. "If you get restless, you're welcome to tour the gardens or get a bite in the kitchen. Make yourself at home. Here's your room. Have a lovely night."

The room is, admittedly, fabulous. The bed is bigger than any I've ever seen and incredibly soft. There is a bathtub that could fit a small nation in it in the bathroom. The shower has multiple shower heads. I think Anne nearly dies when she sees that.

"I'll get the suitcase. Be right back," Carl says.

"Let me come with you. I need to stretch my new body a bit," I say. I toss the cardigan on the bed, keeping just the t-shirt underneath. It's too hot here for a sweater. I didn't make myself a bra because Anne says they're horrible. If I'm only going to be a woman for a brief time, then I refuse to subject myself to torture. "There are, of course, a few kinks that need to be worked out."

When we get outside, and I'm no longer terrified, I'm able to take in how truly lovely the place is. It's surrounded by lush gardens, yes, but also trees. The whole place really does feel like a magical oasis.

"Hey, Ori. You want to go for a quick look around?" Carl asks.

"Hmm?" I'm momentarily distracted by inspecting my cleavage. I don't have nearly as much of it as Anne does. I check behind me. Not as much rear, either. I think I look good, though. A willowy silhouette.

"Ori. Walk?" Carl asks again.

"Oh, right. Sure. I'll work out the new legs." We walk toward a forested area. Lovely, fragrant blooms hang from the branches. I hold a leg in front of me and inspect it. "These legs are quite long. Silly things."

"Mhmm," is all Carl replies. Not very talkative tonight, it seems.

"Carl? I don't really know what Anne likes in women. Do you think she'll like me like this?"

"Yep."

How boring.

"Carl," I turn to face him. I hadn't noticed quite how dark and isolated the path we're on has grown until I look at him and realize how difficult it is to make out his features. "You're being very boring."

"Ori," Carl says in an unusually gruff voice. I startle when he puts his hands on my shoulders and turns me around to face away from him.

"What are you doing?" I ask, confused.

"Ori," he says again, this time, however, his mouth is pressed against my neck, his hot breath in my ear. I hear the desperate rumble in his voice when he says one more word:

"Run."

Chapter Eleven

Carl

Ori turns his—her head to look at me. Her jaw is dropped, eyebrows pinched. The look tells me she's appalled at the idea. This'll be fun.

"Fly, little feather, or I'll take you right here where anyone can see."

Her expression turns to shock. She's not used to being spoken to this way, just as I'm not used to acting like this. But my instincts are kicking in—and *fuck,* she looks good like this.

"How dare—*damn it,*" Ori says before she takes off running.

I'm so excited I can't help but bounce on the toes of my sneakers as I count down from ten in my head. Her little skirt flaps like fins around her hips as she bounces away from me. *Perfect.* I reach ten as she disappears from sight. Time to go.

I take off in her direction. It doesn't take long before she's in my sight again. I slow down so that she doesn't see me—I want this to last a little bit longer. She tugs the hem of her white t-shirt off of a low branch with a frustrated growl. The hardness of her nipples is visible in her shirt. I wonder why she didn't make herself a bra. Huh.

"Fucking fish," Ori mumbles, barely loud enough for me to hear as I approach.

She's gone further into the trees. Low branches are scraping my shins and I'm currently regretting wearing shorts. *'Jorts'*, according to Anne. I'll wait until Ori gets into some kind of clearing before I pounce.

For a second, I lose track of her. I listen for her but find a visible clue first—a feather. She must have gotten snagged on a bush or something. *Poor little pillow.*

And there she is. Running across a grassy area between the trees. The moonlight reflects blue on Ori's shoulder-length black hair. The shadows bring out the sharp proportions of her face. And I can see them well when she turns and sees me coming closer to her.

"Oh, hell. Carl, you better—"

And then I'm on her. I wrap my arms around her and drag her to the grass. Ori struggles against me, cursing at me, nipping at my hands. But I know it's not serious. I know she wants this as much as I do. Because if Ori wanted to hurt me, she could. If Ori wanted me to stop, she'd tell me.

"If you really want me to stop, you know the safe word," I say softly. It's better to be sure.

"That safe word is for you, not me. I don't need safe words. What do you think I am?" Ori snaps back.

I push Ori flat to the ground and twist her head to the side. I grind my hips into her ass as I growl into her ear, "I think you're a slutty little pillow who's gonna take my cock in about thirty seconds. If you have a problem with that, you say the safe word. Got it?"

I sit up on my knees and look down at her, indecision on her face as I push her skirt up. Her little white panties don't slide off her ass as smoothly as they do Anne's—the fabrics catch on each other just a little—but I do drag them down all the way off of her long, pale legs. I toss them behind me.

"Oh, damn it, Carl," Ori whines as she attempts to push herself up, "This is so embarrassing."

I push her back down, lift her ass. "I said, got it?"

"Yes," Ori answers quietly, reluctantly.

I unzip my shorts as I stare at Ori's gorgeous cunt. Whatever magic she took from that lady, she really used it well. I tug my shorts and underwear down, letting my cock spring out. The first touch of my tip against her slit makes her jerk away from me, but I pull her back.

"Really?" she whines.

"You can take it, Ori."

"Of course I can," she replies, that signature Ori cockiness showing itself.

"Oh yeah?" *Might as well take advantage of her little attitude.* "You sure about that? I mean, I know Anne sure likes it, but—"

She squints at me. "Fuck me, Carl. And you better do it right. I'm not wasting my time out here."

I grin as I line myself up with her entrance. *God, I love that attitude.* "You got it."

I drive into Ori with one hard thrust. She loses her position propped on her elbows, falling face-first to the ground. Ori spits out grass as she lifts her head again.

"Is that it?" she taunts. "Are you just going to stay stuffed in there forever?"

I can't help but laugh and shake my head as I begin to push in and out of her insides. She's fabric inside, but it's smooth. There's a squeezing, rippling going along with each of my thrusts, acting almost like a strange sort of machine pushing and pulling me inside, keeping me from getting friction burn. *A conveyor belt of cunt.* The thought makes me laugh harder.

"What are you laughing at?" Ori snaps.

"Not at you. You're perfect. I love what you're doing for me inside. Feels so good," I rasp as I pump faster into her.

"I'm not doing anything. Don't know what you mean," she mumbles. *Sure.*

I slip my hand around her narrow hips to find her swollen clit. As soon as I touch it, Ori moans in a ridiculously delicious way.

"So that's what that feels like," she says, moaning again, as I rub her in brisk circles. "I see why Anne likes it."

"Yeah? Anne loves it when I fuck her Ori. When you're working, we head to the second bedroom, and I fill her with so much cum it drips down her legs when she gets out of bed."

"Carl, you know you can't please her like I can. No one can."

I press her clit firmer as I circle it. Ori drives her fingers into the grass with a clench and a groan.

"She loves it, Ori. Now you know why." I slam into her over and over as her body begins to tense. "Look at that pretty little pillow, stuffed so full."

Ori cries out, her back bowing, head thrown back. "Fuck, yes. Yes!"

The sight is fan-fucking-tastic. Though, I have to wonder if I'll ever take Ori when she's in her regular form. I bet he'd be just as beautiful. Thinking of Ori's other body and what we've done puts a mischievous thought into my head. I put my mouth next to her ear so there's no way she can miss what I'm about to say.

"Ready for my cum, *little omega*?"

An elbow jabs into my side, before I'm tossed flat onto my back with an *oof.* Crouched over me is a ticked-off looking pillow-lady.

"Something I said?" I say with a chuckle.

"I am *not* the omega," she grinds out between clenched teeth. Ori aligns her center with my hard cock and slowly begins to sink onto it. I cup her firm ass in my palms, but she pulls them away, slamming my hands to the ground. "And you'll come when I want you to."

Ori starts a smooth, rhythmic grinding that has me at the edge in no time. Just when I think I'm gonna come, Ori reveals another semi-creepy trick by unfurling short tentacles inside her. She pauses her movements while her internal tentacles squeeze near the head of my dick. Once the immediate urge to come passes, she releases me and continues her motions.

We go on like this a couple more times until finally Ori releases my hands, allowing me to stroke her soft fabric. She rides me faster, both of us moaning now. Ori then clenches around me, coming hard. I groan as I'm at last able to release inside of her. I'm breathing hard as I come down, staring up at the moon. *What a night.*

"Well. That's that then," Ori says as she climbs off of me. "Time for underwear."

I look down only to see a wet mess of little, downy feathers on and around my softening cock. *Huh.* I guess she still comes feathers.

"How romantic of you," I laugh.

"There'll be plenty of time for romance. Right now, we need to get back inside before Anne starts to panic."

Chapter Twelve

Anne

I never want to leave this shower.

It's so fancy. I'm sprayed from several directions at once. She has individually packaged guest soaps, and they smell *so good*. The shampoo and conditioner are the type I will never be able to afford. I am going to smell like a tea tree by the time I get out of here, and I'm perfectly okay with that.

"Anne! Don't worry, we're okay!" Carl shouts from behind the shower door. "I'm sorry it took so long!"

"Yes, please forgive us for the delay, darling," Ori adds.

How long have I been in here? I didn't even realize they'd apparently been gone a long time.

"Oh, uh, it's fine. I totally knew you guys were taking a long time, but, uh, I knew you'd be fine."

"Carl, she didn't even realize we'd been gone!"

"Ori, that's not true. I knew you were gone, I just didn't know I had been in here a long time. This thing is freaking marvelous."

A few seconds later, the door opens and a nude Carl joins me in the spray. *We really just don't have enough boundaries.*

"Wow, this is great!" Carl says as he inspects the various shower heads.

I notice a swirl of feathers getting caught by the drain's hair catcher. My eyes drag up Carl's legs and open wide when I see all the little feathers stuck to his groin.

"So, what did you two do while you were out?" I ask Carl with a raised eyebrow.

"Nothing!" Ori shouts.

"I had sex with Ori. We used her new vagina," Carl says with a grin. "She still comes feathers."

I have to cover my mouth to keep my laugh in. What happened isn't funny—I'm sure it was romantic and beautiful and whatnot—it's just the way he said it. If I laugh, Ori will think I'm making fun of her.

"Carl!" Ori says, tone indignant, "I'm sure Anne doesn't want to hear about that."

"On the contrary, I'm pretty sure I want to know every-thing."

"Well, first Ori and I went on a walk. Then—" Carl starts before the shower door opens.

"I'm sure she's only being polite," she grouses. "Please hurry up, we have driving to do in the morning."

"Okay, grumpy," I say as I close the door. I raise my face to feel the perfect water pressure again. "One more rinse and I'm out."

When my hair is dry and we're all cuddled together in the bed, I wrap my arms around Ori and give her a kiss on the cheek.

"I love you. I'm so happy you're back," I say into her neck as I snuggle her tight.

"Yes, well, you know I'll always find my way to you. And I had full faith that you would bring me back. The three of us are inseparable, darling."

"Absolutely," Carl says as he wraps his arm around Ori's waist. "Isn't it great?"

We sleep for not nearly long enough, but have to get up as early as we can. I'm getting *really* homesick and I'm going to drive as long as possible between stops. We only want to spend two nights at hotels max. No way am I doing three stays on the way back.

"How was your sleep?" Iris asks as she enters the kitchen.

She looks better than she did when we got here. There's more life to her now. She opens the fridge and takes out a bowl of jalapeños.

"We slept really well. Thank you again," I say.

Iris sets the jalapeños on the counter and sprinkles them with a heavy dose of cinnamon, balsamic vinegar, and cayenne pepper. She stabs one of the peppers with a fork and takes a bite. Carl and I exchange confused glances, while Ori taps her chin.

"Is that something people like? I cook for Anne and Carl but would never think of that," Ori says.

"Uh, I think we will pass. No offense, Iris." I cringe.

"None taken. Phoenixes just have a bit of an odd diet."

"Ah, that makes sense," Ori says. Then, suddenly, one of Ori's legs gives out, flattening like it did the first day I met her. She looks up at me with panic as she wobbles on one foot. "I thought this was over with."

"What's going on?" Iris asks.

I explain to her about how when I first met Ori he needed to drain life force from people or else he'd get all floppy, and how when Ori killed those security guards he didn't have to do it anymore.

"I can't very well take life anymore though," Ori says. "After that bird-woman came after me and told me not to mess with life, and turned me back into a pillow when I protested, I think it's safe to say I'm no longer able to intentionally shorten people's life spans without consequence."

"Well, what are we gonna do then? We can't just let you get all flat," Carl says as he holds Ori up by the waist.

"Wait, that's how you were regenerating your powers?" Iris asks, confusion clear on her face. "You know you don't need to do that."

"What do you mean?" Ori asks.

"You just need to spend more time in the sun, Ori. That's how phoenixes replenish our abilities. Yes, we could drain life force, but we wouldn't dare."

"I spend plenty of time in the sun," Ori pouts.

I think about how he spent his beginning in my bedroom, then he was forced to stay indoors for a while, then he got an indoor job, how all his hobbies are indoors...

"Well, not really," I shrug. "We could all probably get out of the house more."

"There. You sit in the front seat of your drive and soak up the sunshine. You'll be back to normal in no time," Iris says as she bites into another pepper.

"Of course, I'll sit in the front," Ori scoffs. *Oh, Ori.* The scowl on her face relaxes as she leans closer to Iris. "I don't suppose you have any other tips and tricks I may want to know, do you?"

"Hmm. Not really sure. I could call you if I think of anything, perhaps?"

Ori returns to her grumpy posture. "How about text?"

"That's fine," Iris laughs. "I'm old and still used to calling."

"You can't be that old," I say. She looks like she's in her late twenties at most.

"Well, I'm not old for a phoenix, but compared to a human I am. I'll be three hundred and fifty soon enough. We do live very long lives." Her eyes turn dull for a brief moment. "Unless we end them by intentional fire, of course."

"How will my life end? I can't set myself on fire. Well, I could, and my fabric would burn, but you're saying for the feather it must be a phoenix flame, correct?" Ori asks.

My stomach gurgles at the thought of Ori dying. I don't know why he would even want to know this. When I look at Carl, I can see his jaw is clenched, and I know he doesn't like the thought either. A familiar anxiety washes over me and I find myself rubbing my fingertips together. *Damn it.*

"Correct. Who knows, though, you could be different. You're not *really* a phoenix, so the normal rules are out the window, aren't they?" Iris shrugs as she bites into another pepper.

"Let's not think about that right now. We just got you back. You can text if you want to talk about it later," I say.

"Yeah, Ori. Let's get you in the sunshine," Carl says as he wraps an arm around Ori's waist.

Ori shoves Carl's arm off. A few seconds later, she wraps her arm around Carl's waist. *Oh, for fuck's sake. What a brat.*

"Fine. Allow us to exchange phone numbers and we'll get on the road," Ori says. She looks thoughtfully at Iris for a moment before speaking. "Despite all the good you've done for us, is it alright if I say I don't think you were punished enough for what happened to the phoenix and the goose?"

Iris sighs, a look of resignation buried deep in the corners of her eyes. "Is it alright if I agree with you?"

A few minutes later, we're in the car and on the way home. Ori is in the front seat, soaking up the sun and telling me about her ideas for future road trips. Carl is in the back looking up potential hotels to stay at tonight. Aside from Ori being a woman, everything is back to normal.

"We could teach Carl to drive if the new identification works for him, make the trips easier on you," Ori says.

"By *we* you mean *me*," I laugh.

"Of course, darling. Oh! We could go to Orlando. I'm sure you'd enjoy seeing the theme parks."

"Ori, I'd rather stay in the house forever than be crowded together with a bunch of sweaty people at a theme park."

"As long as you're in the house with me then I'm happy."

"Okay, found one. Nine-point-five on the cleanliness scale and has an opening today," Carl says.

"Alright then. Load it into the GPS."

We get there in the evening. By then I'm absolutely beat. When we get to the room, I'm too tired to even do most of my preparations. I just check the mattress, strip off the comforter, and lay face down on a pillow.

"Are you okay, Anne?" Carl asks as he sits at the end of the bed.

"Yes. But my back hurts from so much driving and I'm just tired." I stretch my body, my joints making loud popping sounds.

"My poor Anne," Ori says as she climbs onto the bed. "You need a massage."

Ori straddles my hips and settles herself, using my ass as her seat.

"Hey now. I know what your massages lead to," I grumble.

"Oh, but I'm a different woman now. Just relax."

The back rub does feel great, I gotta admit. Especially my lower back. Driving for so long—

I moan as Ori slides down, lifts my skirt, and begins to rub my ass. The muscles there were apparently in great need of a massage. I'm just absolutely lost in the feeling when she starts to rub my inner thighs. *Here we go.* Just as expected Ori slides under my panties and starts to massage my clit with one hand. I can't help but to arch my back a little and follow her moves with my hips.

"Mm. You do love grinding on your pillow, don't you?" Ori says and I can practically hear the smirk in her voice.

I open my mouth to make a comeback, but Carl speaks before me.

"Take them off of her." The bed sinks as Carl lays down next to me. I turn to face him and find his pupils blown out with lust as he watches Ori fondle me.

"Say please," Ori hisses.

"Please. Take them off." Carl unzips his jeans.

"Anything for you, little fishy," Ori says as she slides my panties down my legs.

I take the opportunity to turn over onto my back before she can stop me. Ori gives me a wry look. Carl places his hand on my cheek and brings our faces close together.

"Kiss me, Anne," he whispers. Of course I do—there are few things I love more in the world than kissing Carl. And I know he loves kissing me. If I didn't know it, I would now, considering he's rubbing his cock while we do it. I pull away from the kiss for a second to watch him stroke himself. It's a thing of beauty. He pulls me back to him and we kiss more.

"Kissing without me?" Ori sighs.

I reach my hand in her general direction until she takes it. A gentle tug has her climbing my body until she's back straddling my hips. Ori kisses behind my ear, then down my neck. When she gets to my chest, she lifts the t-shirt over my breasts, then slips each one out of the bra cups. I'm sure I look crazy at this point with my skirt hiked up to my belly button and my shirt like this; and I'm pretty sure I lost a sock at some point.

When Ori starts sucking on my nipple, reaches between her legs to start rubbing my clit again, I stop thinking about clothes entirely.

"I think we need to do a more thorough massage, hmm?" Ori says before spreading my thighs wide apart. "Yes, I'm sure that will help you relax."

I turn away from Carl to speak to her.

"Take off your clothes. I want to see you," I say.

Ori stills, body language wary. "Are you sure?"

"Yes. Let me see."

After a pause, Ori climbs off of me and onto the floor where she stands awkwardly. She lifts her black shirt over her head with a resigned sigh. Next, she unzips her matching skirt and lets it fall to the floor, then pulls her lacy panties down. I take in her new, temporary appearance. She's stunning. I've never been with a woman before, but if I'm going to be with one, I feel incredibly blessed that it's one this gorgeous. Perky little breasts, flat stomach, long legs—pretty much the opposite of me, but somehow exactly how I would expect Ori to look.

"You're so beautiful. You look like a doll," I say as I run a hand down her thigh.

"Enough about me," Ori says as she climbs back onto the bed and makes herself at home between my thighs. Her eyes shine with desire as she kisses up my inner thigh. She licks up my center with a moan matching mine. "It's so good to be back."

I run my fingers through Ori's hair as she goes down on me, her pace slow, all the soft little sounds she makes telling me she's taking her time to enjoy this. Carl takes off his shirt so he can press against me skin-to-skin as we kiss.

Ori lifts her head and huffs out a quiet laugh. "Come on Carl, one more time before I change back, hmm?"

Carl breaks our kiss with a wide grin. He wiggles his eyebrows, making me giggle, before diving to the end of the bed. It takes me a second to realize what's going on, but when Carl lines himself up behind the bent-over Ori, it's pretty clear.

Ori and I lock eyes as Carl inserts himself into her. Her eyelids flutter as she clenches her teeth. The sight of my strong, golden man with his cock inside my beautiful woman is enough to have me reaching down to touch myself. Ori stops my hand with a growl.

"Absolutely not," she bites out before going back to work on me.

The rhythm of Carl pounding into her as she fucks me with her fingers and sucks on my clit has my head spinning. It doesn't take long before I come. Ori smiles at me before going back to try for another one. I stop her, though.

"No. You," I pant out. "On top of Carl."

Ori and Carl reposition so that she can ride his cock while facing away from him. I get between their legs this time. *Maybe my back still hurts a little, but it's worth it.* As Ori and Carl fuck, I lick Ori's clit. Unsurprisingly, she tastes like cotton. I keep an eye on her expression to make sure I'm doing okay.

"You're doing so well, Anne. Lick my cunt while Carl fucks me with his big cock. You're immaculate."

Her encouraging words have me licking with renewed fervor. She grabs my hair and shoves me harder against her as she cries out, "Faster Carl!"

Carl holds tight to her hips as he fucks upwards into her. The expression on Ori's face turns tense just before she gasps. She clamps her thighs around my head and groans loudly as her orgasm tears through her. When her muscles relax I back away to slide something out of my mouth. *A feather.* Carl squeezes her hips tight as he comes next. I look at the place where they intersect and find more little feathers there. I sit up and wipe my face, discovering more down stuck to it. When Ori sighs and climbs off of Carl, she leaves behind a layer of feathers and cum coating Carl's cock.

Ori notices me looking at the downy mess she left behind. "Well, what did you think would happen?"

I break out in a fit of giggles. "Oh sorry, I didn't think about the fact that my girlfriend would come feathers that would get all stuck in my boyfriend's jizz. It's not a normal, everyday thought."

"Our everyday lives seem to come with a lot of surprises. A suspicious number of them involve Ori's feathers though, you gotta admit," Carl says as he heads for the shower.

I continue to laugh and even Ori manages a smile as she pulls me up against her. We snuggle happily until it's my turn to shower. After that I sleep like a baby.

Chapter Thirteen

Ori

The rest of our road trip was uneventful, thankfully. I soaked up enough sun to change myself back into my male form and still have plenty of energy leftover. When we got home, Anne insisted we wash everything we brought with us immediately in case of bugs. After that, she took an incredibly long shower.

I've had to go out every day, sit on a bench, and read while I take in sunlight. It's been several days since we got back, so I've had plenty of time to catch up on my research. I've been looking into what it would take to buy land and live away from the city. How much money I'd need to make to fund a more private lifestyle. The numbers are not looking great, but I believe I can reach them. I can do anything if it's for Anne and Carl.

"Excuse me, son. May I take a seat?" an elderly woman asks.

"Of course, ma'am. Please, rest." I scoot over to make room.

The woman sits quietly, watching the birds while I read. As I'm thinking more and more about how long it might take me to save up, my usual worries creep in. *Will they be alright? What if something happens to them before that?* This anxiety has me in a chokehold. I turn to the woman next to me. Perhaps an outsider has perspective.

"Pardon me," I say, "But I'm wondering how to deal with the fact that all my loved ones will die someday. As an elder, perhaps you have some insight?"

The lady looks at me with pinched eyebrows above her thick glasses. "Well, you're not much for small talk, I guess."

"No."

She chuckles and sits back further on the bench. "Well, you see dear, the key is to enjoy them while you have them."

"But I'm worried about them all the time. They're here now, but one day they'll be gone."

She smiles softly. "That's true. Someday we'll all be gone. It's hard to accept that, but you just have to. My husband died when we were only forty. I'm eighty now and I've never been with anyone since him. I'm waiting to see him again, even though I'm sure that sounds silly to a lot of people."

I take her fragile hand in mine. Living forty years without Anne and Carl seems impossible to me. I could never do something so difficult. This woman is clearly strong and wise.

"What if there isn't any seeing him again? What if when we die there's nothing else? I'll have lost them forever."

"Honey, if there's nothing after we die, then you won't know the difference." She squeezes my hand and leans close. "Every thought you waste worrying about them dying is one you're not using to think of ways to love them even better. You gotta face it—we're all gonna die someday. It's up to you how you spend your time before then."

She's only partially right because we're not all going to die, not at the same time, anyway. *They* will die. *I* won't. I want to stop worrying about them, and this wonderful woman is right that worrying does me no good. But then I'm still left with the knowledge that when something inevitably does happen to them, I'll be left all alone.

There's only one thing I can do.

A few days later, when Anne and Carl are at work, I tidy up the living room for Marlon's visit later today. When that's done, I sit on the sofa, adjust the cuffs of my shirt, and clear my throat.

"Oh my, I have an idea," I say to the empty room. "I am going to find a new way to make my darlings live forever. I certainly hope that bird lady doesn't come back and get angry with me."

I wait a moment, but nothing happens. *I'll try again.*

"I sure am tired of the sun. I think I'll go back to draining people again. Perhaps I'll kill that cashier at the drugstore down the street. She was rude to Anne and I could increase my powers enough to—"

The room goes silent, all of that extra noise from electronics and traffic gone. A crack of lighting and a rumble of thunder later, the woman is in my living room, leaning against my doorway.

"What are you trying to do, Ori? I'm busy, and already annoyed that you're back so soon. Make it quick. I can do worse than make you a pillow."

"Yes, thank you for your time, Ms. Bird-Death-lady. You see—"

She holds up a hand to silence me. A couple of chickadees poke their heads out from her elegantly embroidered sleeve before returning to hiding.

"It's Morana. My name."

"Lovely name!"

"Thank you. Now, get to the point."

"As you know, I don't have a normal life span. Well, I have decided that I would like to die." I hold my hands up and chuckle nervously. "Someday. Not now. Should have worked on my phrasing. Anyway, when Anne and Carl have both gone, I would like my life to end as well. I don't want to go on without them. The idea of an eternity grieving them is too much to bear. I can't do it myself, so I'm hoping you could possibly do me that favor?"

"But certainly you'd want to live on. Think of all the things you can see, the places you could go, with all of that time. Most would see it as a gift"

"None of that matters if they're not there with me. I am only alive because of Anne. Her essence led my spirit out of the void. Carl taught me how to fall in love. They are my everything. Forever without them would be a far worse fate than missing out on some sightseeing."

"But you may not ever see them again. What happens after death is unknown."

"Even to you?" I raise a brow.

"My case is special, and my story is long, Ori. But as far as what happens to regular humans? I have no idea."

"I still want it. Alternatively, you could make them live for—"

"Death it is," she laughs. "Call my name when you're ready to go. But make sure you're *really* ready. You never know what fate has in store for you. You could change your mind."

"Thank you, Morana."

"And don't piss me off in the meantime." She points her scythe at me. "I mean it."

"I will be on my best behavior."

"Mmhm." She stands up straight and waves one hand. "Until then, feather."

"Until death."

Later on, Carl comes home sprinting up the stairs and into the front door with an envelope in his hand and a smile on his face.

"Look what was in the mail," he says as he hands me the envelope.

I take out the items inside and set them on the coffee table. A passport, birth certificate, social security card, and a driver's license meant for Carl. They all look legitimate.

"This is a driver's license. You don't know how to drive," I say.

"I will when Anne teaches me."

"Oh boy," Anne says from the hall.

"Carl," I lean close to his ear. "I have some thoughts for tomorrow."

A short bit later, Marlon, Charlie, and Imani come over again for dinner. We're able to properly chat, this time. Unfortunately, I discover that I *do* like Marlon and I *am* glad to have him as a brother. I suppose he could come around occasionally. Even the child manages to get on my good side, somehow.

"Here, Imani. You with your dad in the back," I tell her as we're setting up for the family photo Anne insists on.

"Which dad?" she asks.

"Doesn't matter. Just don't make any silly faces. My Anne wants a nice photo, so you must behave."

"Uncle Ori," she says as she sets her little hand on my arm. She offers me a gravely serious expression. "I can't make any promises."

"I can't blame you," I say as I look over at my family. "Mischief is simply part of who we are, it would seem."

The next day, Anne and Carl join me for my daily sunshine. Carl walks ahead, Anne and I behind him.

"It's nice to get out of the office, ugh," Anne says.

"Yeah, it was a long week," Carl replies.

"Ori, can you please just tell us where you got the flame?" Anne asks. She asks every day.

I sigh. "Fine."

Carl and Anne both perk up.

"I searched forever until I found someone online who would meet me to sell me what I needed. It was expensive."

"That's not anything weird or embarrassing. Why didn't you just tell us?" Carl asks.

"There's more to the story. The person who sold it to me was the governor."

I'm convinced the man is a part of a secret alien worshipping cabal. Anne thinks it's an insane theory, but there are so many videos online discussing it. They can't all be wrong! And really, why would he have access to magic items if he wasn't involved in something strange? There's a mystery there I intend to solve someday.

"Uh, okay. I mean, I know you're weird about the government, so I suppose I could see why you were being secretive," Anne says with a shrug.

"There's one more thing. He took a shine to me and wanted...well, I also had to give him underwear as part of the deal."

"Oh, well, that's not that embarrassing? You normally work in the erotic transactions field, anyway. It's not that different. Is it? Well, selling your underwear is more intimate, I guess," Anne says.

"Calling my work *erotic transactions* makes it sound very frumpy, Anne, and I am far from that. Anyway, I didn't give him *my* underwear."

"Ori! Why didn't you ask before selling my underwear?" Anne asks in an angry tone.

"It wasn't your underwear either," I shrug.

After a few seconds, Carl pauses. "Wait, huh? Why me?"

"Well, I couldn't give him mine. They're made of *me*. It's far too risky."

"But I called the neighbor across the hall an underwear thief!"

I shove my hands into my pockets and look ahead. "Anyway, let's enjoy the lovely sunshine."

We walk quietly for several long blocks. A smile grows larger and larger on my face. Anne squints at me.

"What's going on with you?" she asks. "You're suspiciously quiet."

"Oh, I'm only enjoying our walk. Aren't the trees lovely this time of year?" I say as we begin down a path leading through the little woods near the park, Carl leading the way.

"I guess. Fall is more my thing," she shrugs.

"What do you think, Carl? When is the forest your favorite?"

He pauses to let us catch up, then stands on the opposite side of Anne. "It's my favorite whenever I'm with you."

Slowly, we veer further and further from the path. Shadows become more frequent than rays of light on the forest floor.

"Hey guys, we're pretty far into these trees. Let's turn around," Anne says.

"No, I don't think we will. Not yet," I say.

"We thought you might want to play a little game with us, Anne," Carl says.

The two of us stand behind her.

"What's going on?" Anne asks.

"All you have to do is run. We'll take care of the rest," Carl says softly against her neck.

"Run?"

"Yes, darling." I say with a kiss to her cheek.

"But I don't—"

I nip her earlobe hard enough to get her full attention, then drag my teeth down her neck. When she shudders, I growl softly into her ear. I can see her pulse racing. Lightly, I let my lips caress her ear as I whisper the word that sends her running.

"Go."

Thank You

Thank you to everyone who has read the Stuffed books. You have all changed my life in ways I can't even explain. Writing this series, building these characters, and getting to share them with you has been fantastic. I have the most wonderful readers in the world.

Thank you also to everyone who has helped me with the books. I have had so much support, and I could not have done this alone.

Special thanks to Latrexa and Cassie for aggressively helping me when I was ready to give up, and Tee and Alijay for being there whenever I drop an anxious mushroom emoji in the chat.

Audiobooks, Etc.

Audiobooks and More

You can find the audiobooks for Stuffed and Double Stuffed on Amazon, Audible, and iTunes today.

The Spanish version of Stuffed, *Repleta,* is now available on eBook at multiple retailers.

If you would like to order the paperback of any of the Stuffed series for your bookstore or library, it's currently available through Ingram.

Bubble Tea

Want More Sentient Object Fun?

If you enjoyed Stuffed, you may enjoy my other sentient object romances, such as My Date with Bubble Tea.

You'll flip your lid for this bubble tea.

Adanna enjoys the sweet side of life: frilly clothes, adorable puppies, and walks in the fresh spring air are the thing for her. When she thinks she's spotted something else sweet to add to her collection—a gorgeous man sitting on a bench sipping a bubble tea—she struts over to get her guy.

Too bad a misfit fairy accidentally turns the man, Harry, into a bubble tea before she can get there!

Thankfully, she can change Harry back. But first, Adanna has to fall in love with him, boba and all. Then they have to prove that love—physically.

How are they supposed to fall in love when one of them is a cup of tea? And does his straw go *there* or not?

www.ingramcontent.com/pod-product-compliance
Lightning Source LLC
Chambersburg PA
CBHW070308310726

48976CB00005B/1628